THE SOJOURNER TRILOGY

Book I – THE GOSPEL ACCORDING TO JUDAS ISCARIOT

A Novel

By

Peter Leighton

ISBN 0-7414-3089-4

Published by:

INFINITY
PUBLISHING.COM

1094 New DeHaven Street, Suite 100
West Conshohocken, PA 19428-2713
Info@buybooksontheweb.com
www.buybooksontheweb.com
Toll-free (877) BUY BOOK
Local Phone (610) 941-9999
Fax (610) 941-9959

Printed in the United States of America

Printed on Recycled Paper

Published July 2006

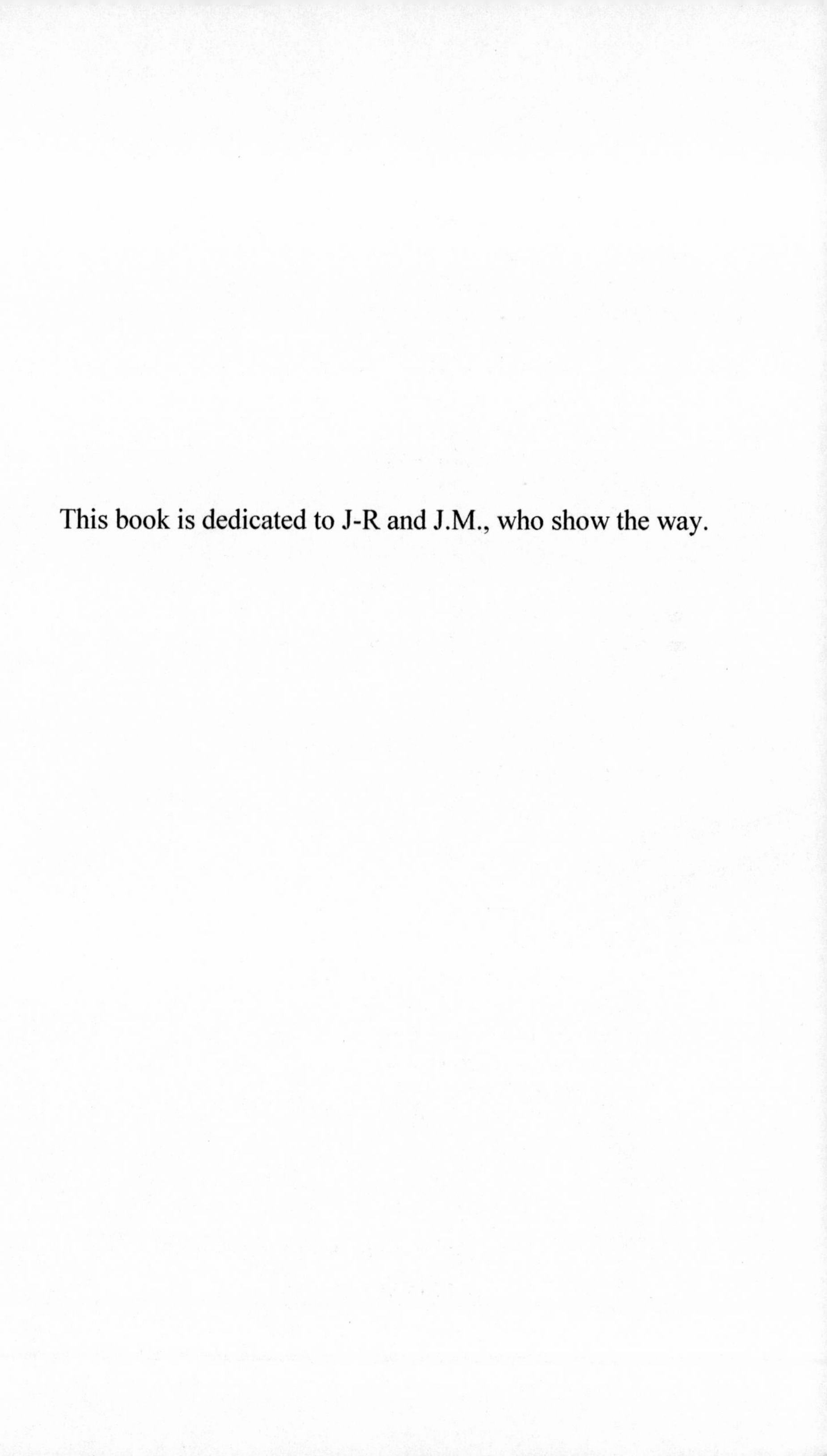

This book is dedicated to J-R and J.M., who show the way.

Special Thanks

A special "thank you" goes to my lovely wife, Andrée Leighton. Andrée wrote "Mary's Chapter" of the manuscript.

Andrée: may you be blessed for your loving support and encouragement during this whole process.

The cover art is the work of the incredibly artistic Julie Finger and Margalit Ward.

Acknowledgments

I would like to acknowledge the support of my parents, Dr. I. M. Levitt and Alice Levitt for their encouragement and belief in me.

There were many sources of information which assisted my research and enhanced my understanding of the historical Jesus. Although I cannot possibly name all of them, the following is a short list of references which helped me create the most accurate historical context available for my story:

The Gnostic Gospels by Elaine Pagels
Beyond Belief: The Secret Gospel of Thomas by Elaine Pagels
The Lost Gospel Q by Marcus J. Borg
James the Brother of Jesus by Robert H. Eisenman
From Jesus to Christ by Paula Fredriksen
The Five Gospels by Robert W. Funk
Judas Iscariot and the Myth of Jewish Evil by Maccoby
The Lost Gospel by Burton L. Mack
Who Wrote the New Testament? by Burton L. Mack
Rabbi Jesus by Bruce Chilton
Misquoting Jesus by Bart Ehrman

This novel blends the historical with the spiritual. There are three readily-available books which reflect the spiritual direction of this novel:

When Are You Coming Home by John-Roger
What's it Like Being You? by John-Roger
The Aquarian Gospel of Jesus the Christ by Levi

P.L.
Los Angeles
8/29/2005

PROLOGUE

OK. Sure. I copied the manuscript. I had to. I really felt there was no other choice. I'm not telling you this as an excuse, but as an explanation. I knew it would get me into trouble when I did it. Was it stealing? I'm not really sure. I didn't actually take the journal. I just took photos of it and had them translated. I suppose you probably think that I'm just deluding myself because I feel guilty about my actions. Well, I can tell you, without being self-righteous, that I probably have just as much right to that journal as The Threshold Foundation. After all, it was I who originally wrote it. And I did let go of my guilt. I paid the price for my actions. I did that gladly and would do it again. That was just the beginning, or at least I thought it was. After I learned the truth concerning the real beginning, I understood why I felt this way. Knowing the beginning gave me a sense of history and a sense of purpose. I always wanted to know, but it seems as if I got much more than I bargained for. If I had not been present when that ancient manuscript was found, I would never have had the history or the purpose, but my life would now be much, much simpler.

I was filming a dig in the Middle East for The Threshold Foundation and the Metropolitan Museum when a certain text in Aramaic was discovered. The document was a journal written by Yehudah bar Joseph, otherwise known as Judas Iscariot.

Here was a find of tremendous proportions. Even though a corporation with known shady business practices was funding the project, I decided to take the job. In fact, I found that I had a lot of trouble, at first, containing my excitement. I couldn't eat. I could hardly sleep as I followed very closely the painstaking process of the text being translated into English. My excitement began to turn to obsession as the process progressed at what appeared to be an ever-declining rate. The scholars of The Threshold Foundation still spend most of their time arguing about interpretations. The process had become a very polarized, political battlefield for them. Meanwhile, my entire being was screaming out in pain for the delivery of each word as if it was to be my next breath of air.

My patience had run out. I was being driven by this obsession and I had to act. Knowing that my camera could take digital photographs as well as video, I acted. I broke into the room where the book was kept and photographed all the pages. Before the sun came up the next day, I had left the dig and traveled to Jerusalem where I went to the home of my friend, Dr. Ernest Wilder.

I knew he would gladly translate the manuscript for me. Dr. Wilder had more experience than all of the other scholars together. His more politicized cohorts on the dig frowned upon his approach, vowing to get rid of this "renegade." However, I knew him to be an expert archeologist who based his interpretations upon historical evidence, not upon preconceived doctrines. I had grown to know him during the dig and became his friend. I was saddened when the foundation fired him. When I delivered my photos of the manuscript to him, he acted as though I had reintroduced him to a dear, long lost relative. I wanted to watch the process of the translation, but he sent me away. "I don't want to see you for four weeks," he said. "After that time you may call and see if I am finished." He gave me his number and practically pushed me out the door.

I buried my almost unbearable obsession in work. For four weeks I hunted and found enough photo jobs to keep me in my Jerusalem hotel room. I had almost forgotten the manuscript when I received a call from Dr. Wilder. "Come to my home immediately," he said. He welcomed me with the same intensity with which he had thrown me out four weeks before. It was as if he was a child with a new toy that he wanted to share with a playmate.

I started reading that very night. I anticipated a great relief. I felt myself strangely drawn into the story as I read it. Soon the words, the images, and the feelings became so familiar they were frightening. I began to relive all the events as if I were there. When I was able to recall events <u>not</u> mentioned in the text, I became truly terrified. I left my room and wandered through Jerusalem aimlessly, wanting to escape what seemed to be, for me, the obvious conclusion: that I had been Judas in another life.

I walked all night, oblivious to others, weakly attempting to find some answers inside of me. As the sun rose, I found myself in a courtyard with an unusual band of tourists. Their leader appeared as a rather ordinary middle-aged man but he had a presence that somehow reminded me of the description of Jesus in the document I had just finished the day before. I heard this man being called "Eric" by his companions or students.

As I edged my way closer through the crowd, our eyes met. I felt as if he was peering into the deepest recesses of my being. I knew that he felt my anguish, my torment, wondering if in a past life, I had been Judas. He said: "The one who now joins us sees his gift through the eyes of pain, but one day he will see that it will bring to him and others a profound sense of freedom. It won't be easy. Karma never is." That was all I heard him say. My awareness seemed to be lifted away from my body and I was plunged into an almost endless stream of other lives encompassing a personal history millions of years long.

He appeared to me again against this backdrop of history. But this time his appearance was somewhat more youthful. No, it was ageless.

"Who are you?" I asked.

"I am what's called a Sojourner or a Spiritual Sojourner. You could say I am a wayshower or guide, but as eventually disciples become teachers, you will only really know exactly what one is when you become one."

"I, of all people, would not be worthy."

"We all have had lives where we have made wrong choices and always God, Spirit has forgiven us. Our most severe judge is always ourselves. You are no different. Remember, God loves ALL of It's creation. There is no such thing as a 'throwaway' soul."

He faded from view and I fell into a deep, dreamless sleep.

When I returned to physical consciousness, I was back in my hotel room in bed and he was looking down at me. He spoke if nothing out of the ordinary had transpired.

"You're Roy Hammer. You make documentaries for T.V."

"It appears that wasn't always the case," I joked feebly.

He smiled and laughed. "Roy, you'd better leave to jokes to me. But, you've had a powerful experience. I was able to share that experience with you. Seeing that book triggered in you a massive recall and you just couldn't handle it in your physical consciousness, so your consciousness left your body behind, in other words, you passed out. We thought while you were gone from your body we might as well make it comfortable, and we went through your identification, found out where you were staying, and brought you back here."

"I am at a loss," I said. "I really don't know what to do."

"You know, you can see this all as a burden or an opportunity to be of service to yourself and others by sharing your experience."

"You mean my experience with the journal of Judas?"

"I shared that out-of-body experience with you," he said. "I was there so I can attest that it was real."

I found that really hard to believe. So I had him describe my experience for me in detail. He described the whole experience, from a slightly different viewpoint, but it was, nevertheless accurate. I found that I could not dispute him so for the moment, I suspended my disbelief and just tried to be open for explanation.

"What I discovered is that the journal was meant to be finished and that you have taken on a responsibility for its completion."

"There is much more," I said. "During my out-of-body experience, I saw that I had lived many lives and each of the lives was linked to a learning pattern set up by my soul ages ago; sort of following a spiritual road map. This experience has turned my whole life around. I have had a direct experience of living other lives. Now I know that the consciousness doesn't evaporate after death. We are all divine beings. We live forever. I don't know whether to be elated or to cry. And I was left with a knowing, a certainty that it was not only me but everyone who makes this journey."

"Nothing happens without a reason. Don't you think that your story might be helpful to others?"

"If they don't all think I'm a dangerous loony. How many times throughout history have people attempted to share the secret of our divine nature and met with disaster? It comes not only from those who wish to deny it, but those who wish to extinguish this knowledge. "

"You're no loonier than anyone else. Take me, for instance. I work as a standup comedian. When people are in the presence of a spiritual teacher, they find it hard to relax. If I come off like the village idiot, they relax and some of what I have to say actually gets in. Then, they find out that they are actually teaching themselves. I'm just a sort of tour guide with a goofy sense of humor. If I make them laugh, I no longer appear so dangerous."

Eric's voice then became very slow and deliberate. "You will find that following what is true inside of you is always the more difficult path. It may seem monumental, but all you have to do is just take each next step guided by your inner voice. You'll find that your vulnerability is also your protection. As for now, get your rest. Come and see me after you return to the States. I won't even charge you the cover. Some of my students have a property. You can stay there."

"You don't live there?"

"Nah, I like my privacy."

I don't think I grasped the full significance of what Eric had told me but I wanted to see more of him. He reminded me of someone I had once known well, perhaps a good friend. I wanted his friendship and his guidance.

I felt like I had been given a tremendous responsibility, yet I was spurred on by the promise of a purpose for my life, something I never really experienced previously. The emotions stirred by the figure of Judas, the betrayer, frightened me. My challenge was to both own that part of me that is the Spirit and the part that betrays the Spirit. That part in all of us called pride, egotism, ignorance, hatred, intolerance and many other "deadly sins." In my case, two thousand years ago, it appeared as jealousy.

So, I was to complete a two-thousand-year-old and perhaps unwanted "Gospel." To my knowledge this was the only one that described the events at the time they occurred. I found myself compelled to finish it. Many of the other disciples of the spiritual master and Sojourner, Jesus, (known then as Master Jeshua bar Joseph) were content to serve, to give their support and their love without being noticed.

From what I had seen of my past lives, I hadn't often been one of those. I mostly wanted to be in the forefront of the action, and, even once, in my vanity, pictured myself as a power behind the throne of an Israel reborn from Roman occupation. I have always had a desire to be recognized, especially as a spiritual adept. I find it somewhat ironic that I, or a prior expression of me, will forever be remembered in somewhat less flattering terms. Through the experiences of many lives, I have learned to forgive myself for my self-judgments. If I, who was Judas, can learn to forgive my self-judgments, others can certainly forgive their self-judgments which are most likely of a different nature. In this way I may be, in this life, of service to others.

So I, a modern "scribe," some two thousand years later, (and hopefully some two thousand years wiser), present to you my journal, my "Gospel," my account of Jesus. But there is more. I will also present to you my story, the story of my soul. I open to you what I have learned throughout time and all my errors and mistakes. It's a story of hope and a story of forgiveness. Eric told me, "Spirit has forgiven us... there is no such thing as a 'throwaway' soul." Jesus, himself, was able to forgive the unforgivable. We just have to start with ourselves.

CHAPTER 1 — A PERSONAL HISTORY

When I returned to the States everything I saw looked different. Could my life have changed so drastically? I had found out that I was more than this life. But then, nothing has ever been ordinary in this life either.

I came from a loving but busy family obsessed with work and performance. I was given the best my family could afford except for time with my mom and dad, who spent most of their time on one project or another. I always had the feeling that I was one of their lesser projects. I always felt that I was "not good enough" to be in their focus, that I had to excel in order to be recognized. Unless I was "a success" I never felt loved. Thus the drive to success.

I tend to be somewhat introverted, so I was not in the habit of making or keeping many friends. To combat loneliness many children create imaginary friends to keep them company. These are supposed to take the form of a playmate. Mine, of course, were of a different sort. Through most of my childhood I had the companionship of 10 hooded monks. I could not see them in the normal sense. I could feel their presence and could just make them out if I saw them from the corner of my eye. They were not playmates but teachers who guided, counseled and instruct me in all the ways I could keep my balance in the world. They remained with me until my teen years when I felt the need to reject any form of authority.

Up until about age five I existed in a state of innocent connection with the Source of Being, having a knowing which surpassed understanding. One evening the worries of the world intruded and I felt like I was cast into a bottomless pit of despair. I could not remember what I was so clear about only a little while before. I felt a fear that I had never before felt: a fear so intense it shook my entire being. It was the fear of death, not the death of leaving this world and going somewhere unpleasant, but of simply ceasing to exist, complete annihilation. I felt a fundamental anguish that God would permit this to happen to an innocent such as myself. Gradually I was able to drift off to sleep again and awoke the next morning back in a sense of belonging. I remembered the feeling but could not for the life of me remember what it was that made me believe that I would not exist forever now that the inner knowing was active. All doubts and fears were answered without words inside of me. I knew who I was again. I resolved to not let anything intrude on this inner knowing again. I asked for protection in my prayers and dreams. A week later the monks visited me for the first time. I made the mistake of telling my parents about them once and found myself being sent to a child psychologist. I learned from this experience that one should keep sacred inner experiences secret. I also learned that these inner experiences are considered unacceptable because of the inability to explain them to others in logical, physical terms. I learned much from my guides. They taught me much about maintaining a degree of inner discipline, so I managed to get in less trouble than many of my contemporaries.

The peak experiences that came to me were ones that I never expected, let alone, had time to prepare for. One day as I was walking home from school, a feeling of total contentment and joy suddenly overtook me. I was at once bathed and surrounded by a column of Light so intense it made me burn inside with a desire to be in the source of this Light continually and forever. It was so rich with pure Spirit, I felt as if I would have been burned up if I did not once again focus my consciousness into the world. Over the next few days the energy subsided but I would never be the same. From that day there would always be a center of absolute joy inside of me to which I could always retreat when I felt under attack by the events of the world. And these events kept coming. My childhood and young adulthood bristled with a series of inner tests as if I was being prepared for something extraordinary, but it never appeared.

I barely squeaked through college. I was more interested in women than I was in studies. You could say that I majored in transitory relationships. I loved the physical closeness of a relationship but was always disappointed when it came to deeper communications. After a while, I began looking for ways to end a relationship for fear of being caught in something that was essentially dead. This did not mean that I stopped trying. The possibility of actually finding someone right for me outweighed the pain my involvement always caused. When the initial pleasure of sex and intimacy faded, I began to feel the relationship becoming mechanical and researched a method of making the woman reject me. If I were the one rejected, I reasoned, I would be causing my ex-partner less pain while assuring my freedom from a wrong entanglement. I began to think that I would never find the right person who could share the inner experiences that were sacred to me.

I ended up with a degree in journalism. My grades were poor and I was cautioned that to continue my education in this direction would be a waste of my time and my parent's money. It was not that I was a bad writer, but a miserable student.

After college, I moved to a different city to get away from family and all who knew me. My only love at that time was motorcycles, and I got a job as a mechanic. During the week, I would work on other people's machines and on the weekend, once I could afford it, raced my own cycle. I got to be pretty good at it. So much so, I took too many chances and one day my luck ran out. While making a sharp turn, I hit a patch of oil and the machine slipped out from under me. I got away with a set of broken legs. While I was in the hospital, I had plenty of time to consider what to do with the direction of my life. I pretty much read and watched TV for the four weeks I was bed-ridden. One night I saw a documentary on ancient Egypt. I immediately thought how great it would be if I could film great discoveries of the ancient world that would bring our history as a species to light. This was the first time that I had ever really become enthusiastic about a field of study. Through force of will, a few contacts and that same enthusiasm, I was able to get into one of the lesser known, smaller film schools. I poured myself into my studies and graduated before my time with close to a 4.0 average and a job waiting for me at Metropolitan Museum as a chronicler of their expeditions. Having control of the camera, I was always able to be close to where the discoveries were being made. The field of archeology fascinated me and I began to read any books on the subject that I could get my hands on. As I learned more about the beginnings of man's civilization, I could not help developing an even deeper questioning concerning the nature of man himself. I dove into philosophy and ended up with Theosophy, or the "study of God." This realm of thought approached an explanation of my youthful experiences but in terms that were too mental for me, too mechanical. I wanted confirmation of my own experiences and a way to continue to access them.

As I participated in digs in the Americas, Europe, and Asia, I found flashes of recognition and connection with diverse ancient cultures. A voice grew in me telling me, that what I was looking for I would find in Israel, but we had no digs planned there. One morning I came to work and we were packing up equipment. The London Museum had given up a dig due to a last minute administrative problem and The Threshold Foundation, working through the Metropolitan Museum, was being called in to do the work. The site was just outside Jerusalem. I didn't know much about it, but I did find out that Empire Investments, a conglomerate known for shady business tactics, was sponsoring the Threshold Foundation in funding the dig. When it came to actually pinning anything on *Empire*, they were like Teflon. I told myself that none of that would affect me since they were only going to be the ones who signed my paycheck.

The rest of the events around the discovery of the journal I've already shared. I returned to the states with Eric and his group. He had called ahead and had a place prepared for me. I was able to stay at the communal residence owned by Eric's group in San Francisco. I was given a job with Eric's video production team, who often recorded his standup routines and more serious seminars. Eric's seminars intrigued me. Here was the type of learning I was looking for since my childhood — it matched my inner experience. I became a student of Eric's. What seemed the most important to me was that I was given time to sort out the flurry of images that had started to pour out of my head since first reading the manuscript. Eric kept telling me how very fortunate I was. If others wanted some information about previous lives, they would have to have a regression session to obtain only a fraction of the information with which I had been flooded.

What came forward for me over a period of a few months was a somewhat disjointed tale of history, my own history, from before the beginning of time to the present. At last my lack of direction had ceased! My obsession for knowledge of myself was replaced by a desire to add additional experiences from that lifetime to the original Judas manuscript and share it with the world. For the next two years, I took the original manuscript and added to it any of my own experiences that might have historical significance. During that time I studied with Eric, got extra video jobs and was able to move out on my own.

I began to send out copies of the manuscript for publication. I was turned down at least thirty times. One of the publishers, one that usually specialized in scientific non-fiction, held onto it for six months and would not get back to me.

During that time, someone had broken into my apartment and only a few valuables were taken. There had been a flurry of "wrong numbers" that hung up when I answered.

I called Eric: "I made a copy of my manuscript on CD-ROM. Would you keep it safe for me? You're the only person I trust," I said, trying not to sound too paranoid.

"And not use parts of it in my routine?" He asked with a laugh.

"Well… it might get you in trouble as well."

"OK," he said, "You send it. I'll try to resist the temptation."

Nothing strange happened for a few days. Then came a knock on the door. It was the police claiming they had a warrant for my arrest. I was taken to the main lockup near city hall. As soon as I could I called Eric and told him what happened.

"Eric, I don't know what you can do, but I really need help here," I said.

He looked at me very seriously. "I'll have to ask my agent first. Nah. Just pulling your leg. Roy, can I help you even if the situation appears to get worse?"

"Sure," I answered. "You're my best chance. Actually you're my only chance."

Over the next few days, I was visited by a few of Eric's students. At my arraignment, I finally found out what the charges were — stealing the Judas manuscript. I was surprised. I didn't actually steal it; I copied its contents. But I took something that didn't belong to me — the information contained in the manuscript — and would have to pay the price for theft of that information. But whose information was it? To whom did it belong? The person that wrote it or the people that found it? I was the original owner. I wrote that manuscript over two thousand years ago and therefore I considered it still my property. Who would believe me? Certainly Eric and his students would, but they were not the ones who would judge me. If this were taken to court, I would probably not stand a chance in claiming it was mine. How could I prove that this book and the information in it was mine? The only way I could see was by proving that I was the man who wrote it two thousand years ago, Judas Iscariot.

My court appointed public defender urged me to plead guilty so I could possibly get a lesser sentence. I admit, I was truly tempted to do just that — accept an "easy out" that would get me out of trouble in the shortest length of time. But I couldn't. There was something inside me that knew I would be going against my very being by giving in. I was the most scared I had ever been in my life. I did not know what lay ahead if I went down this road, but it was something that I had to do.

My public defender was somewhat nondescript in appearance. He seemed to blend in so well with his surroundings that he could almost be invisible.

When I told him what I wanted to do, he looked at me with astonishment. "Look, this really no time to pull this sort of foolishness. You could be put in jail for a very long time. If you insist on this, I may not be able to represent you. The best thing for you to do would be to plead guilty. I might be able to get your sentence reduced if you cooperate."

"I know it sounds insane, but that manuscript belongs to me because I was the one who wrote it."

"Two thousand years ago?"

"Yeah, two thousand years ago!"

He looked at me as if I had just stepped off a flying saucer. "This is crazy. How could we possibly prove that? Where could we possibly find a witness to prove you were there?"

I thought. If I had these memories, perhaps others could also.

He finally did comply with my demand that I plead not guilty. I was taken back to jail, but only stayed there another day. Finally, I was released. Eric's students had taken up a collection so I could make bail.

A man in his early twenties met me at the jail. His name was Josh and he spoke with a pronounced Australian accept. As we let the police building, he asked, "Have you seen the news?"

"What news?"

He opened a copy of the *Chronicle* and showed me an article. A headline lower right side on page one read, "Man Claims to Have Written Two Thousand Year-Old Text."

"You are no longer a nobody," said Josh. "People are talking about you."

This was the type of headline you would expect to see waiting in line at the supermarket, but here it was in a reputable news source. This didn't happen very often.

"Just my fifteen minutes of fame. Well, Eric was right, things do appear worse," I said, under my breath.

"What?"

"Nothing. Could you take me to a library?"

"Right," he said. "Glad to."

My plan was to check some of the historical sources and see if I remembered things that might be different than recorded history that I could readily explain. I spent hours in the library that day with no results. The beginning of my trial was just days away, and I was no closer to setting up a defense than before. Perhaps the public defender was correct, that I really didn't have a case. When Josh brought me back to Eric's I don't know whether I was more exhausted or depressed. I wanted to talk to Eric but he was busy.

I fell into bed and slept for about twelve hours. When I awoke it was about 1 AM. I stumbled downstairs for some cold water and returned to bed. Eric had taught me the ancient "HU" chant, the ancient Sanskrit name for God. I chanted that silently to myself for maybe fifteen minutes before I dropped off to sleep. I was awakened when someone touched my arm. It was Eric. He asked me to get up and follow him. I turned around and saw my body lying on the bed. "Am I dead?" I asked.

"No," said Eric. "You are just traveling where your body cannot follow. You have awakened on a different plane of being. It is called multidimensional awareness. Relax; I'll be your tour guide. It will be easy for you."

Instantly, we were sitting on the front porch where it was sunny and no one else was around. I was fully awake where I was, yet knew that my body was asleep. Things seemed so much more responsive to my thoughts where Eric had taken me. I was thinking about cold water and a glass of it appeared on a small table beside me. I took a deep gulp and it felt good in my mouth, as when I was awake.

After some silence, I said, "Eric, I am really worried about this trial. Things are looking hopeless."

"Just what will happen if you lose?" He asked.

"I would not get to publish the story of my other lifetime. I want to share that story with others. That's what I really want to do. If I couldn't do that, I feel that life would become, well, meaningless for me."

"You do have a bit of drama in you, don't you?" He chuckled.

I laughed. "Yeah, guess I do. But this still something I really want to do."

"I know it was I who suggested it to you, but what if it is just not for you to do?"

"How's that?"

"What if the object of life's game is not to win at it but to master the game — to use either your win or loss to lift above and beyond the game?"

"You mean to not be attached to results."

"Shifting your focus would help. In every Gospel, even the one Judas wrote, it has been stated that if we 'seek first the kingdom of heaven, all else will be added.'"

"I'm not sure what that means."

"Another way of putting it would that the joy is in the travel, not the destination. It's as if life on this planet is a theme park and the theme is learning for awareness. What if you were a child of God, a divine being, sent to this world to learn to be a responsible co-creator when you return to your Father? What if you knew this without the shadow of a doubt? You would then be able to turn your worry and concern to a sense of adventure and an experience of courage."

"I suppose so. But right now I still have a fear of failure."

He looked far into space. "It's only a failure if you judge it as one. This test has been given to you for a reason and that is to use whatever happens in your life for your spiritual advancement, whether you win or lose. You might want to ask yourself, 'what is this situation asking of me? What's the lesson?' First of all it's not a punishment. Most people would look at a difficult situation and be resentful or ask 'Why me?' The easier route would be to accept the situation, cooperate with it and look to master it. The way it is set up in this world is that you are never given anything you cannot handle. If you are that divine being and you created such a situation, you must be larger than that situation." He turned to face me. "Well, that's really all I can tell you now. You're lucky. You got all that without the cover charge."

I was still frightened but I began to consider the alternative view of my coming ordeal being an adventure, an examination that called for me to demonstrate my true being at its most courageous and resourceful self. I resolved myself to avoid any fatalism that might creep into my consciousness. I would also watch out for any feelings of being made a victim. In that I could avoid resentment. It was not natural for me to look at challenges as adventures. I am lazy by nature and want things to be easy as possible for me.

On the first day after jury selection, I approach a table where my public defender was supposed to wait for me before he entered. But he was nowhere in sight. Instead, I saw a young Asian man in a very stylish suit sitting on the table eating a sandwich.

"Oh, sorry," he said as he opened his briefcase for a moment and threw the half-eaten sandwich into a bag inside. "The name's Chris Woo. Some friends of yours hired me to defend you." He went to shake my hand but then halted and first wiped it with a napkin. He shook my hand with a firm grip and quickly gave me his card, as if I would doubt his identity.

"You've got a very interesting case here," he began.

"Does that mean it's un-winnable?" I asked.

He looked at me with a slight grin curling both edges of his mouth as if some inner jester was struggling to get out and shook his finger at me. "Eric said you would be a real bundle!" He quickly put on his "serious lawyer face" and continued: "You say that you have every right to publish your version of a two thousand year-old text because you were the original author, is that correct?" He looked at me with a mock wide-eyed questioning expression.

"Right so far." I said, attempting to appear as natural and serene as possible.

He shook his head. "Well, OK, then what we have to prove is, number one, that you're not crazy, and number two, that you were the actual Judas Iscariot that lived almost two thousand years ago."

He looked at me with his sternest lawyer look. "Well, what do you think?"

"Totally un-winnable!" I said.

We both broke out laughing and he gave me a big smile. "I think I'm going to enjoy this one," he said. "And, you have just proved, at least to me, that you're not crazy."

"I do have one question," I said, "Who exactly was it that hired you?"

"Ah, that's on a need-to-know basis." He said.

I waited for the usual follow-up line, but Chris remained silent. "And, I don't need to know?"

"Right."

Just then, the bailiff told us to rise and Judge Alice Wainright came to the bench.

I looked over at the opposing table and saw a bevy of lawyers with briefcases who all seemed to be wearing the same suit. The one closest to the aisle, presumably the senior partner, motioned to the judge. He was a good-looking, but slightly overweight black man, who was graying prematurely at his temples. He stood up revealing an imposing figure of a man who looked to me like he would be more at home on the front line of an NFL team than in a courtroom.

"That's Fredrick Hastings," Chris whispered. "One of the highest paid corporate litigators in the country. He's extremely detail-oriented and as much of a good detective as a lawyer. Most in the profession are frightened to go against him in the courtroom. This foundation of yours has some heavy connections."

"And you're not afraid of Hastings?" I questioned.

"I know his weak area. I know how to keep him off balance. He depends on his surroundings, his world, to be well ordered. It needs to play by his rules. He is very uncomfortable if he has to fly by the seat of his pants."

"Have you ever faced him?" I asked, hoping for an affirmative answer.

"No, but I watched him numerous times in court." He winked. "Trust me."

The lawyer sitting closest to Mr. Hastings, a severe-looking blond woman in a suit similar to his, motioned to him. She handed him a folder which he opened and read. He closed the file, returned it to the woman and cleared his throat.

"Who's that?" I asked.

"Oh, that's Merissa Crane. Her father is one of the directors of Empire Investments. She's there as a watchdog, I would assume. You know, just in case Hastings starts to lose his taste for blood. Bu-u-u-t, I really don't see that happening."

Hastings' presentation was a straightforward one. The journal was found by The Foundation and is therefore the property of The Foundation. I had copied the information and therefore robbed them of their intellectual property.

"Therefore," he concluded, "the defendant should serve a jail term at the discretion of the court, be blocked from publishing his 'account' of this manuscript and be fined for expenses resulting from his activities."

He looked me sternly in the eye for a few seconds before sitting down. A chill went up my spine. Not because I was afraid, but because I had seen this man somewhere before. Something in his eyes was very familiar. I couldn't place it, but I know that I had known him somewhere before.

"Counselor," said the judge, motioning to Chris, "I have heard of your reputation for theatre and other eccentric approaches to the profession of law, and I just want to remind you that I will not tolerate anything that disrupts this court. Cause any problems and you will be in contempt. Is that clearly understood?"

"Of course, your honor," said Chris.

"Then you may make your opening statement."

"Your honor, my esteemed colleagues, ladies and gentlemen of the jury," he began. "My esteemed opponent has presented to you the facts; facts that can be readily seen and understood. But can there be facts that we can't see? For instance it is a fact that right now there are energy waves of different frequencies all around us. Can we see them? No. But if we find the right device to make them visible…"

Chris pulled a small portable TV out of his briefcase and turned it on. The courtroom was filled with rap music and you could see a small color picture on the screen.

"Counselor, you can turn that off now," said the judge with a somewhat pained expression on her face. "We get your point."

"I intend to do the same thing with the facts in this case. I intend to prove that my client not only has the right to publish this manuscript but to show beyond a doubt that this manuscript is actually his property. I intend to show that it was my client who originally wrote this manuscript almost two thousand years ago. I intend to show that my client was the apostle Judas Iscariot in a previous existence. Furthermore, I intend to have his lawful property returned to him!"

It seemed like five minutes of silence in the courtroom. The lawyers at the opposite table were either staring at Chris or had their heads buried in their hands in disbelief. Out of the corner of my eye, I could see Hastings glaring at Chris.

Chris had already sat down beside me. I whispered in his ear, "You know they may order the same psychiatric tests for you as they will for me."

He whispered back, "*No problema*, I'm ready!" He said with mock seriousness.

The courtroom eventually regained its appearance of normality as the opposing counsel presented all his witnesses. They were very professional and had their entire case stated in perhaps an hour and a half.

The judge did what we expected her to do, called a recess and ordered psychiatric tests for me.

"We are also going to order a polygraph exam for you. It's not admissible as evidence, but it may add an air of legitimacy to your story," said Chris confidently.

As we left, Chris' phone rang.

"Yes sir," he said formally. "I really can't talk now but I want to just say that everything is going the way we planned. OK. No, I haven't said a thing. Honest. OK. I will meet you tonight. OK. Bye."

"OK, Chris, who was that? I have a feeling that whoever that was affects this case a whole lot."

"Need to know," was all he said.

The psychiatric exam took quite some time. When it was over, I was ready for bed. Chris told me to meet him the next morning for the polygraph test.

I slept well that night. I remember only one dream and that was the character of Judas and I appeared and started to merge. Finally, Judas was speaking from my mouth in his own words. I was no longer in control. I awoke. It was about 3 AM. I did some of the breathing exercises that Eric had shown me for calming and then again drifted off to sleep.

The next day I came in for the lie detector test, the polygraph. They asked me endless questions about my present life, as well as all they could ask concerning what I remembered about my lifetime as Judas. I was thoroughly exhausted after this session and went back home (temporarily Eric's place) afterward. I slept about twelve hours but woke up refreshed and ready for the next day of my trial.

Chris looked more professional on the second day of the trial. His energy was all over the place as if flushed from a triumph. He showed me a copy of the newspaper that detailed the first day of the trial. He seemed elated because of the coverage of his courtroom tactics on the first day. His confidence soared and one could not help feel lifted and sustained by all of the positive energy he exuded.

Since the opposition had rested their case, the show belonged to Chris. This was the way he liked it. He was out there center-stage just having the time of his life, while mine (in my opinion) was held in the balance.

I was called as his first witness.

"Would you state your name, please?"

"My name is Roy Hammer."

"What is your profession?"

"I make films. I chronicle the type of expedition that turned up the manuscript."

"OK. After reading the original manuscript, what did you experience?"

"Memories. Memories of the times and places described in the manuscript. But more than that, experiences from that time that were not written down, but that I remembered."

"Did you remember writing the manuscript?"

"Yes."

"Objection!" Boomed Hastings. "How long are we going to put up with these fantasy musings being placed into record as if they are facts?"

"Counselor?" Queried the judge.

"I beg your indulgence with this line of questioning, your honor. I am merely trying to establish the background for building my case. He handed me a printout of the manuscript to which I had added my own recollections. "Do you recognize this?"

"Yes," I answered. "It's my finished manuscript."

"Do you recognize these?" He asked, holding up a few photo print-outs.

"Yes," They're my photos of the original manuscript."

"Your Honor, between this original and this man's additions to that manuscript lies the answer to this puzzle. If we can prove that the additions to the original manuscript are genuine, we can prove that he was there writing the original."

"Overruled," said the judge. "But be careful counselor! You had better start making your point in a direct manner."

"I shall Your Honor," said Chris. "In the end it will all appear rational and logical." He shot Hastings a whimsical smile.

"Then you may continue," said the judge.

Chris then called a doctor to the witness box who had the results of my psychiatric tests.

On the question of my sanity, the doctor reported, "Other than his contention that he remembers a prior lifetime, he appears quite normal. He has a good analytical mind and is quite imaginative."

I glanced over at Hastings. He chafed in his seat as if he couldn't wait to cross-examine. He stood, pulled at his jacket and began: "You spoke about him having a good imagination. Doctor, could he have imagined this whole thing?"

"It is possible. But from what I gather, the level of detail of his recollections is impressive."

"Could all of that, then, have been fabricated?"

"In my opinion, only by someone who has professional knowledge of archeology and the history of the time period."

"Then doctor, we would agree, then, that Mr. Hammer has had an extensive exposure to archeology and had an almost compulsive need to do historical research on his subject.

"Probably."

"Do you think that with all of these factors that he could have the tools to put together a fantastic story like this one?"

"Well, I…"

Chris popped up out of his chair. "Objection! Counselor is leading the witness into conjecture about a subject that is not in his area of expertise."

"Sustained," said Judge Wainright.

"I withdraw the question. Thank you, doctor." Concluded Hastings.

Chris called his next witness, a technician, the one who did the polygraph test.

"So what your results prove," summed Chris, "is that the fact that these experiences my client had are true."

"Well, he perceives them as true." Answered the technician.

"What I'm getting at," said Chris, "is that there is no lying, no fabrication involved here."

"None that appears on the polygraph," answered the technician.

"So, to sum up, my client is of the honest belief that he was this man two thousand years ago who wrote the manuscript. We have already seen that he is not insane nor is he faking his experience. Is this your conclusion?"

"Well, yes."

"Objection!" said Hastings. "Counselor is leading the witness into conjecture about a subject that is not in his area of expertise."

"Sustained," said Judge Wainright.

Chris winked at him and said, "I withdraw the question. Thank you."

The technician took his seat.

Hastings rose slowly and shot Chris a contemptuous glance. "My 'esteemed' opponent," he said with all the irony he could muster, "knows that this evidence is not admissible. Is he trying to waste the court's time?"

Chris' knuckles went white around the pencil he was grasping as if choking some internal rage. To me it looked like Hastings was no fool; he knew Chris' weak point as well. It seemed as though Chris wanted to prove his professionalism to everyone but the one who mattered, himself.

I felt it might compromise his performance on my case, which I could not afford to have happen.

"Well, counselor?" said the judge, with a growing interest.

I tapped Chris on the shoulder and whispered to him, "Go ahead, I believe in you!"

Chris exhaled, nodded and rose from his seat and re-buttoned his jacket. "Your honor, I am merely trying to demonstrate the good faith of my client and to open a crack in the door of plausibility for our argument."

"Then, please, continue counselor, and please try to be direct."

"As I said before, the answer to this puzzle lies in the text itself. The only chance my client has to prove that this is his work is to read it. Only Mr. Hammer, with his gift of recollection can prove he was there. He must have the court's permission to read the manuscript."

Hastings snapped to attention, "I object. This is highly irregular and only seeks to prolong what is a simple case of theft."

Chris was on his feet. "Your honor, this is absolutely necessary to the core of my case. Mr. Hammer will prove who he is, or was, through this process. A similar case, Worley vs. Vargas, was allowed to proceed. It involved a woman who had lost her memory, and through the process of reading her own journal, she remembered certain facts important to the case which were previously forgotten."

"Counselors, approach the bench!" Said the judge. Both took their places in front of Judge Wainright, who then turned off her microphone. Hastings, who dwarfed Chris, looked down upon him with loathing. Chris looked away; choosing not to receive the slight offered him. After a somewhat heated but almost inaudible exchange, the judge spoke. "Objection overruled. We will adjourn until tomorrow so that Mr. Hastings may further familiarize himself with Mr. Hammer's version of the document." She then punctuated this communication with her gavel.

Chris sighed in relief and packed his briefcase to leave.

"Do things look better now?" I asked.

"Better than before," was his evasive answer.

He seemed preoccupied and then he got a call on his phone as he was leaving. "Yes. Perfect. We've got time now, but it won't last. I'll tell you about it when I get there. OK. Bye."

He seemed in a hurry to get somewhere. "I'll see you tomorrow. Bye."

Something inside of me screamed out to follow him. I wanted to find out who it was who was directing Chris because ultimately that person held my future in his or her hands as well.

I followed him down the street feeling like an actor in a grade-B detective movie. Something else inside me took over. I began to do things that I would not ordinarily do. I had a knowing about how to remain undetected, how to remain invisible in a crowd. I remembered! It was Judas or that part of me that was Judas. Judas the Sicarri, Judas the assassin. I had done this before. I surrendered to its direction inside me and just flowed with the feeling. There was something exhilarating in this tracking that I found good for my ego. At last I had the opportunity to discover what seemed to control my destiny.

Chris ducked into a seedy hotel and walked up the stairs. I followed but kept a safe distance away since I saw Chris checking to see if anyone noticed him. When he got to the third floor, his footsteps halted and he knocked quietly on a door.

"Who is it?" A voice inside asked.

"Weasley." He answered.

Oh, a code-name. This was getting to be too much cloak and dagger. A door opened and closed. I could hear muffled voices. I began to get annoyed. I really dislike being tricked and having information withheld from me. I really did not even consider that there might be some danger in this situation.

I listened until I found the door and pounded on it.

"Who's there?" Asked an unfamiliar voice.

I went along with what I thought would be an appropriate answer in code. "Harry Potter."

The door opened and a man with a gun grabbed my shirt and pulled me in.

A tall, muscular man with a decidedly Australian accent held me tightly while turning to Chris said, "bleedin' idiot!"

"And you would be… Hagrid?" I said with much too much sarcasm for someone who had a gun pointed at him.

"Jack Highsmith, mate." He said. Glanced at his gun and quickly holstered it. Offered me his hand, which I shook, happy that there was not a gun in it. "Homeland Security. FBI… officially." He shrugged. "But also the CIA, SEC, NASD, DEA, and perhaps a few others."

I got another look at him. He looked like an agent: blond, tall, well proportioned as if he worked out every day. Not an ounce of fat on him. "I've just made a decision. Rather than kill you, I reckon I'll tell you everything. I owe you that."

"I applaud your decision-making ability," I said. There was something about him. Something I liked immediately. No doubt he could have killed me if he had to but there was something else…

"Don't let the accent fool you. I've been in the states since I was eighteen." He began. "Been working alone on this case; that is until this turkey blew my cover." Pointed his finger at Chris who looked hurt. "I'm going to tell you about it because you are now a part of something much larger. And… I need your help. Actually, my younger brother Josh told me about you. Your situation grabbed my interest because of your connection with The Threshold Foundation and its connection with Empire Investments. I've been on their trail for almost two years now. Their principle business is money laundering. They will accept money from anyone – drug cartels, dictators, terrorists, you name it. They hired the best lawyers to nail you and attempted to keep all of this quiet. You see, one of their money laundering operations is through the expeditions The Threshold Foundation is conducting; it's one of their 'outlets.' I've gotta find where this money is coming from. Once I find the source, I can make an arrest. The longer this trial goes, the more time I have to find that answer and the more chance that they will do something to slip up. That's where Christopher here comes in. I was the one who hired him." Chris gave me a rather sheepish grin.

"I don't see the connection with me. Why am I so important to these people?"

"That's the beauty of it. If The Threshold Foundation blows this trial, there is a good chance that they will lose their matching funding. The mixing of honest with dishonest money is an important ingredient in money laundering. This is one they can't afford to lose. You're in their sights, whether you like it or not. You represent a stack o' money to *Empire*."

I looked over at Chris. "So your only plan is to draw out the trial, no other strategy?"

He smiled back at me. "I have every confidence that by the time I run out of tricks we we'll come up with something."

I must have looked totally horrified. Chris gave me a playful punch on the arm. "You were <u>an apostle</u>, after all. Have a little faith."

CHAPTER 2 - A CHILDHOOD IN GALILEE

The following day Chris met me before the trial began. "Listen, I wasn't kidding when I said that you held the keys to solving the puzzle of proving you were there. As you read your account, try to remember anything that you may have left out of both your recent version and the original. I'm looking for some significance in why you left something out of the original. You've got the answer inside of you, I just know it!"

I did not have the faintest idea how to approach this situation, but I tried to put on a cooperative show for Chris so he could perform at his best.

We rose as the judge entered. She said to Chris, "Your witness, counselor."

I took the stand and read.

In childhood most everything is possible. When we are little children and the veil of forgetfulness has not yet descended, we see so clearly the potential for good in ourselves and for our world. It is only later, when we have been teased by our peers or taught the "facts of life" by our well-meaning but often world-weary and pessimistic parents that we begin to doubt our true vision and turn our backs on the idealism of youth. I saw this happen in many families in our village of Capernaum and those surrounding us. More and more of my friends would gain discouragement along with adulthood. Many would turn to the resistance against Rome and join the Zealots. Others like me turned away from the physical and prayed for the Messiah to deliver his people from under the cruel yoke of a smothering, occupying power.

In our family, there was just me and my older brother, Simon, and our parents, Joseph and Cyborea. My father Joseph was a merchant. He would be gone for months at a time to buy goods at the port city of Cæsaria and bring them back to Galilee. He was quite learned for a Galilean, knowing not only the Torah but also Greek and Roman literature and philosophy. Once, I could not have been more than three or four, I blurted out one of my visions in a paroxysm of joy: "I am to be with the Messiah and help him complete his work." My father did not laugh or rebuke me. He just looked at me with the patience of a master.

"How will you do that, my son?"

"I do not know, Abba, but it was decided before…in the before-time."

My father was a devout Essene, so reincarnation was a part of his belief. He asked me the question that people have been asking for centuries: "Who is the Messiah, little one, and when will he come?"

"He is here, Abba, and he is my elder brother."

This time he did laugh. "Your brother Simon?" He shook his head and the smile slowly disappeared from his face. "That one won't be satisfied until he's hanging on a Roman cross."

"No, Abba, he is also your elder brother."

That one stopped him dead in his tracks. He was a very loving parent. He wanted to see the best for his children. He, of course, would have preferred that one of his sons take over his business, but if one would become a teacher and be known for scholarship, he would not complain. He was interested (and puzzled) enough to see that from then on I was to get the best teachers that he could afford. This was usually given the older brother but Simon had more interest in using a sword than studying Torah.

When I was about seven, the veil of forgetfulness dropped and I was left with only vague memories of the time before this life. There began a desire, an urgency inside me, to gain enlightenment. In this way, I could find the messiah and be by his side. But, what is more, *I wanted people to know it!* I wanted to be recognized as a co-worker with the messiah. And, as things came forward, I didn't have to wait too long.

There were numerous sects in Judaism with many different beliefs. Among these sects were the Sadducees, the Pharisees and the Essenes. The only thing we all really had in common was the Torah, the written law. Some took it in a strictly literal fashion (the Sadducees), some with the addition of an oral tradition (Pharisees), and some focused on the preparation for the return of the Messiah (the Essenes).

My father, being a good and pious Essene, preferred that I study with an Essene teacher. For half of the year I was sent to the Essene monastery at Mt. Carmel. The other half was spent at my family's house in Capernaum where I worked with my father in his business to pay for my lessons. I was truly excited. The reputation of the library at Mt. Carmel was almost legendary. It was second only to the library at Alexandria, Egypt, in depth and breadth of knowledge.

My desire for knowledge and wisdom quickly propelled me through my studies. I was considered a very promising student and came to study under Judith, the foremost teacher at Mt. Carmel. Judith was a truly amazing woman. I had learned from other students that she had undergone several initiations in Egypt. Her understanding of the mystical aspects of being held me entranced and eager to learn more.

Judith told me that I might be able, at some point, to instruct the younger boys. She said that it would help if I began studying under the tutorship of another boy who was already actively teaching younger students. Judith brought me in to watch this boy, Jeshua, teach the younger students. He was the only student at the monastery who was treated with such reverence by older, more experienced scholars. I had the feeling that he was someone very special. Jeshua was a year older than I, had reddish-blond hair (parted in the middle), gray eyes and a piercing glance which could be stern as any chief rabbi or as supportive as one's own mother. When Judith talked to Jeshua, she spoke like she spoke to no other. It was as if every fiber of her being proclaimed some rare special honor upon him. She knew something of majestic purport and was not at liberty to speak it.

As Jeshua was speaking I noticed his command of the law and his ability to interpret complex ideas into practical concepts that one could live by. I had never heard a philosopher, priest or rabbi talk with such inner authority. I was captivated.

Jeshua had been educated by Essene Masters and teachers in Alexandria where he had spent most of his early years. I was surprised to find out that his father was also named Joseph. There was something very familiar about this boy that affected me quite strangely. After a few days, I got up the courage to ask him directly "Jeshua, I feel, well, strange talking with you about this, but… I feel like I've known you before. Jeshua, do you think that we have known each other before?"

"Most assuredly!"

His parents were also Essenes so it followed he would have a belief in reincarnation or "resurrection," as we called it. But the assurance with which he claimed our connection was almost frightening. Could he have kept with him the "far memory?"

"Where...when..." I asked.

"Are you sure you want to know? You might be disappointed."

"I *must*...I *have* to know."

"Very well, then. We were brothers in another time, Yehudah. You were jealous of me and sold me into slavery." He said this as a matter of fact, without any rancor.

I was crestfallen, yet I had to believe him. He said this in his quiet, sincere way.

"How could I have done such a horrible thing to you?" He looked at me with a mixture of sadness and compassion.

"Actually Yehudah," a sweet smile came over his face, "you saved my life. Our other brothers would have killed me!"

I felt a relief so great, tears came to my eyes.

"You see, Yehudah, we really cannot be judge and jury over ourselves. We do not know the result of our actions over the vastness of time. It is the Father's wish that we progress along our own paths toward him. None is better than the other. And since we are His children, none of us will ever be lost! What you need Yehudah is to learn to forgive yourself and not be willing to believe the worst about yourself."

"But, what about evil men?"

"Our law states 'an eye for an eye.' This is often misunderstood as a directive for men to punish each other. What it really means is that what you put into motion will come back upon you."

"Even from prior lives."

"Yes, Yehudah, the law will not be mocked. So often we see people suffering for no reason in this life. It is just a completion of the law."

"Can we ever get beyond this suffering?"

"What I know for a fact is that if each of us will set ourselves at doing our Father's work in this world we burn up the debt much more quickly and with less pain. It is only man that punishes. The Grace of our Father is the greatest law. Your father sent you to study here so I know what a loving father he is to you. Our heavenly Father is even more loving than that."

"And how do we do our Father's work?"

"Love Him and love ourselves and love our neighbors. This is most easily done by not hurting oneself, not hurting others and using all things in this life for the advancement of the Spirit within us. This is most unselfish, for once we become a clearer channel for the Father we most effectively influence others for the good."

I lived for our discussions. Although Judith held me in awe with her knowledge and wisdom, it was Jeshua who really inspired me. For the first time I saw who I could be in looking at him. The formal studies at Mt. Carmel paled in comparison to the easy wisdom that Jeshua shared with me. He took what we were taught and gave it a whole new meaning and a whole new... aliveness! Here was someone my age (or a little older) that I could pattern myself after. I really wanted to be like him. It was easy to see how one could be jealous of such an incredibly gifted individual. Yet, I did not feel jealousy for him but the desire to be included as a part of whatever he was doing.

When we were not at Mt. Carmel, we were at Capernaum, with Jeshua learning the trade of carpentry and I learning that of a merchant.

One day he said to me: "Come over to my house today, I want you to meet someone really special." When I got there I was greeted with a stern look from an Essene monk, dressed entirely in white with a reddish beard.

"Are you from the monastery on Mt. Carmel?" I asked.

He looked all at once very sad. "More and more. I was brought up in a Sadducee family. My father was a priest but he was killed on the altar of the Temple, proclaiming the coming of the messiah. I am torn, yet I find I cannot support a priesthood that kills the messengers of truth. Even if he were proclaiming a <u>false</u> prophet, there would be no reason for him being put to death. There is something more than bitterness inside me. I feel that the way of the Lord will be made straight and that somehow I am to be a part of that."

"So, you have become an Essene monk, and taken the vows of celibacy and poverty."

He chuckled. "If the Essenes did not exist, I would have done these things myself. You have heard how the Zealots proclaim their zealousness for the Lord, for the Law."

"I have heard of them mostly through my brother, Simon."

"Well, I too am zealous, but for the Law alone and not politics... and actually more than the law."

"What is beyond the Law?"

I could hear a passion rise up in his voice that had me riveted to his next word. "Beyond the letter of the Law is the Spirit of the Law. For me the Spirit of the Law <u>is</u> the Law. The trouble with a good number of the Pharisees is not that they don't know the Law, but that they fail to *really live it.* The study of the Law becomes a mental exercise unless you also find love in it. The Law in the Torah is empty unless it is also in your heart. I feel that I cannot be a complete human being unless I live the Law, breath the Law, and do all this from inside of me. That's where the true Law is being written."

"Did you learn this at the Monastery?"

"Actually I found this truth inside of me while walking in the wilderness. I feel so close to God when I am there. I really feel much further away from others when I am with them."

As if on cue, Jeshua appeared. "Yehudah, I see you've met my cousin John. We see very little of this character these days. It took my mother having another son to bring him here."

Both he and his cousin John, who appeared to be about three years older smiled. They had a warm relationship. "Now, Yehudah, like your brother Simon, I have a younger brother also. My mother calls him James."

He seemed really excited about this new addition to his family. I felt that I would envy this child to have Jeshua as an older brother. Just what was my relationship with Simon?

Simon was my older brother by two years and he had a certain nobility to him that brought respect. There was a bond between us to be sure, but I sensed it was more related to duty than to love. He was always a good brother to me. Beyond that, he also had a certain cavalier attitude toward life, that if things were not the way he wanted them he might risk all to change them. Our father was unsure that Simon would live to reach his Bar Mitzvah. Although we were not a noble family, we were not poor either and Simon took it on himself to preserve family honor whenever and wherever it might be in danger. In one instance, he came to my aid as I returned from studying with Judith. A bully named Philomon, about a year older than Simon, blocked my path. Philomon was the son of a representative of the Temple, a Sadducee. He had a great dislike for Essenes. I don't think it was anything special about me that prompted his anger, except, perhaps, that I was present.

"Well, little Rabbi, what did you learn today?"

"That the person next to you might well be the messiah so it is best to offer all men respect."

"I've got your next lesson for you and that is 'the strong get their way.' I want a little of that respect that you are talking about. My sandals are dirty, boy!" The menace in his look appeared to grow more intense. This boy was (what would be today) six inches taller than I was. He also outweighed me by around twenty pounds.

"Then you best clean them," I answered.

At once, I imagined myself bloody and lying on the ground. I knew that I would have to stand up to this boy. Once he found a weakness, he would go out of his way to exploit it and generally make life miserable for me from then on. It would be better to get bloody once than to carry an annoying disease in your heart that slowly eats away at your self-respect. I paused, hoping to find some way out of this situation, when my brother Simon came from behind me and interposed himself between the bully and me.

He spoke in an even tone. I knew that he would always do this so as not to give away what he was going to do next. He had always been successful with this tactic of not appearing threatening until it was too late for the other person to get on guard. He said: "He learned another lesson which he forgot to tell you."

"What was that?"

"You can never achieve respect by showing disrespect for another."

The bully laughed and lunged for Simon. It was all over very quickly. Simon threw him off balance and pushed him down in the mud. The bully struggled for his next breath. When Simon released him, Philomon was coughing up mud and crying.

Simon let the smallest wisp of a smile creep on his face and spoke in a tone almost too soft to hear: "I could have finished it, you know." The message was clear. Philomon gave us wide berth from then on.

I was pulled out of my reverie by a tug on my robe. I recognized Stephen, a close neighbor of Jeshua. Stephen tended to follow Jeshua around when he was in Capernaum (I know how he felt!). "Yehudah, when are you and Jeshua going back to Mt. Carmel?"

"We are supposed to be back in about two months, but anything could happen."

Stephen's family was from the Pharisaic tradition but that did not stop Stephen from seeking wisdom no matter where it could be found. Stephen studied with a rabbi in the village but was released from his lessons today because of the visit of the great rabbi Hillel who was the teacher of Stephen's teacher. Stephen was therefore quite excited and invited us to join him. Before we could leave my brother Simon came and told me that our parents were looking for me.

"Yehudah, you've got to go home and talk to Abba."

"But Simon, Hillel is here today. He is an old man and may not be making this trip again."

"All right, Yehudah, but only on the condition that I go along."

"Sure, Simon, but I thought you weren't interested in teachers."

"I'm not a scholar, Yehudah, but I do enjoy the logical mind and the solving of a good puzzle. He's argued a number of interesting interpretations which are unique and frankly, quite aberrant and peculiar." It seemed to interest Simon's perverse sense of humor.

So there we were — Simon, Jeshua, Stephen, John, and I, going to the synagogue to hear the foremost rabbi in Jerusalem speak in our small Galilean town. Suddenly Stephen turned pale. A boy about Simon's age approached and demanded money from Stephen. Jeshua interposed himself between the large boy and Stephen. His broad, innocent smile never left his face. He asked the boy what the problem was. The boy said that Stephen owed him money in order to protect him while he was going to school. Jeshua said that would no longer be necessary because Jeshua himself would protect him. The boy grew more menacing. "You don't understand..." he began. "Yes, I think I do," Jeshua interposed, "You are protecting him from yourself, a job that should be much less costly." Everyone but the boy saw the humor in this. We all began laughing and Jeshua laughed the loudest. The boy was not able to control his anger. "I'll show how much my protection is worth," he said and swung as hard as he could at Jeshua, who was almost bent over with laughter. The blow hit Jeshua on the right cheek but he laughed even harder. The boy realized that he had hit Jeshua with all his might and most boys his age would not be conscious let alone standing. Blinded by rage, he just stalked off muttering to himself in frustration and Jeshua with a red bruise on his cheek. We were no longer laughing but stood transfixed before him. I managed to spit out a few words, "What...how...." "Oh," Jeshua mused, smile still on his face, "You see, I know this boy. He is very hurt and angry. His father beats him every day. He needs to feel important and worthwhile, he needs to ask for help but does not know how to do it. Instead he tries to become important by having others fear him. I was laughing because he was doing such a poor job of it." We all laughed but were eager for more of his innate wisdom. We noticed one by one that the bruise on Jeshua's cheek was totally gone! He spoke before any of us had a chance to ask, "If you can attune yourself to the joy of being, you cannot be hurt. If you see the humor in life and do not get caught in the illusion of misery, life seems better to you and your attitude starts to influence things on the outside. I think my sides hurt more than my cheek." We all laughed again. Simon then asked, "Should I then allow an attacker to strike and perhaps kill me?" Jeshua said, "Simon, <u>your</u> best choice at this point would be self-defense, although it will not always be so. We are all on different levels of learning in life and it is best to start from where you are. Each of us is a child of the same Father. We each have a miracle within. It will show in His time, not necessarily in ours." Simon looked puzzled, even troubled. This was only the first time when I saw the extent of the power that Jeshua held. Sure, my brother Simon had the power of a warrior, certainly as wild and aggressive as any of the Maccabees might have been. But Jeshua had something way beyond this: Simon had demonstrated real personal power but Jeshua appeared to have control over the very forces of reality.

When we got to the synagogue, we saw not an elderly man but a young man in his late 20's. His name was Gamaliel and he was Hillel's grandson, his foremost disciple and most likely to become Hillel's successor. Nevertheless, I could see Simon's disappointment. Rather than disappointment, Jeshua showed great interest and enthusiasm in getting to talk to Gamaliel.

Gamaliel was addressing several elders of the congregation who were arguing with him concerning the famous decision that brought Hillel to prominence in the Sanhedrin.

"...On the surface it was a simple decision of logic. If the Sabbath and the eve of Passover fell on the same day, which would take precedence? Would the law of the Sabbath preclude the offering of sacrifice?

"The sacrifice would be ordered," rabbis all chimed in unison. It was a well-known decision.

"And why is that?"

"The Sabbath comes weekly and the eve of Passover only once a year."

"Yes, yes, but what made this such a special decision?"

The rabbis were silent.

"Most of us here are Pharisees. We should know this. It is the essence of our tradition," he said with a gleeful look in his eye, enjoying his role as a playful taunter.

Stephen then piped up from the back: "Because it proved the oral tradition and the written law were one and the same!"

"Good! It's the children who lead us. Come to the front here, boys. Now, what further conclusion can we make?"

This time I saw my chance to speak: "That we could now rely on rules of deduction rather than on tradition for our answers..."

"...So that the law could be interpreted equally for everyone..." interjected Simon, not to be outdone. I looked over at him, surprised at his level of scholarship. He beamed back with an "I told you so" look that was playful and loving and openly quite proud of himself.

John: "...and that makes the law something alive which can be constantly interpreted..."

Jeshua: "...by knowing and following the Spirit of the law as it manifests in Spirit and applying it to the mundane."

There was total silence in the synagogue for what appeared to be hours. The energy was electric. The joy of being part of this expression of wisdom of the Spirit brought me almost to tears. Stephen beamed with pride for his hero, Hillel, through the expression of his disciple Gamaliel. John looked lovingly at Jeshua as if Jeshua had confirmed John's very being. There was new strength and resolve in John's countenance. Jeshua just nodded and gave a friendly smile. Simon was very still.

Finally, Gamaliel spoke up. "I offer a standing invitation to you boys. We have been looking for some bright new students. Hillel will not be teaching much longer, he said, his voice trailing off with some sadness, and Hillel wanted to reach out one more time to contact those who hunger for knowledge."

I shot a glance at Simon who looked back at me and knew my mind. I felt the chill of finality in his voice as he spoke in a whisper, "Mother will never let you go."

CHAPTER 3 - FOREIGN LANDS

The chance to study with Hillel! I was determined to convince my father of the necessity of letting me go. If I could convince him, perhaps he could persuade my mother to let me go.

"Yehudah, I think it would be a great idea, but your mother worries constantly and she often wears me down with her concerns." He sighed.

So, it was up to me. I had to face my mother alone and somehow convince her of the reasonableness of my actions even beyond the power of her fears. What would Jeshua do in this circumstance? I remembered how Jeshua handled the fears of others. He was always supportive, never denying another's fears, but he never backed down because of them either.

"...It is like traveling to a foreign land for us Galileans," she said.

"But this is the chance of a lifetime — to study with Hillel!"

"What is so special about this Pharisee teacher?" she asked.

"Mother, he is the finest interpreter of the law in Jerusalem. He is supposed to have descended from King David. He is honored by all sects and is even called 'Nasi'[1]. He is respected even by the Sadducees who respect only themselves."

"There are many of that priestly class in Jerusalem and they have no love for common people, much less Galileans or Essenes."

"That's true mother, but there are too many real threats to them that they will find us totally invisible," I said playfully as I held my hands up in front of my face leaving a slit between my fingers for each eye.

"You tease me when I am only concerned for your welfare," she said, feigning a hurt expression. Then her expression turned cold and a

---

[1]"Prince"

shiver ran up her back as if someone had stepped on her grave. "Be careful of the Romans, they do not abide by our laws and you will have no protection under theirs."

"I will mother." I did my best to allay her fears, but in the end, it was the fact that I would be traveling with Jeshua's mother and father that made this somewhat acceptable.

"And lend a hand with Mary; she is expecting a fourth child soon. After all, you are almost Jeshua's age and he has reached adulthood.

Although I was a full year away from twelve, the age of manhood, I no longer felt like a boy. I felt that I was being prepared to perform the mission for which God brought me back to the world to do. There is no better feeling.

Since I had met Jeshua his family had grown from three to five. After James came Ruth, and now another child was on the way. I thought it must be of some importance that Jeshua's parents had waited ten years after his birth to have another child. Usually parents had their children in quick succession and Joseph, being almost twenty years older than Mary, seemed too old to care for children.

I was eager to make the trip and when the day finally arrived I joined their tiny caravan to Jerusalem.

I looked back at Mary and saw that she held herself with grace even weighed down as she was with Jeshua's youngest brother or sister. Other than Jeshua, Mary was the most enigmatic person I had ever met. It was as though she had volumes of hidden facts inside and the only evidence of it was a gentle look of knowing that poured freely from her eyes. "Is there any way I can help?" I asked.

"You can ask me that question that you are barely holding back inside yourself," she said, smiling.

"Why did you wait so long after Jeshua to have the rest of your family; it was because of Jeshua, wasn't it?"

"Yes. I had to make sure that my part in his training was fulfilled." She looked into my eyes and gently pulled from my being my deepest thoughts. "You feel linked with him, don't you," she said.

"Yes. And the link is somehow stronger than I am."

"Well, I am even more linked. We are in many ways bound as inseparable, yet free in Spirit. What makes it so strong it that it is the will of The Father that Jeshua's work is done. You can't fight it Yehudah; and one day you too will understand it."

I didn't mind that I would be so directed. Perhaps Jeshua was the one that I had been seeking to follow. He could very well be acting like a messiah, but then, I really knew little about what a messiah was. This was one of the lessons that I hoped to learn from Hillel.

Mary seemed to ponder quite a while longer before she spoke. "Jeshua has no doubt told you of your previous life together as his brother, so I need not. If Jeshua should have another brother, he should be named 'Yehudah' so that he will always have someone around who will rescue him from those who would do him harm."

Mary's sensitivity and wisdom of course enchanted me, but I was also quite flattered by her attention. "How did you know that?" I asked.

"I am very closely connected with Jeshua and know many of the things that he knows. While my mission in this life is different than his, I am to support him, be still, and observe."

I swore that this would be the last time I judged someone by appearances. Mary appeared to be just another Galilean wife and mother, yet all at once I saw that she too possessed the wisdom of the ages.

At one point Joseph stopped and faced the rest of us. "Over the next crest you will see Jerusalem."

Jeshua broke away from the rest of us and ran to the top of the crest. I started to follow but Mary's glance held me in check. "He wishes to experience this moment alone," she said "this is a very important moment for him."

Jeshua, meanwhile, had fallen to his knees and was crying. I could hear him saying something like "My city of peace, I have returned to you." Joseph appeared visibly shaken by this, but Mary was calm and supportive. I assumed that Jeshua must have lived there before in one of his remembered lifetimes. How I wished I could remember my own.

Jeshua and his family stayed with relatives near Jerusalem. There was not enough room for me so I stayed with the parents of one of Simon's closest friends, Aaron. Aaron's father, David, was also a merchant, so I was able to be of assistance to him so as to earn my keep while staying in their home.

I rested well that night, for in the morning Jeshua and I were to be examined by the rabbis and perhaps meet Hillel himself. The school was called Bet Hillel, named after the great rabbi. I dreamed of the great Court of Israel where only Jewish males over the age of twelve were permitted to gather and discuss and interpret the Law. I was too young to join in the discussions, but since I was with a school I would be permitted to stay and listen. I was thankful for any chance to be in that environment. If Hillel accepted me, I would be a student in the most respected rabbinical school in the world! Bet Hillel was different from most of the Pharisee schools. While most of the schools only took those who were counted by their fellow men to be perfectly righteous and "respectable," Hillel and his followers were prepared to teach all, in the hope that the world would end up with more good people. While some schools demanded large fees for teaching, Bet Hillel was based on charity. People gave what they could and often were taught without charge. It was said that Hillel believed that charity not only increased the peace between the rich and the poor but also between the poor and God. Hillel has said that when poor people feel deprived, the resentment that is fostered is not only for the rich but also for God who would allow this injustice to happen.

At the appointed time I entered the building where the Bet Hillel School was located. I saw no trace of Jeshua. I was led to a hallway where a lone chair was waiting outside a door. From the hallway I could hear muffled voices inside. It seemed I waited an eternity. Finally the door opened and Jeshua emerged followed by an elderly man who was tall even though he was slightly bent in stature. He spoke directly to me in a voice that conveyed a lifetime of kindness and compassion. "I am sorry we took so long. My discussion with Jeshua was a treat that I am not often allowed. This poor son of man is called Hillel," he said with a friendly smile.

He was not what I had expected as a teacher, not to mention the most respected rabbi in all of Judea. His manner was courteous and self-effacing. The term for himself "this son of man" was one that you didn't often hear. It was similar to the Essene practice of abasement of the body in order to focus on the Spirit. It was a way to mention oneself without ego.

"I expected a Pharisee teacher to be more strict and unbending, more concerned about the letter of the law," I blurted out.

He smiled, seeing my embarrassment. "Well, I hope I do not disappoint you, but there are two schools of Pharisee. The kind you mentioned is the *Parush.* If you are looking for a *Parush* teacher, Shammai is waiting in the more wealthy section of town. We are all *Hasidim* here".

"Where did two roads to piety among the Pharisees begin?" I asked.

"No one knows for certain but I think they are demonstrated most vividly with Moses and his brother Aaron. Moses was as the *Parush.* He would preach holy fire and storm, use judgment and rebuke to frighten sinners back to God. Aaron, on the other hand, was more like the *Hasidim.* He focused on the God and the Spirit within each man and was of the opinion that this inner voice was more effective in bringing a man back to God. Yet as different as these two were, they were brothers; two sides to the same coin. I have already begun to instruct Jeshua from a most ancient document started by Melchizedek with teaching going back to Adam. I have been studying this collection of writings most of my life. It is called the Kabbalah, a practical study of the mystical in all of life. It contains secret oral traditions passed down from Moses. Until now it has never been compiled in its entirety. Now it is time to make this available to all. In codifying it, I intend to share it with all, because it should be practiced in one's everyday life. It does not belong only with the scholars who will discuss it and never see how it affects their very existence."

"What does this Kabbalah say about this pair of opposites you have been discussing?"

"That all comes from the Light of God. When God said 'Let there be Light,' all pairs of opposites were created. Yet how could one tell darkness without light or light without darkness? Both are needed as the day and the night, like good and evil, this is the way of this physical universe. The Orientals call it 'the opposing forces of Yin and Yang.' I have suggested to Jeshua, and I am going to suggest to you, that this would be the essential place for further study to bring a fullness of understanding of the mystical.

"What you are saying, Master, is that the evil is as necessary as good for the fulfillment of God's will on the earth."

"That is correct, Yehudah, and neither is better than the other. I do not criticize my 'rival' Shammai because there are people for whom his philosophy is necessary. He is only doing God's will in another form."

"I have noticed that these people, they are fanatic in their literal interpretation of the scriptures and condemn others who do not believe as they do."

"Yehudah, I have found that the more fanatical people are concerning their beliefs, the more they are seeking external validation for those beliefs. What they are looking for they can never really grasp and hold, so they are never fulfilled. The one who is secure in his own beliefs gets his validation inside all the time. This one is secure no matter what anyone else believes. When he gets to finally experience the spirit, belief is no longer necessary."

"How does one achieve that feeling of security?"

"Not by study, not by learning, but by direct experience. When God comes to talk to you, will you argue with him points of Law or will you just listen to the sweetness of his voice? Both you and Jeshua are most acceptable to Bet Hillel. You will both make me very proud."

The real test was later that day. We were to be presented to the priests in order to be registered among Hillel's students. This would permit free access into the Temple at any time. If we were rejected, we would not be counted among the men of Israel and not permitted to experience the most illustrious of discussions in the temple.

We followed Hillel with the pace of an old man. We were led past the Court of Gentiles where there were booths and stalls for the sale of sacrificial animals and the moneychangers who replaced the Roman coins (with the profane image of Caesar) with Shekels, which were acceptable within the more holy portions of the Temple. Jeshua appeared uneasy and almost irritable in this place. The Court of Women was a little better since it was filled with the gentler cries of women meeting and greeting each other. He appeared to relax a little. Hillel kept on walking, appearing oblivious to the commotion around him. All of him was purpose — to get us into the inner court and have us examined by the priests.

As we entered the Court of Israel, we were assaulted by the sound of beasts being killed and burnt on the altar as sacrifices for God. I felt shaken and disgusted but Jeshua was in tears. He broke away from Hillel and me and faced the priests.

"Why must you do this?" he shouted.

"We sacrifice these animals to erase our sins," the priest said.

"Didn't David and Isaiah tell us that God does not require a sacrifice for sin? Didn't the prophets tell us that God, our Father, requires life, not death as penitence for sin?"

"Aren't you Jeshua, one of Hillel's new pupils? Do you think you know more than we do about the Law? We Sadducees are bred for understanding; we are descendants of the priests of Aaron and we have the authority over Temple practices. You Pharisees, Essenes and the other rabble pretend to know the Law. Well, we will see soon enough!"

Hillel was at once shocked and excited by Jeshua's response. "You have made a rather potent enemy. Caiaphas is in line for the office of High Priest."

It appeared that Jeshua did nothing in a small way. There was an uneasy truce between the Sadducees and the other sects but Jeshua took on the brightest young star on their horizon.

He answered to Hillel, "Sir, you are my master, my teacher, please tell me how man can be just and create such cruelty? Is not God, our Father, a Loving Father? Could He delight in such a spectacle?"

Hillel bowed his head. "While I am chief of the Sanhedrin, I still cannot dictate to the priests. They are sanctioned by a more powerful yet less holy authority."

"Rome." I said through gritted teeth.

At this point the master Hillel looked his age. "Yes, and supported by Herod. There is too much of politics in the religious, and it degrades us all."

The look on Jeshua's face almost made me cry. It was a look of pain and helplessness. "Master, this is not the God I am looking for. I know that our heavenly Father is a God of love, not cruelty. Can you tell me where to find the God of Love?"

Hillel's heart was heavy. He beckoned Jeshua to come to him. He held the boy close to him and he too wept. "My dear Jeshua, there is a God of Love, and if we are truly made in His image, then the place to find him would be inside of us."

"Then that is what I will do." Jeshua had stopped crying and a look of resolve came upon his face. "I will purify my heart so that I will create a worthy temple inside where my Father can reside."

Hillel looked at Jeshua with what looked like a profound respect. "We will find Him together, but first we have the small matter of an examination. Are you boys ready?" The aged master appeared at once elderly but reinvigorated with a spirit of ageless youth.

Caiaphas stood at the head of a seated table of priests. Hillel, Jeshua and I stood at the far end. The deep bass of Caiaphas' voice filled the room: "The High Priest has given me the authority to examine you myself." Then he added with a sneer: "And, I can tell you, this will be a delight!"

His tone was just ominous enough to cause me some worry, yet I saw only confidence in Jeshua and Hillel.

"We'll start with you, Yehudah." He pointed in my direction.

Hillel whispered to me: "Go ahead, it will all be fine!"

Caiaphas asked: "Which is the greatest of the Ten Commandments?"

I took a deep breath and asked for God to grant me the wisdom to respond correctly. Something that Jeshua had said came forward into my mind. I would see where I could go with it. "The greatest commandment is the first 'Thou shalt have no other Gods before me.' If we are created in God's image and focus on being as much like our heavenly Father as possible, then all the other commandments would naturally flow from this first one."

I expected either derisive laughter or an angry or cold dismissal. Instead, the priests conferred among themselves. Hillel was smiling. In a few minutes they pronounced me worthy of being allowed into the court of Israel. At this time I could only observe due to the fact that I hadn't reached my twelfth birthday, but upon that day I would be allowed in the discussion as an adult participant.

"Now Jeshua," said Caiaphas with some menace. "The same question, 'What is the greatest of the commandments?'"

I had never heard Jeshua be so brilliant. "I do not see one being any greater than another, I see them as part of One and that One is Love. If we fill ourselves with Love then we cannot steal, kill or falsely testify. Love needs no commands. Love honors God because God is Love!"

The entire assembly was quiet. Hillel looked as if he had at last found what he was looking for. Finally Caiaphas broke the silence. "Well, it appears that both young men did very well today. I suppose that Jeshua will bring honor upon you, Hillel, his teacher."

Hillel stood up as he faced Caiaphas. "It would be more likely that I might bring some small honor upon him because I believe that he will be more my teacher than I his."

Hillel was known for such self-deprecatory remarks as a sign of his piety, so Caiaphas took no special interest in this remark. Yet something inside me knew that he was in earnest.

The year that we spent at Bet Hillel was one of the happiest of my life. Hillel was becoming more and more infirm during that last year and his grandson and successor, Gamaliel, took over most of the teaching at the school. Hillel took time for us, however, no matter how he was feeling. He always saw us separately. I figured that the lessons that Jeshua learned were way beyond what Hillel taught me, but I was happy just to study with the one who also taught Jeshua.

Hillel's teaching was easily absorbed because of his ability to reach anyone. He had lived a rich, long life and shared his many experiences, which taught me on many levels. He once said to me: "Some of your brother Essenes view the body as a prison for the Soul and focus on the discomfort of this physical life. I see this body as merely a temporary home for the Soul. The Soul is a 'guest' of this body, so it is well for us to focus on being hospitable to our 'guest.' The Soul would prefer kindness to self rather than asceticism."

Hillel saw doing a *mitzvah* (kindness) for others the same as for self. To me he always stressed the necessity of making peace and practicing forgiveness for self and others. Whenever I was angry or frustrated with a lesson he said to me "Yehudah, choose always the way of Aaron."

What I considered a special treat was when I was allowed to accompany Hillel and Jeshua to the Temple and listen to Jeshua debate the priests. I remember one day when a particular section of prophecy was being debated. Jeshua read the section and asked the priests if any could interpret it. All were silent. Hillel reveled in watching his student. Hillel then said: "Now that you've read it, why don't you also interpret the passage."

Jeshua's interpretation foretold the destruction of the Temple, the scattering of Jews to far lands and finally the return of Israel in peace with the rebuilding of the Temple.

This impressed many in the Temple. Many of the Sadducees were angered and many of the Pharisees praised Jeshua as a great prophet in his own right. There were a few who actually proclaimed: "This one must be the Messiah, the Anointed One."

Hillel turned to Jeshua and almost in a whisper said: "It is my prayer that if you are to be a Messiah, that you are the peaceful prophet and not the warrior-king that so many desire."

I turned to Hillel. "Is there more than one messiah?"

"Yehudah, there are legends of two types of Messiah. The priestly prophet I mentioned is called the "Son of God" Messiah and the warrior-king is the "Son of David" Messiah. The one most desired by our countrymen is the Son of David, the military Messiah, the one who is supposed to lead Israel into freedom from oppressors."

"To me, that would seem inherently practical," I said.

"The 'Son of God' Messiah is a great sage who will make great changes in the hearts and minds of men. I cannot support violence even against an unjust oppressor. I feel that one must transform one's enemies rather than conquer them."

"Rome has conquered half the world with the sword. What power is greater than that?"

"The power of the heart and the mind, and the Spirit. If you change an enemy from within, these changes will last when all the swords have turned to dust."

Hillel then turned to Jeshua. "If you are to be the Anointed One, be the 'Son of God.' We live in a world starving for love. Another Zealot won't make the lasting change that a prophet can."

Jeshua appeared as if he was about to answer when a man came over to him and said "Jeshua, your mother and brothers and your sister are waiting. They are going on a short trip to visit a family who would provide you a wife. It is imperative that you go with them."

"I cannot go right now; I am with those who are also my brothers. The needs here are greater. Tell them I will see them later."

Caiaphas, who had been listening silently during most of the discussion, spoke to Jeshua with a voice tinged with sarcasm: "Does our young "Messiah" flaunt the commandment to honor our parents?"

Jeshua responded: "It is true that all parents deserve honor, Caiaphas. However we all have but one heavenly Father and I am honoring Him first. I love my physical family but my spiritual family must be foremost."

The next morning Gamaliel met us on our way to the Temple. "Where is Hillel?" I asked.

"Hillel did not feel well this morning and is staying in bed. He will probably meet you tomorrow. For the time being, you will have to put up with this poor son of man."

Gamaliel said this with a smile, but I could see beneath his composure that he was very concerned about Hillel's condition. For the next five days Gamaliel met us before going to the Temple. He said little about Hillel's health. On the sixth day Gamaliel brought us into Hillel's quarters.

Hillel lay very still. He was not dead because I could see him breathing. Gamaliel gently touched him and his eyes fluttered open.

"Ah, my boys. I am about to pass over into another world. I am truly sorry that I cannot be here to watch you grow into manhood and fulfill your destinies. We live in a time of wonder and there will be many changes. I want both of you to be prepared to meet the challenges of the future. The next step for you both is toward the East. You should study the philosophies and religions of these countries because they contain a different perspective on spirituality. There is no one philosophy that holds the entire truth, but there are places where you can find missing pieces. Take their initiations and learn their mysteries. I also want you to become priests." For a moment I pulled back at the suggestion. "No," Hillel continued, "I do not mean Sadducees, I mean joining a much more ancient order, that which goes back to Melchezidek. In fact, it is called the priesthood of Melchezidek. I myself joined many years ago. This priesthood is not for one lifetime but for all. It is for those who dedicate themselves to the spiritual evolution of all mankind. There are many mystery schools in many lands but I have chosen for you only the ones selected by the *Sojourner*. The *Sojourner* is a consciousness or energy or Spirit that is represented by a man, say, like the office of Chief Rabbi.

When the individual leaves this physical being, another takes his place. As far as I know there has always been a *Sojourner* here in this physical realm of being, for the *Sojourner* helps to bring the Light of God into this realm. I am not permitted to tell you who holds the *Sojourner* consciousness at this time, but you will learn and he will make himself known to you at the right time.

"Is he greater than the Messiah?" I asked.

"The Messiah is for one group of people; the *Sojourner* is for all people."

Hillel wanted to see each of us separately. He called me in first. "Yehudah, you could be an exceptional scholar and I want you to know that I am impressed with your work. Stay as close to Jeshua as you can. Jeshua is bound for great things. To be where he is at his age means that he could possibly reach perfection in this lifetime."

"It's not fair being compared to Jeshua. I could never accomplish what he can."

"Your main problem, Yehudah, is that you allow your ego to dominate you. You feel that being Jeshua's friend will somehow rub off on you and you will become a better person, but it does not happen that way. Jeshua is a good model for you but you need to find who you are inside and to be that person. Jeshua serves for the love of serving. You look for a reward of esteem from others or position. I can tell you now that that will never work for you and you will never be satisfied."

He called in Jeshua and they took almost two hours together. It would have been more but Hillel was getting very tired and we had to leave.

"Jeshua", I questioned, "are you going to avoid marriage? You are at the eligible age."

"Marriage is not a mating of bodies, Yehudah, but souls clothed in them. It is not, therefore to be taken so lightly. I have been married to another soul for many lifetimes. You have also, Yehudah. You will later recognize this soul in the human form when she remembers you. My 'wife' is not for me to marry in this lifetime, for that would avert my focus. I am to be about my Father's work. Nothing must stand in the way, too much is at risk."

The next morning Gamaliel awakened us. He looks like he had been crying. "Hillel is gone. Let us come and say *Kaddish*[2]." After the service, Jeshua looked at me and declared: "I am going to the East." All I could say was, "I am going with you."

---

[2]The prayer for the dead.

It took all morning to get ready. Jeshua said goodbye to his family. They were very supportive of him. If my family had been there, I doubt that they would have even let me go. We said our last good-byes and started out on the road. Just as we were leaving Jerusalem we saw someone chasing us in the distance. It was a tall, dark-haired man with a short beard. When he got close I could tell it was his cousin, John. Jeshua and John embraced.

"John, how did you know that I was leaving?"

"Your mother told me that Hillel was ailing and that soon you would be traveling. Something inside told me I belong with you."

The three of us headed toward Alexandria.

CHAPTER 4 — AN EXPERIENCE OF INITIATION

As I remember it, when he first caught sight of us he flashed us a smile that showed three or four front teeth missing. He was oddly dressed, not like any Arab or Syrian (for which I had first mistaken him). A man of his age would either have a full beard or shave like the Romans. This man had a few straggly hairs attached to his chin as if he had been trying all his life to grow a beard but just could not. His hair was closely cropped.

I remember an uneasy feeling; not only had I never seen this man before but it was also very possible that he might be a robber who preyed upon visitors to this oasis that we had just approached. I looked over at Jeshua and he was calm. I immediately relaxed my wariness and decided just to see where this was going.

"Travelers, I welcome you," he said in a passable peasant Galilean Aramaic with only the slightest accent.

Jeshua was the first to reply. "Peace be with you," he said in the Hebrew of the Jerusalem nobility.

"And with you," the man returned in the exact same dialect, again with the slightest accent. "I see you have come across the desert and are making for the great city of Alexandria, is that not correct?" Jeshua nodded his head.

"Then you will most assuredly need a guide."

Something was going on between this man and Jeshua and it was making me very nervous. "But Jeshua knows Alexandria, he spent part of his childhood there; he needs no guide."

Jeshua turned to me with the slightest hint of a smile on his face: "True, but _you_ have never been to Alexandria, so this man will be _your_ guide."

John looked both bemused and amused but didn't say a word.

This man looked at us and continued giving his analysis of what he saw: "Many scholars come to Alexandria to visit the famed library. You do not have the look of scholars. Some come as merchants, but you bring little money and no wares. I would guess that you would be on a spiritual quest. The spiritual quest is the noblest form of activity there is. And it is one which I always attempt to support in others."

In honoring Jeshua's request (whether in humor or in earnest, I did not know), he directed the rest of his discourse to me. "Allow me to introduce myself. Brothers, I am called Tuzla. I am from the land of Tibet. It is a mountainous country, difficult to reach from the outside, yet serenely beautiful. In my country, it is more common to see people on a spiritual quest than here; it is more a part of our culture. It has been this way since before the Lord Buddha was in flesh over 500 years ago. In my country we are building great monasteries where people can obtain knowledge on their quests."

Jeshua was focused quietly with the same intent that I saw him give our old master, Hillel. "I would very much like to visit your wondrous country one day," he said.

"Ah, I see you shall," Tuzla said, and it would be my honor to be your guide."

"To be a guide, you must know not only the land where you find yourself and your destination, but all lands in between," said John, studying this man.

"Ah... Yes, guides do not survive long unless they are familiar with the subtle distinctions between people and cultures. We must know how to live off the land, in whatever land we find ourselves. We must be able to act as a warrior when the need arises."

This seemed to pique John's interest, "Just how would you live in the wilderness of Galilee?" he asked.

"If I remember correctly there are many locust or carob trees. These have a particularly tasty pod and seeds. It can be eaten fresh or dried. I hear that bread can be made of this, but I have never tasted it. Also there are many wild bees in that area. If the bee stings do not kill you, you can survive on the sweetness of their labors."

I chimed in... "You have been able to defend yourself against robbers and murderers along these routes?"

He again prefaced his affirmative with an "Ah" that I found to be quite endearing in an odd sort of way, and relaxed me even further in his presence. "...Yes, we have not only spiritual masters in Tibet but also those well disciplined in the arts of warfare. We have had little use for these skills for countless ages in Tibet. We of the monastery are recognized and respected as holy men, but outside our country … others do not understand and we must sometimes prove ourselves in action. Many ages before the Lord Buddha came we were a great warrior people. Now we have again turned our focus on the Father of us all."

I began to see that Tuzla had quite a bit to teach me and I began to inwardly thank Jeshua for attaching him to me.

In the next two weeks before we reached Alexandria, Tuzla became the center of our attention. He taught us to find food and water in the most desolate places and I persuaded him to teach me his skills as a warrior.

He was able to teach me skills of hand-to-hand combat and I gained greatly from this, but what I appreciated most was the *twin blades*. He had two small thin swords that he used in combat with skill I have never seen before. Compared to what I saw him do, the best of the Roman or Hebrew swordsmen were slow moving and clumsy. He wasted no motion; all his moves had a specific pattern and logic. He would take me out in the dunes beyond our campfire and teach me the pattern. It looked like a dance when he did it in slow motion for me. He told me that it was an ancient skill his people had acquired when they were great warriors and had conquered much of the East. He explained that his people had come from the eastern colonies of Atlantis and that I could read about Tibetan history in the library at Alexandria. He said that this skill needed to be passed on for it was in danger of being lost forever since his people used it less and less. In learning all that he taught me for only those two weeks, I was confident I could stop almost any attack by robbers on the road.

There was one last question that I had to ask: "What defense is this against an arrow?"

He went into his pack and pulled out a short but powerful bow with a dart-like arrow. He said, "Stand twenty paces back and fire this at me."

I had grown close to Tuzla and in no way wished to harm him. I was frightened, but he insisted. It was a new moon and I could hardly see him by the light of the campfire burning over a hundred paces off. I pulled back his strong little bow until the metallic cord clicked in place. He told me to aim at him and pull a small lever at the base of the strange bow. I did and what followed was almost too fast for my eyes in this dim light. I saw him step aside and heard his *twin blades* swish twice. He stood quietly. I half expected him to fall. I would have to bury my new friend. But as I came closer to him I saw that he was unharmed. The small arrow lay at his feet in three equal pieces.

That night I dreamt I was again with Tuzla. In this dream he looked different but I knew it was he. He led me up a sheer face of a cliff and brought me to the façade of a beautiful mist-covered temple. As we moved inside the mist grew thicker. As we passed through the mist, we emerged on a whole different realm of being. I remember being taught in this dream but did not remember the lessons. Some were taught by Tuzla and some by others who I did not recognize.

The next morning I mentioned my dream to Tuzla. All he said was, "Ah, dreams reveal much."

Soon after we entered Alexandria, Tuzla seemed to melt into the background. I wondered if we would see this combination of a monk and a warrior again.

Jeshua told me that Alexandria was more like Rome than Jerusalem. It was more cosmopolitan, a blend of many peoples and cultures. It had a large community of Hellenistic[3] Jews among whom were a good number of Essenes.

We followed Jeshua around the city for three days, meeting his friends and acquaintances. We saw the famed library at Alexandria. Inside were many scrolls and codices[4]. But what drew my attention was a purplish stone bearing an unknown form of writing. Something about it looked familiar, but I could not place it. Jeshua saw my interest and placed his hand on the stone. To me it had felt cold and lifeless. He just looked at me and said, "This is another old friend. It is one of the stone tablets brought from the Temple of Atlantis." When I heard him mention that it was an old friend, I assumed he meant that he knew it from his childhood in Alexandria. I pondered this again, seeing him as a child touching the stone. I unconsciously placed my hand again on the stone and received a jolt of energy that had me shivering for at least a few minutes. It took me a little longer to regain the full use of my hand and arm.

Near the end of the third day, Jeshua became increasingly quiet. He appeared to seek more time alone as if he were in preparation for something. We came to outskirts of the city and there was Tuzla waiting for us there.

He asked Jeshua, "Are you ready now?" Jeshua nodded.

John and I both spoke up at once, both needing to know what was going on.

Jeshua stopped and sat down in the sand facing us. "Brothers, we are about to tread an ancient path. We are about to attempt spiritual initiations that seekers have taken for ages. These things are hidden from

---

[3] Accepting of Greco-Roman Society
[4] Term for ancient books

most people today. Religious faiths have them couched in mystery. But seekers have always managed to find the way. Go inside of yourself and ask what you want for yourself and what our Father can give you. We are all a part of our Father and to see Him in all things we must first be able to contact Him inside of ourselves. These initiations will give us that opportunity."

Ancient fears surfaced in me. I felt like running. What would I be shown? Would it be that I would not be found worthy? We traveled as a group but we hardly spoke to one another. I was immersed in what Jeshua had said. Why was I even along on this trip? When it was found what fear I had inside, I would surely be found unworthy.

I don't know how many days we spent in the wilderness but we finally came to another, smaller city. It was Heliopolis, the ancient city of *On*. We arrived just as the sun was setting. Tuzla drew Jeshua aside saying, "All has been prepared, and we can begin tomorrow." We bedded down for the night at an inn at the outskirts of town.

I had a fitful sleep full of worry and concern, moving through shadows and voices. John who looked like he did not sleep all night awakened me.

"In fact, I slept poorly," he said. "I have had many things that have been eating away at my mind for quite a long time. I feel I just can't contain them any longer."

"What things, John, if you don't mind telling me?"

"I have these feelings of anger which surface and I have trouble controlling them. As you know, my father was murdered in the Temple, proclaiming the imminent coming of the messiah. He was a respected member of the council but that did not matter. He crossed the priests by proclaiming what would mean the end of their authority. It seems they only exist to sustain their authority and maintain this order with the might of the Romans. I have hatred for these priests and that is my undoing. Hatred, anger, desire for revenge could bar me from attaining these spiritual initiations. But that is not the end of it. When anyone speaks of me, it is of the son of the mad Sadducee who was killed in the Temple. They immediately judge and label me because of my father's actions. It's not that I do not agree with what my father did. I wish I had the fire and conviction that drove him to proclaim his own truth. As for me, I just want to be seen as who I am, not as a son of my father."

Neither of us saw Jeshua approach. "John, if you would truly be who you are, you must drop your concern for the opinions of others. You cannot control them, and to concern yourself with them takes your focus away from your true self. You *do* have that fire and conviction within you. Have the courage to be misunderstood. Why try to push a stone uphill? Some people will simply not be reached. There is a saying: 'It is impossible to teach people who already know everything.' Reach out to those who are open to hearing you."

Tears trickled down John's face. The pressure seemed to lift off his chest. He remained quiet for the rest of the morning.

At mid-day we were met by Tuzla. He said that it was time and that we were to follow him. We were again out in the desert. When we could no longer see what direction we were going he put blindfolds on all of us. He told us that it was necessary to guard the location of the Temple of *On*. Because of the blindfold we could only tell night was approaching because of the rapid fall in temperature out on the desert at dusk.

We were led down an endless series of steps into a chamber where we sat and waited for what seemed to be an eternity. At last a deep voice boomed out into an echo-filled room: "We do not give these initiations casually. We know not only who you are now but also the lives you have led in the past. Our seers have read the *Akasha*[5] and the path is clear toward these tests. If you pass these tests you will be accepted as a Priest-neophyte. If you fail, you will never hear from us again. In this lifetime, there is only one chance. We are a small order but we have been given the authority to initiate spiritual seekers after our Mother-Father-God into the oldest priesthood of this world, the Melchizedek Priesthood. Some of you were priests before; for some of you it is the first time. You may remove your blindfolds."

When my eyes again responded to light, I saw a bald middle-aged man in a white robe. He had a gold Ankh symbol[6] hanging on a gold chain around his neck. I saw Jeshua and John on my right. They also had their blindfolds removed. John was taken first, I second.

The chief priest, called the hierophant, led me down a long corridor about 10 feet wide, the light getting dimmer as we moved on. He put his finger to his lips to indicate that I was not to talk or ask any questions. He reached into a pocket of his robe and pulled out a glowing object. He read the surprise on my face: "The uneducated would think that this is magic but it is the product of a mixture of minerals. It produces a glow not unlike the lightning bug." He handed the lamp to me and we resumed walking. He continued: "What seems to be magic and miracles to the unenlightened are to the initiate just demonstrations of knowing and working a higher law. The tests are physical but the prospective initiate

---

[5] A record of all events from the beginning of time recorded on the ethers.

[6] The Ankh is the ancient Egyptian symbol for life. It is a cross with a circle for the topmost piece.

performs out of the experience of his soul. His reactions to the test tell us about his ability and his character."

We came to a fork in the passageway. The hierophant gave me the lamp and had me proceed alone. When he had gone, every sound seemed to be amplified, every shadow appeared enlarged. The eerie glow of the lamp made the passageway appear smaller. But...wait, the opening WAS shrinking; I could almost touch both sides of the wall with my arms outstretched. I did not see any light at the end of the tunnel that continued to shrink. After a few more steps I had to bend my head. Farther on all I could do was crawl on hands and knees and still the crawl space continued to shrink. I began to entertain fears about this order of priests. I could go so far and be trapped in a tunnel where no one would ever find me. I remembered that this was a test and I would have to overcome my fear of tight spaces. My fear kept growing as I was cramped into tighter and tighter spaces. I was flat on the ground, crawling on my belly when all of a sudden the ground opened up in front of me. I fell into a huge pit onto a pile of straw that broke my fall. I was still shaking when I saw the hierophant in the dim light motioning me to follow him again. He led me to a passageway that seemed to glow on its own. When I came close, I saw why. It was like being beckoned into the mouth of a great furnace. I saw the hierophant come to the edge of the burning coals, remove his sandals and walk across to the other side. He motioned to me to follow him. I held up my hand to let him know that I could not follow directly. I needed to prepare. I remembered some of the meditation techniques that Tuzla had shown me as tools to empty oneself before a battle. I assumed that I could also use these techniques to become totally relaxed and removed from pain or irritation. I don't remember how long I took but it must have been longer than an hour. Finally I saw myself walking on the coals without coming to any harm. Actually, I <u>KNEW</u> that I would not come to harm. Walking quickly, I made it to the other side where the hierophant was waiting. The flames had not burned and there was no searing of flesh.

Without speaking, the hierophant motioned me to follow him. We came to what appeared to be another chamber. When we entered, I saw by the eerie glow of the lamp that we were standing on the shore of a vast underground lake. The surface of the lake was covered with slime and shadows moved and made vague splashing noises. I wondered what monsters awaited an unfortunate who wandered into this lake. You can image my surprise when the hierophant pointed to the far side of the lake and motioned me across. For a moment I stood looking at him in disbelief then turned away to try to see where the shore was on the opposite side. When I turned back to him he was gone. I heard a voice calling to me from the far side of the cavern. It was the hierophant! Still holding the lamp, I entered the water. The level of the water kept rising until it reached my chest. I figured that I had better try to swim across but I would lose the lamp and would be in total darkness. I assumed that the only thing that kept the monsters in the lake away from me would be the glow of my lamp. So, I decided to walk as far as I could. I tried to imagine Jeshua and John going through this test. Yes, I was afraid of the monsters that seemed to hide behind every shadow, but I was more afraid of failing where Jeshua and John would surely succeed. This was what drove me onward.

I labored to keep upright in the water. Although there were no more than ripples on the surface, the water exerted a strong undertow that seemed to shift constantly.

Something large and alive brushed my leg. I tripped, letting go of the lamp in terror. I was almost in total darkness now. I could see the faint glow of another lamp at the other end of the lake. I made for that lamp; swimming with all the strength I could muster. At last it seemed the far shore was getting closer. I would actually survive this test! I kept swimming until my knee scraped along the sandy bottom of the lake. The last ounce of energy in my body pulled me up and set me running to shore. Reaching the beach, I headed straight for the hierophant holding a duplicate of the lamp I dropped. He smiled and gave me the lamp. It was wet.

"Now you may rest. When you are refreshed, you will tell me what you have learned." He turned and was gone. In his place was a bald monk who led me up a long flight of stairs. I began to see just how vast this place really was. When we reached the top, the air was again fresh and clean. I smelled the desert wind. I was again above ground. He led me to a comfortable chamber. I placed the glowing rod down on a table and went straight for bed. There were just so many things I felt gratitude for, and sleep was now at the top of my list.

In my state of exhaustion I should have slept all night but I found myself pulled out of a dreamless sleep by the music of a flute. I sat up in bed. There was no music coming from anywhere but I just barely saw a figure on a chair sitting at the foot of my bed. It was the hierophant.

"Well, Yehudah, what have you learned from your trials today?"

"A few things, I think…I learned that it is quite easy for illusion to masquerade as reality."

"Yes, yes, go on," he said as if impatient with me.

I took a deep breath and let down some of my inner barriers. "I learned that I have much trouble in trusting the Spirit."

"Yes, you have had that for more than this life. Doubt and mistrust stand in the way of your seeing more of the truth in your life experiences. Go on, what else."

"I learned that whatever happens, I cannot lose the Light, the Light of God, of Spirit. It is there to lead me out of darkness."

"If you learn to reconcile these two aspects of your being, you will see much progress. For now you should know that you have passed the initiations. You are accepted into the priesthood as a neophyte. You have much to learn."

"My friends — how did they do?"

"They have also passed the initiations. It did not take them quite so long."

I could accept that. I had always looked up to Jeshua as being beyond my level of spiritual accomplishment. I guess the same now could be said of John. At this point I was just glad to be included in this spiritual quest.

That morning I saw Jeshua and John. We all wore the white robes of the priests. The hierophant motioned us to come forward before an altar on which was depicted the disk of the sun. This was an Egyptian symbol for the All, the Mother-Father God. He placed around our necks the Ankh of a new initiate. It was made of hard, dark wood. His was made of gold.

We did not see much of each other for the next few months. Each of us was to spend much time in meditation and when we were not meditating we were doing menial tasks around the monastery. Yes, it was much like the life I had known before I met Jeshua, only then my teachers were Essenes, and they were much more communicative. When I asked what was to come next, I always received the same answer, "Work and wait." After a time, I gave up asking and settled into the flow of the monastery. I worked and I meditated, meditated and worked. It seemed that one occupation blended into the other. My work became a meditation, my meditation became a labor; yes, but a labor of love. There had been a time not too long ago when I would not let a priest go by without asking a question. Now I could feel the inner support of these priests just by being in the same room.

Without warning my next test came. I was called into the private meditation room of the hierophant.

"Yehudah, it is now time for further dedication. This is a great honor. Some neophytes never get to this test. You are to experience the gates of death and know its meaning and purpose. Then you will also the meaning of rebirth into the life of the Spirit."

They led me down a long flight of stairs. It seemed to me much deeper than when I was led down the first time, blindfolded. At the bottom of these stairs was a chamber with no light and which smelled of dankness. Inside this chamber was an open sarcophagus. It looked truly ancient but it had no dust on it. Was it recently used? I was led into this sarcophagus and the lid was kept open just a crack to permit some airflow.

The hierophant said, "We will return after your resurrection." The lid was closed and locked.

Was this how I was going to die, buried alive? Part of my being was wild with terror at that prospect. Another part of me was so accustomed to meditating alone I just settled in to an easy meditation. I was able to calm the terrified portion of myself through an inner dialogue.

"I am going to lie here until I smother or die of thirst."

"Perhaps, but I can go where I will not feel any pain. I will only feel the joy of service to God."

My purpose was so strong it silenced my fears. I focused intently on my meditation. So the meditation started doing me. I came to the point where I knew neither time nor place. I lifted myself out of the sarcophagus and looked down upon the closed lid. I knew my body was still inside. But I was free! I shot straight up and out, soaring above the desert. Soon the desert, too, disappeared. I felt that if I never came back to that body in the sarcophagus, it would be just fine. I saw a peaceful lake shrouded in mist. Two figures approached me. It was the hierophant with Jeshua. They were talking and laughing together. I leaped up inside myself with joy. They both smiled at me. The hierophant said: "You have gone beyond your physical being and reached into Spirit. In dropping the body you have severed your attachment to it. You have experienced the fact that there is no death for the Spirit. You are done with us for now. Your next lessons are out in the world of men. It is easy to pass tests in this cloistered environment, but to retain your purpose in the world, that will be your real test. Follow Jeshua. He will lead you to your next lessons." Jeshua just smiled and gave me another Ankh. This one was made of copper. The one Jeshua wore was silver. They faded back into the mist. I just stood there and was soaking in all the glory of the experience of contact in the higher planes of existence when I saw another form coming out of the mist. It was a female form. She called me by a name I did not recognize. "I have not yet been born, but I will again be with you," she said.

"Who are you?"

"I am your spiritual sister, your twin soul, and because you have chosen the path of Light and the Soul, you are permitted to see me."

"When will I again see you?"

"I will be one you least expect to be yours. You will see this." She handed me a rose that was a very vibrant red.

Her image faded into the mist. I saw the rose in my hand move. It melted into my hand and was absorbed into my "body" of the level I was on. I felt it as it connected and fused with a hidden part of my consciousness.

I felt a pull from behind me. All of a sudden I was yanked back into physical awareness. The door to the sarcophagus was open and I saw three smiling faces: Jeshua, John and the hierophant.

The Judge's gavel pulled me out of another world. Chris approached me and asked, "Was there something in your version that was not in the original with which you could enlighten us?"

"The purple stone. In my version, I explained all about it. I did not remember it in that lifetime, but in a previous existence, I had programmed that stone. That stone is a memory storage container of enormous capacity. It contains multimedia files of much of the ancient history from before Atlantis. If that could be found, I might be able to access that information. It was in the library of Alexandria."

"The one in Egypt that was destroyed," asked the judge.

"Well, yes." I said. "But it could be anywhere. If I describe it, perhaps it is right now in a museum somewhere."

"Your Honor, if that stone could be located, wouldn't that prove his assertion that he is who he says he is?"

"Yes, counselor, and perhaps a number of other things as well!"

"Well, I make a motion that we recess until the stone is either found or is unable to be located."

"Objection!" Boomed Hastings. "Counsel is stalling for time. I motion that we proceed with the reading. There may be other, more easily proven evidence that we may discover."

"Objection Sustained!" said the judge. "We will adjourn until tomorrow when we will continue with the reading of the manuscript."

I left the stand and walked with Chris. "Nice try," I said. "Jack would be proud of you."

"Hey, it's only the second day of trial," he answered.

CHAPTER 5 - A JOURNEY TO THE EAST

I awoke the next morning after getting a full eight hours of sleep. I convinced myself that I was not going to worry about the outcome of this trial. I was just going to read and be as observant as possible to provide information that might assist Chris in bringing this case to a successful conclusion.

I was called to the stand and began reading.

"JESHUA, JOHN, WERE YOU ALSO ATTACKED BY THE MONSTERS IN THE LAKE?" I ASKED.

JESHUA AND JOHN LAUGHED, "OH, THE DOLPHINS, THEY'RE A FRIENDLY BUNCH, AREN'T THEY? WE HAD FUN PLAYING WITH THEM."

What a great story that would make! It's funny how little adventures on the road could create such great tales to tell family and friends — when we got back to Galilee, that is. Many nights sitting around the campfire, I giggled remembering that one…it happened right after we left Heliopolis. I always wanted to spend some time being a storyteller. It's kind of romantic, wandering around the hills of Galilee, telling tales of adventures in foreign lands. I even thought of writing a journal so that the remembrances did not dim over time.

Thinking about these experiences as being tales told in the future kept me from feeling homesick. I missed my brother and parents. I even missed Jeshua's family. But being on a spiritual quest with Jeshua and John had taken the place of all other family for that period of time.

The calls of some birds nearby yanked me from my reverie. Months, perhaps a year had gone by since we had left Heliopolis. Jeshua, John, Tuzla and I attached ourselves to a band of merchants traveling the trade routes eastward. Tuzla suggested this because it seemed that commerce was the strongest inducement for travel to other lands. He would smile and say, "Ah…here it is profits above prophets; on higher realms, it is the opposite."

Being brought up the son of a merchant, I had experience in doing most of the bargaining for our little group. The merchants told me what was desired in each land we visited. I was able to barter or trade for goods that kept us living in a style far above the homeless spiritual seekers we were. So Jeshua and John deferred to me when it came to our financial "fortunes."

It seemed as though we traveled on forever, but Tuzla always seemed to know where we were. It was obvious to all of us that he had been over this route a number of times. He would always give us the historical account of the regions we visited. At one point, he mentioned: "We are passing through the region where the Aryans first invaded the land of the Hindus over 1500 years ago. It was from their spiritual traditions that Hinduism arose. But from Hinduism sprang other religions such as the Jains and the followers of the Buddha."

That night he told us: "Watch where you step. See that you crush no insects. We are close to the Sindh, where the Indus River fans outward. This is the land of the Jains. These people hold that all life is sacred, and attempt to avoid destroying the forms of any living beings. It is in this way they seek to avoid any repercussions of their past actions. This is called 'Karma' and it means that we are all responsible for the results of all of our actions. They are also strict vegetarians, so if they must kill to eat, it needs to be only the most primitive consciousness."

Tuzla watched us intently for any emotional reaction.

Jeshua was the first to speak: "It would seem like some of the most revered Hebrew traditions would be sacrilege to those people, in particular I am talking about the Temple sacrifices. I have long understood it is not animals that needed to be sacrificed, but the animal-like behaviors of men and women that need to be surrendered and transmuted. Other concepts such as Karma are known in our own mystical traditions. Karma is the true essence of 'an eye for an eye.' It is also stated as 'You reap what you sow." I'm intrigued. Perhaps we might stop and examine their sacred writings."

John was also very excited. The discipline of non-violence to any living being interested him. I think <u>any</u> form of discipline would have interested John. John used to love the rigorous devotion to detail that was practiced with the Essenes, and this went even further. "Tell me, Tuzla," he asked, "we are killing creatures all the time in walking, in eating, perhaps even by breathing. How do the Jains relate to this fact?"

"They are in a constant state of asking forgiveness for these actions."

John was more exuberant than I had seen him in a while. "A constant state of repentance! That is a righteous way of approaching God!" He then became more thoughtful. "Do they worship the One God? I heard that they have many Gods like the pagans."

Tuzla responded, "That is not really correct, it is Hinduism which allows one to worship the aspect of the One God which pleases you the most. It is still One God, however. It just acknowledges that there is no separation. God is not here or there but everywhere in all things, and all things are a part of the One God."

Tuzla continued… "The Jains on the other hand, worship the human aspect of God. When one has completed all the Karmas and is free, he is deemed a divine being and is worshipped as such. In fact if any one of you got to that stage of perfection, you would be a Jain God."

"Have there been many who have done this?" asked John.

"Ah… according to them there have been twenty-four and those were great religious figures in their time."

"I would not want to be worshipped," John said, frowning, "That is placing false Gods before the One true God. I would not mind being as one of the prophets of old, however."

I felt some teasing was in order here. "John, I don't think you are in any danger of being worshipped." Everyone was too wrapped up in the discussion and ignored my remark.

Jeshua broke in, "John, there will be a time in the future when we will be able to look in each other's eyes and see our Father there. In the loving of each other we would be worshipping the Father for we are all his children and our inheritance is His kingdom."

I thought about the rigors of following such a discipline as Tuzla described. "As for me, I want none of such an ordeal. I am already looking for God, why would I need further discipline?"

Tuzla looked at me with a quizzical expression. "You like to study martial arts, don't you?"

"Yes, of course," I replied.

"Well that's a discipline also. You didn't mind that too much, did you?" I didn't have to answer. Tuzla just looked at me and continued. "There are all kinds of physical and spiritual disciplines to follow and some of them can be very joyful and bring you back to God. There is meditation, chanting, and Maun, for instance…"

"What is Maun?"

"That is the discipline of silence. One who keeps Maun only observes, without praising or complaining."

"That would be a discipline perfect for you, Yehudah!" Jeshua said laughing. John and Tuzla joined his laughter. I was a little embarrassed at having my opinionated attitude exhibited to all our company, but I laughed as well. Jeshua regained a serious visage. "You know Yehudah, observation without participation is the best way of learning about things around you. You ought to consider this discipline as a learning technique. This world is our school, not our home."

I thought about that one for the rest of the evening and remained more quiet than usual. I promised myself that I would try to remember that when the passion of the moment swept over me. It seemed that my emotional reactions to people and events blocked out further reasoning.

The next morning Tuzla led us into a village by one of the tributaries of the Indus, a place called Pallipana. He was able to translate the native language and spoke to some inhabitants. We discovered that this was a Jain village and the leader wished to speak to us.

We were led into a huge temple where we were greeted by a wizened, white-haired old man. He looked as if he could not stand still. He was excited about something, but I was not aware of the focus of his consuming interest at the time. I learned later from Tuzla that he was Varadiji, the leader of all the Jains and was much revered by his people. He was not a perfected being but an ascetic. The perfected beings are usually recognized as leaders. When perfected beings are not available, master teachers, scholarly monks, or ascetics are accepted as leaders.

Varadiji spoke to Tuzla but Jeshua was clearly the focus of his attention. "I hear you are interested in examining our sacred texts," Tuzla translated.

"Yes, your traditions are new to me and I would like to learn more of them, said Jeshua."

"Then you will read and we will discuss..."

Jeshua spent almost three months reading texts, learning meditation techniques and joining in the Pratikraman or prayer times. Jeshua was clearly the center of attention but John and I were treated with respect and courtesy.

While I admired the way these people gave respect to every living being, I was becoming bored with the endless ritual and the plethora of rules that this religion demanded. "This is what it must be like to be a *Parush*," I thought.

Once during the Pratikraman, I felt like I was being strangled, like my surroundings were closing in on me. I just had to get out! I was almost in a panic. When I stood up from the floor all eyes were on me like I had done something namelessly horrible. I walked quickly from the room and when I had reached the outside, I took a sweet, long breath of air into my lungs. I spent the rest of the time until dusk outdoors. I appreciated the beauty of nature and the perfection of all things being in harmony.

I learned later from Jeshua that I had done something quite offensive. Jeshua then explained to them that this was not my path and my action was not an insult to their ways. They told Jeshua that they were reading sacred texts given by perfected beings and to walk out on this was an offense to those beings. Jeshua went on to explain that if someone had a path that was different from our path but would eventually get him to God-consciousness, wouldn't you want him to pursue this path? They had to agree and I was not harmed and allowed to go my own way from that time on.

It was not very long after this that Jeshua asked John and me to accompany him on a walk. He appeared quite concerned. He then explained the source of his disquiet. "I can see the beauty in many of these teachings. One must have respect for all living beings, as all are a part of God. I have spoken freely with these people and they are starting to consider me as one of the perfected beings or, at least, a great teacher. I cannot permit them to worship this son of man as such.

"If you are a great teacher, why should not they worship you as such?" asked John.

"If I am the being that they think I am, then they are doing me a disservice through that very worship."

"Why is that?" Asked John.

"A perfected being would want others to follow him to perfection. Worshipping such a being places a barrier between the both of you which doesn't permit you to love in the highest manner."

"Just what is the highest manner of loving a perfected being?"

"To follow him; to walk in his footsteps. The highest form of adoration is to know you are one with that being and move to the same perfection. I cannot stay here."

"Why?"

"It is not my destiny to remain with these people no matter how devoted to God they might be. I have another mission, although it is not yet clear to me. But even if I did decide to stay, sooner or later I would cause a great disruption within this religion. If they worshipped me as a perfected being, I could not practice some of the precepts that they hold sacred from ancient times. That would cause them to question their way and their purpose. If these ways are useful to them to get them to God, why should I change this? I could not disrupt them and say that I truly love them. This religion demands much of their Gods and I could not fulfill this role. I must leave."

The next morning Jeshua appeared before Varadiji and told him of his plan to leave. The old man was visibly saddened but regarded Jeshua with love. "My young holy man, we have learned much from you by spending time with us. I am curious what you have learned from us."

Jeshua seemed to be deep in thought for a moment and then spoke to the old man: "Honored teacher, I found much value in your proof that the Soul is eternal:

> 'The Soul is eternal, never being born, never dying. Since consciousness exists on a higher plane than matter it cannot originate from matter. And so the Soul cannot die because any substance that does not originate from anything, cannot be destroyed by anything.'

Your prayer touched me greatly; the one that goes:

> 'I bow to the enlightened souls. I bow to the liberated souls. I bow to religious leaders. I bow to religious teachers. I bow to all monks of the world.'

This is a demonstration of our unity in Spirit and in your people's dedication to live the knowledge that we are all One. I have been honored by your care of us."

Jeshua bowed to the old man. The old man bowed to Jeshua. I have never seen such emotion conveyed in such simple actions.

As we left the village Tuzla broke the silence: "There is, a few hours from here, a great Temple at Puri called Jagannath. Jagannath means 'Lord of the Universe' and it is one of the major shrines of Hinduism."

It seems that word travels as fast in this part of the world as in Galilee. We entered Jagannath in the morning on the day of a great celebration. It was a grand festival that symbolized the triumph of good over evil. There was a staggering mass of humanity at that festival. We saw priests dressed in white officiating the rituals. We stayed throughout the afternoon enjoying the anonymity the huge crowd offered. But that did not last too long. A priest caught sight of us and pointed in our direction. I had thought it might have been Jeshua's reddish-gold hair that snared their curiosity. But the first question that was asked (translated through Tuzla) was if he was the young holy man who was staying with the Jains.

Jeshua said that we had just left that place: "We are now in search of the holy texts of Hinduism."

"We are eager for you to stay with us and study the Vedas, the basis of our spiritual knowledge."

We were frequent guests at the Hindu Temples in that town. Jeshua was now wary of staying in one place too long so we frequently studied for a time in one city and moved on, often to Varanasi and Sarnath. By being on the move we prevented no one group or city from getting too attached to us.

With Tuzla's help we found the Buddhist monasteries. Since Buddhism was relatively new to India we had to travel to Rajugriha to find a monastery.

After a time we became a common sight and were known to all the traveling Rishis, Sadhus and other holy men on the road. Jeshua focused himself totally on learning the Vedas and the yoga of healing and meditation. He gained quickly in the spiritual sciences and was able to equal or surpass the siddhis or yogic powers of his teachers. When with the Buddhists, Jeshua learned many mysteries. Even the adepts marveled at his abilities in mastering the super-conscious state. I heard that when in meditation he had met with many of these masters and adepts on levels I could not even conceive.

I spent less time in meditation and more time with Tuzla and training in martial arts. I learned unarmed combat and to do with my bare hands what I had only been able to do with the *twin blades*. It gave me a feeling of mastery. I felt no longer helpless inside. I felt that if I could control what was going on around me I could gain some degree of peace inside of me.

John in the meantime had adopted many of the austerities of the Hindu holy men. Through his efforts his own siddhi powers grew. He could go for weeks without food and still maintain his health. He could control most of his physical processes, stop bleeding and inspire people with the tone of his voice. His desire for God mounted with greater and greater intensity.

I knew that Jeshua must have undergone many inner changes before the outward physical expression of the siddhi powers manifested. One day when we were with the Buddhist monks, we heard a tales of how these monks could slow down their heart rate and all body functions to appear as dead for longer periods of time. We even heard of one Holy man who had died and managed to keep his body from putrefying for years with the sheer energy of his being. Jeshua was eager to learn these secrets as well. He was in the habit of surprising his teachers and amazing the rest of us.

One day Jeshua took John, Tuzla and I to an unused room in the Buddhist monastery. He told us he would be leaving but would be back. John and I assumed that he meant either he would be traveling to another town without us or that he would be in a super-conscious state for a long period of time. He stood very still then his body just crumbled into a heap on the floor. John and I rushed over to him and placed him in a chair. We noticed that there was no breathing. John and I were in a panic, but Tuzla said that we should not take appearances so seriously. Both John and I were convinced that we had seen the last of our friend.

We told Tuzla that in this heat it would be necessary to make funeral preparations immediately. Since we could not give the proper burial as proscribed in the Hebrew Law, we would have to resort to the funeral pyres of the Hindus. Tuzla became sterner than I have ever seen him. He announced a few things to the monks in their own language and they bowed to him. The monks promptly removed us from the room. As John and I prayed and meditated continuously, the monks met all our needs, but they would not let us re-enter the room where Jeshua lay dead. On the second night I could no longer remain awake. Grief and frustration that I could do nothing exhausted me. I drifted off to sleep.

I was having fitful fragments of dreams when I felt my arm being shaken. I felt I was being pulled up from the floor where I lay sound asleep. As I looked down I saw my sleeping body breathing erratically. I panicked, "My God, I'm dead, too!"

"Nonsense!" said a familiar voice. It was Jeshua!

"But you're dead!"

"There is <u>no</u> death, Yehudah! I have left my body temporarily. It appears dead because I have learned to stop all functioning and preserve it with my Spirit. It would rot as any dead body would if I did not take that action. It is the Soul that lives and never dies. It is the Soul which has infinite power."

"There is something I must share with you and John, Yehudah. I know what I must do. It has come to me as I have been traveling the high realms of spirit, free from my body. I have been taken up to the highest realms by our Father and shown the results of all actions which I could take from this point and I now know what my mission here will be."

I was transfixed by the blissful look on his face. He continued: "Abba, God, my Father, and I are…One. I am a part of Him and He is in me. I have moved into the essence of His being and I am to express more of Him into the world. I am to fill myself so much with Him and so little of myself so that when you see me you will see Him. Yehudah, do you know why men ignore our Father and focus on things physical, petty greed and jealousies? It is because they fear death. Then they struggle to get as much as they can from a life that is as a moment to our Souls. Many think that when the body dies, it is the end of all. The Sadducees believe this. But the Pharisees believe in rebirth, as do the Hindus, Jains, and Buddhists. They <u>believe</u> it, but they don't <u>**KNOW**</u> it. Why? Because no one has ever returned from this place of after-life to show them that it exists. So they still fear. I must remove this fear so all can know we are immortal and divine. Then we can start to put more of our divine power into expressing our divinity and break the bonds of the physical level. What greater love can you have for your brothers and sisters if you die for them, come back for them, and show them their true nature? If you do this for them they will stop their sins of ignorance. They will know that they already possess what they are looking for."

"If you can do all this, Jeshua, you <u>are</u> the messiah. I would worship you as the messiah."

"No, Yehudah. Don't <u>worship</u> me. <u>Follow</u> me."

"I am unworthy. I am unable to do such things. This is beyond my ability to know."

"We are brothers, Yehudah. We are both immortal souls. The only difference between us is that I have been on this path much longer. I have worked toward this for many lives. If you had been on this path as long as I you would be doing this too. Do you know that saying 'It only takes one man to show others what all can do'? From this time on human beings will know that they can have the Kingdom of God while they are still on the earth. The Kingdom of God is really knowing, for absolute certainty, that there is that connection and it is within you. You can live in that kingdom and you do not have to die to do it. However, <u>I</u> must die to prove it. That is the role I am to play, to show that this is possible."

I was overwhelmed. I could not speak further. Jeshua gently let go of me and I slipped back into my body into a dreamless sleep. When I awoke next morning, I could not speak; I could not communicate with anyone. It seemed like anything I could say would be irrelevant. I saw the world as a different place. I felt a vague buzzing in my head but there was no pain. My comfortable reality had evaporated and what was left was totally alien. At once everything appeared unreal, but then everything appeared to be operating from within its own truth.

John shook me but I could not answer him. Tuzla finally placed his hand on my forehead and chanted something in a melodic foreign tongue. I felt more at ease with myself but still felt totally out of place. I went the whole day in this condition but had a restful sleep that night.

In the morning John awakened me. He was wide-eyed and looked elated. "Jeshua's alive, he spoke to me."

This moment was the closest I have ever felt with John at any time. "I know," I replied. We embraced and both of us wept for joy.

On the third day since Jeshua left. Tuzla brought us into the room. Jeshua was alive and awake. He appeared weak and uncomfortable in his body, however. "The thing is when you leave your body for any time you come back to pain and stiffness," he said.

I knew this after some nights' sleep. But to leave your body for dead for three days must be worse than I could imagine. He explained that he needed this day to do self-healing, so we left him alone for the rest of the day.

I think that was the point when we all were changed. None of us was the same after that experience. I completed my martial arts studies and began to learn more meditation. John spent more and more time alone. Jeshua looked and acted more like a master than a student. He became more serious and outspoken in his communications with people. He could recite the ancient texts in Sanskrit and teach from his inner experiences in the native tongues of the surrounding lands.

He began spending less time with the Hindu priests and more time with the lower caste peoples, the Soudras. The Soudras were treated like slaves and not permitted to study the Vedas. Jeshua told us that a great wrong had been perpetuated through this society. The Soudras were taught to worship likenesses and representations of aspects of God. In not being exposed to the truth, they had accepted these forms to be the forms of God.

Jeshua spoke to Soudras whenever our travels permitted. He told them how they came to be where they are in society: "My brothers, all Souls are equal in the eyes of God. It is necessary for the smooth functioning of society that different jobs are assigned to different individuals. If we see each person, each job as representing a different part of the body of God, we see that all necessary for the well being of the body. No one part is more important. All people and jobs are then equal. When one person began to believe that his job was superior to another's, that was when the system began to decline. At that point people were no longer valued for their divine nature. So the process began to separate us rather than unite us through the fact of mutual divinity. If one organ of the body perishes, it is not too long before the rest do also."

"The Brahmans tell you that the only way you will escape your lot is to die and be reborn. We are all born God's children and He all equally loves us. Those who deprive their brothers of divine happiness will themselves be deprived of it. The Brahmans of this lifetime will become the Soudras of the next. The first shall become the last and the last shall become the first. And that is the law of Karma. Follow instead the God of your hearts and the Law will not bind you. Do not be confused by worshipping aspects of the One, worship the universal Spirit, the Soul of the Universe, for this is what gives life to all. It is this loving Father who has existed always and will exist forever and has divided His power with no other. But He has created us in His image and we are all His children and the heirs to His throne. Into us all he has breathed part of his divine being so that none of us is unworthy of His love and grace."

The Soudras called Jeshua their teacher and were filled with veneration and love for Jeshua. They called him "Master." They asked what actions would bring them the most happiness.

Jeshua responded: "Love others as you would love yourself for you are One. Harm not others or yourself. Seek always the highest good in all things."

I asked Jeshua why he spoke out against the ruling priests of this land.

He answered, "Yehudah, when a priesthood like the Brahmans (or the Sadducees in our own land) exists to perpetuate themselves, they place their vested interests higher than the truth. I must speak out against anything that blocks the direct and unlimited relationship between Man and God. If people can know the truth they can more easily find it within. That is where the kingdom is, Yehudah, within."

All of this was not going on without being noticed. The priest and warrior classes were determined to stop a voice that would have upset their system. One night in Juggernaut we were hailed by a group of Soudras. They said that the soldiers were coming for Jeshua and his party and that they had murder on their minds. John and I had some concern, but Jeshua and Tuzla calmed us. Jeshua told us that we would not be seen. I found this statement to be ridiculous; Jeshua stood out in any crowd. In our own land, his red hair would go unnoticed. But in this land it was a dead giveaway. I figured that Jeshua had planned some disguises that would get us past the soldiers. The soldiers surrounded completely our section of the town. There appeared to be no escape possible. Jeshua closed his eyes for a moment. We joined in with our own meditation. Jeshua had us join hands and follow him. We walked through the ring of soldiers. No one even looked at us. I was astounded at this miracle. After we were gone from the town Jeshua noticed my frightened look and said to me: "It is all quite explainable. It is like one of the siddhi powers John and I were being taught while you were studying martial arts. Yehudah, know that I am able to escape from any situation by this technique. Even if someone tells my pursuers my whereabouts, I am able to escape. Wait, I will show you."

The next moment he was gone from our group. I asked if anyone else saw him. Both John and Tuzla pointed to empty space! The next moment he was there again, smiling.

John said that he saw the masters teach Jeshua dematerialization and re-materialization, but this was something different.

Jeshua countered: "This was taught to me by the Inner Master."

CHAPTER 6 - THE TOP OF THE WORLD AND THE PIT OF DESPAIR

Something was different about Tuzla. Ever since we escaped the Brahman priests he had become more enthusiastic about our traveling. I realized that we were moving in the direction of his homeland, Tibet. Jeshua had expressed eagerness to visit Tuzla's home and I believed that it still was his design to go there. The trip was long and somewhat painful for me. I did not enjoy the cold and the thin air of the mountains. It felt as if the *twin blades* were slashing into my lungs.

As we traveled from Delhi to Nepal the air got thinner and colder. Tuzla tried to take our minds off the discomfort of change by telling us stories of his childhood and youth in Lhasa. "People who have been to Lhasa call it a city of monasteries. Actually the whole city is essentially a monastery since it caters to the desires of the Bön and Buddhist monks who live there. All there are either monks or those that are close to them. Imagine a city where everyone is known to everyone else, not only from this life but also previous existences. Monks often read the Akashic Record[7] and received a small donation from townsfolk. Lhasa is the center of Bön, the native religion, and Tibetan Buddhism. The city is relatively new, however. Many centuries before the Lord Buddha appeared on the planet, my people were both great priests and warriors. Legend says that my people came from a colony of priests who came from the great Temple in Atlantis. They wished to set up a place that was as spiritually pure as possible and protected from outside invasion so this purpose was not polluted. To accomplish this, the founding monks instituted two programs. The first was to create a caste of warriors to protect the settlement. The martial techniques I have been teaching you, Yehudah, come from that ancient time. The warrior caste went too far and became great conquerors in ancient times. This upset the priests, the true rulers of our country who believed in peace and the sanctity of all

[7] Similar to a "celestial tape recorder" where the entire history of the planet has been recorded.

life. They built a great holy city (the second program) called Shamballa and hid it far up in the mountainous regions of our land, almost at the top of the world. It contains a portal into other dimensions where this city really exists in its grandest expression. Only the portal still remains physical so that only those who know exactly where it was can find it. Once you cross over the portal, you leave the physical world and see the incredible beauty of Shamballa. This city still serves a function. Master Beings from other realms use it as a point to enter the physical realm. The purity of energy in Shamballa spills over into our realm and actually 'cushions' a soul's entrance into the physical realm."

Something about this hidden city seemed familiar to me. "Does this city still exist?" I asked.

"Yes…but not very much remains for physical eyes to see. Over many ages more and more structures were converted into the higher realms and disappeared from the physical. Almost nothing of that city remains today. It is well that this happens. An Astral[8] city is harder to find than a physical one." He flashed a smile.

"Have you been there, Tuzla?" I asked.

"Yes."

"Would you take us there?"

"I am forbidden to take anyone there without the permission of our Most High Teacher[9]."

"Will we get to see the Most High Teacher?" asked Jeshua.

"At this moment he is aware of all of us and it waiting in his monastery in Lhasa."

It took almost a month to travel through Nepal into Tibet and make the climb to Lhasa. I had been actively trading on the way so we had plenty of money to buy clothes that would protect us from the cold. The thin air was a problem that we could not fix right away. Our bodies became used to the thin air but it slowed our progress.

Lhasa turned out to be smaller than Alexandria or Jerusalem; it appeared to me to be more of a village. Most of the buildings were monasteries, as Tuzla had told us. The monastery of the Most High Teacher looked like any of the others but it flew a flag that looked like a picture of a mountain in the middle of the ocean. We walked up a flight of stairs at the front entrance and two huge doors slowly swung open. I noticed that Tuzla was no longer with us. Two monks dressed in yellow

---

[8] The realm above the physical — the realm of the imagination.

[9] An ancient equivalent of the Dalai Lama.

robes escorted us to a very large room with some stairs up to what looked like a throne. No one was seated there. Instead a single monk dressed in purple robes sat on the floor with his legs crossed. He motioned us to come closer and sit down. There was not a word for a good five minutes when another monk dressed in blue robes came into the room and spoke to us in a very familiar way: "I have the joy to present to you the Most High Teacher of Tibet." It was Tuzla speaking!

I was even more surprised when the Most High Teacher spoke in passable Aramaic: "I have the joy to present to you the Second High Teacher," he said, motioning to Tuzla.

Jeshua bowed. He did not look at all surprised. I wondered when he knew. He bowed first to the Most High Teacher. "I am honored." Then to Tuzla. "I continue to be honored." There was an easy formality, and a mutual loving that was very evident.

I realized that it must be difficult for just anyone to get an audience with the Most High Teacher, especially foreigners. Here was a master and a great spiritual consciousness that was totally open and almost child-like in his manner. "You know my brother monk here as Tuzla. That is a nickname he had as a child. He is my eyes and ears to the world outside Tibet. What he knows, I know. And so I feel I really know all of you. Jeshua, in your own country they will call you "the Anointed One." Anointed by God you were for a special purpose. One like you we call an Avatar. The Lord Buddha was such an individual. It is our turn to lend our support to your mission and assist you in your preparation. You will all receive final training for what you are about to complete in this lifetime.

He focused his attention again on Jeshua. "I heard that you had quite an adventure with the Brahman priests. Why do you think they were so angry with you?"

"I represented changes they were not ready to accept. They were not ready to acknowledge that our Father equally loves all Souls. They were fooled by the form. Just as it is easy to see Tuzla as a simple guide rather than a great teacher, they judged the people born into lower castes as somehow less in the eyes of God. They had forgotten that we are all made in our Father's image so what we do to the least we do also to Him. And since we are all One in the Father, they did it to me as well. I had to speak."

"Yes, Jeshua, you will find that the problem of being an Avatar is that very few people are ready for you, or are even ready to want you. Avatars are usually hated, discredited, and many times killed in their own time. In years to come they become venerated and often worshipped.

They are hardly ever understood. That is what lies ahead for you. It is a lonely and unforgiving road. Are you ready to make the trip?"

"I have no choice. It is so much of what I am and what I am to become, I would be forsaking myself and betraying my Spirit if I did otherwise."

The Most High Teacher looked fondly at Jeshua. "Jeshua, you have healed many in consciousness already. The teachings you gave against Transmigration removed fear from many Souls. How did you put it...oh...'Our Heavenly Father would not treat his children any less loving than an earthly Father. He would not humiliate any of His children by causing their souls to be placed into the body of an animal. God cannot be contrary to his own laws.'"

He then looked at all of us. "We are all students of the Sojourner Consciousness so you are all welcome here."

I really felt welcomed. I felt a student in my own right, not just someone in Jeshua's shadow. Although Jeshua was his prime focus, both John and I received training and personal time with the Most High Teacher. I felt the same love and acceptance from these Tibetans that I felt from Jeshua. John and I were able to join them at prayer time. We joined a room packed with yellow-robed monks chanting the "AUM" for hours. The energy was compelling and I really knew that I was at the top of the world. Here was the first time that my spiritual practice coincided with John's. I felt that I got to know John better during this period. Jeshua, too, spent some time with us but more often was off with the Most High Teacher. One day he told us that he and the Teacher were to go off in the mountains together.

During the time Jeshua was gone, John and I were able to spend some time with Tuzla (He told me it was fine for me to still call him that. He was not one for protocol and titles.) We learned many things and received another initiation. This initiation was a special one because, like the Most High Teacher, Tuzla was a representative of the Sojourner. We received our own personal tones to chant. Having our own tone helped us build spiritual "muscle" to get beyond levels of illusion and realize the divinity within. I learned that this was actually the second Sojourner initiation that John and I received. The first one was given by the hierophant at Heliopolis just by explaining the Sojourner. The second initiation was for the emotional level of being. We were warned that it would let loose much of the Karma built up over many lifetimes for us to deal with and clear. We were told that we needed to complete the Mental and Unconscious-level initiations before we could realize consciously that our home was in the realm of the Soul.

I sat for hours chanting my new tone. For the first time in that lifetime, I had a sense of self. I was in love — with the Father and the prospect of divinity flowing through me. I could now get a small glimpse of how Jeshua must feel. He knew with absolute certainty his connection with the Father. To me just this glimpse of my own potential was entirely blissful.

But there was something that continued to nag me. I knew that Jeshua and The Most High Teacher were off in the mountains visiting Shamballa. The description that Tuzla provided seemed so familiar to me that I could almost see it. One day I decided to follow them. During the climb I lost sight of them but continued up the mountain. When I came to a ridge I struggled to make it over the top. I knew I was close! At once I had a fright. Something grabbed my ankle and pushed me securely onto the ridge. I turned back and saw Tuzla below me. He had his hand raised. "Well, don't just stand there, pull me up," he said.

"You are beginning to remember, aren't you?" He asked.

"Just what am I trying to remember?" I asked, trying to be cunning but not succeeding.

With a look of incredulity and impatience he said, "Well, all right, just take me to the city. Just stop thinking and go with what your inner knowledge is trying to show you."

I inched our way along the ridge, being careful to avoid looking down. I knew we were close to something when the ridge got even thinner. As we turned the corner, I went for what appeared to be a cave entrance. I was beginning to feel some doubt, but Tuzla just patted me on the shoulder as if to urge me on. All of a sudden the light reappeared and we were above a flat expanse of ground. Where was the city? It was like a sea of stones covered oh-so-lightly with the dust of ages.

I unbuttoned my coat. It felt a few degrees warmer on that dusty plane. The wind picked up and blew the dust into our faces.

Tuzla broke the silence "Less here than before?"

"Yes," I said, pausing, "and I have been here before. And you are the one who took me!"

Tuzla smiled. "Show me the portal." He said.

Somehow my feet found the path through the stones. Up ahead I saw two columns. One was standing straight and the other was tipped over leaning against another column that had collapsed. "That's it… but there was more."

"Yes, there used to be an entire structure at one time."

"I am seeing just the façade of a building."

"Well, that's the condition it was in when you saw it. That was almost five hundred years ago."

As we approached the columns, I could see a mist behind the obscuring whatever lay beyond. "This must be it," I said.

"This is the part that upsets you," said Tuzla.

"What is that?"

"Sit down, we must leave our bodies."

We both went into deep meditation. I felt a feeling of well being come over me.

I heard a voice say, "Come along."

I open my eyes to discover that I was following Tuzla into the mist. When we past through, we found ourselves in a truly magnificent city. Lhasa looked like a pale imitation of what we saw.

All at once Tuzla face brightened. He grabbed my arm. "Here is someone who you will be glad to see!"

A tall bearded man approached and bowed. I did not recognize him at once. But all of a sudden I experienced a rush of memory. It was Master Tsang! I actually remembered him from a lifetime in the past.

"I am very glad to see you again," he began. "It is only fitting that someone who knows you should give you news like this. It may put things into perspective."

I tried to cushion myself with the worst thought I could think of. "Am I going to abandon my spiritual path?"

"No, nothing like that. You will be challenged in a way that will bring the warrior side of your beingness forward. The test will be if you can still return to your peace. That is all I can say about it, but know that the teachers on the inner realms will be supporting you in your test."

We spent some time in meditation together, just the three of us. Then Tuzla motioned that it was time to go. I happened to think of Jeshua and the Most High Teacher. In an instant both shimmered into existence in front of us.

"Jeshua has received an initiation from the Sojourner on the realm of the Soul," said the most High Teacher, clearly beaming with pride and excitement. "There is much now he must do at the monastery. Let us go, I am eager to get back." We passed through the portal together. I noticed that neither Jeshua nor the Most High Teacher had left their physical bodies on the outside. It seems that they released the "physical-ness" from them and then just re-substantiated them.

I turned to Tuzla who looked sad. "Stay with us and we can teach you to do that also."

"Well, I have every intention of staying." I said. "Let's start now."

For the next few days I was deep in study and meditation, feeling that at last I could attain some degree of mastery. Tuzla worked with me but seemed to be preoccupied. With great effort I was able to refine my physical body's energy enough to walk through a wall. This was elementary for the masters at the monastery but for me it was a crowning accomplishment.

My new world of success and accomplishment was not to last long. A messenger arrived at the monastery and was taken in to see the Most High Teacher. A few minutes later Jeshua, John and I were brought in to his private chamber.

"My dear friends and fellow spiritual initiates," he began. "Often the tests in life come very hard and personal. These tests may appear to be life dumping great evil on us but we cannot afford to take these tests personally. We must go on with our spiritual work despite personal loss and setback. To do otherwise is to succumb to both our lower nature and the efforts of the Lord of the Negative Realms, the Great Kal. Kal and his demons are allowed to test us in order that we prove ourselves worthy. That is their job. If we succumb to his temptations and are thrown off our path, there may be more lifetimes of work to make up. If we listen to his cajoling and lies, we are imprisoned again in his illusions, and it may take many lifetimes, even with the help of a Sojourner, to break us free. The news is of death and destruction from your homeland."

I felt that nothing would shake me from my choice to pursue my spiritual path. But I had not yet heard the message.

The Most High Teacher continued: "Jeshua, your father Joseph has died and, as the eldest son, your family has need of you. Yehudah …your father and mother were killed by Romans and all their property was taken. Your brother has disappeared."

All at once I was plunged into a pit of despair. What would all this spiritual work mean if there were none to come home to and share my joy? I sat motionless and only heard faintly Jeshua's answer to the Teacher: "I grieve for the loss of my earthly father, but the work I must do for my Heavenly Father must take precedence over ties to the family. I must serve a greater family and, therefore, surrender my personal feelings for the Highest Good. I will complete my work here. No one lives on this physical plane forever. We go at our appointed time. My sadness at my father's passing cannot bring him back. We all feel loss when a parent dies because we no longer see them physically. I know for a fact that they are alive and progressing on other levels, so they are not really lost from us. They are also in our hearts and we can remember them always with loving there. My time is better spent in completing my spiritual work."

I could feel Jeshua's comforting presence coming close to me and knew what he said was also for me to hear. There was in me such a feeling of injustice and hurt that I could not take in his words. I saw his kind, loving face and noticed a tear running down his face. "Please stay with me, Yehudah, and follow me. You will see later the wisdom of this."

I spoke from my feelings of hurt and despair: "My family really meant something to me. They were harmless merchants probably slaughtered for their money. This is a thing no just God would permit. How do you know that it is not up to me to fulfill the need for balance? What I feel inside with every fiber of my being is the need for vengeance!"

Jeshua put his hand on my shoulder. "I beg you to stay and meditate on this for a few days. Allow the Light of your own Soul to come through and give you direction."

That night I tried to meditate; I tried to see what happened from a different perspective but the fury inside me just increased. I kept of seeing pictures of my mother and father crucified in the street for everyone to see. Hanging there until the flesh fell from their bones… That night seemed to go on forever but when it finally did end, I resolved to find and punish the murderers of my parents. I felt that God, himself, was telling me it was the righteous thing to do. Jeshua, Tuzla, and the Most High Teacher waited for me in the main court. I announced: "I must go now. I thank you for all your love and care of me. What I must do must come first. I will return afterward to complete the further initiations. I must clear this Karma <u>NOW</u>."

Jeshua came before me. "Yehudah, think for one minute. Any merchant will tell you that there is no profit in revenge. Eventually you will be doing more hurt to yourself than others if you choose this path. There is enough hatred in the world, try if you can to return forgiveness. You will find that it is yourself you are trying to forgive. Stay a little longer so that we can assist you in this process."

"No, Jeshua. The time for meditation is past. I know that all things come from God but I just cannot accept this as part of my life. The powerful feel they can do anything they want to poor, honest men. I am through being a slave to their whims. This is a matter of justice. If I do not wipe this injustice away, I will not be able to believe in pursing my spiritual path. I need to handle this first. I will use my share of the remaining money to get back to Galilee as soon as possible. The ones who did this must be found and punished."

As I left the room I heard the last words I would hear from Jeshua for a long time. "Then go with God, Yehudah. Our Father is still close to you. When the despair gets too great, call on Him inside of you. You might reject Him, but He will never reject you."

At the time I did not know that my anger was mostly at God and myself. I was consumed with rage against the murderers of my parents. I bought a horse in Lhasa. I rode that horse until it was spent, trading one for another and whatever additional money was required to get another one. My rage built and boiled over. I plotted and schemed the demise of the unknown murderers. I saw myself extracting punishment from each with the efficient techniques that I had learned from Tuzla. The idyllic life I had led at the monastery became a faded dream. My meditation was now only upon revenge.

CHAPTER 7 - AMONG MURDERERS

It was the thought of the immense injustice done to my family that brought me such rage. I could not get a full night's sleep. My thoughts became disjointed. I couldn't look at a Roman soldier without wondering if he was the one who killed my parents. I spent two days on the outskirts of Capernaum more afraid of my reaction than what I might find.

I don't remember whether it was hunger, desperation or just curiosity that finally propelled me, but I finally entered the city. I was drawn inexorably to our home. I was half expecting to see my parents there waiting for me, older, for sure, but there. The door was bolted. I knocked. An elderly man opened the door.

"Where is Joseph, son of Ephraham?" I demanded.

"How should I know?" he said and was ready to slam the door shut. I quickly wedged my body inside of the opening and pushed him back inside and against the wall. My hand was at his throat, making it very difficult for him to breathe. "What do you want?" he managed to choke out.

"My father and mother used to live in this house and I want to know what happened to them."

"I promise you that I know nothing. I bought this house from a Roman centurion who told me that the previous occupants had left suddenly and were not going to return."

"Didn't the neighbors tell you what happened?" I asked.

"Why should they? I have only been here a short time. For all they know I might be a Roman agent, or worse – a tax collector. My neighbors do not often talk to me, let alone confide in me concerning community affairs."

I relaxed my hold on him. He was visibly shaken but seemed to be compliant. I had also relaxed from my fighting posture. "I asked you these questions because I have just returned from a long journey. I had received notice that the Romans had killed my parents. My brother is also missing. I am looking for those responsible."

"I may be able to help you, if you do not tell anyone who gave you the information."

I relaxed my grip on him. "You have no more to fear from me," I said.

He began: "The centurion who sold me this property was named Marcus Sextus. He took whatever there was in gold or silver except for religious articles. A young man, only a few years older than you also told me that he was a relative. He took a silver menorah. I am a Samaritan and we Samaritans worship the same God as you Galileans so these religious articles were of great value to me. They are yours if you want them. Feel free to take what is of value to you."

I took some bread off the table, a cup of wine and a simple blanket. I put my hand on his shoulder. "Please keep the rest. I nearly killed you and I never even asked your name."

"I am Osmandius, son of Rashon."

"Well, Osmandius," I said, "You are a good man. You would be about the same age as my father. If circumstances were different, I would enjoy spending time with you. But, there are things to which I must attend."

"It is hard to lose one's family. My wife died many years ago and my son was killed in an uprising at Cæsarea. I am somewhat familiar with loss and death. If you ever need a place to stay, feel free to come here. If I still live and you need a father to talk to, I would gladly fulfill that role. It would be good to be useful to a son again."

"I am honored," I said. We shook hands and I felt the hardness within both of us melting. "Peace be with you."

"And with you."

I knew peace would not be with me, perhaps for a very long time. As I left, a tear burst from my eye and rolled down my cheek, but I turned my face so it was not visible.

As I walked down familiar streets, I had new hope. It was possible that my brother, Simon, was still alive. Another joyous thought pulled me from grief. I could find Mary, Jeshua's mother! She was the closest to real family that I could immediately find.

It was almost mid-day when I got to her house. At first I was not recognized. I had grown a short beard since I had last seen Mary.

I saw her from afar and knew immediately it was she. It was as if she had not changed at all. I shouted from a short distance, "It is Yehudah, son of Joseph, I have news of Jeshua!" When she recognized me, she ran to me at top speed and gave me a big hug. A tear flowed from her eyes. "We received the news about Joseph," I said. "I am, sorry. Jeshua was greatly moved by the news…"

"…But he will not be following you," she said completing my sentence.

It was, for me, an awkward moment. I felt as though I should be making excuses for Jeshua. But Mary saved me this embarrassment by noting: "I understand that the tasks that are given Jeshua by our Heavenly Father may conflict at times with the duties to his earthly family. I have learned to accept this." She smiled, "I wonder where we would be if the prophets had to first fulfill all their requirements to their families before doing their work." We both laughed and she called to the house: "Come out and see who has come home!"

A number of children of different ages poured out the front door. I realized that most of these I had never met. The eldest child startled me for a moment. It was James. James looked almost exactly like Jeshua did at his age. The resemblance was truly astounding.

"Yehudah?" He looked at me quizzically. I nodded my head.

I received a hug from Ruth who recognized me instantly. I saw a male child who would have been born at about the time of my first trip to Jerusalem. "You must be my namesake," I smiled. He appeared shy and hid behind the twins Joses and Simon.

The youngest was a daughter. "And who are you?" I asked.

"My name is Elizabeth," she said. She looked very much like her mother with reddish-blond hair, whereas Ruth had dark hair like her father Joseph.

"We heard about your parents, Yehudah," Mary said. "You are most welcome to stay with us. But first, you have news of Jeshua?"

I spent the afternoon and evening with them. I thoroughly enjoyed the role of storyteller as I delved into great detail concerning our adventures. It was nice to be held as the center of attention by such a loving family. I could have closed my eyes and I would have been back in my childhood. But that moment didn't last, for as soon as I lay down to sleep, my consciousness again became troubled with recent events.

I left early the next morning and was able to get some information from our neighbors. Each one I talked to told me the same thing. It seems as though my brother Simon had joined the Zealots a few years before. Simon had become well known among them and, therefore, well known among the Romans and their Sadducee puppets. They came looking for Simon and didn't find him at our home. My parents were pulled out of their home and put to the sword on their front steps because they could not tell the Romans Simon's whereabouts.

Now I was really confused. I didn't know who to hate more, the Romans for killing my parents or Simon for causing it to happen. I knew that I must go and find Simon. I did not know, however, what I would do once I found him.

Like Jeshua, I had been taught the art of invisibility. The version I practiced was not as literal as his. Tuzla had instructed me in the art of disguise. I could become part of a forest or a field and no man would see me unless he happened to step on me. I could easily blend into a crowd and not be recognized. This was almost as effective as Jeshua's true invisibility and it would serve me much better for what I had to do.

I had to make contact with the Zealots. There was a tavern outside of Capernaum where outlaws sometimes met. Common folks knew it, so Roman spies also most likely knew it as well. I certainly could not go as Simon's brother but I could go as a beggar looking for some payment for "important" information about his brother.

Tuzla had shown me the meditation and techniques used to actually become another individual. To convince another, you must be fully convinced yourself that you are that person. The only problem, Tuzla admitted, was coming back. He said, "Yehudah, after a while you get so good at becoming another identity that you can create a whole different set of karmic situations for yourself. You can get lost and forget who you were in the beginning. I had been away so long from Tibet that I had trouble assuming my 'real' identity there. But there is an ultimate good in all this. You get to ask yourself: 'Well, then, just who am I?' And the answer to that Yehudah is, 'I am the Soul'."

"Well, Tuzla, my friend," I thought, "I cannot yet say that. I cannot yet see beyond what I need to do today or tomorrow. But when this is all over I will get closer to know my true self and all that entails."

I had plenty of time to think and meditate. I had found a spot not far from the tavern among the underbrush. I was not so far away that I couldn't see anyone who came or left by the front door. I dug a hole, planted the belongings that would contradict my assumed identity, and dug in for the night. I had picked up some old, torn clothing on the road to the tavern. Lying in the dirt would help the effect of camouflage. The next day was very hot and I had to lie perfectly still or be discovered by passersby. I was certain that I would both look (and smell like) an authentic beggar. During the day I was able to practice meditation and allow my consciousness to leave my body for long periods of time. In this way the day went quickly.

I was usually able to meditate for long periods, but I kept being interrupted by a vision of Jeshua. He was repeating his philosophy concerning revenge: "Turn the other cheek," he said. He explained that by turning your other side you were walking away from a negative direction and toward a positive one. This was something you could do in all aspects of your life. Being in his presence always kept me focused on the positive. I would have gladly followed his advice this time as well, but I felt I would always have this lingering thought eating away at me: that I was brought to dishonor by the Romans with their cruelty and injustice. If I did not do something about it then the deed would go unpunished. I had to complete this. My war was going to be a long one.

When the sun set, I separated myself from the camouflage of my surroundings and made my way to the front door. I knocked the door with a beggars' staff as to make lots of noise. An eye appeared in a knothole and told me to step away from the door. It took a full minute looking at me and decided that I was harmless enough. A burly man interposed himself in the door's opening. "There is no place for beggars here."

"But I do not beg tonight. I am selling information to those who might make very good use of it."

"And what would this information be?" he demanded.

"If I told you, I would have nothing to sell would I? I would go hungry and get thinner while you would sell my information and get fatter."

"Let him in," said a voice from inside.

"Very well," said the guard at the door, "but he smells worse than you do, Jacob."

They all laughed and I was permitted in. The room was not well lit. My eyes quickly adapted to the dingy interior.

The one called Jacob asked, "Well, just who would you be looking for?"

"Some patriots," I said, "those who could carry a message to Simon, the Zealot, Simon son of Joseph."

"Now why do you think WE would know such a person?" He backed slowly away toward the bar. "Someone who knew this Simon would be wanted by the Romans for questioning. Not too many people survive their questioning."

In the next few minutes most of them left. Another, shorter man approached me. "I know of some people who would be interested in what you have. Follow me. They're around back."

They led me around back of the inn, the side that was close to the woods. There were six men. I assumed things would then be pretty evenly matched.

I sensed one behind me and readied myself for an attack.

The short one beside me spoke: "I don't think you are a beggar but a Roman spy."

I reached down into a dirty old bag and pulled out the *twin blades* saying, "would a Roman fight with these?"

My blades slashed the one behind me on both cheeks. Another one came at me with a drawn sword from the side. I dropped to the ground, rolled past him and slashed the rear tendon on his right ankle. He went down and stayed there. As I got up I drove my knee into the crotch of the man with the bleeding cheeks. Another down. Not a movement wasted. Tuzla would be proud.

With two out of the fight, the remaining three hung back, trying to circle me and looked for an opening.

"Now you have to be extra careful," I quipped, "you're outnumbered."

"You have even more arrogance than the Romans," said Jacob, "Just what is it that you want?"

"I have important information for Simon, son of Joseph, I would tell him in person. I also wish that we now treat each other as brothers and go in peace. I do not want to reduce your ranks further."

"'Go in peace, heh.' You are an Essene, then," said Jacob "You people used to <u>practice</u> peace as well as speak of it."

"I may be a special case."

His voice softened: "Well it does explain the arrogance; I always suspected that arrogance would lie under all that holy attitude." He showed a thin smile.

"I am afraid that I alone must take credit for my arrogance. I did not learn it from the Essene teachers."

"I suspect you may have learned it from whoever taught you to fight. You do both with equal aplomb."

"And I suspect that you are either Zealots or have close contacts with them. Is that correct?"

"That we do. Let us go back to the Inn. We will stay the night and find the person you are looking for."

"I also know a few things about healing," I said. "I will attend to the wounds of your comrades, if you wish."

The fight was over. We went back to the Inn. I let my body and senses relax somewhat. I knew they did not entirely trust me, but I was reasonably certain that I would not be killed in my sleep. They were too curious about the news I had for Simon. Since I would not tell it to anyone and could not be frightened into revealing any information, I knew I would be safe at least until I reached Simon. I found a very thin cord used for sewing and a needle. I stitched one man's ankle and the other's cheeks.

The next day saw us move toward the hills. I had been there when Tuzla taught John how to live off the land. I remembered exactly what he had to say about our own land, where to find water and food. I knew the terrain as well as these bandits and they appeared even to be somewhat impressed. I could use that to my advantage. Being mysterious seems to be quite beneficial to one's survival!

We reached an old fortification around midday. I recognized it as one used by the Maccabees many years before. Compared to its heyday, it was in a shambles, but it provided shelter. I was brought to a large room with open windows and an open porch overlooking a courtyard. There was a thick, long wooden table stained with drink and scarred by knives and swords. On the wall hung all forms of battle attire, swords, shields, flags, bows and spears. I could almost feel the martial spirit of the Maccabee prince with my name. "What a long way from Yehudah Maccabee's armies to this pathetic band of robbers," I thought. "From that glory to this squalor in only a few hundred years." And then I saw it: the silver menorah of our parents on a side table. Simon was here, to be sure.

I heard voices coming down the hall toward my room. The door opened, revealing a number of men dressed for battle. There were four of them. Two had their swords drawn. The leader spoke: "I was told you are a very dangerous man. You have a set of daggers. Place them on the table and step away from them."

"That would leave me at your mercy. I'm afraid I can't do that," I said, "especially with two swords drawn."

He motioned for his men to put their swords on the table. I did the same with the *twin blades*. After an uncomfortable silence he began again. He spoke with a slow, calm manner that triggered recognition within me; it was Simon! "I heard you had some important news for me."

"Yes," I began, "your brother Yehudah is alive, in Galilee, and looking for you."

His voice got louder, a sure sign that he was now off-guard. "You saw him? What did he look like?"

It took me less than a second to assess the situation. I acted. I grabbed Simon by the throat, smashing him into a section of the wall where a shield hung. It was an Assyrian Shield with a pointy tip. He winced; it probably pierced his flesh under the ribs. At same time I reached up and pulled a rusty sword off the wall and held it to his throat. "He looks a lot like me," I said.

His men went for their swords. "If you pick up those swords, I will kill him immediately, and then you afterward. He may die anyway but at least there will be a chance for him to try and talk me out of killing him."

Simon struggled against my hand but I had clamped down hard on his windpipe. "Are you really Yehudah?" He was my older brother and assumed he could still overpower me.

"I suggest you stop fighting and start talking," I said. My rusty sword pressed harder against Simon's throat. A drop of blood appeared. "By talking you will make me less nervous."

"Are you really Yehudah?"

"I remember when you almost smothered that boy in the mud who was bullying me."

"If you are my brother, why are you trying to kill me?"

"You killed our parents."

"It was the Romans who killed our parents."

"It was because of you that they did it."

"We are at war, Yehudah, and there are often many innocent casualties of war. Our parents were not the first and they will not be the last."

"Give me one reason, Simon, why I should not kill you."

"All right. But I will give you two reasons. First, I am now the only family you have that is left alive. Second, I know the location of the man who killed Mother and Father."

"Give me your word you will help me slaughter the Roman pig that killed our parents."

"I will, brother, but it is next to impossible."

I relaxed my hold on him and beckoned everyone to sit at the table. "That does not sound like the Simon I used to know."

"Yehudah, I have been trying to get at him for months, but we just can't get close enough to him. When we attack a caravan, there is no danger of being surprised. In a town, there is always a garrison and often that is behind stone. This centurion never leaves the town and is usually surrounded by his guards. Even if we could get in, none could get back out. If only we had the *Sicarri,* the assassins, they used to be able to get anywhere, kill anyone, and escape without harm."

"What happened to them?"

"They are probably all too old to carry a knife. They may have all disappeared by now."

As I listened to the tales of the *Sicarri*, I became more and more certain that Tuzla's instruction could be applied to these situations. "Simon, would you like to see the *Sicarri* reborn?"

"Now how could that happen?"

"Will you get me all I ask for?"

"If you could do this, I would do my best!"

He did do his very best. In the next few months I took ignorant, frightened bandits and put them through an extremely rigorous martial arts training. I took all that applied. Those who met the most demanding standards became lone assassins, *Sicarri.* Those that were less able but still superb fighters were inducted in my attack teams. The ones who gave it their best but were less able, I saved for my spy network. Everyone was given a responsibility and a duty he could be proud of. I was a harsh teacher but I rewarded excellence.

Simon came to me one night and sat down. He looked me in the eye. "Yehudah, I am in your debt. You have given these men more than I have ever been able to give them. They now have a sense of pride and a sense of certainty that they will fight and survive. I regret my part in the death of our parents and I do not know what to do about that."

This was the first time I had ever seen my brother express grief.

I felt a wave of regret pass over me. "I was a man of peace, now I am a warrior. Soon, when I find the man who killed our parents, I will be a murderer. It is because of you that I am becoming this." My voice was tinged with blame.

Simon put his arm on my shoulder. "I am truly sorry for all that has happened. I joined the Zealots because it was the only thing in which I truly believed. You had Jeshua and the inner mysteries. I needed something more solid, more immediate. I believe in this with fervor equal to that of your own. I cannot change that. If you still wish to kill me after we balance the scales for our parents, I will offer myself to you without resistance. But if you let me live I will find a way to bring you back to your peace, brother. I do not know how, but this I will do!"

My anger was spent. He opened the floodgates for me. I pulled him to me and wept on his shoulder. Between sobs I managed to say, "Simon, I can't kill you. I chose my own path and am responsible for my actions. If I choose the life of a murderer, it is my action and I will reap the result. You need not do more."

"I have promised to bring peace to you, Yehudah. Nothing can change that."

As time progressed, Simon and I got closer as brothers. We were even closer than we were as children. We were fighting for the same cause. Simon continued leading attacks against caravans. From the riches that he received I paid our network of spies and their operatives. With the gold and gems we took from the Romans, we could have retired rich men. It was used instead to supply our fight for freedom and, in our own way we gave it back to the people.

I spent more time teaching than fighting. I taught the techniques that Tuzla had taught me concerning camouflage, hand-to-hand fighting and the use of the *Twin Blades*. Very few of my *Sicarri* were ever caught. They could lose themselves in a crowd, get close to a target, kill without being seen, and fade away back into the masses. My targets were Romans or Jewish collaborators. The Sadducees and their functionaries were secondary targets as well as Herod's officials.

Our presence was being felt from Galilee to Jerusalem to Cæsarea. I became to be seen as a shadowy figure, "Yehudah the *Sicarri*," or in the Latin, "Judas Iscariot." My brother's reputation grew as well, "Simon Zealotes" (Simon the Zealot), striking terror in the hearts of Roman troops traveling across the open plane. We found that terror of our <u>possible</u> presence was enough to consume Roman resources. Many crimes and killings that we had nothing to do with us were credited to us. Many unfortunate men who had their own agendas were crucified as Zealots and *Sicarri* but were just in the wrong place at the wrong time. This served our purposes as well, since it brought more awareness of Roman cruelty to the general population. The general population saw us as liberators. The Romans saw us as bandits, and Herod and the Sadducees saw us as traitors.

I always chose the Roman targets hoping to get more information about Marcus Sextus. I received help from an unexpected source. Simon had captured a prisoner of the Romans during one of his raids. This prisoner would have been a great find for any Roman official stationed in Galilee. To them, Galilee was like the armpit of the world and they would have been eager to turn in a prisoner like this and perhaps earn a trip back to Rome. This prisoner was Petronius, a runaway Gladiator. It appeared that not only had he escaped the games but killed many soldiers and a few officials while doing it.

Simon had him chained to a wall in one of the underground rooms. I motioned to the guard to open the door for me. The guard appeared nervous and explained to me just how dangerous this man was. That only engaged me more. I shouted an order to the guard. "Remove his chains and leave us. Oh, and make a horse and provisions ready for the man who leaves this cell alive."

"You are taking quite a chance, challenging someone you haven't seen fight," Petronius growled in plebeian Latin.

"I might say the same for you if you accept my challenge," I said in a Latin, which was quite rusty but more formal.

"What choice do I have?"

"A lot more than you'd expect," I said. "But for now take this sword and defend yourself."

I threw him the sword and watched his movements. He was trained well. He had more cunning and ability than I had ever seen in a Roman soldier. After a few jabs and parries we got a pretty good look at each other's capabilities.

"You are toying with me," he said suspiciously. "You are much more skilled than the usual Jewish bandit. What is your name?"

"Your people call me Judas Iscariot."

"You are somewhat famous, or rather infamous, from what I have heard."

We circled each other cautiously.

"And you have defeated the Emperor's best troops," I said.

"Why are you not trying to kill me? You have given me a few scratches to demonstrate your skill with those two knives, but you show no interest in finishing the job."

"That's because killing you would be a great waste. You are a master with a short sword and perhaps other weapons as well. I am sure that you have no love for the empire and would probably enjoy fighting against it. I can offer you that choice, or you can leave."

"You would let me leave alive?" he asked with a quiet laugh.

"Certainly. You cannot harm us. You are more wanted among your own people than we are. You could not get close enough to them to tell them where we are. But…I told the guard outside that only one of us would be coming out alive to leave this place so if you want to leave you will have to kill me," I said. I threw the twin blades over toward him and left myself without weapons.

"Then I prefer to stay," he said, "I would rather fight along side of you than against you."

"Good, for I have a battle worthy of your talents. But first I must train you."

He looked hurt and angry. "I am a seasoned Gladiator, one who has survived long enough to tell about it. What can you teach me?"

I smiled; dropping down on one bent leg and swept the back of both his knees. He came crashing down on his back. I placed a foot on his chest, pried the sword out of his hand and pointed it at his neck. "Unarmed combat, for a start," I said.

"You could have done that before, right?"

I smiled and nodded, helping him up. "I studied with a master of the Martial Arts from the East. We all have <u>something</u> to learn. It is when we stop learning that we die."

"<u>This</u> is the notorious Judas Iscariot?" He smirked. "I get captured by a Julius Cæsar and find out that he is actually Plato after all. Are you a master philosopher as well?"

"No, but I have been exposed to them," I said wistfully. "I would give anything to have that life back. If it weren't for vengeance, I would still be on a path of spirit."

"Well, perhaps one day you will return to that path," he said with a smile. "And I resign myself to have you as a teacher. But I give you fair warning, I am a fast learner when it comes to fighting. I will become as good as you or perhaps better."

"I am counting on that," I said.

We walked out of the room and a dozen men came running toward us. "Everything is fine, he's now with us." As he went off with the others I whispered to Jacob, "Just keep an eye on him and report anything that should not be."

"My pleasure, I will become his best friend."

"I'd prefer that you would be subtle," I said.

Survival demanded that I become extremely cautious. But Petronius appeared true to his word. He did learn quickly and in a few months was an able *Sicarri.* Simon was happy to use him to get close to Roman encampments. He could mimic the manner and the attitude of any number of ranks of Roman soldier. Once he earned their trust, my other *Sicarri* could enter and do their damage. Simon lost fewer men and won more prizes.

Petronius became an accomplished spy as well. He was able to learn many important facts from visiting Roman garrisons. One day he came to me with news that set my blood afire. "Judas, I have found your Marcus Sextus. He is in a garrison close to Nazareth. The Feast of Venus will be coming soon and most of the soldiers will be drunk. I can get us in. We will need Roman armor, swords, helmets and quite a bit of luck in order to get out again."

Petronius showed us the layout of the fortress and the easiest access points. Beyond that, there was no way to tell where Marcus Sextus would be. So we practiced our entrance and our escape and hoped that there would be something in between that would support the risks we were taking.

On the night before we were to go I said, "Petronius, I would die for this chance. I would go even if I knew I would not survive. I am only worried that I will die before finding him."

"Revenge has been the focus of your life for so long, what will you do after it is complete?"

I smiled and teased, "Now who is the philosopher?" But the question was a valid one, one I did not even wish to look at. "I really don't know. Perhaps my life is over."

"Or perhaps after this long side street, you will again get back to the main road of your life. With all your skill and ability, Judas, you are not a fighter. Your heart is not in this. As someone who has done it all his life I can tell. You have given me another chance by rescuing me. Perhaps I will give you another chance by fulfilling your quest for revenge."

He showed more wisdom that day than I had ever seen from him before. It was almost like Jeshua spoke through this man. He was the only Roman who had earned my respect. He was truthful and honorable, and I promised myself if I ever ran into Jeshua again, I would have Petronius meet him.

The assembled group of *Sicarri* jolted me out of my reverie. They carried packages of Roman armor. We were dressed in the usual night-dress of *Sicarri* – black robes and a black scarf wound around our faces. We made good time on horseback and in a few hours we were at the garrison. We changed into Roman armor and buried our traveling clothes and marked the spot with a sword.

Petronius took the role of a centurion and led us to one of the side gates. The guard looked suspiciously at us, but Petronius convinced him that we were stationed in Nazareth and had come to join the celebrations. We were almost all inside when Petronius, who had been keeping the guard busy, slit his throat. This guard was replaced by one of our men who spoke passable Latin. We made our way down the halls and got our first look at a Roman festival. There were whole groups of people in the throws of sexual passion. There were people who were eating to capacity and when they could not eat anymore, would vomit and start all over again. Others were drinking themselves into a stupor. We often entered rooms where people were entwined in numerous sexual positions. Few even noticed us. Petronius said that if we looked like we were enjoying ourselves we had the right to watch whoever we wished. Petronius had the presence of mind to keep asking where Marcus Sextus could be found. He was on the top floor in a closed room. We tried the door but it was bolted from the inside.

Petronius and I looked at each other, blades in hand, brought a leg up and broke down the door. A rather greasy-looking man with a pocked-marked face turned toward us with a wild rage. He was raping a woman who was chained facing a wall. "Who are you to interrupt me? Aren't there enough woman downstairs?"

"I am known as Judas Iscariot and I am here to collect on a debt you owe me."

"I owe you nothing, bandit, but an early death. I have never even seen you before."

"You knew my parents, at least a short time before you killed them."

I was slightly distracted. There was another conversation going on at the same time. The woman reacted with surprise. It seems as though this slave girl, named Julia, had known Petronius in Rome. I missed a lot of the conversation but it seems that she was once from a noble family that had done something to cross the Emperor. Petronius, who was a servant of her father, had fallen in love with her. They met secretly. One day the Emperor's guard came, killing her father, mother and most of her family and she was sold into slavery. Petronius had been sent to the games.

While I kept my twin blades at the throat of Marcus Sextus, Petronius was freeing Julia.

"Your parents deserved to die as do you."

An enraged Petronius came at Marcus Sextus with his blades. I pushed him aside. "Do not ruin this for me, I have waited too long."

"My cause is as just as yours, and the insult is as great."

"Let's not fight over this carrion. Perhaps we can both kill him."

While we were arguing Julia had picked up a dagger and with one slice opened the abdomen of Marcus Sextus. He screamed with pain. A second slice of her knife opened his throat and ended his miserable life.

We were both stunned.

"I could not let friends become enemies over one such as this," she said.

Petronius and I were both angry and confused but we knew that it would be better if we left. We could sort it all out later.

We found some clothes for her that were not covered with blood and made our way to the side entrance. Most of our group were already there, pockets filled with stolen articles.

Our group made for where we had buried our clothes. Petronius told her to take his clothing and that he would wear the armor back to our camp. Petronius buried her clothing deep. Perhaps he thought he could also bury her previous identity forever.

On the way back to camp, no one spoke. It was like a funeral. At last we could see the camp on the horizon with the first dim glow of morning. I went straight to my bed and slept until noon.

When I awoke, the sun was high in the sky. I spent time meditating and trying to sort out all that had happened last night. Had I failed my parents? Had I wasted years of my life on a quest doomed to failure? Petronius would appreciate the irony. Everything now was meaningless. I did not know how to return to my old life and there did not appear to be anything else left for me. I had even thought of suicide, but I knew that would be a sure trip back to the earth plane in perhaps worse circumstances. So fear and a vision kept me from taking my own life. The vision was one I had not experienced in quite a long time. I saw Julia in a fresh, white robe. I looked again and her face changed into another woman's face, one with copper hair (Julia's was almost black) and thin features. "I will be with you soon and you will not know me."

I was interrupted by a quiet knock on the door. A female voice asked in Latin if she could enter. Julia and Petronius entered. They had bathed. Julia was quite striking and I had never seen Petronius that clean.

"I wish to tell you how sorry I am. I robbed you of your just revenge. I just wanted my nightmare to end." By now she was sobbing.

"I am not angry," I responded, "What I feel now is mostly relief. I am at a crossroads in my life, but there are no signposts, and I have no plans."

I found out that they did. They could not go back to Rome. They found a new life here in Galilee and wanted to spend the rest of it together. Petronius enjoyed his life as a fighter and wanted to continue. Women were not part of our encampment so she could not stay with him. I suggested that she could stay with a family I knew who lived near Mt. Carmel.

The next few days I must have spent telling them my entire life story from childhood in Galilee with the Essenes to visiting the holy men of the east. Story by story I regained my feeling of being alive. I enjoyed telling the tale and watching the reaction of others. I had remembered my experiences writing on scrolls at Mt. Carmel and the thought came to me of writing about my thoughts and travels. That is when I began writing this manuscript. I thought first of using the scrolls as did the Essenes do but scrolls do not travel well. The Romans used the codex or book form but pages were made of copper laced together. What if I placed sheets of papyrus or parchment between the copper sheets as a front and back cover to protect the sheets? Books in this way I would not only have something more portable, but able to be preserved from damage to a great extent. I could also use the Essene technique of coating scrolls to keep pages from sticking together. It came to me to use a two-step process. My father had used parchment for his accounting because it could be erased. I could use parchment with my charcoal to take down the stories. I could then transfer the stories to papyrus using a permanent ink.

I had lost all interest in fighting and was no longer active in the training of *Sicarri*. Our people were intensely loyal and spies continued to report to me on the events of the outside world.

I thought it would be a good idea to travel to Mt. Carmel. I wanted to see the latest in scroll preservation techniques. I did not want my book to fall apart before I finished it. I discovered some of the scribes were experimenting with a form of ink that had a component that actually etched itself into the papyrus. After a short period of time, they would have to treat it again with another solution to halt the etching process. I saw the scribes busy copying scrolls. It started me thinking. What if the scribes made one copper codex with lettering that was indented? If this special ink was made to cover that surface, it could be pressed onto sheets of papyrus, cutting down the time required to create texts. The result would be codex pages, however. Scribes were loathe to use codices. It was a Roman practice.

Petronius and Julia accompanied me. They were curious about the Essenes that I had woven into my tales. After a few weeks, they announced to me that they wanted to join the order. I explained that it would take much study for them, perhaps many months. They were glad that this was not a celibate order for they wished to marry.

I told Petronius that if he wanted to join the order, he would have to be circumcised. He went white as milk.

"Don't worry," I said, "give it three weeks; it will be good as new, or almost." Petronius laughed nervously. Julia smiled broadly.

The love that Julia gave to Petronius seemed to burn up all the anger and the hatred Petronius had carried since I knew him. I wondered if there would ever be a woman who could do that for me. Our Heavenly Father knows that I needed that comfort as much as Petronius. All I had was a dream, a phantom that told me I won't know her when she comes…

Both Petronius and I had stopped killing people. We could just tell by looking at each other that the fight was out of us. I felt like there was nothing left, like the only thing remaining was to sit at camp and wait for death to overtake me. Instead, I found that Our Father <u>does</u> extend his Grace to us! Petronius, who was always a master spy, came and informed me of a meeting that was taking place at the River Jordan. It seems that a "rogue Essene" was baptizing anyone who promised to repent or turn away from error. His name was John.

At this point the gavel came down. The judge was again going to have Chris ask me about the information contained in both documents. My head was swimming with possibilities.

"Mr. Hammer," said Chris, "is there an item you can give us to show us you were there?

"I believe so." I said. "In the original book I did not go into so much detail concerning early Tibetan society. When my memories came back the history of the two castes, warriors and the priests, were again shown to me. I did not know this information in this life. In fact, I did not hear anything about them from any of the archeologists or historians that I have known."

"Can we check to see if this information is common knowledge?" Asked Chris.

"Yes, you may." Said the judge. We will reconvene after the week-end.

This gave us a few days to prepare.

"Chris, I know someone who knows almost everyone in the world of archeology and is also well versed in the history of just about every-where." I gave him Dr. Wilder's number in Jerusalem. "If someone exists who could check the validity of this, Dr. Wilder would know."

"That's really great, Roy. That gives us some hope. I didn't want to tell you this during the trial but we came up with nothing in regards to your stone. No one has seen or heard of anything like it. It could have been destroyed or may still be buried, but there is not even any mention of it in any text or catalog."

I tried not to sound as hopeless as I felt. "I know I look wacko to you but there is something else I must reveal to you. I've known Jack before but I could not place him until now. Chris, Jack was Petronius!"

"Yeah, and I was Julia." He said in his best sarcastic manner.

I chose to ignore the sarcasm. "I don't know who you were yet or if you were even someone I knew."

He saw that I was very serious and asked, "So what do you pro-pose?"

"Eric told me that he knows someone who does past life regressions. This person will bring you back to a past life and, if you wish, allow you to retain the memories, if they are not too painful. Eric does not usually recommend such a thing because often it is good that these memories do not show up. Some lives we have lived left some severe scars on our consciousness. Those would be better left unconscious."

"Let's run it by Jack."

Chris made his call to Jack and I made one to Eric. During the next day we coordinated getting Jack and the psychologist together. Jack, at first was dead set against it. "This is total rubbish, you called me for this?"

When Chris and I explained that it might help the case (or at least extend the trial), he cautiously agreed to participate.

We met at Jack's temporary home.

"Jack, meet Dr. Jane Collins." I said.

"Hello, Doc," he said rolling his eyes. "You know, this is not going to work on me. I can't be hypnotized."

"All right," she said, neutrally. "Then you need not be concerned."

"OK, fire away then."

At first, Dr. Collins brought Jack back to his childhood in this lifetime. She left the suggestion that Jack would remember everything. Jack awoke with some memories of childhood that were forgotten, but memories he could corroborate. He was then taken back again, but this time to the year 26 A.D. He was asked to describe the events as he experienced them. He described being captured by Zealots and meeting me. I then asked him a question about that time, one that was not written in the manuscript, and one that only Yehudah and Petronius would know: "Petronius, who was your tutor at Mt. Carmel?"

"An elderly woman, Judith was her name. She told me she taught you when you were a pup."

"He's right. That's not in the text and there is no way that Jack would know that."

Chris grabbed my arm and said: "Damn, Roy, this shit is real! I really didn't think…" He just stood silent for a few minutes just grasping what had just occurred.

"Shall we have him remember?" I asked Chris.

"That was what we had decided. I don't know if he is going to be too happy about this but I think we need to prove to him the validity of your argument. He may take a different view of this case."

I told Dr. Collins to suggest that he remember nothing too traumatic about that lifetime, but to remember all else.

When Jack awoke he stared at Chris and me for a few minutes. "Do you have any idea what I just been through?"

"Yeah, I think I know exactly what you've been through," I said.

He pointed at me. "I do remember you."

"Judas."

"Right, OK. If you were Judas, can you tell me the color of the *Sicarri* robes used during the daytime?"

"Tan, of course."

"What was your brother Simon's favorite weapon?"

"The bow."

"Right, OK. Then who was the best man at my wedding?"

"You're looking at him!"

"Amazing!"

But his sense of wonderment faded fast and he became "practical Jack" again.

Jack looked at Chris. "You know that you can't put me on the stand. That would blow my cover and compromise my mission. I could never allow that to happen."

"What if you completed your assignment before the end of the trial? It wouldn't matter then, would it?"

"I was planning for the results of this trial to solve my problem, not the other way around. But if on the outside chance that my mission is complete before the end of the trial… well, we'll have to see."

Chris saw a possible opening in that personal armor that was built around Jack. He actually cared a whole lot more than he let on. "Thanks, Jack."

"Man, you guys know that I'm really busy and you have the balls to dump something like this on me and knock me off my focus. Now bugger off and let me get back to work."

I stopped in the doorway. "You must admit, Jack, we had some interesting times."

"That we did, mate."

CHAPTER 8 - OUT OF THE WILDERNESS

A dreary day. The fog seemed to keep rolling in waves. That didn't affect my mood but it did make us late for court.

When we finally got there, it was noisy inside the courtroom. It seems the fog had made the judge late as well. I ran outside the courtroom and dialed my phone. I pressed it close to my ear so I could hear and spoke: "Eric, Chris seems to think that the answer lies within me. But I'm no further along in understanding than I was at the beginning of this trial."

"You must really learn to trust that inner voice," said Eric. "It is your best guide. You will learn to cooperate with it, even surrender to it. Give it a try. I do. It even tells me jokes once and a while."

A memory came back to me that nearly knocked me off my feet. "I know why Chris is certain that I know the answer!"

"More memories surfacing?"

"With all that's happening, I don't know how much more I can handle."

"You'll learn that, too." He said and hung up.

Perfect timing. Court was being called into session.

"You have new evidence counselor?" Asked the judge.

"Yes." Said Chris. "There was one historian and archeologist who had been studying ancient Tibetan culture all his life who held to the two caste view as one of his theories, but is still looking for definite proof. I have it here in his deposition."

When Hastings cross-examined he would always draw himself up to look taller and more menacing. "So, what you're saying is that all you have is one man's theories, which are yet unproven?"

"He is an expert in the field," said Chris.

"Sure, until the next expert comes along with his theory. I'm sorry gentlemen. You're going to have to come up with something better than this to show the jury, they are looking for real proof."

Hastings sat down. He knew he had made his point.

Chris and I looked at each other. There was nothing left to do but go back to manuscript.

He called me to the stand and I read.

John had changed. But, no more than me, I guess. I expected to see the same John I left in the mountains of Tibet. John perhaps expected the same concerning me, for the first words he said to me were in an accusatory tone: "Where have you been?" To me this was almost comical, but I saw the wild look of total zeal in his eye and knew that he was deadly serious. He had the same fire as of old but something had changed. It seemed as though he had attained an absolute certainty of purpose. His appearance had also changed. Gone was the look of the devout Essene. His look was as unkempt as his manner. He had clothed himself in hairy animal skins as a tunic with leggings of the same material reaching to the knees. I would think that such clothing would scratch and irritate his body to the extreme, but John used everything to focus on God. He would tell me later that he used the irritation as the yogis we had seen in India: to train him to focus solely on his love for God and man and to ignore the flesh.

On my way to meet John at the Jordan, I heard many stories about him. He was quickly earning a following. John, who had hardly been able to maintain a conversation for five minutes without going into reverie, had become eloquent in his speech. To those who didn't know of his love for man and God, he appeared fierce and frightening, even mad. He had voiced so many of the injustices perpetrated by men in power that friends and foes alike listened. The Sadducees and scribes feared him. The Romans eyed him with deep mistrust. Herod would probably have had him arrested but John's following was too powerful. Many of them were Zealots. His manner and attitude fit the description of the "Son of David," the Military Messiah, but he was accepted by the Essenes as the Priestly Messiah since part of his lineage was priestly. I had always thought it would be Jeshua; could it be John? John, who had but recently come out of the wilderness, was pulling me out of the wilderness as well.

"Well, where have you been?" He demanded a second time.

"Fighting the enemies of our people," I said, somewhat shaken at obtaining the full focus of his scrutiny.

"You have killed?"

"Yes, I have killed."

"Are you still killing?"

"No, in the many years since I saw you, I could not kill all the enemies of our people. I was not even a successful murderer. I am looking for better way." I look toward him expectantly. "I just haven't found it yet."

He placed his hand on my shoulder. "You have taken the first step by turning away from wrongdoing." His manner had softened as he talked. "Do you remember the rite of Baptism we practiced daily on Mt. Carmel?"

"Of course."

"Then tomorrow I will baptize you in the name of the Father of us all. Tonight I want to hear your story. I want to close the gap of years that lies between us."

The sun was setting and as I sat down in front of the fire I was greeted by some of John's companions and disciples. At the fire closest to John's tent sat his closest followers, three sets of brothers.

Andrew and his brother Simon were fishermen from my hometown of Capernaum. These two were like night and day. While Andrew was calm and modest, Simon was always pushing his way into things. Everything became his business. It was like he had no roots. He had a wife and daughter but he could go off and leave them, on a moment's notice without telling them. He was a fisherman, but he had also had a number of other jobs: a farmer, a bricklayer, a builder, and even carried arms at one time. He was a drifter. I wondered how long he would remain with John.

A second set of brothers, James and John, sons of Zebedee, were also from Capernaum. James really irritated me. If there was a time that he had any manners, that time had long past. Here was a man who just could not see beyond himself. Everything was in terms of him. He HAD to be the center of attention at all times and had no compunction about interrupting another's tale and telling all present how much greater or better his experience had been. I can't say that I had ever met one more selfish than James. His brother John, on the other hand, was extremely caring and passionate, devoted and supportive of his friends and just as passionately aggressive concerning his enemies. He was wonderfully uncomplicated. I felt I could readily understand John and hoped he would become my friend.

Philip and Nathaniel were the third pair. They came from Bethsaida, east of the Sea of Galilee. Philip was pragmatic and cautious. He wanted to see things and how they worked before he would jump into anything. In fact, he really didn't ever jump. He wasn't very trusting, but I was sure that no one could put anything over on Philip. If I were looking to buy a horse I would want Philip along to assure me that it had everything it was supposed to have. Nathaniel had set ideas about everything and everybody. You could say that he was prejudiced. Perhaps if you could convince *Philip* about something, then Nathaniel *might* be willing to change his opinion.

"So, Yehudah, son of Joseph," began Nathaniel, "I hear you were with the Zealots. I'll bet that you did your share of murdering and stealing."

"Well, I…"

James interrupted: "No, I've heard of him, he was with the elite, the *Sicarri*, in fact he was their leader, the one the Romans call 'Judas Iscariot.'"

"It is as James told you. But I have given that up now. I am looking to get back to a more spiritual way of life."

"And you think you will find it here with the Baptizer?" asked Philip.

Somewhat surprised, I retorted, "Don't you?"

"I'm just waiting and watching. Perhaps something better may come along."

"I think that John deserves our loyalty," said the brother of James, "after all, he has been willing to teach us and help us prepare to serve the Messiah and be at his right hand."

"Well, that's if the true Messiah ever comes. It seems like every week there is another false Messiah raising Israel's hopes," returned Philip.

"As for me, I agree with John," said Andrew, "the Baptizer may prove himself as the Messiah, although he denies it, and he might just be testing us in our resolve."

Simon pulled me aside, "Say, I had a bit of military training myself. Would you take some time to show me some of the things you learned about weaponry?"

"If you wish," I said with a sigh.

After about an hour I felt like I had been accepted in this company of diverse characters. There was something comforting in the fact that John's disciples seemed to be as confused about the future as I was. It was like I may not have missed much in the years I spent as a *Sicarri.* Everyone went quiet as the Baptizer came close. He put his hand on my shoulder and told me to follow him into his tent.

He asked me to tell him all that happened since I left Tibet. It was painful to go through the story of that time in my life, but I did it. I was judging myself as a failure and as a weakling to succumb to the emotional pull of revenge.

John seemed like the friend of old. He looked me in the eye for some time and then said, "Suspend judgment on yourself until after my story. I, too, have done things I am not proud of, things that are not worthy of me as a soul. I have misrepresented myself horribly in thought, consciousness and deed."

He had my full, rapt attention. I suspended my self-pity and self-judgment only because curiosity took over completely.

"The first thing I can tell you is that Jeshua said that you would regret for a long time leaving us. He said that you would blame and judge yourself harshly. He told me to tell you to learn to forgive yourself now, because it would be too difficult later."

I understood because I did feel the regret of these past few years deep within my bones. I did not understand what he meant by "because it would be too difficult later." What could happen that would make me do something so bad that I could not forgive myself? I had tried to make these last few years be acceptable within myself, but I still had regret.

"John, I can't help but regret leaving. There is always the thought in my mind of all I might have attained spiritually had I stayed with Jeshua and you."

"Thank our heavenly father that you left when you did. You might have met the same discouragement as I did in our travels. Let me explain. One day Jeshua wandered off in the hills of Tibet and did not return for two days. On his return he told me that he had slid into a crevice on the side of a hill. He had gone into deep meditation and was visited by Kal, the Lord of the Negative realms who promised to lift him out and save him if only Jeshua would worship him. Jeshua replied, "You are the god of religion and not the It of Itself, the Father of us all." Jeshua reproached this god and said that he could not, in truth, even worship Kal because the god was too small for him. He was left alone, and assumed that he would die. He accepted his fate and left his body for a time. He told me that he received initiation in the Spirit and then was returned to his body. On his return, he was able to lift himself out of the crevice as if weightless. He returned looking better than when he left, full of power and Spirit. He attended a meeting in the Temple at Lhasa where they celebrated his initiation. I was not allowed to attend. He told me later what occurred after that initiation."

"Some in the temple were engaged in a discussion concerning man's fate. They had decided that after many lives, man would again reach his heaven on the higher planes. Jeshua was asked his opinion and said that they were mistaken. God never made a heaven or a hell, and that we are co-creators with God and we have made our own. He told them to seek not for a heaven in the higher planes after countless millennia, but that they should open up their hearts and see the perfection of God in all things. In this way they would know that heaven is right here if we would own it."

"It was there he began teaching in the temples and in the very streets. We were taken in by many of the common people and Jeshua taught and healed a good number of them. One night of celebration he told a parable of a king who sent his son to spread his gifts to all. The priests of the land were angry because the king did not proffer his gifts through them. They sought to turn the people against the son, saying that his gifts, precious stone, gold and silver, were fake and were worthless. They believed the words of these men and so when they looked at precious gems and gold they saw stones and rusted iron. They threw away these precious gifts, captured and beat the son and finally drove him away. The son did not resent their cruelty toward him and prayed that they be forgiven because they did not know what they were doing. He blessed equally those that beat him and those that welcomed him, as this was the way of his Father. He never stayed in one place because the whole world and its entire people had become his home. Then Jeshua said to the crowds, 'This king is our Heavenly Father and he has sent me, his eldest, to shower his Love upon all peoples. This son of man has no place to lay his head for he must tend to all his brothers and sisters.'"

"We stayed a few more weeks until the approach of winter. Then Jeshua and I left for Persia. Word of our imminent arrival in Persepolis had spread. The common people of the nearby towns were glad to see Jeshua; word of his deeds had spread. The priests and officials were less than happy to see him, since he had criticized their treatment of the lower classes. To them he appeared as a rabble-rouser and troublemaker. They tried to forbid him from healing the sick or teaching the crowds but he ignored their threats. Right before we reached Persepolis we were met by wise men. Jeshua appeared to know them but did not tell me when he had last seen them. They proceeded to honor him and said something about the fact that at last the "elder brother" was going to fulfill his mastership. They stood together and chanted a tone that I had never heard. The four of them shone with the intensity of bonfires in the night. When we reached their home, Jeshua told them of his life and travels. They said that they were proceeding with the next initiation that he would go through, and that it would also be open to me, if I desired. I should have packed up and gone then rather than to have failed a spiritual test."

"What happened that caused you to fail?" I asked.

"I am still not sure of it," said John. "We had to sit still for seven days and nights without a word or making the slightest sound. This was not a problem for me. I was able to use what I had learned in Tibet to leave my body. I had some experiences while out of my body that prompted me in a certain direction. I ignored these requests. I found out later that I was being asked to a meeting. If I would have come with them, I might have passed the tests and had experienced the masters in the higher realms. Instead, I felt that I gained nothing from the experience. Believe me, Yehudah, this was a difficult and subtle test, you would have failed as I did."

I had no doubt that I also would have failed such a test and was not irritated at him for telling me so.

"The next morning I saw Jeshua," continued John, "and told him of my plans to leave. He did nothing to stop me but told me that he understood. For a moment, as he looked into my eyes, I thought I saw a look of sadness. But that was momentary and he was again his smiling, friendly and caring self."

"Where did you go from there?" I asked, astounded at the turn of events.

"I went back to my old Essene teacher, Philo of Alexandria," he explained. "I had decided that if I could not be a part of Jeshua's pathway I would find my own. I looked within and saw that where I was lacking was not in my devotion but in my discipline. I followed the path of the most ascetic of the Essenes and then I actually found ways of going beyond them in their zeal. I found that I was capable of many things I would not have believed possible. I again tried the test of sitting for seven days and nights. I was at last successful. I did not join Jeshua, but other masters on the higher realms. I asked them to guide me, but they gave no answer. That only made me go inside for answers. I began to spend much time alone in the wilderness and took on many of the traits of the Indian ascetics, for their discipline suited me best. I could tell I was unnerving Philo, but his love for me made his support for me unwavering. One day I had spent quite a long time in the desert. I was very thirsty and thought I might have passed out quite soon. I thought I heard a voice, and when I turned around I thought I saw the form of my dead father looking at me sternly as he was occasioned to and said to me 'If you would be an Essene, why are you not preparing for the Messiah's coming?' It was a rhetorical question, of course. He was chastising me for not completing what I started. All at once I knew that it would not be enough to prepare myself, I had to bring this message of being prepared to all Israelites."

"So, you received a revelation while in the wilderness. Was that vision you saw actually your father?"

"I may never know," he sighed. "But whoever or whatever it was focused me on the task at hand. At last I have a purpose. I began using the Essene ritual cleansing for groups of people outside the order."

"They must have been pretty upset about this," I mused.

"Upset, ha," he said with a tinge of bitterness, "they tossed me right out! They told me that they could never have outside groups corrupting their rituals. I argued that this was at last the time for everyone to prepare. They told me that they had not seen a sign, nor was there anything astrologically evident that something was going to happen soon. Even Philo finally had to turn his back on me; else he would have been shunned also. I don't hold any bitterness toward Philo. He did the best he could. The others, however, were more complicit in their blindness. They could not expel me because of my zeal for the Lord. Instead they sent me among the Nazarenes, this group of non-cloistered Essenes that wander the land, proclaiming the power of the Lord. Then these Essenes proclaimed me their leader. Anyway, I continued my baptizing and picked up a follower or two. Some heard me chanting while on my wilderness walks and called me 'the Wild Man of the Hills' and 'the Voice in the Wilderness.' "The Voice in the Wilderness" seemed to me an apt description of myself."

"So you kept it," I chuckled.

"Yes, I kept it!" he smiled back. "But I was not always in the wilderness. Last year I traveled to Jerusalem and sat down in the marketplace. I stayed, silent, in one position for another seven days. Crowds gathered around and left, probably many times. I do not know since I was minimally aware on the physical level of things. I do not remember much during this time except when I returned to physical consciousness on the seventh day I was greatly strengthened in resolve. There was a crowd gathered about me. I knew the time had come to speak. I said to the crowd, 'Prepare, O Israel, prepare to meet your king.' I got up and left. It appears that I created somewhat of a stir among the rulers and officials." He chuckled and said, "They thought I might be leading an army to conquer them."

"But it was then that I began to feel that I was finally out of the wilderness since I had found a clear path to follow. I knew that the Essenes are essentially correct when they prepare for the Messiah to come. Many call me the priestly messiah, but I know that I am too imperfect to be that. I rather feel that it is I who prepare the way for the Messiah. The Essenes agree with my leadership but they restrict the preparedness to their own order. If we really want his coming we must get others prepared now!"

"The more voices that are here to call out, the less he can ignore it, right?"

"I know you are teasing me," he said in mock sternness, "but that is essentially correct. We must not only expect his coming, but we must live lives worthy of his coming."

"How did you gain all this following?" I asked.

"When I returned home to Capernaum I decided to practice the rite of Baptism for all in the Jordan. It was there I acquired the three sets of brothers that you met."

I saw the earnestness in his eyes that shone even greater than his zeal. "Well, I for one will follow and support you…even if Jeshua is not here to be a part of this. It's funny; I always thought I would be following him."

"We will both be following the one for whom we are preparing," he said, correcting me, "but as of yet we do not know who that will be."

I learned the next day that John had planned a return to Jerusalem in the next month. My main concern was being recognized if I were to go along. There would certainly be Roman spies who were on the lookout for "bandits" such as myself, and might arrest anyone who even loosely fit the description of a *Sicarri*. I thought of my friend Petronius who once told me "Judas, Romans need to be familiar with their surroundings. They feel much more comfortable when that which is around them reflects to them their own style of living. If you want to be invisible among Romans, you must be Roman." Well, I figured, at least I could look more Roman. So I shaved my beard and cut my hair in Roman style the next day. I received disapproving glances and some embarrassing questions for a few days, but after a while, everyone in John's camp became used to me in my new appearance. They realized that it was the only way I could move through areas like Jerusalem with impunity.

I could not delude myself that I was showing courage in the face of my enemies. It was John who was truly courageous. John moved everywhere with impunity without disguise. It was like he traveled under a tent of protection at all times. He feared nothing. It was like the angels protected most strongly those who were divinely inspired or “mad” as John was often called. While many of us lagged behind he made great haste to Jerusalem, strode down the main streets and entered the Temple court with seven shy, scared disciples tentatively following at a respectful distance.

Reaching the center of the court, people turned and noticed him. “It’s the Wild Man of the hills,” they shouted, eager to hear what he had to say. John turned to the crowd and shouted over the mob, “Prepare, O Israel, prepare to meet your king.”

The crowd fell silent. You could not hear a raised voice at all. John began again: “You have been living lives at odds with God and nature. The poor cry in the streets and you refuse to hear them. God has instructed us to love our neighbor, but do you know who your neighbor is? You have cheated friend and foe alike.” John raised both hands to the sky and then placed them on his heart. “Your prayers to God are abandoned to your mouths and are nowhere found in your hearts. In your hearts there is only desire for gold.”

The priests and Sadducees began to gather in an angry mass, blocking the door to the sanctuary. John pointed in their direction. “The priests live in comfort upon the hard labor of the poor. Their prayers and sacrifices are as empty as yours. They burden you with rules but give you no peace. Your doctors, lawyers and scribes are but tumors on the body of society. They do not toil yet they deplete the profits of your labors.”

A group of Herod’s troops gathered at the rear of the court and slowly made their way through the crowd. Roman troops from Pilate’s palace began to gather in the Court of Gentiles. John saw them but did not change his tone. “Your rulers are adulterers, murderers and thieves. They ignore the rights of all men.”

As they approached him his voice seemed to turn to thunder and all were frozen in their tracks. “Hear me, people of Jerusalem! Reform and turn from your evil deeds. Turn from your evil ways or God will turn from you. The heathen will overcome you and what is left of your honor and eminence will be ripped from you. Prepare, Jerusalem, prepare to meet your king.”

The silence in the hall was deafening. John strode for the exit. No one dared stop him. It seemed like the very air was on fire with his words. We were just as stunned but recognized that this was the perfect time to leave.

We went straight to an inn on the outskirts of the city, and stayed there for the night. I had been sleeping for a while when I heard the door open. Had some Roman spy noticed me and come to kill me? He had entered and was moving quietly among us. I had my hands on both blades, ready to strike, if needed. By the light of the dying fire in the fireplace I could see the figure of a man. He appeared to hold no sword or weapon. I sat up and he approached. When he pulled back the shawl he was wearing I could see who it was.

"Petronius! How good it is to see you! Quick, come outside and talk so that we do not wake the others."

"Judas, it has been a while. You are looking much better than the last time I saw you."

"I have found an old friend."

"You are following the Wild Man."

"Yes."

"I saw him in the city today. That was some fine oratory. It enraged the priests and the scribes. It made the soldiers quite uneasy. They thought he was going to stir up a riot."

"What happened then?" I asked expectantly.

"The plebeians, uh, common people stood in his defense. They were shamed by his speech but they seemed to see the truth of it in their hearts. I would caution you, Judas, stay away from Jerusalem. If you stay with this Wild Man, they will take you when they take him. Then they will find out who you really are. They will crucify him for promoting rebellion, and hang you for murder."

I looked deeply into my friend's eyes, so full of concern for my well-being. "After I put my revenge to rest, I had no direction left in my life. John is my best chance to regain what I lost when I left my teachers for revenge. This is the first time since my youth that I have felt any inner direction. I feel I am going somewhere, but I know not where. I would gladly give my life to continue along this path."

Petronius looked at me with continued concern. "I will always be your friend; I owe you my life. If you wish to pursue spiritual goals which become your undoing, I will continue to support you, but I will always tell you what I see, for I owe you a clear view of the truth in my being. You trained me well, Judas. Unless you are dead, I will be able to find you." Petronius smiled. "Perhaps even if you are dead I will still be able to find you."

I laughed with him.

"Petronius," I said, looking him in the eye, "You have the best quality of the Roman people, a true sense of honor. In the years we fought together I have seen you as my brother, like Simon – perhaps more than Simon."

"I'll be more than that, Judas. I will be your shadow; I will be with you when you need me. May you walk in peace and walk with God."

He took my forearm in the Roman handshake, but there was too much emotion and we embraced. "I wish the same for you Petronius."

He walked away in the night and I walked back to the inn.

I entered silently and made way to my bed.

"Someone from your '*Sicarri* days,'" a voice said, slightly above a whisper. It was John, the brother of James.

"Yes. But don't be concerned. He is just a messenger. He supplies me with information."

"That could be useful. What news did he bring?"

I told John, son of Zebedee, of the effect our teacher had on the crowd. "John should know this," he said.

The next morning John called me to him. "In light of what I have heard, I believe that I should pay another call on our friends at the Temple."

"Is that wise?"

He studied me for a moment and smiled. "I hope this does not frighten you, Yehudah, but I am no longer driven by wisdom, only the fire in the heart. If I am killed in the Temple, I will merely suffer the same fate as my father. I find more than a little honor in that. You do not have to follow me if you are concerned."

"Where else would I go?"

The next day we went back to the Temple. This time the priests observed our entrance into the Temple court. They seemed over their rage and wanted to know more of this Wild Man who invaded their peace.

The chief priest came forward to address us. Blessed God, I knew this man! It was Caiaphas. "Hermit, what is the meaning of your message? Are you a prophet? If you are, tell us plainly who sent you."

John answered: "I am the voice of one who cries out in the wilderness: Prepare the way, make straight the paths of the Lord. The prophet Malachi wrote down the words of God: 'And I will send Elijah unto you before the retribution day shall come, to turn the hearts of men to God, and if they will not turn, lo I will smite them with a curse.'"

Caiaphas laughed cruelly, "Do you mean that you are Elijah returned? Only a Pharisee or an Essene would spout such nonsense."

John was not deterred. "Of whom I was before…I cannot tell you, but that is of no importance because time is short. My message is urgent: reform, O Israel, reform, and meet your king."

"Then you are not claiming to be the messiah?"

"I am preparing the way for the messiah to appear."

Caiaphas laughed again. "This is a first! A pious madman who actually denies that he is the messiah."

"But I am here to prepare the way, make the paths straight, for the time of retribution is quickly coming. You priests of Israel: while you stand there and ridicule me you are arrogant in your sin. You trample righteousness underfoot and have sold Justice to foreign oppressors. You have committed spiritual crimes against all the people who come to you. You sell forgiveness in the marketplace and deny the people the truth that would set them free. Within your gold vestments and your powerful office you look with disdain at the common peasant, while in his simplicity and innocence, he is closer to God than yourselves. If you have nothing to give him, to ease his load or make lighter his burden, then step aside and let him find truth, for he will not find it within these walls. You wallow in hypocrisy, pretending to speak for God when your only course of action is to preserve your own ranks. Before it is too late, reform, and prepare to meet your king."

There was no one that was not affected by John's words. The cheers of the common people who had come to make sacrifice broke the silence. After hearing John's words, they slowly turned and left.

Caiaphas lost his composure. "How dare you criticize us, Wild Man! We have been chosen by God and you cannot even name your parents."

"My father was Zacharias and he was one of you. He was inspired by God to speak out the truth and was rewarded for this by your guards with an arrow while standing in the holy place. So, you see I am of the same breeding as you and yet I am worthier to speak. Your priesthood has decayed since the time of Aaron and even in that time they were the uninitiated priesthood. Melchizedek founded the priesthood to which I belong on God's direct authority. Blow the dust off your most secret texts, and you will see. As for your authority, the whole of Israel knows that you have been chosen by the Romans."

Now Caiaphas was stammering, on the defensive. "We perform an important service. We represent Israel to the Romans. Think what would happen if rabble like you were to deal with them directly, all of us would be slaughtered. We know how to speak to these people so that all of Israel can be safe and continue to exist."

"It seems to me, Caiaphas, that we continually give more than we have been getting. When the Messiah comes, all of this will cease to be. He will drive the Romans from our shores and you from our Temple. Heaven will reign on earth and only the righteous will enjoy it. I know these things to be true and so I must prepare all Israel for his coming. I care about our people enough to warn them, to get them to change their ways and reform their actions. Everyone I can reach makes me joyful. I would be happy to reach even you, Caiaphas."

"Do you mean to stand in this doorway from now on and prevent the people from entering?" asked Caiaphas.

"No," answered John. "I have said what I needed to say to you and the rest. I will come no more to this court. I am going to the Jordan, where Israel first crossed into the Promised Land. I tell you this so that if the Holy Spirit touches any one of you, you will know where to come and be cleansed."

John did not wait for the retort of Caiaphas. I heard him say to John, the brother of James, "We must stop and stay a while with my relatives in Bethany."

I, for one was glad to get out of Jerusalem. As a *Sicarri*, I was able to use the crowds to blend in. As a follower of a very visible Baptist, there was a chance, however small, that I might be recognized. In Bethany I would remain unknown.

After a few days we arrived at the home of John's cousin, Lazarus. This was a beautiful home. In large cities such as Cæsarea it would be unaffordable by all those but the rich. I am not a student of architecture but I could see that it was very much out of place. It appeared to be Greek Style but had not the high ceilings of those dwellings. It had trees growing around every side.

Lazarus saw us coming and came out to meet us. He was an exceptionally likable man. He had the refinement that one would find in a Hellenized Jew that had been well educated in the Greek manner. But he had none of the self-importance of that type; he was prone to sharing his ideas about many subjects. In fact, when I ask him about the home he told me that he had seen it in a vision and had proceeded to build it. He explained that above the shortened ceiling was another floor that had certain ducts that pulled the hot air up so it was cooler during the day. Not all the inside was on the same level. He told me that he also envisioned a way to keep the home bright as the outdoors during the day and at the same time have a ready water supply. He envisioned a huge column of glass that would be hollow so that water could be held in it. It would reach above the top of the roof so that sunlight would travel down its shaft. He pulled me aside and showed me drawings but was sad because there was no way he knew to construct such a structure.

Out of the corner of my eye I saw Philip make a sneer of disbelief. Later, his brother Nathaniel pulled me aside and asked, “Can you believe the ranting of that man?” I just looked at him and said, “Yes.”

All his sisters were home with him – Ruth, Martha and Mary who was called “Magdalene.” When I first saw Mary a shiver ran up my spine. She was not the most beautiful woman that I had ever seen, but she was certainly the most striking. Her bright, light red hair framed an attractive yet strong face. Her every look told of her determination to live life in her own way. I found myself drawn to her without knowing why. She reached out her arm to touch her brother and on her forearm was painted a rose. She quickly covered it up, as this was not a customary adornment for a proper Jewish woman. This provoked a memory within me, but one that I could not recall.

Her presence was pleasant, yet disturbing. I tried to start a conversation with her but her answers were short. It was like she was always elsewhere. I even tried to ask her sisters about her but they would not volunteer any information. They seemed to be hiding something. I had never been involved with a woman so I did not know what to expect. Like John and Jeshua, I had avoided the usual marriage at fourteen. Either my spiritual studies or my desire for revenge had monopolized my emotional energy, until now. We left for the Jordan the next day, but part of me stayed in Bethany.

On the night before leaving Bethany a feast was prepared for John and our whole company. As the people were gathered together, John began to speak; “Reform, O Israel and prepare to meet your king. The sins of Israel do not all belong to the priest and scribe, or with rulers and men of wealth. Because a man is poor does not mean he is pure. The very men that cheered because I told the priests of their injustice to the people, judge and condemn their fellow man with word and deed.”

I did not hear all of the speech since I was looking at Mary. When John said, “You steal from your neighbor and sleep with his wife or her husband…” Mary quickly turned away and went into the house. I did not see her the next morning when we left. With Mary gone, my focus was again on John who continued “…and drown yourself in deadly brew.” He took a cup of wine that was offered to him and threw it out into the street. I had some wine earlier. Did John mean to make us all ascetics, denying all the pleasures of life? To me this did not seem consistent with my path, but I put my doubts aside and watched John.

The next morning we left Bethany and John did not say a word. He was deep in thought. When we reached the Jordan, John performed the Essene ritual cleansing with us, his disciples. He called out to the growing crowd, "Come to me and in the waters of this stream be cleansed. This is symbolic of the inner cleansing of the soul."

We were immersed fully in the cold water, one by one. When it was my turn I felt the cold in my bones and came up gasping for air. I was only under the water for a few seconds but it felt like much longer. Coming back into the air brought joy forward in my being. The way was being made straight! Life was open to me again. For the next few months I was again practicing meditation techniques that I had learned in my travels. Had I contacted that "inner master" that Jeshua often mentioned? <u>This</u> is what I followed, but I <u>served</u> John.

Many came to hear John plead for righteousness and purity. The honest seekers confessed their sins and were baptized. The Pharisees and the Essenes were generally accepting of John but were afraid to become his followers. But as John lingered, more came to scorn him. The Sadducees and their followers came to question and attack John.

John asked them, "Are you not disturbed at the news of the coming wrath? If you are, I need not baptize you, but go and do the things that prove true repentance. It is not enough to be children of Abraham. The wicked that are also children of Abraham are as wrong as any heathen. In God's forest, every tree which does not bear wholesome fruit will be chopped down and its roots pulled out."

There were those among the Pharisees, the Essenes, and even the Sadducees who stepped forward and asked, "What must we do?"

John answered, "Take up the ministry of helpfulness for all mankind, Jew and Gentile, Greek and Roman, male and female, and let go of your selfishness. If you have two coats, give one to him that has none. Share your food with those who do not have any."

The listeners who were repentant were also uplifted. I was glad that John was not as harsh as I had feared. He would not require all to embrace his asceticism. At last I felt secure following John.

Tax collectors, some of the most hated people in Israel, came to John and offered themselves to him and asked what they should do.

John answered, "Be honest and do not increase the amount you collect to line your own pockets. Collect only what the king demands."

Soldiers, both Jewish and Roman came to John and offered themselves, asking what they must do.

John answered them: "Hold back your violence, do not do vengeance, and be content with your lot in life."

There were others who were so moved by John's words and deeds that they proclaimed him the Messiah.

John readily denied this, but they continued unabated. He explained, "I cleanse with water which is symbolic of the cleansing of the soul. The true Messiah will purify and cleanse with the fire of the Holy Spirit. He will separate the pure from the impure and all that are pure will be saved. He is here and when he comes forward you will not know him because he will come not as you expect him to come. It is <u>he</u> who is the king and I am one not worthy to unbind his shoes."

"If not John, then who?" I asked myself. I was again in confusion and doubt and slept a troubled sleep that night by the Jordan.

The next day saw even more people flock to John by the Jordan. Word had spread throughout Galilee and I saw many faces I knew. I scanned the crowd briefly and my gaze became fixed on someone in a white robe with sandy red-blond hair hanging down to his shoulders. I caught his eye and I felt that every atom of my body was stirred. Jeshua! Jeshua has returned!

He slowly made his way forward toward John. When John saw him, Jeshua shouted above the crowd, "Behold the greatest of the seers, behold Elijah has returned. Behold whom God has sent to open the way. The kingdom of heaven is at hand."

John opened his great arms and shouted, "Behold the king who God has sent."

When Jeshua called John 'Elijah,' I understood what had transpired. Jeshua was at last stepping forward as the Promised One. I had always wanted to serve the Messiah and now I would finally be able to serve him directly. I felt ecstatic. If I died at that moment, I would have been content. But that was not to be my fate.

Jeshua and John embraced. The crowd was filled with wonder and excitement. Jeshua asked John to baptize him.

John replied, "You are the master, the one initiated. It is you who should be cleansing me."

Jeshua then explained to him: "John, it is my role to be a pattern for those to follow into the heart of God. What I ask of them I must do myself, for all men must be cleansed. Let the rite of the Essenes be used now to remind all of the cleansing of the soul."

"What shall I do now, my master?"

"John, your work is to prepare the way and to reveal the hidden truth. My work is to manifest the consciousness of the chosen one, to demonstrate the path back to God that all might learn to follow. I am the Wayshower of the Father of us all who calls all His children back to Him. From now on, the way will be clear and open to all who wish to be again one with their Father."

As Jeshua and John entered the Jordan, a hush came over the crowd. Jeshua was immersed in the water. When he again surfaced, the pressure inside me was too great and I burst out crying for joy. I felt a twinge of self-consciousness until I looked around at the crowd and saw others who were similarly affected. I felt the Holy Spirit descend on us all and at once I knew that Jeshua was truly the chosen one, the Messiah, the one who would free his people. It felt like a voice inside of me saying "This son of Mine I have chosen to manifest Me among you."

John must have heard this too, and understood, because as Jeshua left, John again continued his ministry. Many more now confessed their sins, turning from evil to ways of light. John baptized many and preached to the multitude, but his fire had calmed and nothing would ever be the same.

CHAPTER 9 — A CHANGE IN THE WIND

For the first time since I joined the followers of John, things became easy. It was like all of us hung suspended between our past and our future. Each day became like the day before, days of summer heat and clouds, one blending into the next as if the earth itself was waiting for a resolution. John appeared to ride a wave of contentment (for John), more than I had ever seen.

Foremost among the followers of John was Jeshua's brother James. He looked like a younger version of Jeshua. The resemblance was truly astonishing. He fell at his brother's feet. He said, "Brother, forgive me! For a long time after the death of our father I judged you for not coming home and instead leaving me as the head of the family. Part of me still feels abandoned and cast aside by you. It may take time to get over that. I am a follower of John, and as such, I recognize his loyalty to you and offer mine as well."

Jeshua responded with compassion. "I realize the pain I must have caused you and others of our family. It was not on purpose that I hurt any of you. It was my duties to the Father of us all that stole my time away from the rest. I can only hope that some day you will understand and allow me back into your loving."

A long time they gazed into each other's eyes. Then Jeshua outstretched his arms and motioned to James. The hardness dropped from James' features as they embraced. "Anytime you wish to talk, James, I am available for you."

I slowly eyed the crowd. We could generally pick out the Roman or Sadducee spies fairly easily. Their manner of dress was always "off." It was not that they could not find the appropriate dress, but that there was always something out of place, something included that did not belong with a Galilean peasant or something missing that no Galilean would be without. On the other hand, our spies managed quite well in a Hellenistic environment. Since we had to deal with Greek influence and culture long before the Romans came, it was easy enough to fit into the popular culture. I was no longer active with the *Sicarri*, but I could count on a very personal intelligence report from Petronius each week. A well-dressed man in Roman merchant attire pulled me into the shadows. I recognized him immediately.

"Peace be with you, Petronius, what do you hear?"

"And with you, Judas. Your Baptist has made many enemies in some very high places. Plans have been put into motion to silence him."

"From what direction does this come?"

"Less from Jerusalem; more from Galilee."

"Herod?"

"The Baptizer has attacked Herod and his wife directly. This has become a situation of personal vengeance. That does not make it less dangerous than a political motive, but it may be more assured, as you well know, Judas."

"How then, Petronius, can this be prevented?"

"The only way is for him to be surrounded by the crowds at all times. Herod will not make a move where there is popular support."

"John would never go for that. He is adamant about getting away from all of us and walking in the wilderness. He says he needs to do this to remain in touch with himself."

"Then it is only a matter of time before he rots in Herod's dungeon. Once deposited there, people are never heard from again."

At once, I felt a need to be in control. It was like the promise of life was slipping away and I was the only one who could stand against it. I took a deep breath, sighed, and shook my head. "I will do what I can, but once John has made up his mind, heaven and earth cannot move him."

Petronius adopted my serious demeanor. "If they can't, I'm afraid Herod will."

As Petronius slipped back into the crowd, I resolved to put things right. I figured that the only one who could make John listen was Jeshua.

I had not seen Jeshua in almost two months when one morning he came into our camp with my brother Simon in tow. I wasn't at all diplomatic; I quickly threw my arms around both of them. "I have come with someone who has always brought peace to you, Yehudah," said Simon. I was about to tell my brother that I had forgiven him completely for what happened to our parents and had forgotten his promise to bring me back to peace when I heard John bellow, "Behold, The Messiah!"

Andrew, Philip, and John, son of Zebedee followed quickly after the Baptist. They were as eager to meet Jeshua for the first time as I was to see him in this new role, one that I always hoped he would claim.

Jeshua appeared to be in good humor, talking and joking with John's disciples. I was amazed to see the degree that he could draw people to him. "Well, my new friends," Jeshua began, "what is it that you seek?" It was like a whole world balanced on one question.

Andrew was the first to respond: "I want to be a bearer of Light to men."

Jeshua answered the question that was not on Andrew's lips, but within his heart: "Andrew, if you follow me, you will become the spiritual master you always wanted to become, and what's more, you will know it."

A light of reverence and enthusiasm shown from Andrew's face. It was as if you could see the spirit coming forward in his eyes. In the midst of all this bringing forward of spirit, Andrew could have said many things. What he did say seemed to surprise all of us (other than Jeshua): "Wait, wait right here, while I get my brother." He was off like a flash. In a few minutes he returned with his brother Simon, both panting from running.

While we were standing there, John, son of Zebedee, reached inside himself and pronounced: "I want to know Perfect Love, I want to Love perfectly."

Jeshua placed his hand on John's shoulder. "Follow me and you will discover that what you seek is what you already are. You are beloved of God, our Father."

Philip who had been watching and waiting silently answered Jeshua's question with a question: "Where do you live?"

Jeshua answered: "Follow me and find out." He had appealed to the one thing that would activate Philip, curiosity.

The silence was broken by Andrew panting and still out of breath, "Master, here is my brother Simon."

Jeshua looked at Andrew's brother and exclaimed, "Behold, the rock!"

We all knew Simon and burst out laughing. He was the one among all of us whose life was most built on sand. He looked annoyed at being ridiculed, but his good humor quickly returned. "Sure, from now on, I'll be 'Peter,' 'the Rock.'"

We all started chuckling except my brother, Simon. He looked a little perturbed. "Great! Then I can still be Simon. Can't I?"

This time we all laughed out loud. Jeshua laughed the loudest. "With the addition of Yehudah the *Sicarri* and Simon the Zealot, we almost have the whole of Galilean life represented."

Philip surprised all of us by actually expressing enthusiasm. "Yeah, all we need is a tax-collector and a few prostitutes." We all laughed except for Jeshua. He just seemed to smile and nod in agreement. Philip interjected: "My brother's right over there; I'll be right back!"

"Nathaniel, come with me, I've found The Messiah!"

Nathaniel gave his brother a somewhat suspicious look. "Who is this Messiah, and where does he come from?"

"He is Jeshua Bar Joseph and he comes from Nazareth."

Even from where we were approaching I could clearly experience Nathaniel's prejudiced attitude. "Really, brother, can anything good come out of Nazareth?"

Philip was not in the least put off. "Well you're not going to know from where you're sitting. Come with us and find out."

Nathaniel looked like the last thing he wanted to do was to get up from where he was sitting. He got up, dusted himself off, and grumbled something. As we approached his eyes met Jeshua's and he was stopped cold in his tracks. At last he said, "Behold an Israelite in whom there is no deception." Something about Jeshua's presence would not allow Nathaniel to regain his suspicious and jaded attitude. It was like Jeshua kept breaking down Nathaniel's expectations, keeping him off-guard. It was truly wondrous to see.

After John found his brother James, the company of Jeshua and four pairs of brothers camped for the night not far from the Baptist's camp.

As we sat around the fire, we bathed ourselves in the magical quality of Jeshua's presence.

Peter broke the silence. "For quite a long time we have been looking for the Messiah. When John came to Galilee, we joined him, but he assured us he was not the Messiah but one to clear the way. Then when you appeared, he said, 'Behold, the Messiah.' Now there is a knowing inside of me that tells me that here is where I am supposed to be. As for me, I would follow you to the ends of the earth, just tell me what to do and I will do it." Peter had most effectively expressed that which we all were thinking.

"The foxes have their homes," Jeshua began, "the birds have their nests, but this son of man has no place to lay his head. My brothers, we are not of this earth but our true home is in the realms of Light. If you would follow me, you will have to give up any and all attachments to things of this earth. We can still enjoy and partake of what our Father has provided here for us, but it does not control or lead us. We all enjoy a good meal, but when the meal is done, we can shift our attention to meditating on our relationship with our Father. One is food for the body; the other is food for the Soul."

"I can't speak for anyone else," Peter said, "but I am ready to leave all else behind to follow you." We all spoke as with one mind and heart. It was like a brotherhood was forming. We felt closer than we ever had before. We told Jeshua that from our experience, and from deep inside our beings, we knew that what he told us was true and that he spoke with the truth of the Father. It was like there was no other choice than to follow him. Any other choice would be to miss the way.

"Will you teach us to feed our Souls?" asked Peter.

With that, Jeshua gave us sacred tones to chant and taught us techniques of meditation. I felt almost as if I could explode with joy. I was getting all that I had ever asked for.

When the fire had burned low and many had retired for the night, I approached Jeshua and asked him about the events since John left him.

He laughed, "Yehudah, I doubt that you will leave me alone until you are brought up to date on my adventures. Very well."

I smiled and listened eagerly.

"After John left," he began, "I stayed to teach the Magians more of the inner mysteries. They were curious as to the source of my wisdom. I explained to them that it was from Spirit because, by myself, I could do nothing. I continued by telling them that the same divine direction is available to anyone who wishes to enter into the place were man meets God. This kingdom is within the Soul and is the source of Light, wisdom, Love and power. I explained that in order to find God, one has to make God's will one's own. The desire for this union with the divine must consume you and you must follow it above, but not to the exclusion of, all other things. You must still fulfill your responsibilities in this world. The Law will not be mocked, but it is the Grace of our Father that can change it all in a moment! We must all see ourselves as His messengers into the world. I told them that even as I spoke, it was the Spirit that provided the words. You see, Yehudah, that is how the Sojourner works. I stayed there a short time but then I could tell that it was time to come home and I passed through Assyria on the way to Galilee."

"Then you had actually returned home before now."

"Yes, but I didn't stay for very long. My mother and sisters were happy to see me but my brothers judged me to be a worthless fortune-hunter who had not brought home any riches." His face fell. "It saddens me that I cannot provide my whole family with these riches. In my travels I had amassed a fortune, but none of it was physical. I shared this wisdom with my mother for only she would listen. I knew it was not yet time for me to speak the truth I had learned in my own country. I made for Greece. I was welcomed in Athens by the foremost master of the Greeks, Apollonius of Tyana. Apollonius is a great sage and is only a few years my senior. He is best known in Greece for speaking great wisdom and being able to see the future. Like us, he has traveled in the East."

I was curious as to what this sage looked like. I asked Jeshua to describe him.

"He is a tall, slender man with long, dark, flowing hair. He possesses great physical beauty. He is not shaven as are the Romans, so his beard is also quite long. He is a follower of the Pythagorean School of philosophy and they are strict vegetarians and will wear nothing from animals. He would appear strange to other Greeks, but would not be so different from our most devout Essenes. But, let me continue. He foresaw my coming and had invited the wisest masters of Greece to hear me." Jeshua chuckled. "I really did not know what to say to those masters until the Holy Spirit swept through me and I spoke to them in their own tongue. I told them that they set the standard for culture in the world, being masters of Science, Art and Philosophy. I explained that this could only get them as far as the realm of the mind, and there is nothing in the mind that recognizes the Soul. I said that if they wanted to discover their true nature, they needed to open themselves to the Spirit. I told them not to abandon their pursuit of knowledge but to infuse it with spirit consciousness and their science and philosophy would then become a tool of divine awakening. When I had finished there was total silence. Only Apollonius was able to speak. He took me aside from the crowd and revealed himself to me, speaking my name in Greek: 'Jesus of Nazareth, I have been waiting for you to come. It is my job in this lifetime to be a keeper of the sacred keys to the Consciousness of the Sojourner. They have been in my safekeeping since I was young. In each time there must be a sage to be the focus of this master consciousness out into the world. There will be a number of Masters who will hold these sacred keys during my lifetime, but you are the first and will be the greatest.' What followed I cannot share with you, Yehudah, but I can tell you that it brought my purpose for this lifetime clearly into focus."

"Where did you go from there?" I asked.

"Egypt. Apollonius traveled the entire way with me. Tell me, do you remember the Temple at Heliopolis?"

I smiled. "How could I forget?"

"Apollonius also had been initiated there and brought me to the hierophant who presided over our earlier initiations. The hierophant was puzzled. He said that the wisdom of the gods was already mine, and wondered what use these initiations would be to me. I explained to him that physical initiations were only symbolic of the inner initiations that we must pass in order to return to our Father. Of their tests, I have been sworn to secrecy, but what I can tell you is that they provided me with what I needed to conclude the inner tests. When these were over, a council was called. It was Apollonius who presided over a meeting of sages from all over our world. These sages were all students of the Sojourner and at a future time each may be the focal point of that energy on the earth. They all offered their support, spiritual and physical for my mission in this life. I will make all of this clear to you and the others later since you are all to be a part of it."

"Did they proclaim you The Messiah?" I asked.

"Well, in a manner of speaking," he said hesitantly, "They recognized that my path and my actions are under control of The Father. I know that this is what it is to be 'anointed' of God. It is giving yourself over to Him. This is our higher purpose and it is what we must choose in order to be an anointed one of God. I do not like using the term 'messiah.' There is just too much confusion among our people. I am sure you are aware of the teachings concerning the coming of The Messiah. In the scriptures there were always <u>two</u> Messiahs: one is the warrior and the other the wise man. I have the birthright of the warrior, but I am more a warrior in spirit. This son of man is not here to fight Romans. My enemies are much more powerful and universal. They are ignorance, doubt, fear and death. This son of man is here to be an example for all who wish to find their own divinity. That is why I ask all of you to <u>follow</u> me. Speak of me <u>not</u> as The Messiah. Learn that you may also do as I do. From now on the expression of God through man will be the true Messiah. From now on men will learn to look for The Messiah within because that is where our Father speaks to us. Perhaps the Greek term *Christos* or 'The Christ' should be used in this more universal manner, to serve all peoples. Prepare for this, Yehudah, so you too can be the Christ. The most joy you can have on this earth is allowing God's will to act through you. Follow me, Yehudah, because I have been chosen as the pattern for men to follow in expressing their divinity."

"I'll tell you," I said, "many will not accept that you are not here to free your people. They will not accept a scholar as the Davidic Messiah.

They want a warrior. I don't know that I can accept that if you will do nothing to free us from the Roman yoke."

"I don't expect you to understand all of this, Yehudah," he said to me, speaking softly and clearly, "but such a Messiah would be too small for our Father. I would speak to the entire world rather than fill the needs of one people, even my own people. There is a time coming when we will get beyond nationality and religious traditions and see everyone as a brother. There must be a pattern for all of us to follow into expressing our individual divinity."

"But your own people need you NOW!"

"Yehudah, we, in this world are all one people. We must learn to accept each other with our differences and Love the Spirit of the Father that expresses through each of us. Until you can look at that Roman soldier expressing his arrogance and cruelty and see the same divine spark as is within yourself, you haven't grown into your true adulthood as a Son of God. You will come back here again and again until you learn."

"Do you suggest that we allow ourselves to sit idly by and be exterminated by an oppressor? Who then will be left to spread the message of this pattern, Jeshua?"

"There have been a number of times since my return when I have felt the anger of a man whose people have been enslaved. I have seen both physical and spiritual oppression. I saw an old man being knocked down by Roman soldiers because he did not show proper respect by getting out of their way in time. Part of me wanted to knock over that Roman soldier and ask, 'See, now how do you like that.' That would have given that part of me some inner satisfaction. But when I saw the old man lying there, helpless, I saw where my action was most needed. I went over and picked him up, dusted him off and checked to see if he was injured. I had a choice, Yehudah: to give in to my anger, or act out of support. If I had fought the soldier, I would have had to flee and the old man might still be lying on the ground, perhaps dead. I made the choice that would help the most. We are all presented with these types of choices, to help or to harm. I felt that it was a better choice to help the victim rather than harm the oppressor.

"That same old man is unfairly taxed by our own priesthood who are the puppets of the Romans. Our people need to be free in their relationship with their heavenly Father. They must be taught that the closest way to the Father is inside each of us. It is their lack of trust in their own worthiness to go to the Father directly that gives these priests so much power. The abuse of this power also angers a part of me inside and I want to denounce these deceivers of the innocent. Yet, I am faced with another choice. And that is either to express the position of againstness toward the priesthood, or to help the victims by teaching them that their authority comes from within."

"That time, in our youth, when you stood up to the bully… did you have the same type of process going on inside of you?" I asked.

"Yes, Yehudah, I did."

"Then why did you not share that with us? I thought you were perfect since the first time I met you."

"I am a man, Yehudah, like you. I did not share what I was thinking and feeling with you because I was ashamed of that."

"<u>You</u>? Really?"

"I did not mean to deceive. I have parts of myself that get angry, grow fearful, wish revenge, and are resistant to change. I have spent a long, long, time learning to choose not to express these parts of myself. I have also learned not to judge or condemn myself for having these parts. Everyone who is in a human body has them, they are a part of this experience, and we cannot escape them. What I had to help me was the understanding that I could not just put this off until later. I realized I could choose to go beyond my limitations. I also continually kept giving it all over to the Father, since it is He that is the source of all of this anyway."

He continued: "Yehudah, we have both fought and died in many lives and this has kept us coming back to learn and re-learn these lessons. We have to say, '<u>Now</u> is the time!' '<u>Now</u> I will have the courage to follow a new path!' '<u>Now</u> I will listen to the voice of the Father within me and choose His way rather than my own.' I would much rather die attempting to follow the path that our Father has set for me, than to follow the path of my mind and emotions that has led me so many times into folly. I am so grateful to the Father who has given me the consciousness of the Sojourner to share with humanity."

"Jeshua, just what is this consciousness of the Sojourner?"

"The Sojourner is the wayshower, the one who teaches us what we need to fulfill our debt so we can learn, so we can overcome the earth and leave it. We can be the new pattern to show a new way for people to treat each other, with loving – like brothers. The Sojourner teaches by example, so I must live what I teach. Believe me, Yehudah, it is a world of difference when one's every action is on view. Each choice must be from the higher perspective, the perspective of Spirit. I am often exhausted but I find my time alone with our Father renews me. So, I could fight Romans, Yehudah, but then what would that teach the oppressor? Only that he was not strong enough to keep us in our place. If we live free then we are free. You are always free inside of you, Yehudah. You must choose if your attitude will be that of a free man or a slave."

"What kind weapon is one's attitude against a Roman sword?"

"The best kind of weapon because it is not a violent one. Violence never brings real peace. Only love will heal wounds of war. Do you remember the lessons taught by Hillel?"

"Yes, before I learned about weapons. But they seem inappropriate to our present condition."

"The problem you have, Yehudah, is that you see the ideal in the future and you are trying to control that future by what you know in the present. That is not yours to do, but God's. The best way to make that happen is to surrender to God's will and be a willing instrument of that inevitable change. Are you so sure that your time is better than God's time?" he teased.

"And this is the whole of your mission?"

"Part of it. I cannot say more at this time."

I then told Jeshua about the danger that awaited John and asked him to talk John into taking the necessary steps to protect himself. Jeshua said he would do this, but that John was very willful in his expression and might not listen to him.

It was getting late and I was somewhat confused by certain things Jeshua had told me. I was filled with worry and concern. I was hoping for something simple to sweep all the problems of the earth aside. What Jeshua shared with me just seemed to stir up more questions. When I told him this he exuded a wistful smile and said, "Well, it appears as if my presence comforts the disturbed and disturbs the comfortable."

We arose early the next morning. When we approached the Jordan, John was already teaching his followers. As Jeshua approached, John called to him and asked him to speak. I readied my piece of charcoal to take down the words of Jeshua. Perhaps I could understand better what was said in private by learning the lessons of what was being said in public. I felt that the words of Jeshua should have a place in my story since they always affected me to such a great degree.

"Men of Israel," he began, "the kingdom of heaven is at hand."

He pointed to John. "You see before you the great key-keeper of the age. It is John who has the Spirit of Elijah within him. He heralds the opening of a new age where men, women, and children may seek the kingdom within. But beware! There is a keeper to this gate. Those who would enter must overcome the attachments of the lower self. If we could enter the kingdom with our attachments to the desires of the lower self, we all would have left this world a long time ago. When men realize that they cannot take these with them, they turn away, for few are ready to give all that up to see the King."

He paused for a moment and looked back at John. "They call the Nazarenes fishers of men. Well, John is a most excellent fisherman. He fishes for the souls of men. He brings those human fish back to this river so that they may be cleansed of sins. But many confess only with their lips and not with their hearts. The next day finds them back in their old ways. If we should enter the kingdom our actions must speak for us. To see the King we must be strong and pure in our hearts. However it is human to be weak and most of us do not change our actions. But do not despair, for even those who are caught in their weakness will someday come again to the gate and will have the joy of entering the kingdom of our Father. Be glad for our Father has decreed <u>that not one soul will be lost</u>."

He pointed again to John. "People of Israel, learn from this prophet. Strengthen your minds, open your hearts and help yourselves so that you may be available to help others. The kingdom is at hand, and it is as close to you as your next breath."

Jeshua was not a quick speaker so I was able to write most of this down. I would redo it in ink at a later time. I found that I would have little time that day, however, because Jeshua was preparing to visit Bethany.

Bethany! I would get another chance to speak with Jeshua's cousin, that mysterious girl called Mary Magdalene. When we got to Bethany I did not see her in the crowd that had gathered in the center of town. I stopped looking after a time because Jeshua was about to speak. I took out my charcoal and paper and followed his words.

He began: "The kingdom is at hand! It is here! As I speak it is all about you and within you, and you cannot see it with your physical eyes. It does not replace the kingdoms of the earth nor does it look to."

"Our sacred texts have said that a Messiah will come. There has been much argument and discussion about this. People have been led to believe that a Messiah will raise up armies against Rome and free Israel. If this is the Messiah you are looking for, it is not I. I have no designs on the thrones of Cæsar or of Herod. They need not fear me. Yet there is no other term that successfully describes the office of 'The Anointed One.' By the Grace of our Father, I have been anointed by Spirit to show the way back to him. I hold another office, that of the 'Sojourner,' but you would understand that term even less. I would call myself 'The Christ' for it is the Greek translation of 'The Anointed One,' but even this can be misunderstood. I use it only to distinguish the difference from Messianic expectations. Yet, I have no desire to distinguish myself. This son of man, Jeshua, son of Joseph, the one who stands before you, is a man, like you. One who has been tested by temptations, trials, and misfortunes. I, too, have failed my tests, but have always gone on. The Christ is not a man but is a force of unconditional and universal Love. I am here to manifest this to you and to show you how you can manifest this within yourselves. Don't judge the Christ by this body; it is the Christ that is the king, not this son of man. I have this Christ spirit within me and I know it. The only difference between us is that I know it and I am familiar with it. You do not yet see this within yourselves and it is easier for you to see it in others. Find the Christ within you, for that Christ knows me and knows our Father."

All were silent and Jeshua got up and left. We scrambled to follow for he was going back home to Nazareth.

On the way to Nazareth, I found myself in conversation with Peter.

"Yehudah, you and your brother have known Jeshua much longer than any of us. What do you think his next move will be?"

I shook my head and smiled. "I might as well try to predict the next earthquake or volcanic eruption. I have never been able to predict what he would do. It has always been like he existed in another reality…" I mused and was quiet for a moment. But Peter was still looking at me expectantly as if to get some shred of information that would clarify what our collective future would look like. Remembering what Jeshua had told me about his feeling anger and sadness like other men, I began to look at our situation a little differently. "Well, I may be completely wrong, you understand…" Peter's look communicated to me: "Well, go on!" I began again: "If I were him, I would be looking for a center of operations, like for a military campaign."

Peter chimed in, "Like a home base."

"Yes. Somewhere to begin… although I don't know what. And what better place to start than in your home town where things are familiar and people know you."

Peter looked relieved and happy that he had some information on which to base his expectation, erroneous though it might be.

When we reached Nazareth, I split off from the rest, since it was my job as keeper of the purse, to provide for accommodations for our group. If it had been only Jeshua, John and I, as of old, we could have stayed with Jeshua's mother. But her home could never provide for all seven of us. I also suspected that things were not yet right between Jeshua and his brothers. James, especially, would have frowned on us staying there. James had too much of the Essene in him, as did John. But, I figure that it served him well enough. I was able to get one night's lodging at an inn, as by Jeshua's instruction. It seemed as though we were not settling down just yet; more travel was ahead.

I completed my business and headed back to Mary's home when I met Peter running toward me. "Did you make the accommodations for tonight?"

"Yes. I was just coming…"

"Well, you're going to have to cancel them. It seems as though we are moving on."

I felt somewhat irritated by all this. I had handled (and very well, I might add) all preparation for our stay and now I find out it was all for nothing! I was feeling really unappreciated.

"What's all this about?" I asked, not bothering to hide my irritation.

"Jeshua was going to speak in the synagogue but that has changed. The rabbi at this synagogue is a *Parush,* a follower of Shammai, and did not know Jeshua as a young man. He sent for Jeshua to come to the synagogue where he would ask for proof of Jeshua's messiahship. Jeshua, of course, ignored this demand and went to his mother's house. Later this *Parush* came to Mary's and asked Jeshua why he had not come when he was summoned. I tell you, Yehudah, Jeshua looked as irritated as you do now."

I suddenly felt a little embarrassed at my reaction to Peter.

"Jeshua told him that he was not anyone's slave to come when others call. He said that he heeded only that call of God, our Father. He went on to ask by what authority this man asked for proof. It was about this time that he again found his composure and told the man that if he followed him, he would not lack for any proof of Jeshua's authenticity. But the man just left. Jeshua got up, shook his head and said that a prophet has no honor in his own town and that he would not speak again in Nazareth until he had won the faith of men in other towns."

I was beginning to feel a little better. If someone as masterful as Jeshua could express his irritation, I guess it was all right for me, one of his disciples, to do so. But I learned also that I could take that energy of irritation and frustration and use it in a positive direction as Peter had told me. It seems as though Jeshua taught me even when he wasn't present.

Jeshua and his family were invited to a wedding in Cana and it would be an opportune time for him to speak.

The rabbi at Cana was either a *Hasidim* or at least not opposing Hillel's view of the law; he asked Jeshua to speak at the wedding. I was ready with my charcoal to get all of his teachings when I spied Mary of Magdala in the crowd. I assumed she would be with Mary, Jeshua's mother or with her brother Lazarus. But she stood alone. Her radiant beauty could almost hide the uneasiness she projected. I decided to keep one eye on her during the wedding while writing, so I am sure that I did not get all of Jeshua's words.

He spoke on marriage: "When a marriage is truly made in heaven, there is no tie that is more sacred. It is the love that is made in heaven that binds the two souls as one and no man can break it asunder. However, when a marriage is based on the lower passions, it is like the blending of oil and water, the two are never really joined. Their union is one of adultery…"

As he said this Mary of Magdala went white as a cloud and melted into the background. I could not follow her as she left, but it seemed as though she was trying very hard to escape hearing any more of Jeshua's words.

"… It is not a genuine marriage. Even though the ceremony has been consecrated by a priest, it is a counterfeit marriage."

Jeshua had finished his thoughts on marriage when his mother rushed up to him with a look of some urgency. "Jeshua, the wine has soured and the party will be ruined."

Jeshua looked at her and said, "What is wine, after all but water flavored by grapes." He asked the servants to bring six large water pots, filled to the brim. The guests at the wedding had stopped their merriment. They seemed aware the something of importance was going to happen. He sat down in front of the pots in the lotus position of eastern contemplation and explained the spiritual laws of manifestation to the forming crowd, "And grapes are just a manifestation of a divine thought. In manifesting that thought the water will transform to wine."

He went into a deep state of meditation. I don't know how long he stayed that way. It seemed like a long time but all were transfixed, curious to see the outcome of this. When his meditation ended, he stepped away from the pots, not waiting to see what he had done.

The servants opened the pots and poured the contents into the cup of the bridegroom. This poor man was so surprised that he nearly dropped the cup.

The servants, on the other hand, were laughing and enjoying the spectacle. They had tasted the wine. Normally this behavior would have been out of place, but these were certainly not normal times.

"They usually use the best wine first at a feast like this, but it appears they saved the best wine for last," one joked. They laughed again and looked uplifted while performing their chores.

The guests looked on in amazement at what had been done. Although Jeshua had calmly explained the action rationally in terms of the laws of the universe, people looked at him as though he were a magician. Many called him messiah, and would have gladly followed him as such if he hadn't hastened us together to leave the celebration. More than a few of the disciples were also dumbfounded by what Jeshua did but heroically closed ranks. He said just one thing: "Since my home town doesn't want us, we will set up our base in your home town." He was looking at Peter, Andrew, John and James. The center of our activity was to be Capernaum.

CHAPTER 10 - SIDES ARE CHOSEN

The sun was setting by the Sea of Galilee. As we sat on the sandy shore, Jeshua taught us about the Kingdom of God.

"You have asked me the location of The Kingdom. You must know this because people will one day ask you and you will need to tell them. By that time you will know what I tell you is true because you will have experienced this for yourselves. It is a part of that deepest essence of your being, so you know it as true in that place. When you hear it, you will know it as true.

"The Kingdom of God is inside of you. The way to this kingdom is to go inside of you. You will find it in the stillness, where the emotions and the mind cannot go. You can never see the Kingdom through the emotions or the mind. The only way you can see the Kingdom is through the eyes of the soul. The soul is the holy of holies. It is that part of us which expresses our true God-nature.

"Certain Greek philosophers, through their science, have surmised that all matter is made from tiny units called 'atoms'. Each one of our bodies must be made of a staggering number of these tiny particles. In the same way, each us is an atom in the body of God. We have our life within His being and the only part of us which is aware of this all of the time is the soul. It alone knows who we truly are. For that reason it is already in the Kingdom. The Soul is the true child of God, for it was made most perfectly in His image. So, each one of us, in our truest sense, is a child of God. The Christ also dwells in the soul of each of you. So if you find the Son, you also find the Father. They are as one.

"You might see a criminal or a leper and think, 'How could a man such as this be a son of the Father?' Yet, seen in the spirit, the criminal, the leper, the priest, are all equal in the eyes of God. For each of them, when they step into their inner kingdom, will see the Father in each other and judge not by the outer appearance."

With my charcoal in hand, I struggled furiously to keep up with Jeshua.

He continued: "You might wonder, then, why are not all people given the same chances in life? Why are some born to wealth and power while others wallow in filth and disease? You might wonder how a loving Father could allow that to happen to any of his children. Let me tell you a story:

> "A great king ruled a vast empire that had no boundaries. What gave this ruler the most joy was in training his son to someday rule a domain such as his. He did all he could to teach the boy inside the castle but it was no use. The boy only saw clearly inside his father's castle. Each time he left this castle, he forgot all he had learned and behaved badly, mistreating people and causing suffering to others. The king understood what had to be done. One night the son was placed outside the castle in rags. When he awoke, he had forgotten his identity and who his father was. He treated people just as badly as before, but because he had no protection offered by the fine clothes of his station and others saw him as a troublemaker. They scorned him and finally had him stoned to death. This happened a number of times so that he was returned outside his father's castle after returning to life. In the beginning of each life the boy had no memory of what had occurred before but awakened outside the castle fully grown and went through the same type of pain and anguish each time. In some of these existences he was a slave among slaves such as aboard a Roman barge. Little was offered and he had always fought for each morsel of food or drop of water. After many times as a slave, he finally saw each of the other slaves as his brothers. A man next to him was near death and the boy gave all his food and water to that man. He did this for many days and as the other man got stronger, he, himself, grew weaker. The other man recovered, but it was too late for the boy. He finally died. He had developed compassion and love for his brother slaves. This time, when the boy awoke, he was in his bed in his father's castle. At once he remembered all his lives. His father was very proud of him because his son had finally learned compassion for others. He told his son that this was the time. This son was ready to rule at his side because he had learned to see himself inside of his brothers. The question is, was the father cruel in subjecting the son to all of these horrible experiences? The answer is that the son gained understanding that only experience could have taught him. He then gained his own kingdom. In the same way, mankind goes through many lives to experience that which is needed to gain the ability

to see the soul and the Christ in each other. Some experiences are quite horrible, some can be quite pleasurable but all are to awaken this ability in each of us."

"When will we get to see others the way they truly are, as souls?" Peter asked.

"When you can see yourself as a true son of Our Father," Jeshua replied.

There were other talks that Jeshua gave to us by the sea. I had scraps of paper with incomplete notes that I took from these other talks. These somehow were missing when it became time to travel to Jerusalem. But what I clearly remember most from those talks was when Jeshua told us that people would get impatient with teachers, but they seemed to have infinite patience with storytellers. So, he decided he would clothe his teachings in a form with which people would most easily relate – a story.

The festival of Passover was approaching. Jeshua mentioned that it was time for us to make our presence known in Jerusalem. A warning bell went off inside of me at the mention of this. I knew the politics that we would encounter in this city could be extremely dangerous. As we made ready, he assured us that this was according to God's plan and that we would be protected. As we entered the city a crowd of people who had heard of Jeshua greeted us. There were cries of "Hail to the King" and "The Messiah has come." I was nervous. Any one in this crowd could have been a Roman or Sadducee spy. Jeshua wisely paid no attention to them and went straight for the Temple.

Arriving at the proper Temple gate, Jeshua stopped in his tracks as if he has hit an invisible wall. He saw the usual business of money changing and the booths selling sacrificial animals for use as offerings inside the Temple. His body appeared to tense and there was first a look of anguish on his face, then anger, and then he looked up at the sky for a moment and took a deep breath of air. When he again looked at the booths he appeared calm and at ease. It appeared as if a glow of ecstasy surrounded him and his eyes burned with understanding. Then all of a sudden he ran into the thick of the bustle, throwing over tables and scattering items, breaking cages so that many of the hapless animals were set free. The look on his face was still ecstatic, as if God was moving his body and his being. His voice boomed out strong and with a laugh in his voice: "You don't have to do any of this to speak with Our Father. The way to our Father is much simpler! Our God is a loving Father. You don't have to exchange your money, perform animal sacrifices, or pay a priest to pray for you. Our Father is closer to you than your next breath (if you would only take that breath)."

He stretched his arms out wide. “The Kingdom of Heaven is all around you, if you would open your eyes to see. If God is truly your goal, turn your back on all of this foolishness. The only sacrifice our Father requires is for you to let go of your fear, your judgments, and your doubts. The only authority you will ever need is inside of you. Your body itself is the temple where God lives, neither in a building nor in the pronouncement of a priest. The God that is the Father of us all knows you and loves you better than you do yourself. Do you think He would make your path to him as difficult as you make it?”

A temple priest arrived with four of the temple guard. Their hands were on the hilts of their swords, but the crowd had gathered around Jeshua and they were not permitted to advance further toward him. The priest had overheard what Jeshua had said and was not amused by any of it. This man barely held back a sneer: “What gives you the right to upset the order of the holy Temple?”

“The same right as any Judean who loves God and God’s Law,” Jeshua replied. He spoke to the crowd. “How many of you follow the sects of the Pharisees?” A majority of the crowd raised their voices in the affirmative. “Should I be any less zealous for the Law than Hillel who was my teacher?”

There was a murmur of agreement in the crowd. “Does it not read in Psalms, ‘Thou dost not call for sacrifice nor offerings of blood; burnt offerings and offerings for sin thou dost not want?’”

Hearing that, many left the temple with the joy of the possibility of knowing God within, but many also stayed to hear what Jeshua would say next. The temple guard again attempted to approach Jeshua, but a booming voice from inside the Temple told them to halt. It was Philo of Alexandra, a great sage in his own right, who stood between Jeshua and the guard. “This man is a sage and great Master and a righteous teacher, and I, for one, would have him teach inside.”

We followed Philo and Jeshua inside the Temple. The priest, feeling himself now on “home ground,” went on the offensive. “You mentioned that your body is the temple of God. Are you claiming to be God?”

Jeshua smiled. He knew what this priest was attempting to do. If Jeshua replied “yes”, he could be charged with blasphemy. If he said “no”, it would look like Jeshua was not being consistent. But Jeshua had dealt with adversaries much more clever than this priest and was able to turn the situation easily to his advantage.

“No man has ever heard me make any special claim to divinity. But, follow this, if you will: When God created all things, all things came from God, is that correct?”

"Yes," said the priest warily.

"Well, then would it not follow that all things, then, are <u>of</u> God?"

"Yes."

"And in Genesis, is it not said that man is made in the image of God."

The priest was getting quite annoyed. "You presume to teach me, peasant…"

"Will you just be patient until I am finished?" Jeshua said, unruffled.

"Very well, man is made in the image of God."

"Then would not there be a part of man that is the divine co-creator, and would not that part be the true child of God?"

"I do not know," the priest said, finally.

"Then that is the only difference between us," Jeshua said, "for I <u>do</u> know that I am a son of the Most High and dearly beloved of our Father. And that this body <u>is</u> the temple of God. You are this also yet do not know it." He looked straight at the priest and his guards: "And, if you would tear this temple down, in three days it will be rebuilt more glorious than before."

The priest was silent for at least a minute. He must have been deciding which tack to take in order to trip Jeshua into condemning himself from his own words. By the look on the man's face, however, I could see that this priest knew he was in way over his head.

"I have heard that you call yourself the Messiah. Is that true?"

"The Messiah you refer to is a king. I have never said that I am a king. I could not sit on Cæsar's throne and be who I am. My kingdom is God's kingdom and it is not a place on this earth."

"What would you call yourself then?"

"The Christ."

"What is 'The Christ,' then, if not 'The Messiah?'"

"The Christ is not a leader of one people but a servant of all people. The Christ is not understood in the intellect but in the heart. The Christ does not preside over an earthly kingdom but rules with love and mercy over a heavenly kingdom. He is also a Wayshower, teaching others to follow in his footsteps. He is the pattern that man must follow to be truly free."

The priest soon vanished and Jeshua continued teaching in the Temple. I found that I was too lightheaded with the flush of Jeshua's victory to take notes on what was said.

On our way back to Bethany we passed a procession of wailing women and sorrowful men. It seems as if a young child had just drowned in a pool of water in which he had been playing. Jeshua asked them how long had the child been dead. They told him that it was not long, perhaps a few minutes before they had discovered him lying face-down in the pool. Jeshua lifted the child up by the feet and water poured from his mouth and lungs. Jeshua then placed the child on his back and opened the child's mouth. He breathed into the child's lungs in the manner we were taught in Tibet as part of our healing work. He prayed over the child and then resumed the breathing technique. In a manner of minutes the child began coughing and breathing again. The group of men and women were crying with joy. They asked his name because they wished to place him in prayers. He told them, "Jeshua, son of Joseph."

He then asked us to gather around him after the joyous procession had left. He explained to us that this was not as simple as it looked. The Soul of the little boy had left the body. He had to check and see if the action of bringing it back were for the highest good of the boy's soul and spiritual development. The soul of the boy chose to re-enter the body when the coughing began.

It seemed like I was back in Tibet. There was one teaching situation after another, as if we were being prepared to do more of this work. This was thrilling, but I was feeling that I had not been able to get close to Jeshua lately. He seemed too involved in his plans and I found that I was wishing for the "old Jeshua," the one with whom I could sit and talk, alone, for more than a few minutes. He must have sensed that, because he approached me that evening when we had all returned to Bethany.

"Yehudah, did you want to ask me something?"

"Yes. I've been feeling like I have been pushed aside for… well… ever since you came back from the wilderness. I guess there is a part of me that feels hurt because of that. I feel that I am no longer central to what's going on. It's like I don't matter anymore."

He looked at me with tenderness. "Yehudah, I know for a fact that you will have a major role in this unfolding plan and in my life. You have not been forgotten, old friend. You may want to consider, however, that being in the midst of drama does not always mean that you are at the head of the class spiritually. Spirit works with us all in different ways and we can never judge our inner growth by that outer drama. Often it is the ones who work quietly in the background who make the steadiest gains. Watch your desire for recognition; it can take you to places you may not want to go."

I must have looked troubled by this so he asked me if there was any specific thing I wanted to know.

"Yes, Jeshua, I want to know what happened to you in the wilderness where you stayed for forty days."

"I am uneasy talking about it, Yehudah. It was a very personal and difficult time for me. My lower self is strong and it binds me to the earth life. I was faced with my worst fears and saw parts of myself of which I felt ashamed. I was presented with three tests to clear the Karma which I had accrued over many ages."

He continued: "I knew that if I could overcome this Karma, there would be a better chance for me to finally complete my tasks on this earth. I had been given the task of being a willing sacrifice for mankind and I feared that I would not be up to the task. I began to doubt my real identity — that of my soul. Part of me asked, 'If I really am the Chosen One, then I should be able to turn these stones to bread.' Then I asked myself, 'Who is requiring a test?' It is no sign of being God's chosen to perform a miracle. Any master of the lower realms can do the same. The Soul does not require a miracle. The proof shall be in the way I lead my life, in what I say and do, and in my attitude to all things."

"No sooner had I overcome that doubt, another came in. I doubted that people would listen to me and then think me the fool. I though that if I could jump from the pinnacle of the Temple and through use of the Eastern techniques, save myself from harm, then people would believe that I was the Messiah sent from God. This would be easy for I have done such things before, while in Tibet. But I realized that it was that part of me which requires the approval of others that longed for that recognition and that was of this world. This was not needed to fulfill my purpose here in this lifetime. Furthermore, such an act would be an affront to the Lord, from who all power comes."

"The third test was for me to confront my own ambition and pride. I knew that with the power and vision I have been given I could easily win the honors and fame of the world and live to an old age in wealth and splendor. All that was required was for me to renounce my goals and pathway to the Father and instead focus on healing the troubles of the world. I tell you, Yehudah, this was the most difficult test for me because I am not insensitive to the cries of our people for freedom. Even you, your brother Simon, Peter, John, and the others expect that I should fulfill the traditional role of Davidic Messiah."

When I heard this I was crestfallen, but I still hoped that he would change his mind and bring in the Messianic age that was to come. I knew that if this was what the Lord wanted, then His chosen would have to bring that forward.

"It took me all of those forty days to overcome my inner temptations, but when I did, the Holy Spirit was with me and the joy I felt was incomparable. It was another initiation, Yehudah, one from Spirit because from this point on, only Spirit, not man, can initiate me."

I was troubled hearing this and could not sleep. I was awake to hear someone approach in the dead of night. My reaction was to go for the *twin blades*, which I still carried.

"Judas, you can put those blades away. It's me, Petronius."

"I heard you, old friend, are you getting out of practice?"

"No more than you, Judas. As a disciple of Jesus, you are out of practice slitting Roman throats."

"I guess so. Perhaps that might change later… I don't really know. What have you heard?"

"Your little band of Nazarenes has drawn some attention from a few quarters. Many of the Essenes and the *Hasidim* look on your group with great favor. The followers of Shammai, the *Parush*, on the other hand, heard Jesus praise his old teacher Hillel and are looking to dim your Master's light. The Sadducees are the most angered at your Master. They are devious and ruthless. I heard that they are scheming with the *Parush* on this one issue and have procured the services of one over-zealous *Parush* named "Saul." I warn you, Judas, this is a very dangerous man. Almost as dangerous as you," he smiled.

"Can you tell me anything about him," I asked.

He shrugged. "As of yet there is nothing to tell. He is a man of mystery."

"You know, Petronius, it has always been the intrigue that thrills me…" I said, as if this were news to him, "…but I would know more about this 'Saul;' he sounds like a worthy adversary among all these transparent politicians."

"I will tell you more when I have more information. But, for now, be careful! There may be other parties watching you."

"The Romans?"

"Not yet, Judas. The Roman command is like a sleeping dog. Flies can land on it without notice, but if they bite, the Beast can awaken and then nothing can hold it back. No, you have not drawn any interest from the Jerusalem garrison as yet."

Having received what seemed to be his full report I turned to more personal information. "Petronius, how is Julia?"

"As well as can be expected being the mother of two boys."

"That's great news! How is their health?"

"They are excellent, healthy boys. They have the fine Patrician looks of their mother and the Plebian stubbornness of their father."

We both laughed. "I hope they also have your strength, Petronius. They will need it growing up in these times."

"I will teach them to use a sword as soon as they can lift one. By the way, Judas, is there anyone special in your life or are you determined to be alone for the rest of your life?"

"Well, actually, there is someone special but…"

"…Or, perhaps you Nazarenes are not permitted to marry?"

"No, Peter is married. His wife is back in Galilee, though. He doesn't see much of her. There is no rule against marriage here as long as it doesn't stand between you and 'The Way', as Jeshua calls it. There is someone special for me but she doesn't even notice me."

Petronius gave me a sympathetic look. "Don't worry my friend, she will, and one day our children will play with one another and we will gather our grandchildren together and tell them stories of the battles we fought."

We smiled and shook hands in the Roman style and I watched him disappear into the shadows.

The next morning was the Sabbath day. Jeshua went again to be with the people at the Temple. Many were there because they must have heard of Jeshua's healing of the little boy the day before and came that they might also be healed.

Jeshua spoke the sacred name of God that is a part of us all. This word of power, being said in Spirit, healed many. Jeshua laid hands on others, causing them to be healed. He also employed herbs, oils and suggestions that some wash themselves in certain waters.

A doctor in the crowd asked him how he healed. Jeshua explained to the doctor that the human exists on many levels of being and sometimes the cure for an individual is not just something that can be done physically. He went on to explain that one should go to whatever level on which is an imbalance and perform a cure for that level. He compared the human body to a harp that has many strings. He said that one must tune each to the other so that the whole is in perfect tune. But he did say that the string of the Spirit was the most important, for when that is tuned, many times it brings all the others into harmony.

The *Parush*, followers of Shammai, were there and observed him. They came forward and raged against Jeshua for healing on the Sabbath and commanded him to quit immediately saying that it was a violation of Sacred Law.

Jeshua welcomed this intrusion. It provided him an opportunity to teach. "You *Parush* follow the letter of the Law and expect that others do the same, but you are hypocrites in your zeal for the Law! If you fell into a pit on the Sabbath and could not get out, would you not cry out for help? Do you mean to say that you would lie in the midst of disease and filth for a day and tell others to pass you by because it was the Sabbath and that you would have them rescue you another day? Not likely! You would be happy to be pulled out as soon as possible. If that were the case, why would you curse me now? These souls have found themselves in a pit and are crying for me to pull them out. Shall I ignore them?"

The *Parush* were silent and Jeshua continued: "The question here is 'Was man made for the Sabbath? or was the Sabbath made for man?'" When people fear transgressing the smallest portion of the Law (which was made as a guide for our benefit) they miss the Spirit of the Law. This is a great pity since the Spirit of the law gives freedom. The letter of the Law generates fear. For my part, I choose the joy that freedom brings. Then I know I am serving the Lord in the way which was intended, with freedom and joy."

As if the joy that Jeshua was expressing was too much for the *Parush*, they backed away and disappeared. Jeshua turned to the disciples and said to us, "Friends, here is how we can test the Law. If it does not hurt others or ourselves and if it allows us to take better care of ourselves so that we can take better care of others, it is in the Spirit of the Law. If the Law excludes rather than includes it is not of the Spirit. Look inside and you will be able to evaluate the Law for yourselves."

Just then, a man from the crowd approached Jeshua and said that he was a messenger from a powerful individual and that he needed to talk. After a few minutes he turned to us and said, "I will be meeting Nicodemus, a member of the Sanhedrin. Do not expect me back tonight, but be ready to go in the morning. I will go to Bethlehem."

The next morning Jeshua was more quiet than usual. Peter asked him if everything was all right. He smiled at Peter to let him know all was fine but his smile was tinged with sadness. This was where Jeshua told us of one of his previous lives, the priest Melchizedek. I felt entranced by the revelation and eager to learn the lessons that were being shared.

Jeshua began to speak: "Bethlehem is the place where Abraham tithed to Melchizedek, The Prince of Peace." Jeshua's eyes seemed to be staring at another world. "He fought many battles. Not one was fought with a sword, lance, or shield. His sword, his lance and his shield were love. He demonstrated to all nations the role of the Warrior of Spirit. He won glories that you cannot imagine, and was king over all Kings for he was King of Righteousness. Now he has come again to do battle, but not with man. His enemies are fear, ignorance, hatred, and death. These things are illusions and cannot last, they are not of the Spirit, so in the end, Love will be victorious. But the final grave of Melchizedek shall be in Jerusalem, not here."

Jeshua taught many of the mysteries that day, and it was one time when I wished I could both learn and write at the same time because I would have wished to pass on more of his wisdom.

Jeshua heard that there were some problems with his family that needed his attention. It had something to do with his cousins Ruth and Mary. John "the Beloved" and I volunteered to make the trip with Jeshua. John had a very tender feeling for Jeshua's family and wanted to lend his support. I nodded as I too agreed but my reason for going was more selfish; it was because I wanted to see the mysterious Mary again.

Ruth was crying as she met us. She told Jeshua that her husband, Asher was a *Parush*, a loyal follower of Shammai and forbade her to support the Nazarenes or even speak of Jeshua in the house. She had explained to him that even as his faith was strong, so was hers in following Jeshua. He had thrown her out of the house and so harsh was his treatment of her she feared for her life.

"Ruth," Jeshua began, "the problem here is intolerance."

"You are right, Jeshua," she answered. "My husband reacts this way whenever I mentioned The Way or any of your teachings."

"The intolerance is not his alone, Ruth. We all have given in to intolerance and felt quite justified in our attitudes. It is a human failing that can be overcome with loving. You, too, have been intolerant of his beliefs. No one has the monopoly on the truth of our Father and "The Way" may not be Asher's way. We all must come to God by the inner Christ, but there are as many pathways to the inner Christ as there are people. He believes just as strongly in his pathway as you do in yours, Ruth. To assume another is less because of his or her beliefs is to deny the Christ inside that person. Some will do this with the smug self-righteousness that comes from the authority of scripture. Others will compare their experiences with those of others and make themselves appear to be more holy than their brothers and sisters. The Father God that I know does not care what your beliefs are because He is a loving

God. He just wants you back in His kingdom, and anyway you can get there is fine with Him. The best way, however, is to follow the path inside because there reside the keys to the Kingdom."

"What could I have done better, Jeshua, so as not to cause this split in my family?"

"What you could have done you can still do. The key is not to preach the teaching but to live the teaching. Return to your home with loving, forgiveness, and understanding. These deeds will open his heart and mind more quickly than a scriptural argument. Perhaps, in time, the Light will come to Asher and your pathways will be in the same direction. At that time you will be repaid in full for all your loving and kindness. If this never does occur, then you will be rewarded by our Father for being true to your path and you will find the Kingdom."

The tenderness and understanding that Jeshua offered his cousin brought tears to my eyes and to John's.

Ruth continued, "I fear greatly for Mary. I fear your reaction to hearing this almost as much as I fear for the consequences of her actions, but I have nowhere else to turn. If I told Asher, he would make sure she was stoned. She… she has been the mistress of a wealthy married man in the town of Magdala. I have told her of the dangers which await her but she says that this is the only thing a woman can do to keep her family fed and clothed. Lazarus, God bless him, is not a businessman, not a farmer, he is a dreamer. Martha can cook and clean but she is not in any demand. Mary has been seeing this man for a while. Your father Joseph was a good provider so your mother had a surplus of funds. She used to provide for Lazarus, Mary and Martha for some time. Funds dwindled, and Mary found this wealthy man, and his gifts over time have been lavish. I am afraid now because of the religious fervor throughout the land. If she is found out, she will be stoned to death for adultery. I know Mary is a good girl at heart but she is overcome by the demons of fear."

Hearing this brought me face to face with my own demon. I felt like someone shoved a sword through my heart. The woman that I was ready to worship, the woman who I had dreamed about for all this time was an adulterous prostitute. I felt as though she was cheating on ME! How awful she must be, I thought, to reject me and choose a married man with whom to sin. Damn her! I felt humiliated and betrayed. I made a mental note to avoid trusting people with any things that were important to me, least of all my heart. Bitterness raced through me. I hadn't felt like this since my parents were killed. But this time there was no enemy to fight, no Roman soldier to kill. "Control is the only answer," I concluded. I turned away and sat in the corner of another room in the house where I could hear but not be seen.

Jeshua was comforting Ruth. He said things that made no sense. "Ruth, I know of a way which will help Mary. I tell you this now and ask you to believe. All will be well. She will not be harmed and will change her course. She will marry one she has married before and he will be the right one for her. The house of Lazarus will prosper and continue. Trust our Father. There is not one of us who is beyond his care."

"Except for me, that is," I thought. "I am never to be a part of her life; she will marry another. How could a loving father abandon me like this? How can I trust in the Spirit? He must want me to have more control over what is going on around me. I must have been a lazy initiate. The more I am able to control, the more worthy I will be. There is to be no love in my life other than Spirit. Very well, I can do that!"

Jeshua was ready to leave. He gathered up John "the Beloved" and me and we headed toward the Jordan to visit with John, the Baptizer. Anger seethed within me. Jeshua looked as if he were going to tell me something but did not. I saw sadness in his eyes. It would not matter if he had said something to me. No one could have helped me.

After a day we met the rest of Jeshua's disciples and John the Baptizer at the Jordan and he began to teach us about discipleship. "John, here, has baptized many in the waters of the Jordan. This is a symbol of the cleansing that must be done to enter the Kingdom. It will be a symbol and a pledge of discipleship for this age."

He drew us near. "Come into the Jordan with me and be my disciples." The eight of us followed. "You are the first to enter the gate and know the kingdom. In the next age the initiation will be a baptism in the fire of the Holy Spirit. All who now believe in the Christ will also have to <u>know</u> the Christ from within to be an Initiate of the Christ."

John ("The Beloved") asked Jeshua, "What is the inner meaning of these symbols, water and fire?"

Jeshua explained, "In this new age we are entering, people will find the Christ within mostly through the fervor of their emotions. In the next age, they will find it directly through the perception of the Holy Spirit. This experience is not one of an emotional quality but one of inner knowing and inner joy. The emotions can still cause separation between peoples. Joy is calming and sees all as a part of the One. Baptism by fire burns away that which is not of the Spirit."

The crowd that was gathering expected to hear John speak. A Pharisee follower of John asked him, "Is this Jeshua now your foe? He has taken many of your disciples and is here to seek more. Why is he here?"

John stood and faced him: "Jeshua is the one for whom we have been waiting. My role was to pave the way for him so that he could do his work. I can testify that he has been through the highest initiation that a man can attain and has demonstrated the consciousness of Master. He has overcome the tests of the world and stands forward as a guide and a pattern for us to follow on our search for the Kingdom. I am pleased with your loyalty to me but I cannot be the teacher that Jeshua is; he is the Master and I, like you, am the student. In our age, power is seen as either force or wealth. Jeshua will show that Love is stronger. Jeshua has said that I am Elijah returned. If this be the case, I have done my part in preparing the way for him who must be Melchizedek returned, for his presence has brought me peace, more than I have known in this life."

We made for Galilee and left John the Baptizer at the Jordan. As many times before, we passed through Samaria. The trail was dusty and dry so we stopped at Sychar to drink at Jacob's Well. Jeshua told me to take the other seven disciples with me into town and purchase some bread.

When we returned the Master was talking with a Samaritan woman. "She is probably a prostitute," offered Nathaniel. "When you see an unescorted Samaritan woman, she is probably a prostitute." I admit I was a little irritated with his attitude because the Samaritans I had known were good people and I felt their honor was being needlessly soiled.

Before we approached she was off toward town and none of us made any mention of it to the Master. Jeshua bade us sit with him for a while. Philip offered Jeshua some food, for none of us had eaten since breakfast. "No, you eat," he said, "I find myself being fed from inside by my Father."

As he was talking, a crowd had arrived led by the woman that Jeshua had spoken to at the well. At once he got up and addressed us all, disciples and townsfolk: "You seem to think it is strange that I, a Galilean Jew, should talk with you. After all, we have our Temple and you have your Sacred Mountain and it is not likely that the mountain should come to the Temple or the Temple go to the Mountain."

Jeshua's words of wisdom and humor opened the hearts of all of us. I felt so filled up with joy that I momentarily forgot my own problems. He continued: "I tell you that the sun shines equally on the flowers here as there. There has been mistrust among our peoples. Judeans against Samaritans, Samaritans against Galileans, and Galileans against Judeans… it is all foolish, since we are all children of the same God. It does not matter whether we pray to him on the Sacred Mountain or in the Temple or in any synagogue, no place is more holy than any other. No matter where we are on the earth we can worship our Father from the Temple of the Heart, which is truly the Holiest of Holies. There are truly only two groups of people on this earth: those that turn to the Light and those who turn from the Light. It does not matter whether they are Judean, Galilean, Samaritans, Assyrian, Greek, or even Roman. We who turn to the Light must stand united."

An official of the local synagogue pushed his way to the front of the crowd and spoke to Jeshua. "It seems as though your reputation has preceded you. When we heard that Jeshua of Nazareth and the Nazarenes were here preaching in town, we thought you were here to stir up trouble. But in listening to what you have to say, I must disagree with that notion. I have heard nothing but Love, acceptance, and a true understanding and application of the Law. I offer you our synagogue in which to teach."

The crowd cheered as we walked to the synagogue. Jeshua stood on the pulpit and read from the Torah: *"In thee and in thy seed all the nations shall be blest."*

He replaced the scroll and said, "The children of Israel have been blessed by being chosen to teach the unity of God and Man. We cannot, however, teach what we do not practice in our daily lives. You who are priests, you must be the example of what you teach. One life lived from the perspective of the Soul is worth ten thousand written prayers and lessons. Let your life be a living lesson to those around you."

As he was teaching, a woman cried out from the congregation to be healed. Jeshua approached her but did not touch her body. A chill ran through my body and, as I looked around, others moved as if twitching from being pinched. The woman, who just a few moments ago looked close to death, stood up and thanked God. People were amazed and asked her what happened. She said she not only asked for healing from the Master, but actually saw it occurring.

Jeshua used this to bring forward another teaching. "It was this woman's intention to be healed. The strongest power in the universe is intention. Intention comes from the absolute knowing inside of you of what is to happen. It asks that you put your entire beingness in its power to follow it. It is more than faith; it is action. As you have seen, intention can change death to life. It can also change our flesh to spirit."

Saying that, he disappeared. I remembered that this was one of the techniques he had mastered in Tibet. He did not forget any of what he had learned, and used it to teach and enlighten. I had seen him do this before but it was the first time for the other disciples.

We headed back to Nazareth without Jeshua. The others were silent because they were still shaken by the Master's disappearance. After a while I thought it would be a good time to put all at ease with some stories about our times in Tibet. Just then, Jeshua appeared next to me and said, "Save the stories for your written account of our lives. The others will be able to read of it later."

While on our way back to Galilee we saw a large figure on horseback in the distance riding toward us at great speed. It was my old friend Petronius. It took him a moment to catch his breath, as if the world could not wait for him to speak. He bent down on one knee before Jeshua as a Roman soldier would do before the Emperor. "Master Jesus, forgive me... I have news. The Baptizer has been captured and taken by Herod to the castle of Machaerus. I know of many men who would gladly break in to set him free."

I probably would have been one of them and was ready to join Petronius but then the Master spoke. "Hold, good Petronius. We all feel hurt that John has been taken away from us and may never see daylight again. But think of him on our last encounter. He had the peace of the Holy Spirit with him. He knew that he had finished his task for this life and was at peace with it. All things in the eyes of God are perfect. All are a part of His plan. Life is not fair, my brothers, but it is just. Believe me when I say that all is in balance here. When I am done with my tasks, the powerful will do to me what they have done to John, for, as Joshua, I have also been the slayer of peoples. But be assured that no one escapes the consequences of his actions. The Law of Karma will not be mocked!"

I left Jeshua and the other disciples and went to Capernaum and waited for them. I needed to be alone and meditate and sort things out for myself. Just what in life did I have to look forward to? I ended up feeling uneasy so I took all my scraps of paper written in charcoal and penned them in permanent fashion for my book. For me writing was a great comforter. It was also quite beautiful by the sea. I enjoyed sitting on the shore and writing, listening to the crashing of the waves.

One day, I saw a boat off in the distance. Somehow I knew that Jeshua was on that boat. I packed up my gear and ran down the shore to get closer to the boat. I saw that Jeshua had Peter, John and James out on the boat with him, and I burst out laughing when I saw that they were <u>fishing</u>! My brother, Simon, and the others were on shore. There were two more, James and Thaddeus. These were cousins to Jeshua, the sons of Alpheus and Miriam. They were carpenters of Nazareth who were now set to follow Jeshua. They told me what had happened in Nazareth when Jeshua passed through. It seems that Jeshua had been teaching in the synagogue and had angered the *Parush.* They had actually grabbed him and tied him up and were about to throw him off a cliff when he disappeared. When they returned, they found him again in the synagogue, teaching. Their fear presided over their anger and they left

Jeshua alone from then on. Seeing all this, James and Thaddeus decided to follow their cousin on his path.

When the boat came back to shore, it was filled with fish. Peter jumped off the boat and fell on his knees. His face was filled with wonder as he talked of the miracle of the catch. Jeshua asked him, "Peter, does this convince you that our Father offers us abundance rather than scarcity?"

"Oh, yes, Master, I believe," he said.

"From now on you shall all be fishing for souls and there will be no scarcity of those who will come to you seeking peace and the blessings of Spirit. Those are the ones you shall catch."

We went walking on the beach and came to a tribute house, the office of a tax collector. The tax collector was a man named Matthew. Tax collectors were some of the most hated individuals in all of Judea. I had seen this particular tax collector in Jerusalem when Jeshua knocked over the tables, but I thought he might be a spy. I was glad to see I was wrong. Jeshua approached him as a friend. "Hail, servant of Cæsar. I have more important work for you if you will follow me."

He did not hesitate. With him was a Pharisee and a student of Greek philosophy named Thomas. He had come from Antioch to study with the Master in the school of the Sojourner. He approached Jeshua and said: "I had been a student of Apollonius of Tyana for a number of years. I believe that I was one of his most difficult students. It's not that I want to be difficult, but I just need to see the reality, the solid evidence of something before I can accept it as truth. I can't follow anyone blindly. I used to ask Apollonius for proof but he would always laugh and tell me that it was the student's job to prove himself to the Master, not the other way around. One day he told me that I should go to Galilee and follow you. He spoke very highly of you and said if anyone could convince me of the reality of Spirit, it would be you."

"Well Thomas," Jeshua said, "you are not the most trusting of men and I will not ask you for faith." The rest of us laughed quietly and Thomas appeared somewhat uncomfortable. "However, you do have a very sharp, critical mind. I cannot convince you of anything, and so I will not attempt to. If you decide to follow me, Thomas, it will be you who convinces yourself from your own experience. Come along. I have need of men of learning as well as men of faith, follow me."

We weren't sure whether Thomas came along out of his sense of duty to his prior master, Apollonius or his desire to try to figure out this peasant Galilean Teacher.

The next day Jeshua brought us all together, all twelve of us. "This is a taste of what is to come," he said. When we were together, we chanted the name of the Most High and were filled with a Light brighter than the sun. Then we were quiet. We all heard the name of God spoken inside of us and knew that the rest of us knew also. "You have been baptized in the flame of the Holy Spirit. Focus on this Word within you, within your souls, and you will have the keys to the Kingdom of God. You are my twelve initiates and apostles and you will be the ones who will spread the teachings of the Kingdom. Just as there were twelve tribes of Israel there will be twelve pillars of the Sojourner's School."

It seemed as though Jeshua had the full complement of spiritual warriors he needed for his battle with darkness. I wondered if the forces of darkness that would be pitted against us would have already been prepared and were in waiting for us. But I think my greatest fear was that I would not be worthy of the honor of serving. There were just so many personal issues that plagued me. When would the rest find me out?

Again the gavel sounded. I was ready this time with information that was esoteric enough so it was not common knowledge, yet was available to check to determine it authenticity.

On the stand again, I explained, "Jeshua told me (as Yehudah) that Apollonius had also visited the east, India, to be exact and that while there, there was a great meeting of the initiates of the Sojourner."

It took three days to research the material I supplied. Chris presented it to the court as further evidence that I was there to hear it directly.

When it came to cross-examine, Hastings replied, "Ladies and gentlemen of the jury, this is hardly evidence that confirms Mr. Hammer being there. Yes, it can be confirmed that Apollonius did visit India, it is available to be read by anyone in two books by Philostratus on Apollonius' life. The information that there was a meeting of initiates could just be another fanciful dream cooked up by Mr. Hammer and his vivid imagination. Gentlemen, you will have to do much better than this.

"Objection!" said Chris. But was silent afterwards.

"Yes, counselor?"

"Your honor, I object to the fact that whatever facts we can bring forward from memory here are either too available or not available enough."

"It could be, counselor, you are just not being as imaginative as you could be in presenting your information," answered the judge.

I could see that comment was being taken by Chris as a challenge and a very personal one at that.

I leaned over to Chris and in a whisper said, "Life is not fair, my brothers, but it is just."

"What's that?"

"From the manuscript."

"Oh," He said, looking somewhat perturbed.

There was an uncomfortable silence. Then I looked over at Chris. "We're running out of pages in this manuscript."

"I know, but something gonna turn up. I'm sure of it! It's <u>in</u> there."

As I left the courthouse for the night, I was deep in thought. I wanted very much to believe Chris. I fought against a sense of desperation that hugged me at every turn. When I got home, I called Eric for help but he was not available. I had myself and only myself. The manuscript had so many times told me that the place to turn was inside.

I turned every fiber of my being from desperation to intention. I WAS going to get beyond this! I started to focus inside and did the chant that Eric had taught me. My intention took over and I was again floating free. Eric's face came into view. "Reclaim your initiations," he said. I sent my focus back to the first century, back to mysteries. It was like I was dreaming. Sounds came to me. They were chants. I saw myself receiving the initiations and hearing the tones as they were given. They became familiar as I repeated them silently. I could feel the energy building inside of me. The pressure in my chest built up to a point where I thought I was about to have a heart attack. Then the pressure subsided and my body felt alive with electricity. I felt connected to the source of this energy and it was pulling me in. I lost consciousness and floated into an ocean of bliss.

I could have just remained there forever, but an alarm woke me. The sun was already rising. I didn't remember exactly where I had been but I felt more confident. It wasn't confidence in the outcome of the trial, but a more universal confidence that I would somehow be able to handle whatever was coming my way. There <u>was</u> an inner guide that I could access! And I knew it was in all of us.

CHAPTER 11 — THE NAZARENES

"Well, a new day, a new chapter to read," I said, "might as well begin."

"We are positively 'chipper' today, aren't we," said Chris, giving me a look of mock annoyance. "I haven't even had my coffee yet."

"I'm just going to surrender today. I'm just going to take this day as it comes."

"Just keep your wits about you."

"Just remember what you are here to do. You need to find an item in that manuscript you can use as evidence."

Chris called me to the stand yet another time and I began.

The boy who sat beside me in the small synagogue in Capernaum marveled at the way Jeshua taught. I studied the boy's smooth face and he appeared perhaps only a little older than I when I first met Jeshua. Jeshua had begun early this morning. He had been out walking alone before most of us, his twelve closest disciples, had awakened. It is entirely possible that he may have been the first in the synagogue this morning.

The boy looked up at me and into my eyes and spoke with a wisdom that I considered to be beyond his years: "He does not teach like the scribes and the *Parush*. He teaches as if he has the authority to speak, as if he knows."

I nodded to him and then I experienced clarity of thought that I had not had for some time. I wondered, "How would the world see Jeshua years from now?" Those disciples who are Roman and Greek see him almost as one of their gods. It would take very little coaxing to get them to worship him as some otherworldly being as they do with their own gods, quite removed from earthly life. If they were more aware of spiritual law, they would know that Jeshua is a man who is a master of that law. When one understands that spirituality follows laws and one is familiar with those laws, spiritual manifestations no longer appear to be magic, but a result of spiritual law.

I was taken deep into my own thoughts and I took the time to write them down:

"And I see him as being a hero, a hero in the truest sense. To me, he stands forward as a demonstration of what we could all attain in life. He has sacrificed all selfish aspirations that are the usual ones for human beings, and has allowed himself to be an instrument of the will of the Father of us all. He is a descendant of King David, so he actually has royal blood and could claim the throne. True, he is a rather poor relation, but how many descendants of King David are remaining? He could claim this leadership legally, but he chooses another path. Sometimes I wish he had claimed this throne. It sure would have made things easier. It would have united the factions and made us strong again. Instead he chose not to assume a political role. But then, perhaps that was wise. The Romans would have crucified him for sure. Still, he manages to do wondrous things for our people. I wish I had the courage to do it. I can, however, endeavor to be more like him. I can try to look beyond my petty jealousies, hatreds and fears and be the best disciple I can be. He is my friend; I feel I owe him that. No, it is my responsibility to do that. And it won't matter if I am not acknowledged for it. He is my master and teacher. Thank God that he isn't a god. It would make his accomplishments unattainable by us mere mortals. It would remove us from our responsibility to follow him and strive to attain his closeness to Spirit. It would then be more appropriate to stay where we are and worship him, rather than getting up and following him. It makes life all the more difficult but it also gives us an ultimate goal to pursue.

I wonder how many others see him as I do. I guess it depends upon one's definition of 'heroic.' I can see it in the eyes of his other disciples. I see it in the eyes of the people he has healed or touched in some way. I often see it in the eyes of the followers of Hillel's teachings and many of the Essenes also. Certainly not the *Parush* or the Sadducees. They see him as a destroyer of their way of life. Someone whose philosophy makes their own appear invalid would indeed be seen as an enemy. Their natural allies in this would be the Roman command. I shudder to think what will happen when that sleeping dog awakes."

My thoughts were shattered by the noise of Peter running through the synagogue to get to Jeshua. At once Jeshua was silent, but there was some grumbling in the congregation. These folks did not like their prayer time interrupted by anything. Peter spoke loudly so that most everyone in the neighborhood could hear: "It's my wife's mother, she's come down with a high fever and she needs your help, Master."

Jeshua nodded and spoke to the congregation. "You see that the plans of men are not considered by God. Things from the world can intrude even into our holy time. Do not let this disturb you, my brothers and sisters. If you think of our Father all day long, then you will not miss a time to talk to Him. If you chant the names of God continually, your whole life will be a prayer."

With that, he moved toward the door of the synagogue with us, his disciples, in tow. I noticed two additional faces in the exiting entourage, Jeshua's brothers, James and Yehudah (my namesake). I embraced both of them and shared with them how good it was that they had joined us. Now there were three from the past (these two and my brother, Simon) that I could talk to on a regular basis. I had felt like an arm had been amputated when John was imprisoned. I had not yet felt as comfortable with the other disciples as I did with these old friends.

A crowd followed us to the house of Peter's mother-in-law. They had flocked to the house but were prevented from entering by the imposing figure of Peter at the door. Among the people outside were those who were crying out for healing. Jeshua came from behind Peter and addressed the crowd, "I will be coming out after I see this woman. Be patient and quiet. Focus on the power of God within each of you that performs the healing." The crowd became silent and reverent.

Jeshua looked lovingly at Peter's wife and mother-in-law. All he said was, "There is nothing to fear."

He placed one hand on her forehead. The other hand he held over different parts of her abdomen. He closed his eyes and chanted in barely audible tones. In minutes the fever had broken and she arose from the bed. She was still a little wobbly from the fever but could walk with the help of Peter's wife. Jeshua gave her instructions on what to do to in order to complete the cleansing. The rest of us moved outside into the middle of the silent crowd.

Jeshua then emerged from the house. He was met by a number of people seeking to be healed. A man in the crowd suddenly went to the ground as if he had been thrown. This man was possessed and the spirits fought for the voice of the man. The din was awful. They screamed, "Please, master, do not destroy us!"

Jeshua spoke a few holy words and the spirits fled. The man awoke as if after a dream and asked what had happened. The last thing that he remembered was standing in the crowd. Jeshua explained to him that the spirits would be back unless this man changed his behavior. "You know what you do and how to stop it," he told the man. The man bowed his head. "I know this man's transgressions," Jeshua said. "They are little different from those of the rest of us, but this man has judged and condemned himself for them and has given away his power to lead his own life." He looked into the man's eyes. "I would tell you, brother, that you cannot escape your own creations because you are a child of God, and therefore are responsible for what you create. You really have no choice in the matter. You can either go on condemning your life and wishing to escape from it (in which case, the spirits will be back) or you can forgive yourself and heal the inner wounds that you suffer. The choice is yours."

With that Jeshua moved on to the next man, a follower of the Sadducees, who was a leper. He spent a long time with this man talking about the Kingdom of God.

"How could one such as I ever hope to attain it?" the man asked.

Jeshua said, "If that is your primary focus and your ultimate intention, no one will be able to prevent you from having it."

"How..."

"By wanting it more than your next breath," Jeshua answered the unfinished sentence. "You can start now. Take a deep breath and hold it and I'll tell you when to release it."

It seemed like forever. The man's face became as red as a beet. Finally as if his lungs were about to explode, the man let out the stale air that was in his lungs and gasped for his next breath.

"Do you see how much your body wanted that breath?" Jeshua asked. When you want the kingdom that much, it will be yours. <u>This</u> is a clear intention. Now do the same with your illness. Want your healing as much as you want your breath."

Jeshua never touched the man but held his hands over the areas of the man's body that had the rash. The man let out a whelp of surprise. He had felt a burning sensation in the area under Jeshua's hands. The reddened skin peeled off revealing unmarked skin underneath.

"Thank you, Master..."

"You need not thank me. It was you, your Soul, which did the healing. Tell no one about this healing. Instead, following your tradition, show yourself to the priests and make the offering for your healing what the law demands of you."

The man was overcome with joy and rather than go to the priests, he went to the market and told everyone he could find.

The crowd had grown by now to a few times what it had been in the beginning. There were other followers of the Sadducees in the crowd now who were not as joyful at Jeshua's deeds.

"We hear that you heal on the Sabbath and the law strictly forbids it."

Jeshua, seeing an opportunity to teach, responded: "I ask you, then, do people get well on the Sabbath?"

The Sadducees answered warily. They had heard of Jeshua's ability to master a debate. "Yes, of course."

"All healing actually comes from the Father. And if the Father works on the Sabbath, why not the Son?"

"What tradition do you follow that you would claim to be a Son of God, the most high?"

"I follow our own. Who was Adam's father? Where did Adam come from? He came from God. Was he not God's offspring? And since we are all children of Adam, are we not all sons of the same God? Those that live a holy life are more conscious of that fact and can manifest that fact by being a co-creator with the Father. Did He not give us dominion over everything on the Earth? Human beings are truly God's emissaries to the earth. This means that we are able to heal the sick, send away trouble-some spirits and even raise the dead. All people are sons of God so these abilities are part of our birthright. God, in His wisdom, will not let us use these powers until we are ready and can use them in a responsible fashion. This is why we must take the first step toward His kingdom. A person who is not living in God's kingdom inside of himself is still an unknowing servant of the negative power. He is still ruled by his emotions and ignorance. Living separated from God's Kingdom is like a living death. Most walk around dead but never know it. If you would only break the bonds that hold you and step into the Light, you would see all that is possible for you. When one masters his lower self, only then is he able to manifest his creatorship from his higher self. This I have done, so think it not strange. It takes but one man to accomplish something. Then others can know it can be done."

Words flowed from Jeshua effortlessly. He continued. "If you live your life from the body and consciousness of God then you are as one with the Father and when someone sees you, they will, then, also be seeing the Father. This takes the sacrifice of all earthly attachments you hold dear, since you must allow God, the Father, to live through you, the Son. You do not lose your individuality and you can still participate at will in what is of this world but you gain much more in surrendering your own desires and illusions. If you do this you will learn that your life is eternal because you are living it in and through the Father, who is eternal. But if you turn away from your Father's kingdom, you will be subject to return to this world again and again to pay the debts you owe to yourselves and others. The problem is that this earth is set up so that you may not be able to pay faster than you accrue. But since our Father is a loving father, He would not see you abandoned in your own ignorance. He sends a comforter to you and this comforter is called "The Sojourner." The Sojourner is a part of all humanity and it speaks to you from inside with a voice such as mine. Many have tried to get to The Sojourner by attempting to quiet the mind and the emotions. You might as well try to hold back the Nile! Instead, place your focus and attention on God, and The Father will place his attention on you. Chant the names of God! When something good happens to you, chant the names of God. When you come to some evil, chant the names of God. If nothing is happening, chant the names of God. If you spend your every waking moment in God's consciousness, you offer yourself to that consciousness. Do you understand?"

The Sadducees had long since left but Jeshua continued teaching and talking to those in the crowd about God's Kingdom. This lasted most of the day and I became too weary to write most of it. I knew that in the morning we had to leave early, so that Jeshua could visit with Lazarus and his family.

When we arrived in Bethany we were treated to a great feast. Lazarus and Ruth had heard how the number of Jeshua's followers had grown and wished to celebrate and honor both him and his disciples. Ruth ran up and threw her arms around Jeshua. She was gushing and tears of joy were pouring down her face. "All is now fine with Asher and me. Thank you so much for your loving, caring and good advice."

Jeshua smiled broadly as he hugged her. "Nothing that I said would have had any value if the loving was not already present. When love is there, it desires a way to communicate and let itself be known. You were talking in different languages so the loving was not perceived. I was merely the translator."

Jeshua would often speak to people who doubted or hated themselves in this manner. He would not only give them hope, but also show that they had some power of choice in their lives. My thinking was halted by a shock. I was almost knocked over by a *Parush* who was trying to get to Jeshua as fast as he could. Normally, I would have reacted in a martial fashion, but I saw the face of this *Parush* and his look of gratitude. It was Ruth's husband, Asher.

"Jeshua," he said, "I am so grateful for what you said to Ruth. We are getting along so much better now."

When this *Parush* clasped Jeshua's hand in friendship I almost dropped my teeth.

"I am not yet ready to join you Nazarenes on your path, but you are good men and you have my blessing. You and your disciples are welcome in my house any time."

Jeshua smiled at Asher. "If your path is one of loving you stand with us. Then you and I are disciples of the same inner master, whose pathway is loving."

Jeshua's conversation was cut short by the smell of smoke and the screams of townspeople. A woman was shouting that her child was trapped on an upper floor of a burning building. Jeshua stopped all movement and appeared to go into a state of deep meditation. He took a deep breath and rushed off to the site of the burning building. The fire was raging and the heat from the flames kept all but the bravest away from the house. Jeshua held up his hands to the fire and uttered a prayer in Sanskrit. I could feel that the heat was immediately reduced. He sped into the house and up the stairs. I thought for sure that he would not return with anyone who was alive. It seemed like only a moment but he reappeared with a child in his arms. It was a bittersweet moment. The townspeople were joyful that no one had lost their life in the fire, but more than a few families had lost all their possessions.

A number of people had seen the rescue and were amazed by Jeshua's control of the fire. "The energy of the Father is in all things and all things are alive. When man learns to communicate with the elements, he will be able to work with them. That, too, is our birthright."

Then Jeshua felt a pull on his sleeve. A young girl asked him to help her father and mother. Her father had become the town drunk. He had been an important member of the community before he lost his self-respect. After that the rest of the townspeople lost respect for him too. This man was a carpenter as was Jeshua in his youth, so he was able to make a good living, but he would spend all his money on drink and the rest of the family went hungry. His time would be spent either drinking or recovering from drinking. "Please open his heart," the little girl asked. "When he's not drinking, he's kindest, most gentle man I know."

Jeshua returned a few minutes later with the man and showed him the destruction that had occurred. "These people need your help to rebuild their homes."

When this man saw the suffering of his neighbors, he stood motionless and tears rolled down his face. "It's not that I don't feel the suffering of your loss," he said to them, "but I feel great joy that I am again useful and needed." He reached out and brought his wife, daughter, and two sons close to him. "And as I rebuild your homes, I will rebuild my own."

Jeshua saw the amazement in my eyes. He beckoned me closer so only I could hear. "Here is a man reborn, Yehudah. All he ever wanted to feel was a little hope, and he was rewarded with a trusted place in his community. We all need to feel wanted and worthy, Yehudah. I know that you have been feeling left out when it comes to sharing time with me, and this may have affected you emotionally, but things have changed and I must take on a larger role. I need you not only to maintain our finances but also to be a silent support system for our group. I need you to stay in the background and allow the newer disciples to feel useful and needed as well. If you remember the chants we learned in Tibet to hold and maintain the Light, I need you to do that for us."

Jeshua was always loving, always teaching, always trying to get whoever he was with to step into their full potential as a spiritual being. He never separated himself from others but was always quick to include himself with those he taught. There were times when those among us questioned his attention to one group of people or another. He would just say, "The sun shines equally on all places and so does the love of God. If that is the case for my Father, why should it be any different for me?"

The next morning Jeshua alerted us that it would be a day for learning, so I took my paper and charcoal with me on our visit to a mountain near the sea.

"I am going to talk to you about prayer," Jeshua began. "What it is and what it is not. Prayer is the communication of the soul with God. It is done purely to communicate with the Father. It is <u>not</u> done so that others can see how pious you are and judge you a 'good person.' It does not matter if you pray alone or in the midst of hundreds in a large synagogue, our Father will always hear your prayers. We worship our Father in Spirit, and the form matters little. But in this physical existence we often need a form as a means to relate to something we cannot see, so I will provide a form which you can use."

"The first part of a prayer is to call on the name of God. We have chanted together the names of God so you know that this will differ depending upon what realm of existence we are dealing with. The most effective way is to reach the highest realm possible and call on 'the highest God.' If we call on our ancient, tribal God, Jehovah, we are talking to a God who is too small. We would do no better than calling on Jupiter or Zeus or any of the Pagan gods. The true nature of God is too immense for man to comprehend when man is not experiencing the consciousness of God. The Sanskrit name 'HU' is the ancient term for the true nature of God, that which is everywhere and is all things seen and unseen. In our Aramaic, it is *Alaha*, in Arabic, *Allah*, but it means the same thing, the Oneness of God. This God is both our Father and Mother and indeed all things. This God encompasses the male, the female, the 'good,' the 'evil' and there is nothing that is not a part of this God. You have heard me talk of 'my Father' and 'our Father' but remember that I am talking about the whole nature of God that is both masculine and feminine and all pairs of opposites. There is no separation. The correct name would be 'our Father-Mother-God' but you may use 'our heavenly Father' if you wish, if you understand that this also includes the feminine aspect of creation.

"The ultimate source of the Light of God comes from the sound of God's Name. So I ask that His name be resonant within me and that my life be lived in His name.

"I also ask that I be kept aware of the presence of His kingdom continually. But more than that, I desire that I might be the Emissary of that kingdom to all, that all might see as I do. Therefore I ask that His Kingdom be universally present.

"I ask that the intention of God also be my intention, for the more we ally ourselves with His intention the more our life becomes one of ease and bliss. I ask that I be a clear vessel that His Light could shine through. I ask that His desires and goals be also mine.

"I ask Him to grant me what I need to fulfill my tasks each day. This means food for both the body and the Soul. I not only ask for our daily bread but our daily wisdom to fuel our understanding of how to get closer to God in our purpose.

"Our Father knows us in our hearts and he forgives our errors in judgment, our failures, and our mistakes. He forgives often more than we are able to forgive ourselves. I would ask him to allow me to let go of these judgments I have placed on myself and also that I may be like him in forgiving others as he forgives me. For as I deal with others God will deal with me. Many times Karmic debts just need to be 'let go' to be done. Ask for the wisdom to know when to let these go.

"The job of the negative forces is to delude us from our true purpose, that of coming back to our father. We ask that we are not deluded by the appearances of this level and then act in an inappropriate manner, thus bringing more karmic debt. Since the Law of Karma is that of Cause and Effect, seek to be the Cause rather than the effect. Choose not reaction for that is effect. Decide what is for the highest good and act upon that. In this way we become co-creators with our Father. We get to fulfill the circle. We are cause and create on the higher levels and reap the benefit of the effect on earth.

"Such a prayer might sound like this:

'Father-Mother God,
may your name resonate inside of me,
may Thy kingdom be known by all,
may Thy will be my will.
Grant us each day what life requires
and let us forgive our debts as we forgive others'
and don't allow appearances to delude us, but
strengthen us in our purpose.
For out of You comes all things, in power, in beauty,
and in Love for all time.
The blessings were, and are, and ever will be.
So be it.'

"I will not always be with you, so you will have to go forth alone as bearers of Light to the world and as emissaries to God's kingdom. Go first to our countrymen, then to the world. Tell them: 'The Kingdom is already present, it is at hand.'

"Tell them also: 'If the Kingdom is in your heart, then truly, you will see the Kingdom everywhere you go.' For every destination there are signposts, and it is no different with God's kingdom. But these signposts are inside of you and they appear as blessings:

Blessed are those whose intention is Spirit, for theirs is the Kingdom.

Blessed are those who are ordinary and seek not greatness, for they will be truly great.

Blessed are those who ache for truth, for they shall find it.

Blessed are those who extend Grace to their brothers, for they shall receive Grace from our Father.

Blessed are those who master the self, for they shall have the keys to the Kingdom.

Blessed are the pure in heart, for they shall see God in all things.

Blessed are those who reach out to others in peace, for they are manifesting God's Kingdom.

"Do not be discouraged when the world persecutes and curses you. Instead be glad, for your way of loving is not of this world. Thus were vilified the prophets and masters before you; cursed during their lives only to be honored later, after they had gone. Know that your Father honors you now. The curses of the world only show your worthiness in Spirit. For those that vilify you are ignorant and do not know what they do; they curse you one day and praise you the next. Emotions change with the tides, but our Father's love is constant. And do not rejoice when they reap the rewards of their foolishness, but offer them understanding and forgiveness for your kindness will be a beacon to God's kingdom. Do not hide your Light under a bushel, place it high so that others can see and be guided by it and honor God."

"Many see me as dangerous to their way of life. They say I speak and act against the Law. I have not come to revoke the Law, but to fulfill it. Man's law changes daily. God's Law is fixed in Spirit and cannot be nullified. The heavens and the earth will pass away long before the Laws of Spirit. These will pass only when they have been fulfilled. Those who disregard God's laws and teach others to do the same will pay the price of return. Those that keep God's Laws and live in harmony with them shall live within the Christ. Follow the Spirit of the Law — it is written in your heart."

When Jeshua had finished he answered many of our questions. Many were of a personal nature that I will not reveal here. There were also a number of discussions that dealt with scriptural points. These were much like discussions that students had with their teachers for thousands of years. These teachings always had more hidden within them, waiting for the student to get to the next level.

After that long day of teaching we headed back to Capernaum. I had received a note from Petronius to meet him in a certain place and to bring Jeshua with me.

As we approached the place of meeting I saw that Petronius had with him a Roman Centurion. Petronius hated the Roman military more than I did, if that was possible; how could he have turned? I grabbed hold of Jeshua's arm to hold him back, but he just laughed and told me that everything was all right. We approached at Jeshua's normally speedy pace.

Petronius stepped forward, "Please, Master Jesus, this man is not your enemy and he desperately needs your help." We learned that this particular centurion who lived in Capernaum had a great love for the local Jewish community. He used some of his wealth to help them build a synagogue. It happens that a beloved servant of this centurion had become ill and paralyzed. He had heard of Jeshua and how he healed the sick and had faith that Jeshua could heal his servant.

Getting down on one knee and bowing, the centurion said, "Master Jesus, I ask you to help my servant for he is deathly ill, but you should not come to my house for it is not worthy. I am a man of war who commands men to take the lives of others in battle. If you speak the names of God, I know that my servant will be healed."

Jeshua placed his hand on the shoulder of the kneeling officer. "Rise, for you have great faith and that will be rewarded. Your servant will be well. And I would not be accepting any dishonor by visiting you. Some of the people who are my closest friends are also men of war. Is that not true, Yehudah?"

I thought for sure that it would be the cross for me, but Spirit was truly shining on me that day for the centurion said, "Yes, Judas Iscariot, Judas the *Sicarri*, that is a name I have not heard for a while. I do not think there is any Roman officer who has not heard of you," he said without a trace of malice. "None will admit it, but the Roman command has a grudging admiration for your strategy and methods of warfare. I am sorry we are on opposite sides, I would appreciate the opportunity to fight side-by-side with you."

"Yehudah is wondering why you do not arrest him right now," Jeshua said.

"I have no political ambitions. I am happy with my life the way it is, so I do not need to ingratiate myself through the capture of Judas. As long as he is a follower of yours, Master Jesus, I do not fear for the lives of the men under my command. Do you not teach the forgiveness of past actions?"

Jeshua smiled and nodded. "It would seem that the two of you are fighting on the same side after all."

People came from all over the known world to our "home base" in Capernaum to learn wisdom at Jeshua's feet. They came to learn the mysteries of "The Way." He taught them to learn, he taught them to teach, and he taught them to be. He was the living example of what a human life could be when touched by God-consciousness. He showed what man could attain.

Word of Jeshua's teachings spread to places as far as Tibet and as dark as Herod's prison. John had heard of the works that Jeshua was doing and he must have expected that things would be otherwise because he sent messengers to Jeshua. These messengers asked him "Are you the one of whom the prophets wrote or did I err, is the one yet to come?"

Jeshua just told these messengers to observe him for a few days about his work and then report what they saw back to John and he would know. We stepped out onto the street and a crowd began to gather in the anticipation of some words of wisdom from Jeshua.

Peter asked Jeshua if he was going to do anything about John.

"I hold John in my dearest heart of hearts for he was not only a lifelong friend but a fellow co-creator of Light. I ask that the Holy Spirit be sent to comfort him. I ask that the Sojourner be felt inside him to lift him in times of doubt and fear. I place it all into the hands of the Father because he is the One here in command. Then if the Father is the one running everything (and He is), then I tell you, all is as it should be. We will not be taken away before our time so there is nothing to fear. Our Father has a plan for each of us and all is perfect within that plan."

Peter asked: "How does John fit into that plan?"

"We are all lanterns on the way to a greater expression of God in man," said Jeshua. "John came to pave the way for the work that I do. I will pave the way for even greater advances. In my opinion, there is none greater than John. This man that Herod bound and cast into the depths of prison is Elijah re-embodied. He lived as he taught and he taught repentance and preparation for the coming of the kingdom. He spoke and many listened, were baptized, and found their path to the Kingdom of God. Others missed this opportunity to come back from the wilderness.

"John's manner was austere, he lived as an Essene monk and he drank no wine. For this people called him an obsessed wild-man and made jokes at his expense. Now I come, eating and drinking with the common man, and I am judged as having no morals." He shook his head and his laugh was tinged with sadness. "When the Light comes into the darkness, darkness does not know it. People ask for signs and yet they cannot see the truth right in front of them. There is also no pleasing those who will not find themselves pleasing. If John and I descended from heaven on white horses, in golden chariots with fire erupting from our heels, and came down right into the center of town, we would be judged that we did not clean up after our horses."

We all chuckled but felt Jeshua's frustration at the inability to reach those who needed it most. He lifted his eyes to heaven and spoke, "*Abba*[10], I thank you for unveiling the Light and the truth to the innocent for it appears to be hidden from the wise."

He turned to the crowd that had gathered and said, "Of myself, I can do nothing. The wisdom that I share with you comes from Spirit. These are not my words; I merely pass on what I receive. In this way, the Father talks through his children. Take up with me the burden of the

---

10 Father (familiar).

Christ. It is not a heavy burden. It is a labor of love. The more of us who pull this load, the easier it gets. Follow me."

A rich, prominent *Parush* in the town, Simon, son of Nathaniel, gave a banquet in Jeshua's honor. I had the impression that this man's heart was not in it. His manner was condescending and he did not offer us the care that one would find in a simple meal with friends. I was sure that he was doing this merely for appearance, but *why*?

A woman who had been a prostitute and had decided to change her ways after hearing Jeshua, came to the feast uninvited. Her face shone with the glow of freedom as someone who has just recovered control of her life after a long period of slavery. After the meal, she sat at Jeshua's feet. Tears of joy streamed down her face. With these tears she washed his feet and anointed them with costly oil.

Jeshua saw the look of disdain in the eyes of the *Parush.* He turned to one of his guards and whispered so he could barely be heard: "What kind of prophet is this who would accept favors from this type of woman?"

Jeshua could not have heard this from where he was sitting but he did get the essence of the communication. "My host, may I have a word with you?"

"Certainly."

"What is sin?" asked Jeshua.

"Sin is wrongdoing." The *Parush* answered.

"Sins can be large or small, something done or left undone, any instance of 'missing the mark' or inappropriate action. Would you agree?"

"Yes."

Jeshua continued: "One person leads a life of wrongdoing and then decides to leave it all behind and sin no more. Another person, unconcerned, careless, forgets to do the things he should do and is forgiven. Which of these is more worthy of praise for his actions?"

Simon answered: "The one who changed his life, of course."

"You are right, Simon. This woman washed my feet with her tears, dried them with her hair, and anointed them with costly oil. She did this to express her gratitude because, after hearing me speak, decided to change her life and was forgiven. On the other hand you did not even offer me a bowl of water to wash my hands and feet, which is a common courtesy in a Jewish household. I ask you again, Simon, who is most worthy of praise?"

The *Parush* did not answer. Jeshua turned to the woman and said, "Your sins are forgiven, go with the Father."

Simon then asked Jeshua, "Who are you to forgive her sins? That can be done only by God."

"I am but stating the obvious, Simon. Look at her face if you doubt that she is forgiven. Any fool can tell that she is already forgiven by the way the Light shines in her eyes and through her tears. Our Father forgives us all, but <u>you</u> must take this forgiveness inside of you and forgive your own sins and turn your back on unworthiness."

Again, Simon said nothing to Jeshua, but turned to the guard and said, "Make sure that Saul knows all about this."

Ah, that mystery man again. I decided to follow this guard and discover more about this Saul.

I hid myself in the shadows until this man left. I had to be careful about being seen since I was wearing white robes, not the black night clothes of the *Sicarri*. By the actions of this man, I knew that he had no idea he was being followed. He was headed to Jerusalem. Knowing his route, I could comfortably hang back and did not need special measures to avoid his gaze. The one difficulty in this was avoiding other travelers. Those that passed us on the way to Jerusalem might let him know that someone else is behind. If this man were the least bit suspicious, he would then not head for his true destination. It was a good feeling to be living in nature again. I had missed the clarity it often brings. Traveling for days alone was a truly refreshing experience.

All went well entering Jerusalem. As I surmised, this man headed right for the Temple. He was going to meet someone inside and since it was by then daylight, I would have a very difficult time getting past the guard. I had a plan, but I had to act quickly. I swung my leg across a low stone wall to take the first layer of skin off and create the appearance of much blood for a very slight wound. I assumed a bent posture and called a guard over as if I needed help. After that, it was easy. I simply and easily rendered him unconscious and exchanged clothes with him. In his uniform, I could easily go to almost anywhere in the Temple. I chuckled thinking about Petronius and him wondering if I had lost my touch. If he could see me now, he would take notice!

I assumed the purposeful stride of a Temple guard and headed toward the chambers that I knew to be empty of activity at this time of day. My foresight was rewarded. I heard muted voices coming from a chamber down the hall. The man who I was following was talking to a twisted figure of a man. This man was dressed as a *Parush* but walked with a decided limp as though one leg was shorter than the other. His accent was decidedly foreign, tinged with Greek, a Jew of the Diaspora. From the accent I heard, I would place it somewhere near Tarsus.

Pacing up and down this chamber, he was formulating plans concerning Jeshua. “We must expand our network to keep up with the travels of these Nazarenes. We need more agents. We also need some who would be willing to join this group and give us regular reports.”

At last I knew what this Saul was up to. Right now his game was espionage. What he could do, I could do (and had done) better. Through Petronius, I still had links to the *Sicarri* and through my brother, Simon, links to Zealots. I had what I had come for and returned to where I had placed the unconscious body of the guard. I quickly exchanged clothes with him and disappeared from the city. As soon as I could, I washed my scraped leg and placed some healing cream upon it. I felt more of a sense of ease knowing what our opposition was, and alternated my periods of chanting with internal strategy sessions. Alone, I moved quickly and was back in Capernaum in a few days. When I arrived, I discovered that Jeshua and his disciples had left for Magdala.

When I arrived in that company, Nathaniel filled me in on the events that occurred. Jeshua’s cousin Mary (of Magdala) had ended her relationship with the wealthy man of Magdala and came to Jeshua, asking for forgiveness for her sins of adultery. Jeshua offered her forgiveness. She wished to devote the rest of her life to our group and asked Jeshua if she could join the disciples. Many of Jeshua’s followers were upset concerning this, especially Peter. Not only would she be the first female disciple (not just a follower) but one with a decidedly unsavory past. Jeshua had rebuked him and taught again about forgiveness.

I listened but there was a part of me that was beyond listening. I wanted Mary of Magdala and she didn’t even notice me. Now she would be a fellow disciple and near me all the time. I would not be able to escape my hurt since it was to be in front of me all the time.

She had accumulated some possessions, no doubt from being this rich man’s mistress. She had her own home in Magdala to which she had the audacity to invite us. As we dined Jeshua talked about the Kingdom. “Do not fear my disciples; you shall all be rulers in the kingdom of the soul. There is one thing of which you must be aware, and that is the ruler in the kingdom of the Soul is the servant of mankind. To whom much is given, much is expected. This is a job that must be performed full-time.”

The next day Jeshua taught in the great hall of Mary’s house. A man came forward and asked Jeshua to convince the man’s brother to give him a fair share of the inheritance of their father.

To this Jeshua said, "I did not come to force men to do the right thing. In all men there exists knowledge of what is right and what is wrong, but many do not listen to it. Greed and selfishness cloud their eyes so that they cannot sense the rights of others. But, in truth, all things belong to God. What we 'own' is merely borrowed for a very limited time. The real wealth lies in the Soul and it lasts forever. It consists of the wisdom and experience that one gathers while here. If you spend all of your time chasing after the wealth of the world that will be gone in an instant, what time will you have to stockpile the eternal treasures? If you are so focused on wealth that you avoid the spirit, then it is better that you give away your remaining wealth to the poor and learn to trust in God."

"But Master, it is so difficult to trust when I have no wealth to keep me from prison due to debt."

Jeshua continued: "Do you not think that your Father knows of your difficulties? He cares for every living thing, birds, flowers, trees, insects, stars, planets and moons. He knows every hair on your head and every angel in heaven. Without his knowledge and consent a sparrow would not fall to earth. If he cares for a sparrow, two of which you could purchase for a farthing in the marketplace, would he not care for one who bears His image in the Soul?"

"Master, then why are there poor who struggle to stay alive and often starve?"

Jeshua answered: "When you understand <u>why</u> we are here on earth you will understand the answer to this question. Our souls are immortal. The lives we live here on earth are for the education of the Soul. Our Father placed us here to gain understanding and that is the reason why we are here. If a person in one lifetime cannot sense the rights of others, and metes out abuse, it is through ignorance that he acts. The debt that is built through ignorance must be paid in this lifetime or another. It is not for punishment but for understanding that the individual soul may come into the same circumstances of the ones he may have abused, in order to know what that behavior is and to avoid it in the next life or in lives to come. It is merely cause and effect. On the other hand, a starving person may have agreed to take on that role for the benefit of others, so we cannot look at someone and judge him for his situation in life. It is for this reason that our best response is love and forgiveness. If you only look at one lifetime, life and God seem unfair indeed. But things <u>are</u> all in order. Let God balance the scales, for He is the only one who knows how. Bless your brother, for he will reap what he sows, and then make the best choices <u>you</u> can to go on with <u>your</u> life."

Then I saw Jeshua break in a great smile. It was Tuzla! I went over to where Tuzla was in the crowd and hugged him. Following him was

Jeshua's brother James. "I knew that I came here for a purpose," Tuzla began, "and I did not know what that purpose was when I began my trip from Tibet, but I think it may have been to deliver to you some bad news."

Jeshua made his way over to us and said to Tuzla, "Your purpose is much more than that but it is good that bad news be brought by someone who is such a dear friend."

"Nevertheless I must share this with you, that John, the Baptizer, is dead."

James, quiet until now, began to sob. Jeshua did the best to comfort his brother, but I could see that there was something deeper here. "Jeshua, John is gone and I am lost. Now I am wondering: are <u>you</u> to be my new master? I feel that no one can take the place of John."

"My dear brother," said Jeshua, "John would want you to follow your heart. What John taught and what I teach are not so different. I may be your master for a short time, but soon it will be you who is master, and your mastership will be a beacon for all who love truth. Take leadership of the followers of John; give them the love that he imparted to you. Soon you will lead my followers as well."

The presence of Tuzla softened the blow of losing John. Tuzla told us the entire story of the murder of John and that his body was buried in Hebron. James told us that there was great sadness among the Essenes and John's followers in the Nazarenes. Jeshua spoke to all who were there: "If you seek a safe haven from the evils of the world, leave me now, for I will be dealt with as was John."

CHAPTER 12 - FROM DISCIPLE TO APOSTLE

Jeshua began: "'Hear O Israel, the Lord thy God, the Lord is One.' Those words are very powerful since they speak a great truth to us. God is One and All is God. There is nothing that is not God. God is the constant in all activities. Let's look at the action of loving. When you love someone, it is God that is doing the loving. It is also God that is being loved. In fact, it is God that is the Love itself. God is a part of every element of our being and there is no place you can go where God is not. When you read from the scriptures that we have our coming and going in the body of God, that body is not an empty shell. We are the living parts of that body and when we begin to know this inside of us, we have entered God's Kingdom. When you are in God's kingdom you truly know and are known by God. When you have entered the Kingdom of God, the eyes with which you see God are the same eyes with which He sees you. It is the most intimate and the most natural of all relationships. Are you beginning to understand just how close we are to our Father?"

We were attending a great feast, which Matthew had prepared in order to welcome Jeshua home to Capernaum. I had really begun to respect Matthew. Though he had been a tax collector and may have, as tax collectors are known to do, collected more than what was due, he had a keen mind for business and had amassed quite a fortune. But here he was spending it not only to give back some of what he had taken, but also to give more. He was bringing others the teaching of The Way. He even brought some of his old friends to meet Jeshua. He's still a great businessman. He keeps more accurate records than I could do. I suggested to Jeshua that he take over the handling of our finances.

Over the short period of time that I have known Matthew, he has been changing. Many of us had been changed through our desire to live Jeshua's teachings. Mary of Magdala's appearance had changed. She is no longer gaudy in order to attract. She has removed much of her makeup and is dressing more simply, allowing her natural beauty to shine through. I can see her becoming a truly devoted disciple. I see the loving that she bears in her eyes. I still find it very difficult to talk to her, because it still brings up an ache inside of me. I ache for her, but I have lost my anger towards her, so, perhaps even I can change.

Today, all in the town were invited to this feast and most were having a good time. However, there were some *Parush* sitting at the table next to me and instead of enjoying themselves, they were finding fault with Jeshua. They complained that if this teacher, meaning Jeshua, was supposed to be a man of God, then how could he spend his time eating and drinking with tax collectors, loose women and all manner of common men?

I had had enough. I turned to them and spoke: "If you are so wise, then how can you focus on the outer appearances of a teacher and ignore his teaching? Look at those who you call 'common,' for you have much to learn from them. They are taking in these teachings as the parched take in their first cup of water. They know wisdom when they hear it. If a donkey gave true wisdom, they would have the sense to listen. You are wasting your time here and irritating those around you. I suggest you leave." I would have had great pleasure in personally escorting them from the street, but Jeshua had overheard and drew near and put his hand on my shoulder to stay further action on my part.

"You question the company that I keep. It is true that I often spend time with sinners. You claim to be 'learned men.' How can you miss the obvious? Does a doctor spend his time with those that are well? Would you not expect him to be found among the sick? Sinners too, are my brothers and sisters, and they deserve no less than I would give to you. I often spend my time with those upon whom the world has turned its back. I spend my time comforting them because their need is greater. They thirst and hunger for the truth of Spirit. They sin because they do not know the way back to their Father. I act as their wayshower for this path. Those who are not sick do not need to be healed. They need less of my time. Are you like jealous siblings competing for their mother's affections? I have also spent time healing lepers. Would you trade your life with theirs for more of my time?"

The *Parush* were shamed, and most left. There was one who stood his ground and spoke to Jeshua with a sneer in his voice. "You people are transparent. We see the falseness in your inconsistency. What are we to believe when the followers of John wear badges of mourning and you do not? They fast out of devotion to the dead and you feast."

There was something familiar about this *Parush*. His voice was different and his appearance changed, but I knew him. I had a hunch that he was very familiar, indeed! I got up from my chair and walked toward him, making like I was going for the exit. I pushed him ever so gently in order to see what he would do when off-balance. He took a few steps to recover and glared at me with hatred I had never seen outside of battle. He could hide his appearance and his voice and his manner, but not his limp. It was Saul! "If I had my sword close to me, I would change your appearance for the better," he hissed.

My calm smile seemed to increase his fury. I spoke slowly and in lower tones, as if I were my brother Simon, but with more sarcasm than threat. "Even with your skill of changing <u>your</u> appearance, the pious demeanor of Saul still shines through!"

Being discovered seemed to dissipate his fury (although, it might have been just part of the character he was acting out). "I do not know who you are, but you have made a dangerous enemy," he said, pulling his lethal gaze from me and allowing his eyes to wander round the room. "You all have." A companion whispered something in his ear. "Oh," he said, "we have the murderer Yehudah the *Sicarri* in this 'holy band.'"

Then tension between us was building to a point where we might have actually fought. Suddenly Jeshua appeared between us. We both took a step backwards and then he faced Saul.

Jeshua spoke: "John is dead and his followers rightly show their love and respect for him by fasting. My followers and I do not love and respect him any less by not fasting. Men must follow what the spirit inside of them dictates. What is proper and holy for one group might be a sin for another. Is there a set of clothes made that will fit all men? One may fast in sincerity and he is blessed. Another may take on the trappings of grief but he sins because it is against the spirit inside of him to do so. The Laws of Spirit supercede those of man. We honor John not by fasting, but maintaining our health to carry on the work that he started. Which way is correct? It depends on what is inside each man. There is no universal measure of good and evil, since all is of God and is pleasing in his sight."

Saul evinced his most mocking expression: "So what if my conscience told me to draw my sword and kill this follower of yours because he offends every fiber of my being?" he said, pointing at me.

"Many times the pious get so wrapped into their own vision of what is holy, they make those who do not believe as they do wrong, and therefore, unholy. This then gives them the license, in their self-righteousness, to inflict their will on these others, even to the point of taking their lives. If you set such an action in motion you will most surely reap the results of your actions. This comes not under grace but the law, and the law will be fulfilled. It is that way not because I have said so but because God has willed it. You, Saul, listen but do not hear, so convinced are you of your righteousness. God will allow you to have your way and you will do to me what Herod did to John, and, still, John's followers will fast, and mine will weep."

At Jeshua's words, a chill ran up my spine and held me motionless for a few minutes so that I did not see Saul depart. In the meantime, Jeshua began talking to Nicodemus, one of our few friends among the Sanhedrin. Nicodemus wanted a closer cooperation and relationship between the Nazarenes and the Sanhedrin. Jeshua explained that the priesthood ruled the council and that the priesthood was an old form that was marked for extinction. He explained that it was not his task to keep the people under the control of a self-serving authority, no matter how good their intentions might be for the good of the people and the nation. The fact was that people no longer needed a spiritual authority between themselves and their Father. The Priesthood has hidden the truth from the people and will not even use it for their own advancement. Jeshua was most adamant on this point. He put it this way: "You should not pour new wine into ancient skins. During fermentation there is expansion and the brittle old form cannot hold the vital spirits. The skins will crack and burst, wasting the wine. Trust instead that the Father will continually provide new forms to hold the Spirit. He has been doing so since original creation."

Nicodemus' face reflected a certain sadness and regret at these words. Nicodemus was an intelligent man and a man of peace. He wanted to smooth over as many rifts as possible between the Nazarenes and the Sanhedrin. He was aware of a coming storm of opposition from the rulers of the Temple and our group. It must have been a difficult choice for Jeshua as well. Here was a way to remove him from danger by forming a political alliance and protect the future of this group. Instead he chose to hold to his integrity and remain faithful to his purpose. That was more the heroic pathway, although it was also the more dangerous one. There are many more tales of the premature deaths of heroes than their dying in old age.

For seven days we stayed with Jeshua and meditated. I had the feeling that we were being prepared for some task of which only Jeshua knew. At the end of this time, Jeshua brought us together and said, "You are now very comfortable in your following me. There will be a time when <u>you</u> will be followed and you must know what it means to lead. It means that you must be a more responsible follower of God, our Father."

There were looks of uncertainty and downright fear on the faces of his twelve chosen. "Do not worry," he added, "I will make sure that you are prepared and imbued with enough Spirit to accomplish your task."

He began: "The harvest is ready but I am the only harvester in the field. You have watched as I have healed, performed 'miracles' and taught. In essence, you know what you need to carry on this work. It is the Spirit always that does the work if you are willing to be an open receptacle for the Spirit. That is what I have done and it takes only one man to accomplish something to show that it can be done by all."

He brought us, the twelve, in a circle around him, raised up both arms and said, "Receive now the Holy Spirit."

The next breath that I took was like I had breathed in the pure Light of Spirit. I felt every cell in my body quickened by that energy. Jeshua then came around to each of us and whispered in our ears a Word of Power, an initiatory tone, for each of us.

He said, "With this word you shall heal the sick, clear the possessed, and teach those who are hungry for knowledge. Go not beyond the borders of Galilee. Proclaim that the kingdom of the Father is here. Trust in Spirit, your faith will protect you. Give as you have received, freely and abundantly. Go as my emissaries, you will be representing me and my support will be with you. I will be sending you as sheep among wolves, but I will tell you how you can assure your protection:

"Do not focus on any negative or evil thought. Remember you are not responsible for any thought that goes through your mind. You are responsible for any thought you choose to keep there. Any negative thoughts you hold to you will dissipate your energy.

"Do not resist the evil of others. There are places you will go where you will not be well received. They may shut their doors in your face and refuse to welcome you. Bear them no ill will, for they are only exercising their choice. Do not push on them with the attitude of righteousness, for they may be doing what is best for them at the time. At the first sign of irritation or anger, thank them for their time and go. Remember that your job is to make this good news available to others, not to enlist them forcefully. One who freely chooses is a truer disciple than one who has been tricked, cajoled, or coerced.

"Do not be concerned as to what you should say. It will not be you that speaks but the Holy Spirit who breathes the words and guides the lips. Do not be concerned that those who listen may be angered at your words. They are like those who get too much sleep and are infuriated at any disturbance to their mindless slumber. You do not know what will come of this. Perhaps later in life they may step forward into Light or maybe in some other lifetime… we cannot presume what is best for another. Never force this good news on anyone. When you are rejected in one place, seek another place.

"Take simple precautions but do not fear. There are those who will try to trap you and arrest you for what you say. If you do not make overblown claims and speak only of your direct experience, you cannot be harmed. Even when, at a time not too distant, they take your lives in the name of God, you will not see death. They can destroy the body but not the Soul. You hold inside you the power of the Christ. The Christ puts the love of God before the love of life, so cling not to life or you will lose the authenticity of your life and therefore your conscious connection to Spirit. Remember, while this present life may seem real to you, it is a momentary play in the drama of your real existence."

He ended his lecture thusly: "I will send you out in pairs. When you have completed your tasks, meet me back in Capernaum."

I left with my brother Simon, who chose to travel with me. We decided to try Nazareth and the surrounding areas. I thought that we would have a better chance to communicate than Jeshua since we were not as well known, or more accurately, known for things other than God's Kingdom.

Simon was worried. "I do not abide with all this talk of sacrifice and dying. How will Jeshua fulfill his tasks as the chosen one if he dies? Is he giving up and sending us out to accomplish what he will not?"

"Simon, would you please use your brain. Jeshua is merely preparing us for being his devotees[11], his closest initiates. The task that he has taken on is monumental. It may take many years to complete and since we are the generation who is introducing it, it may be future generations who will complete it."

"But the scriptures tell us it is not supposed to happen this way. It is supposed to happen very quickly. The Kingdom is supposed to come about in the twinkling of an eye."

"You know as well as I, Simon, that Jeshua does nothing that is expected, yet he seems to accomplish what he sets out to do. Sometimes, it frustrates me beyond belief, but so far he has produced amazing results."

"What about <u>us</u>, Yehudah? We can't do what he does. I am a fighter like you. How can I be a healer?"

"Simon, we are his initiates. In Tibet I learned that an initiate carries the energy of the Master who initiates him. I am willing to try and see this through."

"What about teaching? My only experience is teaching others to fight."

"What was it that kept you going? What provided you your passion?"

---

[11] *Apostle*, in Greek

"I felt like what I was doing was directly affecting our country. What I was doing was bringing forward a lasting freedom for our people."

All of a sudden, Spirit brought forward an idea to me. "Perhaps you could substitute the Kingdom of God for the Kingdom of Israel. It may be just another form of patriotism and another way of having our brothers and sisters gain freedom."

"Yehudah, I am willing to try anything that will clarify my understanding and harmonize parts of my life that do not seem to fit at all."

In Nazareth we would be familiar to many people and not as "controversial" as Jeshua. Perhaps we might have better luck in the city of our childhood than did Jeshua.

When we entered Nazareth, we headed for Jeshua's family home. Mary, Jeshua's mother, and her daughters Elizabeth and Ruth were the only ones at home. The boys were either working or following Jeshua.

As of old, I told her news of Jeshua. She seemed to be more interested in our mission to Nazareth. "The people here have some of the best and worst qualities of Galileans," she began. "They can be intensely loyal to people and causes, but they can also be stubborn and hard-headed. If I can offer some advice, I would tell you to seek those things in your past to which you were attached and bring them present now."

I had always known Mary to be an extremely wise woman. Her suggestion was as enigmatic and esoteric as some of Jeshua's statements. She spoke with both his kindness and determination. I suspect that she had been a disciple right from the beginning, but was very willing to stay in the background and allow the twelve to receive the greater portion of Jeshua's attention.

Later, while attempting to fully understand Mary's suggestion, we stopped into the inn. The place was almost deserted. A burly man sat at a table in one corner of the room and the innkeeper was sweeping the floor.

"Any news Benjamin," I asked?

"None, Yehudah."

The man in the corner looked at us with recognition. "Are you Yehudah and Simon? I am Philomon."

"Yes," said Simon, "the one who used to torment Yehudah." I sensed Simon's uneasiness and placed my hand on his arm.

"Please forgive me, I was young…"

"You have long been forgiven, I hold no ill will toward you," I said.

"I saw you with Jeshua, the healer, son of Joseph. I admit that I had little faith in him, but I need his help now. My wife lies dying in our bed and there is no one else who can help her. Would you send for him before it is too late?"

I remembered what Jeshua had told us and I spoke, uncertain, but willing to bring forward whatever Spirit would allow. "Philomon, I would be happy to send for him, but it would take some time for him to get here and it might be too late. We have been given the abilities of healing by our Master; he will be working through us. If we cannot help your wife, we will be happy to send for him."

He seemed to be absorbed in thought for a moment and then just said, "Please, come to my home."

I remembered that his home was just a bit further up the Marmion Way, past Jeshua's house. As we were walking I wondered what I had gotten us into. If we failed to help this woman, word would spread quickly through the town and we might even be stoned for being false prophets. My fears ran rampant but I was able to control my outer appearance by resigning myself to be already dead. I figured that I would be proud to die for Jeshua's plan. He was both my friend and Master. This resolve nullified my fear and numbed my frantic brain.

All too soon I was standing over the bed where the woman was lying. Truly, she looked already dead.

If this were ever going to work, I would have to let go completely of trying to do anything. I relaxed, and invoked the Spirit as Jeshua taught us:

"Father-Mother God,
we ask for the presence
of the Christ
and the consciousness
of the Sojourner to
be with us,
work through us,
and guide us at this time.
We ask that anything
that is not of Spirit
be taken into that Holy Light
and transformed.
We ask for healing and rebalancing
for this woman in all realms
if that is for her highest good.
We place all of this into
the Light of the Holy Spirit,
and we step clear. Amen."

I stood there with my hands outstretched and gave up all my expectations. I may have moved or stood still, I do not remember. I wanted to flee, to be somewhere else. I felt my body but I did not feel a direct connection with it. I felt some energy move in through the top of my head, down the neck and into my hands. I felt like a puppet suspended from a string at the top of my head and a string each for each of my hands. I was not even holding them up any longer. They just stayed in placed and pulsed with energy. I saw no emanation from them but I could feel something like a prolonged version of the shock I received from wearing shoes on a carpet during a dry day. When the power went from me, my hands dropped like the strings were cut. I looked directly at the woman for the first time since the beginning. Her eyes were wide open and she was staring intently at me.

"Your Master is proud of you," was all she said.

My own awareness was dimmed. I felt like I had been trying to run through thick soup. "What?"

"While I was… not here… you and your Master were with me. He told me that you would be standing in for him and for you not to fear. It is true. I saw you both very clearly." Her look of intensity did not waver. She described Jeshua accurately.

Philomon, on the other hand, had the look of wild enthusiasm. "Rebecca, we have been part of a miracle. We too should follow the teachings of this master. Yehudah, could we accompany you on your trip back to your master?"

"Of course. I do not see why it should not be," I said, still amazed at what had transpired. Rebecca was still weak, but whatever her illness, she showed no trace of it. "We will be in Capernaum for a while longer, but you are welcome to be with us here and also to travel with us." I think that what was most amazing to me was that with a great effort she mustered all of her energy and followed us around all that day.

As we walked down the street, people noticed that she was better and began asking how she recovered so quickly. The pair was only too willing to share every detail of the story.

At first there was some ridicule from our hometown neighbors. "Our two famous murderers, Yehudah and Simon are now <u>healers?</u> This must be some type of trick. Bring them to the Synagogue. The Rabbi will know what to do with them."

We could have fought them off, but for some reason we went willingly. We were taken to Malcholus, a Pharisee who had *Hasid* leanings, and would therefore be more open to listen.

"I hold no enmity toward you or your teacher. I would just like to know the purpose of your visit."

I looked at Simon and he looked back at me. Simon was used to addressing (or more precisely, inflaming) crowds and he naturally stood forward and commanded attention. "Our purpose is merely to spread the word that the Kingdom of Heaven is present and available for all. This Kingdom is nowhere physical but is in us and all around us."

"Look at this couple," he said, pointing to Rebecca and Philomon. "They are already in the Kingdom. Look at their joy. They have created the Kingdom for themselves with the gratitude they have for their lives. They have done this for themselves and so can you. I enlist you, if you would, to follow them into the place inside of yourself where you hold your attitude toward life. If you change your attitude as they have done you can have more power over your lives. I used to expend my energy killing Romans, but no sooner is one killed, and then there is another to take his place. I have found it too much work to try to change the outer world so much. If I change, instead, my <u>attitude</u> to the outer world, I have not given over my power to it. I am a happier man today because of this."

I had never heard Simon talk like this before. He had the crowd silent and waiting for his every word. The *Hasid* invited the four of us to his home. He was very impressed with Simon's teaching and asked him at dinner about his training. Simon laughed and said that his experience was that of addressing his troops or to inflame crowds. He told Malcholus that <u>I</u> was the one with the religious and spiritual education. Malcholus seemed puzzled so I explained to him that it was not really we performing these deeds but the energy and guidance of Spirit. He just could not grasp that and felt that we were just being modest.

Later, when I was able to get Simon alone I told him that I noticed a change in him and asked him what happened.

"It all happened in an instant," he said. "For what seemed to be quite a long time, I was taken away from this place. Jeshua was guiding me through the realms of Light. He showed me the realm of the imagination, the emotions, the mind, the unconscious, and then the realm of the Soul, which is our true home. Above that are the realms of Spirit, which are, to me, incomprehensible. He taught me about the Kingdom. It all happened in an instant as it is written! Then I was back with you and the crowd with knowledge I never had before."

"Jeshua has done this so we could see ourselves as being useful as his high initiates. I know that I have more confidence in doing this work, that there are useful things that I can accomplish in my life. I..."

The experiences of the past few days were too much for me. I remained silent for the rest of the trip back. When we returned to Capernaum we heard similar experiences from the other high initiates. Each of the six pairs had returned with new disciples and a whole lot more confidence in their work.

Then began a period of intense training. We learned many hidden things concerning the Christ and the Sojourner Consciousness. Jeshua was the perfect one to teach us, since he was the physical anchor point of both those consciousnesses for this world.

The result of our mission to Galilee was that it vastly increased the number of followers of The Way. Jeshua taught the multitudes by day and us, his apostles, by night. It seemed like he was always busy and yet refreshed.

Thomas expressed the concern that we were all feeling. "Master, the multitudes are weak from hunger and have nothing to eat."

Jeshua replied, "Then feed them."

I spoke, "Master, I have money left from my trip. Perhaps if we put all of what we have left together, we can feed at least some of them."

Andrew spoke, "That will not be anywhere close to what we need. I have also found a boy with five loaves of barley bread and two fish. But, we would perhaps be able to feed 50 of 5000 men, women and children, but even then not to capacity."

Jeshua's gaze turned somewhat intense as it did sometimes when he was teaching us. "Have all the followers sit in groups of twelve and do not waste a crumb."

As some were fed, Jeshua gave further instructions: "Gather up what is left from this group and fill the baskets with the fragments."

An amazing thing happened. There was as much left as the amount of food with which we began. The people were astonished by this miracle but Jeshua, as always, used it to teach.

He first spoke to his disciples: "What you have witnessed is something anyone can do, perhaps not on this scale, but certainly in the same manner. One just has to know the laws of manifestation. In India I have seen masters pluck objects out of the ethers and give them to followers. The prime mover is intention. If your intention is strong concerning where you want to go in this life you will be able to create things ahead of you that will benefit you when you reach a point where you can use them. That is not as dramatic as what I have demonstrated to you today but it will have much more meaning for you in your lives. Remember this event when your doubt surfaces, it will give you courage."

He then spoke to the multitudes: "You have eaten of the flesh of fish and the bread of life which is food for the body. We offer you also food for the Soul. This food is not physical and cannot be consumed as such. It is the flesh of the Christ. It is the knowledge you have inside of you that your Father is with you and protecting you. It sustains and invigorates every part of your being. It gives meaning to your lives and makes you joyful sons and daughters of your loving Father. But there is more. When two or more are gathered in this awareness of the Christ inside of you, a fellowship of Loving appears. The flesh of your neighbor is your flesh and yours is his. In this Loving, the illusion of being separate melts away. This is the blood of the Christ. It is the flowing spring that Moses brought out of the rock when he smote it in the desert. The knowledge that our God is inside us is the Flesh of the Christ, and the knowledge that God is also in our neighbor is the Blood of Christ. He that eats and drinks of these shall never hunger or thirst and will not be lost because he will have found the Kingdom. No man shall enter the Kingdom who has not eaten and drunk of the Christ."

Jeshua told us we needed further training as his high initiates, his apostles, and suggested that we go into retreat. Jeshua knew of a place in the mountains near Decapolis where we would not be known and could have solitude. We spent three days in meditation and prayer, building our energy and becoming more familiar with more of the inner truths by experience.

When he felt that we had prepared enough, Jeshua called us together and said, "My time on this realm is running out and there is much you still need to know. I came to be a pattern for men to follow to return to our Father. I have shown how to overcome the trials that plague those who would choose the spiritual in life. I have taught you to use the names of God, the words of power to teach and heal and lift, but the greatest gift that I can give is the assurance that life is eternal and I need to get on with that part of my work. For that to happen one of you must turn me over to the *Parush* and the Priests who will, in turn, give me to the Romans to be crucified. They will be driven to do this through the demons of their own fear, but I will slay the worst of all fears."

Peter jumped up and said, "They will have to go through the twelve of us to get to you." The rest of us immediately jumped up and intoned hearty agreement.

"No. You cannot stop this process," said Jeshua. "It needs to occur and you shall assist me in making this happen. I have brought your names up before the Lord of the highest realm and you need not fear, for your paths are those of the Masters. You will all be renowned in history and one of you will be disgraced, but in name only. He will be the one who turns me over to the Sadducees."

We looked at each other in disbelief. Which among us would do such a thing?

"It will not be with malice but with necessity that this happens. And the one who does willingly sacrifice his good name for my plan will be the most devout disciple among you. But you all will take up my banner and bring forward the knowledge of the Christ that lives inside of all."

All of a sudden, Jeshua got up and his whole manner changed. "Who do people say that I am?"

Matthew said, "I have heard others call you David, Enoch, Solomon, and Seth."

"… And Jeremiah," Andrew interjected.

Nathaniel said, "Your friend, Tuzla, while he was here, expressed the belief that you were Gautama the Buddha returned."

James said, "Many believe that you are Elijah reborn."

Then John said that he heard a man of great wisdom in Jerusalem say that he knew for a fact that Jeshua was Melchizedek in a previous life.

Thomas laughed and said, "Well, <u>Herod</u>, thinks that you are John who has come back to plague him."

Then Jeshua asked us, "Who do you think I am?"

John said, "You are a Master Soul who was many of those figures in our history and returns again as a pattern for us to follow."

We all nodded our heads in agreement.

"You are also the 'Elder Brother' who is the anchor point of the Sojourner Consciousness on the Physical Level," I said.

Again there was general agreement.

"You are the Physical manifestation of the Consciousness of the Christ who has returned to show us the way into the Kingdom and the heart of God," said Peter.

We, as disciples, never before reflected so much of the consciousness of our teacher.

Jeshua looked at all of us and said, "It was not man who told you these things but this knowledge came from Spirit. I will pass the keys on to all of you that you may awaken all people to their special relationship with the Father. These words I am about to tell are for you alone for they are the Words of God."

We were opened up and we were taught.

We continued on our journeys. We found ourselves passing through Cæsarea. Jeshua told us that there was a mountain close by that he wished to climb and he chose Peter, James and John to go with him. All of a sudden I felt terribly left out. Why was I not one of the ones chosen, although I did not have any idea what all this was about? I decided to follow at a distance to see what was going on.

Andrew said, "Don't you think that if Jeshua wanted you to come along, he would have asked you?"

But I was not in the mood to listen. "How will it hurt anyone if I just watch what takes place. I won't interfere," I retorted.

He just shrugged and I went on my way, following from a discrete distance. When they got to the top, I positioned myself so that my presence would not be detected but that I could still hear what was going on.

Jeshua instructed Peter, James and John to go into meditation. As they meditated, I could see a Light growing around Jeshua. It became so brilliant that I had to avert my eyes. When I looked back I saw the faint outlines of Jeshua and two other glowing figures standing before Peter, James, and John. They were talking but I could not hear a thing. It dawned on me that these were things that I was not meant to hear so I went back down the mountain.

When I reached the others, who were back in Cæsarea, I shared what I had seen (and the lack of what I had heard). We were summoned to heal an epileptic child, but no matter what any of us did, we could not accomplish what was needed for the child to recover.

The next day Jeshua returned with Peter, James, and John. He asked about what we had accomplished in his absence. We told him of our failure with the child and he took us back to the child's home where he healed the child in a few minutes.

Thomas asked, "Why did we not heal him? We spoke the words of power you gave us, but we still failed to heal him."

"Yes," said Jeshua, "That is the problem. Your prior successes have gone to your head and you forgot where to place your faith. Your personalities have judged you and told you that you failed. But this experience may yet be positive for you. You learn most through 'failures.' But did you fail? There is no way that an individual can 'fail' in the work of Spirit when the individual is in the consciousness of acceptance. A clear intention and purity of heart in love and acceptance is all that is required. Then you are a clear receptacle for the Holy Spirit allowing God to work through you. The Spirit will not follow the wishes of your personalities. Your intention should be to be open and to serve Spirit no matter what the outcome of your work. Yet, it may be part of Spirit's plan for that person to continue with their illness and die from it. The true intention should not be 'to be healers' but to support a person in his or her healing, which may or may not include a cure for a condition. In our human physical consciousness, we cannot know why someone might be required by Spirit to remain ill or to die. We are called on in those moments to accept that God's love is in the action even when we do not understand how it is working. Always let those you work with know that it is the Father who does the work and that there are no guaranteed outcomes other than the highest good of all concerned. You must keep this in mind when you work with people, because I will not always be with you in the flesh."

We were all silent. No one dared to press Jeshua into explaining his meaning, but all too soon we were back in Capernaum and were greeted by one of Matthew's old friends, a tax collector, Aaron. "Are you strangers or residents of this town?" he asked.

"We have lived here for over a year, but many of us are originally from other towns. To settle this, we will pay the tax." Said Jeshua.

We all looked for money, but not even Matthew was carrying any.

Jeshua smiled at me and winked. He waved his hand in the air as I have seen the Holy men in India and Tibet. He produced a shekel out of the air and gave it to the astonished tax collector. The tax collector must have thought it an illusion because he bit it with greater force than usual in order to test its reality. He let out a short scream and held his mouth. "As far as I am concerned, you have met your obligations," he said, and hurried away with his hand holding the side of his mouth.

That afternoon, as we were resting from our trip, an argument ensued. James said that Jeshua was probably considering him as the foremost Apostle to lead while Jeshua was elsewhere. Peter laughed and said "if that were the case then why didn't he reveal to just you what he revealed to you, John, and I?"

"Well, you are most likely to be my lieutenants," said James.

"How could any of us claim that position," asked Andrew, "when none of us had success with the healing?"

Philip interjected, "Perhaps the offices and responsibilities could be split so that a few of us..."

Nathaniel was angry, "How can you compare yourselves to Jeshua? It would take you lifetimes to get his wisdom."

John said, "This is truly laughable. You are fighting like schoolchildren for the favors of your teacher. I am disgusted with all of you."

I was silent during this battle of words but part of me was gleeful at their childishness. Perhaps Jeshua would now see that I was the one with whom he should spend more time.

Jeshua came over to them with a little child in his arms. "If you are wondering which among you is the greatest, it is this child that I hold in my arms. He is the most innocent and without pretense. If you too wish to truly be great, you must become as unassuming and humble as this child. It is the innocents who are closest to the Father. An innocent does not plan another's undoing. Woe to him who connives to make another man fall. It is a price that you would not enjoy paying. The wise man does not wish to pull himself up by pushing others down, for this merely digs his hole deeper. The wise man has learned that the only way one can truly lift himself is to help others lift also.

"Your fighting amongst yourselves is foolish, as John has said. What makes you think that you are the only ones who are doing God's work? This is something all may do and over this you have no control. The best you can do is support them in their work, for as they are lifting they are also lifting you."

Just then a soldier dragging a man in chains passed through the street. Jeshua just said, "Come along, everyone," and was off after the commotion.

The man was in rags and was held tightly by a guard that worked for the town magistrate. It appeared that a wealthy woman who demanded he be sent to jail was accusing him of theft.

When all had testified as to this man's guilt, Jeshua stood forward before the magistrate and said, "Hold. Do not take this man away just yet. Under Roman law, he has the right to speak in his own behalf, yet he was not permitted to do so."

The magistrate agreed to hear the man's story. This man was a beggar who had been refused food and had stolen to feed his wife and children. This woman snatched back the bread and fed it to the dogs. The man ended by saying, "Do what you wish to me, but have mercy on my family whose only crime is that they are hungry."

Jeshua argued his point as well as any lawyer: "Who here is guilty of a crime? Was it this man who stole to keep his family from starvation? Was it this woman who acted without mercy to deny that which would give life? Was it this court that is blind to human suffering? Is it the town of Capernaum that ignores cries of destitution and hopelessness? To say in a smug manner that the world is imperfect and do nothing to help your brothers and sisters is a crime against God, for you are misusing what He has given to you. You are all a party to this crime because you have withheld life from the helpless. Tell me, where is the righteousness in this?"

The people, and even the magistrate, remained silent. Jeshua concluded his argument: "I ask every one of you, if you were this man and faced with these hopeless circumstances, what would you do? Look in your heart for what is right. Let this man go and give him what he needs to feed his wife and children."

The magistrate raised his lowered head and made a movement with his hand. The man was set free and all those in the town gave a small amount but when taken together it was a sizable gift. We heard at a later time the man was also given employment in the stables and was able to feed his family through his own efforts.

Jeshua sent us ahead to Jerusalem and said that he would catch up with us later. But before we left, he told us, "I am selecting seventy of my disciples to go out as you did, to teach and to heal. Some are not Jews and they will go to lands other than Judea. I do this because the Kingdom of Heaven is not only for one people but for all people. People will more often listen to their own countrymen than to you or I."

Our trip to Jerusalem was uneventful. We stopped only once at an inn along the way to rest and take some nourishment. I was aware that we were headed into the lion's den. This city was the sanctuary of the Sadducees and the *Parush* and they would have spies to tell them of the arrival of the Nazarenes. I cautioned everyone to keep a low profile because I expected that we would run into Saul again in Jerusalem. I had cautioned Peter to carry his sword, as did my brother Simon. I had my *twin blades* hidden in my clothing but did not expect that I would need them — Peter's sword as well as his size appeared quite formidable.

As we entered the gate of the city we heard a familiar voice, "Ho, travelers, are you not afraid to travel without your leader?" I knew that Saul was clever, but I did not expect that he would find us so soon.

Saul had positioned himself so that he had the sun behind him, making him difficult to see. "I will be watching you very carefully. Be careful that the poison that you spew does not infringe on our laws. It would be a pleasure for me personally to send you all to the dungeons."

"We are at peace with all men," said Peter.

"We have nothing to fear, Saul," I said, "since our only occupation is to heal the sick and speak the truth."

"My occupation is to protect the rights of our people to remain free and unharmed under this Roman occupation. When trouble occurs they do not distinguish between troublemakers and honest people. If troublemakers like yourselves continue to speak your 'truth,' the Romans will make us all suffer for your causing unrest among the people. When you talk about any other kingdom than the one the Emperor rules, you speak not heresy but sedition. The Sadducees are here to keep order so that the Romans do not slaughter us. If you endanger that balance you endanger all of us, and it will be you who are slaughtered. Our people must survive."

"Ours is not a political movement," said John, "but one of the Spirit. We cannot deny that there may be political changes that result from man's greater awareness of God, but we are not looking to overthrow the power of the Priests in political issues. But in issues of religion, they represent only themselves."

Saul stood gazing down upon us for a while as if contemplating the worthiness of our arguments. He said, "I will be watching you," and melted back into the city that was his home.

We were hungry from our journey and we went directly to the marketplace for food. As we fed ourselves others recognized us in the crowd. A group formed around us, asking us more questions than we could answer all at once.

"Is your leader The Messiah as foretold?" one man asked.

John spoke, "Jeshua, son of Joseph, is not the traditional Messiah that you expect. He is no earthly king and will lead no military victory against our oppressors. But he is much more; he is the wayshower into a better life for all. He is a king in the unseen world of the Spirit."

"How does he heal lepers and save people from the madness of possessions?" one woman asked.

This time Peter answered, "We have done these things, too, and as far as we can tell, these powers appear when you are ready for them. It is the Spirit of God that is doing the work through us. If any man, or woman, allows the Holy Spirit to overshadow them, they will speak the words, live the life and do the deeds of the Christ, which Jeshua, son of Joseph, represents."

There were many questions from those both friendly and unfriendly to us and Spirit helped us answer them all.

The next day was the Sabbath and the Master met us as he promised. As Jeshua and we, his twelve apostles, walked through the streets of Jerusalem Simon and I knew that we were being watched. I looked over at Simon to see if he was aware and he looked back at me. His gaze confirmed what I had experienced. As if we found ourselves in a Greek tragedy, priests and scribes appeared with a few officers of the Temple. I had my hands on the *Twin Blades* as they approached but they did not have a direct assault in mind. They had a crying, half-clothed woman in tow that was found in the act of prostitution. To me, it was a transparent set-up by Saul and his minions. The officers approached Jeshua and the priests said: "Rabbi, the Law of Moses demands that she be stoned to death for her crime of adultery. What do you say her punishment should be?

Jeshua crouched down and with a stick drew a figure in the dust. It was too far away for me to make out what it was. When he got up again, he looked into all the eyes of the priests who were gathered around the pitiful-looking woman and said, "I know everything that you have done in this life as well as or better than you. If there is truly <u>one</u> of you that can stand forward and say he is without sin, let him cast the first stone."

He stooped again and brushed away the figure he had drawn in the sand. When he again arose, he and the woman were alone with his disciples. "Where are the men who accused you?" he asked.

"They are gone," she replied.

"Then there is no one left to condemn you. I certainly cannot condemn you. I am sensitive to your plight. There was a member of <u>my</u> family who was involved in adultery. She discovered that she was hurting herself more than those around her. Her actions came about because of her lack of valuing who she was. In that, she degraded the Spirit of God inside of her. You too, have that Spirit of God inside of you. Honor your body because in it resides the Living God. Go in peace.

I knew that Jeshua was talking about Mary of Magdala. I realized that what she did was out of a feeling of desperation in her life, it had nothing to do with me personally. I had judged her harshly and unfairly. I would ask her forgiveness the next time I saw her. I felt my eyes well up. I turned my head away from the other twelve.

Jeshua decided to teach outside the Temple. Since only Jews were allowed in the sanctuary, Jeshua decided to teach in the court, so that everyone might hear what he had to say. There were many questions from the crowd that day, both the honest and the goading kind. But Jeshua used everything in order to teach about the Kingdom and how it works.

"You say you are <u>not</u> the Messiah, are you a prophet such as John the Baptizer?" asked one lawyer.

Jeshua tailored his answer to the active mind of the lawyer. "We can see in the daytime because it is light. In the night time we can only see if we have a lamp. While we are in this world, it is as night time for our Souls. There is little we see in clarity. Once in a while there comes a bearer of Light to awaken our understanding. I am the wayshower to the Light. I am also the lamp that holds the Light." He continued the analogy. "The Christ is the oil in the lamp and the Holy Spirit is the fire."

"You speak in riddles and you testify for yourself. If you were in a court of law that testimony would be held untrue."

Jeshua answered: "The words you hear from me are from Spirit, so it is actually my Father that testifies for me."

This lawyer was having a difficult time with Jeshua. "I do not know your father. Where does he live?"

I chuckled to myself. This lawyer assumed that Jeshua meant his <u>physical</u> father.

"If you truly knew yourself, you would know my Father and you would also know me."

Another man asked: "Why have you come, wise man?"

"I have come to demonstrate the awakening of Christ as it lives inside us. Many will be open to see and will follow the Light into God's kingdom. Most will not listen to me and will live in darkness until they understand the true meaning of my words. Many have heard of 'the Way', as we call it and ask us 'What is the way?' You are the way. When you know the truth you shall be set free."

Another man challenged Jeshua: "We are all here free men. Where are we not free?"

"Nearly all that still live are slaves to this world or they would not be here. It is the passions, the diversions and the problems of this world that keep them in chains. They live in chains, die in chains and are reborn with the chains in place. If you but listen to me, I can free you from your chains and you can be truly free."

A priest leveled his anger at Jeshua, thinking what Jeshua said was said in pride. "Are you claiming to be greater than the Prophets, greater than our Father Abraham?"

"Abraham rejoiced in my coming," he answered.

"You must be an idiot," said the priest with a scornful laugh, "you are no more than forty years and you claim to have seen Abraham?"

"Before the days of Abraham, I am," he answered.

The priest shook his head and walked away. I understood that Jeshua was talking about his lifetime as Melchezidek, the king of Salem, who was Abraham's spiritual advisor.

There were others whose questions were the questions that Jeshua used to teach the people.

"What can I do, Master, to reach the Kingdom that you are talking about?"

"Do you know what is said in the scriptures?"

The man answered, "You shall love the Lord your God with all your heart, with all your soul, with all your strength, and love your neighbor as yourself."

"If you live your answer, you shall do well."

"Master, exactly who is my neighbor?"

"When you truly realize who you are you will find that there is nowhere you can go where you will not find your neighbor. But for right now, to be realistic, love the person next to you. If all of us could do just that, we could change the direction of our future. This is no small thing. You have to take into account his or her race, religion, class, circumstances in life and environment. If you can accept all those things about him, and do not judge, then you are being truly loving. Then you are also clearly and accurately fulfilling your destiny as God's representative on the earth." Jeshua then related the parable of the Good Samaritan. (The purpose of this, I believe, was to show him that the man from Samaria was truly being a neighbor to the unfortunate man, because he showed mercy without compromise and was of loving service to this stranger.)

A woman asked: "What is the meaning of 'an eye for an eye' as it is in the scriptures?"

"Not what most people think," Jeshua began. "Just because you think someone has wronged you, it does not give you license to extract equal payment from that person as a punishment. All judgment belongs to the Father, not to his children. We do not have the ability to see as our Father. The Lord will extract payment from the individual in His own place and time. When you see a man afflicted with a disease, he might be paying a debt accrued in a prior embodiment. On the other hand, do not judge this man as a sinner, he might have taken on such as burden to serve others and is a master-soul. We can not look at the man and know the total of his existences."

"Can this re-embodiment ever end?" she asked.

"It can now," Jeshua replied. "When a man or woman accepts The Way and enters into the Kingdom of God, these debts are either released or quickly paid off. It is a sign that an individual is ready to accept a greater responsibility in lifting himself and his neighbors, which is actually all of humanity."

We returned to Capernaum because we had received word that the seventy, which Jeshua had sent out, had returned. They rejoiced to see him. There was felt a greater fellowship now that other disciples of Jeshua had gone out and taught and healed. They offered many stories of the lame and the blind being healed and the powerful effects that had occurred when the names of God were spoken.

Jeshua then brought us together to teach and give his blessing on the work of the seventy.

"I tell you, well done! I say this not only for myself but also for all the Masters of Light who I have heard in many realms. You have joined a tradition of ministers of Light who serve mankind. These are the Priests of Melchizedek, not those of Aaron that we speak of. They minister to all people, regardless of their beliefs and regardless of their willingness to accept 'The Way.' All nations will now be available to hear the news of the Kingdom and many will accept it. But do not rejoice in your abilities to do what I have done, for that is the puffing up of the personal self. Remember that it is the Father who is doing all the work. Instead, I suggest that you rejoice that so many of your brothers and sisters were open to hear the truth and that so many hearts were opened to Spirit."

Jeshua then began his blessing:

"Dear Father-Mother God,
I thank you for revealing yourself
to the innocent and teaching them
to light the way for the wise.
I have shared with them
what you have given to me
and you have opened them up to understanding.
Bless them that they will forever
know You inside of them and
let them honor you forever
through honoring the Christ that
lives in their hearts.

"Through your Word, I proclaim them
Priests of Melchezidek
who need neither Temple nor synagogue
to tend.
Their sanctuary is the world
and allegiance is to You alone.

"For these, Spirit places
a blessing of Understanding,
knowing that the greatest knowledge
one can ever receive is located
inside the Spiritual Heart.
That when they stand with you,
they never stand alone.
That wherever they go
they bring with them
your Kingdom
whose door they open for others.

"Go, then, and make this understanding
available to others
no matter what be their belief
or circumstance for they are all
your brothers and sisters."

"You have started upon a path of discipleship which is a serious task. It means that you will have to release all of your attachments to this earth. Be sure that you are willing to let go of your attachments before you follow me. Your Love of our Father must be paramount above all other things. If you love your wealth before the Father, you cannot follow me. If you love your family before our Father, you cannot follow me. And if you love the praise of others more than our Father, then I tell you to stay at home, for this discipleship exacts a price, a price that you can only pay by following one Master. Many are accustomed to following the master of this world and so this will be difficult to change. You must decide whether you will continue to follow that master or follow me into the heart of our Father. This will be different for each of you. Some may only need to give up the yearning for things material and that will be enough. Some of you may feel that you have to sell all you have and give your money to the poor in order to be free. It is individual. It is between you and your Soul. There is no formula for freedom."

Nathaniel, being quite the practical-minded asked, "Master, what then will be our reward for following you?"

"Those that follow me shall share with me the throne of power. It is the power that comes from knowing that God is truly your Father and that you are the Son or Daughter of God. I can tell you from my experience that all wealth on earth pales in comparison to the wealth of the Spirit."

That same week we were invited to a wedding. Two of Jeshua's disciples, Aaron and Naomi, were getting married and we were all invited. I summoned my nerve and asked Mary of Magdala if she would attend with me. Her response was one of surprise. "I thought you despised me. I didn't think that you would ever want to be in my company."

"I did judge you at one time," I admitted, "but since then, I've found that I wanted to get to know you. I see how you've changed and I would want that kind of inner change for myself."

"Yes, I will go with you, but I want you to know that it cannot mean anything more," she said.

I felt wounded. "How come?"

"It is better that I do not place myself into any situations where I could be tempted. I have already degraded marriage and I would not like to do it again in any way."

"Does this mean that you plan never to marry?" I asked.

"I don't think so," she said, "but if I ever did, it would have to be one who did not know me before, someone who would not look at me and know my shame."

"Jeshua always tells me about the necessity of self-forgiveness. Perhaps this is one you should look at also," I offered.

I noticed a quantity of pain etched into her face. It acted like a barrier to her expressing her feelings. "It is easier to say than to do. You and I do not have the same *Karma* and probably have different ways of dealing with it as well."

I took this as being told politely to mind my own business. I felt a minute or two of hurt and then I decided that I would be silent and serve her as a friend. If there were no way I could have her, I would just be there for her to depend on if she needed me. I just wanted to be close to her and if she could never be my wife, I would be her friend.

Jeshua, of course, presided over the wedding ceremony. As usual, Jeshua used the occasion to teach. I brought my charcoal and a large quantity of paper. This seemed to fascinate Mary who did not know writing although she could read well enough.

He did not begin the ceremony in the traditional way. "My friends, I see there is plenty of wine here today, so I suspect that my services will not be needed, at least, in that one area."

He prompted joyous chuckling from the congregants, for most had heard the story of his turning water to wine at a previous wedding.

"It is my joy to bless these two people as they have decided to become partners in this life. They have been so before in other existences and it is likely that they will do so again. You see, their commitment to each other was made in heaven and the vows they take today are merely a poor reflection of the depth of that commitment. The divine marriage for all of us is when we marry our souls to the will of our Father. On this level, we are not aware of this so we desire to seek this union mirrored in another individual. When these two look into each other's eyes it is the loving of their Father that they see reflected to them. This is a union that no man can pull asunder.

"Is it lawful for a man to divorce his wife," asked a *Parush* in the congregation?

"You know the law, what does it say?" answered Jeshua.

"It says that a man may divorce his wife."

"There is the common marriage and then there is the spiritual marriage that I have mentioned. It makes sense that if two people enter into a marriage and they do not really know or love each other, that there would be a law to counteract that union. This law, however, makes it too easy for men and women to repeat the same pattern with a different partner, not loving and not gaining the least understanding of what a true spiritual marriage is. If they made an agreement to stay with each other and discover the *karma*, which drives them, they might gain from each other knowledge that is priceless. The law was at one time more strict. It used to be that unless at least one partner engages in adultery, the two were to be bound in their agreement. The changes in the law came because most marriages are not of the spiritual variety. Most people marry with a sense of social obligation to their families. It is no wonder that there is no loving in these pairings, at most a sense of duty. They will last as long as that sense of duty prevails. Then others marry because there is a sense of attraction between them. These marriages may last a few years, more if there is also a sense of duty involved. Still, one or both may harbor an empty, betrayed feeling if they do not share interests. If they <u>do</u> share interests and can talk and have compatible feelings with each other, these may truly be happy marriages and may last for a lifetime. However, these are not yet the spiritual marriages of which I speak.

"There is no way for man-made laws to bind two hearts. This occurs in spirit and man's law does not apply. As far as a spiritual marriage is concerned, even lusting for another is adultery. When two enter into a spiritual marriage, there are no thoughts of lusting for other partners and there is no desire for the man to leave the woman or for the woman to leave the man. When they are truly joined by God, the man sees all women in his wife and the woman sees all men in her husband. Others are unnecessary. They are forever 'lovers' in the sense that they always feel the compelling joy of their romancing. They also learn to communicate on all levels of awareness, even to the level of the Soul. They assist each other naturally in clearing the karma that keeps each from leaving this world, and they fully support each other on all levels. In a true spiritual marriage one sees God in each other and all else is a secondary consideration."

While taking down Jeshua's words, I was affected to my core. I wished to reach over and take Mary's hand and hold it and never let it go. It was only my fear of how she would react that kept me from doing this. There was something inside awakened by Jeshua's words that recognized Mary as one who could be such a partner for me. As he spoke I took sidelong glances at her for a reaction. I saw her swallow a few times. Could this have frightened her? Would it change her attitude toward marriage?

I was floating in a sea of confusion. The feast after the ceremony was anything but joyful for me. There were so many questions unanswered, so many possibilities…

A messenger staggered toward Jeshua. It appeared that he had been running for some time and was exhausted. The messenger barely got out the words that Lazarus was sick and close to death. Martha had sent this messenger to get Mary and Jeshua back to Bethany immediately. Mary acted in haste. Jeshua, on the other hand, did not. Mary was surprised at his relaxed manner.

"Please cousin," she said, "let us hurry. If you get there in time, I know you can save him."

"There is no need to worry," said Jeshua, "Lazarus will be fine. You must trust me. We will rest tonight and head out in the morning."

Peter said, "Don't go, Master. This is the kind of situation Saul will use to trap you and turn you over to the priests."

Jeshua responded, "No one may take my life until the appointed time and that is not yet. Peace, be still."

Thomas said, "If you go, Master, so shall we. We will die with you if we must."

The next morning Jeshua started toward Bethany, but not in haste. Mary had pulled away from me. She was not seeking anyone's company and appeared very hurt that Jeshua was not moving faster. The trip took longer than usual and when we arrived, Ruth and Martha met us weeping. "You are too late, my brother Lazarus is dead. If you had come only a few days earlier, he would not have died, you would have been able to heal him." Mary went inside the house in order to be alone with her grief.

Martha did not move from her spot. "Jeshua, I know that you can still bring him back if you wish. If you say the names of God, I know you can bring him back."

"You have faith in what I have told you. I have told you that death is but a sleep and that the dead can awaken."

Mary came back out of the house with tears streaming down her face. She said in an accusatory tone like a hurt child, "Why did you take so long to get here? If we would have come earlier my brother would not have died."

Jeshua was not without feeling. He held Mary, Martha and Ruth for a moment as they wept. The house was filled with grief; all of us felt it. Jeshua wept with them and held them closer.

At last he said, "I miss my cousin Lazarus. I experience grief because I feel that I have lost someone who is close. But we never truly lose anyone. Yes, their spirit is no longer in their body and we cannot touch them, but they are not gone. The spirit lives without the body. I will show you that Lazarus in truth is not dead. Show me where he was buried."

We went a down the road until we came to a sepulcher which had been carved out of rock. There was a huge boulder in from of the doorway. Jeshua took a few deep breaths and said, "Take away the stone."

Martha looked at him with worry in her eyes and said, "It has been a few days now, the body will be decaying, it is not right that we should see it."

"What has happened to your faith, Martha? Jeshua asked. Only minutes ago you said that he would be raised. Never doubt the power of the Lord. He has created this world and given us the tools to be creators also. Let us not disappoint him!"

The rest of us rolled the stone from the opening. We smelled no odor of decay.

Meanwhile, Jeshua lifted up his eyes and chanted first in Sanskrit then in some languages I had never heard and finally in Hebrew he chanted:

"Father-Mother God,
I am the son who is grateful
that you have always heard my prayers.
Assist me now so that your children
can know the extent of your power.
Let them know that you have sent me
to show them what power we can manifest
in your name.
Place all your power in the words
of your name.
So be it."

He spoke the words. And finally called into the dark cave, "Lazarus awake!"

Nothing.

Jeshua was unruffled. "Lazarus awake!"

We heard rustling of clothing inside the tomb. Finally Lazarus emerged bound in grave clothes.

"Let him loose," said Jeshua.

Lazarus appeared to be more dazed and confused than usual (for those who knew him). "I was dead. I know I was dead. I was bathed in Light and was led by messengers to a place of healing. I was getting used to being there when you came, dear cousin," he said pointing at Jeshua, "and told me that it was not yet my time to stay. Suddenly I felt myself back in this body and my illness is gone. I feel weak but I am glad to be back among you. I could have stayed, you know. It was beautiful where I was."

"As you see," Jeshua said, "there is no more reason to fear death. It is but another step in continuation."

Mary, Martha, and Ruth were beside themselves with joy. They had their brother back.

Jeshua spoke again, but to no one in particular, "Some of you may still doubt. The time will be soon when I give you even greater proof of our divinity."

CHAPTER 13 - THE PRICE OF POLITICS

We had received word that a wealthy and influential member of the ruling council wished to speak with Jeshua. His name was Zaccheus and he lived in Jericho. We traveled to Jericho in order to spend some time with this man. Jeshua was not at all blind to politics. Some influential people among the Sanhedrin were either his friends or disciples. His popularity with the common people was on the rise. He had already gained many supporters among the *Hasid* sect of the Pharisees. I did not trust politics and was of the opinion that a strong sword had the loudest voice. Others in our group felt that the Nazarenes might gain respect in the council and have some real power to do good.

The main town square in Jericho was filled with people. They were getting ready for the trip to Jerusalem for Passover. We had no description of this Zaccheus except that he was a short man. Jeshua look about the crowd and spied a man sitting on one of the lower branches of a sycamore tree, just above the level of the tallest in the crowd.

Zaccheus caught Jeshua's eye and waved. Jeshua, looking amused, offered a broad grin and said, "Zaccheus, come down from there and spend some time with me." The little man made his way through the crowd and embraced Jeshua as if they were old friends. "Many of our *Parush* brothers have condemned me for supporting you," he said, "but I believe that your approach to living should be made available to all our people. You have practical as well as spiritual insight."

Zaccheus appeared to be ashamed of his role in the politics of Judea. It was as if he felt that he could not really live a spiritual life doing what he did. Jeshua told him that this was an illusion. "You are valuable as a spiritual being right where you are. One must always attempt to use everything for the advancement of all. Talents are not to be wasted. Do not judge your profession for God has placed you there for a reason. If you judge that, you judge the wisdom of the Father who placed you there. If you are not happy where you are, you may change your profession, but do have a good look and see if you can do spirit's work in your current situation with the talent you have been given. Remember, you have been given talents to use and not to waste. In fact, it might be a blessing in disguise for you to enjoy!"

Jeshua then told a parable of a king with three servants, two of whom made an increase from what they were given and one who did not. The king then took what he had given to the man who failed his task and gave it to the others. I took it to mean that he who uses what he has gains, and those who hide away their talents and gifts shall lose what they have. "Our Father is not unlike that king," Jeshua said. "Let us not thwart his trust in us to do his work on earth. One should always use everything to the greatest advancement of the Soul, for that is our main task while on this earth."

"Politics, like anything else in this life, can be used to lift or to undermine," Jeshua continued. "We are given mastery over all things on the earth. The test is how we use them. Nothing is evil in and of itself. So politics, too, has its positive aspects. The kind of politics I envision is one that encompasses rather than separates people, a politics of the heart, so to speak. We will always have differences of opinion on many subjects, but there will always be areas where we can agree. We must always start from our similarities and look at each other as partners rather than adversaries. For instance, there are many sects represented in the Sanhedrin. They disagree on many issues but they all do agree that one must be free to worship according to one's practice. That benefits everyone. We must always see politics from that perspective — what is for the highest good for all concerned, and start from that point."

This Zaccheus was a scholar at heart and Jeshua's time with him was mostly spent in discussing holy writings with which Zaccheus was not clear nor wished to debate. I personally had enough of that in my youth and in the East, so I paid little attention to much of what went on that day, but I was aware that Zaccheus left as a man with greater faith and joy for life.

On our way to Jerusalem, we stopped at Bethany. Many had heard about the resurrection of Lazarus and we had crowds awaiting our arrival. Jeshua was in the midst of the crowd answering questions. A blind beggar named Bartimæus called out to Jeshua and thanked him. "You have given my simple life meaning," he said, "by opening me up to understanding."

"What is it that you now understand?" Jeshua asked.

"I now know that there can be nobility in my attitude toward my disability. I no longer judge myself for being less than others because of it. I understand that it can be used to lift myself and others."

Jeshua placed his hand on the man's shoulder and said to the crowd, "Bartimæus, here, is a wise man. He looks to God with gratitude instead of anger and he has chosen to see further than most." He then spoke to Bartimæus; "Your faith will make you complete."

Jeshua knelt down and scooped some dirt from the ground. He spat on that soil and made it as a paste that he applied to the eyes of Bartimæus. In a matter of moments Bartimæus began to see faint images and within the hour his sight was restored. The crowd sang and praised God.

I felt a strong hand on my shoulder. A deep voice accompanied the vise-like grip on my shoulder, "We have to talk."

Petronius caught me by surprise. "What is so important that you would meet me like this?" I asked.

"The sleeping dog has awakened."

"Rome? How?"

"It was the miracle of Lazarus' resurrection. Word has reached Pilate. His power is already shaky. Something like this would make his power even less stable."

"How could that be, Petronius? Raising a man from the dead is hardly a political act."

"On the surface it would not seem as such, but the effects might be devastating to a ruler who wants to maintain control over an often hostile population. The main preventive measure to general uprising is the fear of death. What if someone came along and actually proved that it was an illusion? What if that happened not only here, but all over the Empire?"

"What's going to happen?"

"Pilate is putting all the pressure he can on the Sadducees to get Jeshua out of the picture. Your Sadducees, who do not believe in an afterlife, cling to this existence too strongly to resist that pressure. In fact, they will tend to be somewhat zealous in protecting themselves. They will instruct your friend Saul to take more serious measures against you."

"Perhaps now is the time that Jeshua should act against the Romans. If he is proclaimed King, then he will have enough to stand with him. The Romans would be outnumbered. It may be again like the old days, in the hills, on the run. Petronius, have you forgotten how to use a sword?"

"Do you think me a peasant farmer?" He asked with a sneer. "I will always be a warrior."

"I have a plan. You have many contacts in Jerusalem. Make sure that when Jeshua arrives in Jerusalem that there are many who will sing his praises. Make sure that they call him King. The rest will follow. This demonstration will convince Jeshua that it is time to act and accept his throne. When this is accomplished, come back to me. We will see this through together."

"What if he does not act?"

"Jeshua is no fool," I said. "It is in the interest of all of us that he continues. His work is just getting started. We cannot afford to lose him."

Petronius and I grasped arms, and looked into each other's eyes with resolve, as he slipped back into the crowd. I knew now that I had to take charge, to plan our tactics as if I were going into battle. It was obvious that history was calling Jeshua to be great and I would be the one to assist most in bringing that about. The moment would be soon when Jeshua would have his throne and I would be the planner behind the throne. It did not seem as ego to me at the time. After all, no one would ever know what I was doing; Jeshua would have the focus of the world. I would be left with the knowledge that I was the prime mover in bringing about the thousand years of peace that was described in the scriptures.

The next day, our arrival in Jerusalem, was just perfect. There was a sweet wind from the east that was passing over the town, removing the usual smells of a large city. It was the wind that usually comes before a downpour, but today there was not a cloud in the sky.

Just outside the gates of the city Jeshua told us to wait as the disciples were gathering for the entrance. After about half an hour two disciples came from over a hill leading an ass. Jeshua climbed upon the ass and rode through the gates into the city. This was turning out wonderfully! Much better than I expected! The biblical prophecy stated that the Messiah should ride into Jerusalem on an ass. I did not think that Petronius would have the knowledge for such detail, but it was brilliant and I would tell him so.

Once inside the gates, we were greeted by a multitude of people. They showered him with blessings and praised God for sending the Messiah. "All glory to God, All hail to the King!" They shouted. It was an awesome sight. Children came carrying flowers. Many were thrown in Jeshua's path. Others had cut branches from trees and cast them in the way.

"Hosanna to the Lord of Hosts." "This king shall sit on the throne of David," they shouted. You could feel the joy and expectation of the crowd. It was as if their dream was finally coming true. I could well understand. It seemed as if my dream was coming true also.

Jeshua did not waste any time. He headed into the Temple. The priests could not continue their prayers over the din of the multitude and they shouted out to Jeshua, "Quiet your followers. They bring the marketplace inside this holy house of worship."

Jeshua truly looked the entire king that they wanted him to be and more. He shrugged his shoulders and showed a wistful smile. "It is useless to resist this. If all were quiet, the rocks and stones would shout. Joy is the spirit of this day, for people are discovering their divine heritage."

The priests at the Temple were emboldened with the order from Caiaphas to proceed against Jeshua without hesitation. They were looking for any reason to say that Jeshua was a troublemaker and a law-breaker, so that they could take him into custody. "By what authority do you come here to teach?"

Jeshua answered them, "I will answer your question if you answer one of mine: 'Was John the Baptizer a man of God, or a spreader of sedition?'"

The priests were caught in their own trap. Either way they answered, Jeshua could use that answer to his advantage. If they answered to the first, then Jeshua could prove John's support of him. If they answered the latter, they would make many enemies with the people because they considered John a prophet of God.

"We do not know," they finally answered.

Jeshua replied: "If you cannot answer my question and have not the knowledge of the truth, then my authority is at least as great as yours. One day, perhaps, you will learn the true source of authority for any of us originates directly from God. But God does not give authority to those who are too proud to listen."

Jeshua again turned a dangerous situation into an opportunity to teach. "Let me share a story with you. A man gave a sumptuous banquet for the surrounding nobility. They all came to his banquet hall, but found the doorway to be so low that they would have to bend their knees and bow their heads to enter. They took this as a grave insult and refused to enter the feast. The man, seeing that his guests had all turned away, opened his doors to the common people of his town, who did not have a problem with bending their knees and bowing their heads. They all entered and experienced the joyous feast."

"What is the point of this story?" the priest asked with an air of irritation and impatience.

"Those who are not puffed up with their own importance are usually the ones who will listen and gain wisdom. Those who accept themselves as ordinary are most open to hearing God speak to them. Sometimes, God will even speak to them through others. Will they listen? Judge not from where wisdom comes because, like the nobles in the story, you may miss the feast. You must be diligent and ready to heed God's call, for He may call out at any time. It is, in fact, that He is calling out all the time for those who would hear Him. He called to you from the mouth of John and you ignored him. He calls out again using the lips of this son of man. These followers you see have heeded the call and are enjoying the feast. No one should complain that they have not been called. Many have been called, few have been chosen. Why? Because few chose back."

Other followers of the Sadducees in the crowd attempted to discredit Jeshua. One posed a question of Law to Jeshua: "The Law of Moses states that if a married man dies and has no child, that the widow shall become his brother's bride. Let's say there are seven brothers. The first takes a wife and dies before she could bear a child. She becomes the wife of the next younger brother. Each brother dies in turn until she marries the last brother with whom she has a family. Which brother would have this woman as a wife in the afterlife?"

Jeshua chuckled at this man, who seemed to get more and more uncomfortable as Jeshua spoke. "A Sadducee asks me about an afterlife in which he has no belief. Anyone can see the falseness in this question, but I will answer it regardless of the motive of the poser. The law you talk of is for the flesh and not the spirit. The laws we follow on the earth are to provide order and a uniform code. They do not apply to the Spirit. In the Spirit we have but one Beloved and that is our Father-Mother God. You cannot understand this because you believe that death is the end of all life. Man is made in the image of God and God is eternal, and so man shall live as long as God lives. A man may seem to go to the grave, yet he is reborn again and again."

I felt a change in the atmosphere of the sanctuary. Jeshua had driven a wedge between the Sadducees and the *Parush*, who do believe in the afterlife.

An honest *Parush* came forward and asked Jeshua: "You speak as one who had been touched by God's wisdom. Tell me, Master, which is the greatest of all the Commandments?"

Jeshua answered in the way that this man would understand: "It is thus: *You shall place no other gods before the Lord.* The Lord is All and the Lord is One. From that we can do nothing else but love God with all our heart, mind, and soul <u>and</u> love our neighbors as ourselves, because our God resides in both. From this comes all the Law, the psalms and the prophets."

It was, to me, a miracle. Jeshua was actually winning over some of his greatest detractors. But Jeshua seemed to be troubled. His tone changed and the crowd became quiet. "Do not be caught up in the emotions that you feel today. Those who follow and call me 'Master' must remember that it is only by God's will that I bring forward His Light. There is truly but one Master and we are all His students. Those who will follow me ascend into the Light and wisdom of our Father's love. Those of you who scorn me will continue to curse the darkness you walk in. You can have it, it is yours. You created it. I have done what I could to show you the Light, to reacquaint you with your Heavenly Father as his very children, to open the door of His kingdom to you. I know you well but will not judge you. Only God has the authority to do that. Farewell."

Jeshua left in a hurry and we had to move quickly to keep up with him. We came to a familiar hill outside the gates. This was where he chose to finally rest. He dropped to the ground like a wounded beast. He just sat there on his knees with the tears streaming down his face. We were all a bit scared and did not know what to think, seeing him so troubled.

"Oh, Jerusalem, my Jerusalem, my holy city of peace," Jeshua sobbed. "You will not know peace for many centuries to come. You will see death and destruction until men again see The Father in all their brothers and sisters. Men will actually hate and slaughter the innocent in my name and in Your name. Those who follow me falsely will cast down our people for my sake. We could have led the world into God's kingdom and into the truth of our Being. I would have shown you the way, but you chose to ignore my meaning. I would have held you in my arms as tenderly as a mother suckling a newborn son, and fed you with wisdom straight from God… but man has chosen a different path. We who see are so few… when you take me, Lord, my only regret will be that I could have had more people listen and hear the truth. Come, my twelve, join me in meditation."

We went deep into meditation and left our physical bodies. We traveled with Jeshua to places where grief and turmoil could not follow. I was as aware of things in those realms of being as I was with the physical reality, and even more, because things seemed so much clearer on those other realms. We were taught many things there although I cannot write them down. Even if I did have words for them, I am bound to silence for these were teachings of the Masters.

He initiated us into the Holy Breath, the Sound of God. We were now all initiates of The Sojourner, the highest initiation one could receive and still be in a physical body. We were shown how to access the Akashic Record, where the history of the earth is written in the greatest detail imaginable. We caught a glimpse into probable futures for our world and probable outcomes of different actions. It was a dizzying experience when I now recall it, but it made perfect sense on the higher realms. Jeshua then told us that he was going to teach us what we could teach to other men. At that point we were back on that hill and it was dark. Seven hours had passed in what seemed to be a few minutes.

"Teach them to meditate as we do. To chant the names of God until they hear the sound of the Holy Breath and then to give up chanting and allow themselves to be taken into that Sound. From there, we can all travel the higher realms of Spirit as I have shown you. The Sound can come as a tone or a feeling or a wave of inner intellect; for each it is different, but you will know it when it comes. Teach them to be prepared! The Sound of God may come at any time, even when they least expect it. Let me relate a story…

"There was to be a great marriage in the town. Ten virgins were picked to have the honor of meeting the bridegroom and bringing him to the feast. Five of these were wise and brought oil for their lamps in case they had to wait long into the night. The bridegroom did not come at the expected time and the virgins, who were all weary, slept. At midnight came the call, 'The bridegroom has arrived!' The wise virgins lit their lamps and were ready to receive the bridegroom. The foolish virgins had no oil for their lamps and rushed to a merchant to purchase oil. While they were gone, the bridegroom left with the wise virgins to the marriage feast. When the foolish virgins arrived at the feast, they knocked on the door but were not let in. The owner of the banquet hall did not know them and sent them on their way. Because of this, they did not get to enjoy the feast.

"Be like the wise virgins and be ready every moment to receive the Lord inside of you. Also, it is wise to prepare now for the banquet that awaits you after this lifetime is over. Tend to Spiritual matters now, don't put these off! The end of this life may also come at any time. Be ready! Between each life, the Book of Life, the Akashic record, is opened and read. This Book of Life has all your thoughts and deeds of all your lifetimes written down. Everyone can read for himself or for herself what is written. The ultimate judge then, is your own soul. It will determine if you will ascend to the house of your Father or come back again to this earth. Each will know his place. If you want to stay with your Father in heaven, you must, while you are here on earth, pursue the highest form of relationship — that of service. Minister to all that come to you. Not for hope of reward, but because that person next to you is linked with you forever through our Heavenly Father. There is no person that you will meet who is not 'family.' And whatever you do to another, you also do to me, since that person is also part of <u>my</u> family. If you serve only yourself in this life you will certainly be back. No one lifts himself without lifting his brothers and sisters.

"Come, let us return to Bethany."

In Bethany we attended a feast in Jeshua's honor at the home of Joshua Bar-Simon. This man was once a leper whom Jeshua had healed. Jeshua was more quiet than usual but seemed to be in better spirits. I was fortunate enough to sit next to Mary of Magdala. She was in a somber mood that day and did not seem to enjoy the feast very much. I did my best to be attentive and caring with her, but her mood remained. At a point in the evening she muttered 'It is time' to herself and approached Jeshua. I was caught by surprise. She produced a small contained of perfume from the sleeve of her dress and preceded to perfume Jeshua's hair and feet.

"Mary, why are you doing this?" I asked.

The scent had quickly filled the whole room and was noticed by everyone. Matthew, the new treasurer of our group, took a whiff and said. "Mary, you have used the most expensive perfume. We could have made better use of the money."

Money was really not the issue for me. What was irritating me was that something was going on here of which I had no previous knowledge and I felt things out of control. One anoints a body in this way before burial. What was the cause of Jeshua's preoccupation with his own death?

"Men! Leave her alone," Jeshua finally said. "She is doing what is right and proper. She is demonstrating what none of you men are able to comprehend; that of acceptance and surrender to the wishes of Spirit. She has accepted that my time here will not be much longer and she is providing me the most loving service fitting the circumstance."

I saw Petronius behind a portal and moved toward him. "That was brilliant, what you did," I said.

"I only told a few people to cheer him," he said.

"No, I meant having him ride into Jerusalem on an ass, as in the prophecy."

"That was <u>not</u> I. I didn't come up with that, but I wished I had."

"Jeshua must have done this himself. He must be waiting for the right moment to proclaim his kingdom. Then all this talk of leaving and death must be serving another purpose. Could Jeshua be at cross-purposes? Things don't seem to add up. What am I missing?"

"This business is very confusing," Petronius said in an effort to support and comfort me, "Difficult to understand. But there is much that I have heard. Jeshua should move soon. Ananias, second to the High Priest, has personally taken over Saul's duties and is handling the problem of Jeshua personally. He wishes to find Jeshua alone or with only a few disciples so that he can be captured without the knowledge of the populace. I must go, Judas, it is not healthy to be seen in public together. There are those who watch all the time now."

"You're right. We need to stay in contact. Something is about to happen."

That night was the first night of Passover. Nicodemus had graciously provided a home for Jeshua and the rest of us, his apostles, to share a Passover meal. Something was going to happen, tension was in the air. Simon and Matthew started an argument concerning who should sit closest to the Master. The rest of us, I'm sorry to say, got pulled into this. We were like harlots fighting over a dress. I really don't know how Jeshua maintained his patience and loving for us at these times, but he shown forth again and used the episode to teach.

"Why do you fight?" Jeshua asked. "Is it for prominence among you? Is it to gain more favor with me? Unlike the politics of an organization, the most prominent position at heaven's table is the one who is of greatest service."

Jeshua then got up from his seat. He took a large bowl of water, soap and a towel, knelt to each of us in turn and washed our feet. I understood immediately what this meant. Jeshua had sacrificed the prominence that was due him at the table to serve us. No man is above serving his brother. The real Master is truly the servant. I felt like weeping, but maintained my composure.

I was not the only one affected like this. When he got to Peter, Peter protested, "Master, you will not wash my feet!"

"Then we are not in fellowship."

"In that case," said Peter, "wash my hands and face as well!"

"There is no need. You have bathed in the Jordan, so have all the rest of you; right to your soul is clean. The feet, however, get soiled in our travels on this earth. The feet represent understanding and all need to clear their understanding each day. If you call me Master and truly believe it, then you should seek prominence in Spirit by washing each other's feet and open yourselves to serving each other. I have taught you these things before. These are lessons from Spirit. If you take them to heart and live them, then you will be truly blessed.

"I wanted to share this meal with all of you in the true spirit of the Passover, in love and service. When evil comes to your door it will pass you by if you are one of God's children. While all are God's children, only very few know the true meaning of this. Even fewer will live their lives as the expression of this truth. To truly celebrate this festival one must accept one's own self as a divine son or daughter of a loving God and, most importantly, live your life from that understanding. Then you will know evil, but it will pass by you and not touch to your heart.

"I wanted to share this last meal with all of you because I will not eat with you again before I pass into the realms of Spirit. Soon after I will again eat with you in the Kingdom."

Jeshua led us in the prayers and songs that were at the heart of the festival, adding his own interpretation of the ageless wisdom. We then enjoyed the meal. Peter summoned more courage than the rest of us and asked the question, "Why will you not be eating with us on the other nights?"

"I will soon be turned over to those that would do me harm."

"Who would turn you over to our enemies, Master?" Peter asked again, pressing Jeshua for more information.

"It is the one who has his hand in the dish with me," Jeshua said.

I had reached onto the plate that held the matzo at the same time as Jeshua. I saw that my hand was on the same dish as Jeshua's. Why would I want to turn him over to those that would kill him?

I looked at him with a heavy heart and pain in my eyes. "Master, is it me?"

Jeshua did not answer me directly. "It is not with malice that this happens, but as a circumstance which must occur if I am to lead the way to the Kingdom."

Just then there was a knock at the door. It was a young boy who pointed at me and beckoned me to come to him. I got up from the table and motioned that he talk in low tones so as not to disturb the rest.

"Petronius has need to talk to you. Follow me."

This was strange. It was not the usual way of our communication. Perhaps something had happened to him. I motioned to Jeshua.

"Go and do what you must," he said. "And when you see Nicodemus, tell him to make ready the cave."

I agreed but this made no sense. I did not expect to see Nicodemus where I was going. I should have suspected something was not right when we went along a path that was shrouded in bushes and undergrowth. I heard a noise and turned around to see myself surrounded by Temple guards with swords drawn and ready. I quelled my natural reaction to fight. I expected to see Saul with these guards. He did not disappoint me. But I didn't expect to see Ananias.

"Well, it's Ananias, the High Priest's hatchet-man who holds Saul's leash," I said, mustering all the contempt I could.

"We could kill you right now..." Saul moved toward me in a rage, but was halted in his tracks by Ananias.

"Stop! We need him alive and well if he is going to betray his Master and turn him over to us."

I chuckled. "What makes you think that I am going to do that? I would die before turning Jeshua over to you."

Saul had regained much of his composure. "We know you would. You would jump at the chance. But what if you are laying your life down for a false prophet? What if he is no more a Messiah than you are? Would not we find that hysterical that the great Judas Iscariot should be taken into such a transparent ruse? This son of a carpenter is a nobody and he will die a common criminal like you. You will die right next to him and I will be laughing at you both."

"When he comes forward as Messiah, he will show all of you. He has powers that you cannot even conceive." I fumed.

Saul laughed and said, "I pity you both."

I felt myself giving in to the rage that stirred within me. I could take death and torture, it was a part of being a soldier. But my weakness had always been being ridiculed. I would now do anything to prove that bastard Saul a liar and a fool.

"Very well," I said. "I will tell where he is. But it is you who will pay the price for your arrogance."

"Ha," he said. "I knew I could get you to listen to reason." He gloated. "I have grown to know you well, Yehudah, almost as well as I know myself. One must know one's enemies in that way if one is to succeed. And now for the business at hand. I do not want him to be warned, so you will remain our guest until the morning when you will tell us where he stays. If you try to trick us, we will kill him and all his followers too. This includes Jeshua's entire family. We cannot have the "king's" heirs looking for revenge, can we?"

I then realized that this meant Mary of Magdala as well. I could not bear to think of her put to the sword.

"I am sure you do not want to be the cause of all that needless bloodshed." He continued. "Would you like to be known from now on as the cause of death of so many, just like your brother Simon, who was the cause of your parent's death? If you even try to escape, they will all be killed."

"Just what do you get out of this, Saul?"

"I receive the knowledge that I have done my job well. My duty is to protect the citizens of this land from harm. If we anger the Romans we are asking for wholesale slaughter. Why are the Romans so powerful? Because they know the meaning of order. They are also powerful because they do not know the meaning of compassion. Why should we be any less powerful? In fact, we should be greater. We have the Law. That Law must be followed to the letter if we are to have order. This means both civil and religious law. To do this there must be a strong authority to maintain order. I represent that authority. I am that authority."

"Just remember from where that authority comes," chimed in Ananias. "Do not just get information of his whereabouts, have this man lead you to him. Have him point out his Master. Have him betray his Master with a kiss." Ananias began to cackle like some old hag.

I was quickly sinking into desperation so I went inside to chant my sacred tones. I began to realize that things could still turn out as I had intended. Jeshua has always been able to easily elude mobs by disappearing. He would certainly do this again. Furthermore, when he saw them act against him, he would know the time would be right for him to move into his kingship. Why else would he have gone to the trouble of following the prophesy of riding into Jerusalem on an ass if he did not intend to follow the rest of it? This seemed better and better. I would save the lives of the disciples and Jeshua would accept his rightful kingship. I would be known as the active force in bringing this all about.

I tried to ignore the odious Ananias and concentrate on Saul. At least he was another man of action. I could talk to him. "Saul, are you a man of your word?"

"To lie is to sin. I do not go back on my word."

"If I do all you ask and you still cannot take Jeshua into custody, will you honor your promise to allow his disciples and family to live?"

"If you lead us to Jeshua, that will suffice. Why do you ask?"

"He just might slip past you, it has happened before."

"You have my word and God will deal with me if I break it," Saul concluded.

"Tell us now where he will be. Then lead us later," said an untrusting Ananias, who would think nothing of breaking his word.

"We are to meet at the garden of Gethsemane, do you know the place?"

"It is an open space… not good," mused Ananias.

"Hold to the agreement or be ready to kill me now," I stated with finality.

"Very well," said Ananias with a frown, "do not trick us, we can still have Jeshua and his disciples killed later. Do not think us so awful, we punish, but we can also reward. You are the treasurer for your band; you will appreciate this, a small donation."

He tossed me a small pouch. I looked inside and it contained about thirty pieces of silver. "What's this, blood money?"

He shrugged, "Call it what you will."

I threw it back in his face as hard as I could. In the dim light I still noticed that I had knocked him off his feet. What I didn't see was the hilt of a sword coming down on my head.

I was not unconscious for very long. Night passed at a painfully slow pace, my back up against a tree trunk, surrounded by guards who were even more dangerous to me because they feared me. I do not think I actually slept but I went into a haze wondering what Jeshua was doing now. Did he know what was about to occur? Was he planning anything of his own? I may have appeared to be sleeping because I got a shove from Saul to awaken me.

"It's about an hour before daylight, time to go."

I took the path to the garden followed by Saul, the boy who first summoned me, Ananias, and a company of guards. And yet, it was the loneliest walk I have ever taken.

I found it foolish that they were carrying lanterns. Jeshua and the other apostles would easily be able to see us coming from far off and get away. As we approached, Jeshua, alone, came out to meet us.

Malchus, captain of the guard and Saul's second in command, stepped forward to make the arrest.

"Whom do you seek?" Jeshua asked.

"Jeshua, son of Joseph, the one who calls himself Christ."

"I am he," Jeshua said and raised up both arms. The whole garden was immediately filled with Light. Many of the guard ran off, but enough stayed to outnumber Jeshua's group.

"At last," I thought, "Jeshua is going to act!"

"Yehudah!" said Ananias, motioning to me.

I came up to Jeshua and kissed him on the right cheek. "Master, forgive me."

"This needs to be done to fulfill God's plan so there is no need for forgiveness, I do not judge you. It is not from me that you should fear judgment. You have been blinded by ambition and you will soon come to your senses and understand how you have erred. But I understand how you feel so I say to the part of you that will need it, 'I forgive you.'"

The other apostles, seeing what went on, but not hearing, grabbed me and were ready to kill me. Peter had already drawn his sword. Believe me, at that point, I would have welcomed death!

"Hold," said Jeshua. "You have no right to harm or to judge this man, this is God's will and all of us are subject to it." Peter took me and shoved me to the ground in disgust.

"Come on, this has taken long enough," said Malchus. He bound Jeshua in chains.

"I tell you I have no wish to escape, I will go willingly with you," said Jeshua. "You do not need these."

Jeshua raised his arms, and again the light became brighter and the chains crumbled and fell away.

Malchus, fearing the Master would then escape, drew his sword, but Peter was ready and slashed the face of Malchus, causing a great deal of bleeding.

"Peter, put away your sword," said Jeshua. "I have no need for man's protection, since I could call up legions of God's forces to assist me, but then I would not be fulfilling my goal."

He placed his hand on the side of Malchus' face and the light shown again brightly. "I would not have any man harmed on my behalf. He who follows the road of peace shall have peace inside of him; he that lives by the sword shall die by it."

Then he said to Malchus. "I told you I would not run to save my life. You may do with me what you will."

Malchus stood up and motioned to his remaining troops to arrest Jeshua's disciples. Not being able to fight, they ran to save their lives. I wished that they had also taken me.

"What about me?" I asked Malchus.

"Don't worry, you are free to go and your Mary of Magdala will not be harmed."

Mary! I would go to her and see if they had kept their word not to go after Jeshua's family.

I stood, untouched by the outside circumstance, yet I was probably the most deeply hurt of all. I was not alone. The boy who had summoned me looked at me as if I were a demon from the depths. "Please, I did not know it would come to this," he cried. I approach him as he wept. He cowered at my approach but was too wounded inside himself to run.

"You may kill me if you wish; I did not mean you any harm. I would have been punished if I didn't obey," he whimpered.

I reached out and held him close to me. I ruffled his hair. One tear streamed down my cheek as my body somewhat muffled his sobs.

When he became silent, I moved away. I had other things to attend to. Mary! I must get a horse. I rushed to the nearest stables that were unguarded and took a horse. I rode for what seemed to be forever until I got to Bethany.

The sun was just breaking when I got to the house of Lazarus. I knocked on the door and saw Mary, Martha, and Lazarus. I must have awakened all of them.

"Are you alright?" I asked Mary.

She looked puzzled. "Yes, what's the matter?" she asked.

"Jeshua has been taken by the Temple guard. I do not know whether he will escape. They might kill him. Mary, I must tell you…" I pulled her away from the other to speak with her in private.

"…That you will hear some really bad things about me. I want you to know that I did not willingly betray Jeshua to the authorities."

"You did what?"

"I was told that his entire family would be killed by soldiers if I did not bring them to where Jeshua spent the early morning."

"What are you talking about? I did not see any soldiers."

"Then it was another lie," I said, shaking my head, "they would not have killed you."

"You betrayed the Master for me?" she asked incredulously. "Do you know what you have done?"

I saw that she would not understand in her present state. She filled up with tears and shouted at me in anger: "Never, never, talk to me again!"

I saw that I could do no more good there and I left; perhaps I could help the other disciples free Jeshua, that is, if they didn't kill me first.

The sun was getting high when I returned to Jerusalem. I asked all those I saw if they had seen Jeshua. Word of my part in this had not yet spread; I still might be able to get some answers. I found out that Jeshua had been taken that morning to the Temple to be tried by the Sanhedrin, before Caiaphas, the High Priest.

By the time I got there I spied Nicodemus. "What has happened?" I asked.

"Yehudah, what is this I hear about you? Did you betray The Master?"

"You know me well enough to know that I would not do such a thing willingly. I was given a choice of his life or that of all his family and followers. I assumed he would escape as he was used to doing many times before. What has happened since I have been gone?"

"Caiaphas and the Sadducees brought him to trial on a number of charges, a false prophet, a blasphemer, and a profaner of the Sabbath. They had even paid people to bear false witness against him. I pleaded that those men who would speak against him do so separately to the assembly. None of them had a story that supported the other. It only showed them as perjurers. I then pressed the council to find him not guilty. The Sanhedrin acted well this day by resisting Caiaphas and not condemning Jeshua to stoning, but Caiaphas would not let him go free. He sent him to Herod, hoping that perhaps Herod would do to Jeshua what he did to John. That is all that I know. Where are you going?"

"I must see what I can do to free him," I said.

"I am afraid that this is out of our hands now, Yehudah."

"Oh, Jeshua also told me to tell you when I saw you to make ready the cave."

Nicodemus' frown relaxed and turned to a smile. "It may not appear so, but I am sure Jeshua is still in control of the situation."

"I cannot accept that he would go willingly like a lamb to slaughter," I said, "I just can't permit it."

"Things are not always what they seem," he said, "especially where Jeshua is concerned. You of all people should know this. This is bigger than you are, Yehudah, and you can't stop it."

"Then I'll die trying," I said and stormed off.

I walked at a very fast pace to get to Herod's court in Jerusalem. As I turned a corner, a blow knocked me off my feet. "I could kill you, you scum." A voice boomed out.

It was Petronius. "I didn't only because I want to know what made you do this. Mary came to me and told me what you said. I could not believe it at first, but then it began to make sense. This was stupid and foolish. In the earlier days you would have died before doing what you did. And, you would have let Mary die too. You have let your own desires rule out your loyalty and good sense. I am very ashamed to call you friend."

"I am ashamed of myself as well, Petronius, and if you kill me you would be doing me a favor. I would like to free him but the whole Roman garrison will be guarding him if he is taken to Pilate. I have never felt this helpless since my parents were killed."

"I do not think I will kill you. You will punish yourself more than I could punish you. If you want to see the end of this, go to Pilate. That is the seat of power. That is where things will be decided."

He sheathed his sword and turned away.

I ran as fast as I could to the Governor's Palace. The square outside the palace was filled with Sadducees and their followers. I ducked into a corner so as not to be noticed. I was close enough, however, to hear what was going on. Was it here where Jeshua would manifest his kingship and start the thousand years of peace? I strained to hear the proceedings. Pilate was the center of the proceedings and used everything to let all know that his will was law.

"We have the man you wanted here," said Ananias.

"Why have you brought him?" queried Pilate in a mocking manner.

"We have evidence that he is an enemy of Rome, *sir*," said Ananias, holding back his distaste or, at least, keeping in mind the consequences of crossing Pilate.

"Why would you care about enemies of Rome?" Pilate pressed him.

"You know as well as I that it is our people who will suffer most if a rebellion ensues," Ananias replied. "Our only protection is bound to Roman Law."

"You answer well and with wisdom," Pilate said "Let us bring forward the prisoner. State the charges against him."

I then saw Jeshua, bruised and bleeding, bound in chains, but with a resolve in his eyes and on his face that I had not seen before.

"We have evidence that he has plotted to overthrow Roman authority in Judea, Samaria, and Galilee. He claims to be a king, a descendant of David, and therefore a traitor to Tiberius," said Ananias, experiencing more and more distaste for his role. "My assistant will continue. I have urgent business at the Temple."

It was Saul who stepped forward to represent the Sadducees at the trial. "All the Zealots need is a powerful leader to whip up the populace and cause rebellion and destruction of our homeland. This man's own words have condemned him as an enemy of Rome. He claims to be a king."

Pilate continued this mockery of a trial. He turned to Jeshua. "Well, are these charges true or false?"

"Yes, I am a king, but not in the earthly sense. My kingdom is not of this earth, and therefore no threat to your power. If my intent was to carve out an earthly kingdom, do you think I would have been taken peacefully? You are a man of thought, Pilate; does this make sense to you? If I make no claims on a physical kingdom, why should I be tried in an earthly court? You have the evidence of perjured men who would twist my words only to ease their own fears. My kingdom resides within each of you and those who would come to the truth inside of themselves would perceive the truth of my words."

Pilate shuddered and quickly regained his composure. He was a man who enjoyed being in power, one who also enjoyed exercising it and did not like his authority challenged on any level. But somewhere, Jeshua's words had touched a part of Pilate in which he knew there was truth (or at least there was doubt), so he quickly moved back to the position of command to quash that uncomfortable feeling.

"What, then, <u>is</u> the truth?" He countered, more as a command than a question.

"There is only one truth and that is God, the Holy Spirit, which is all things and knows all things. If one would know Spirit, one would know truth."

Pilate's frustration appeared to be growing. Here was a man before him, in chains, who spoke as well as the most enlightened of philosophers in the Empire. Pilate was no match for Jeshua in terms of rhetoric and that annoyed him. Pilate often fancied himself a philosopher and because of his position, there were few who would contend with him. Now here was a man without fear, about to die, who made Pilate appear the fool.

He was getting nowhere with Jeshua. Talking to Jeshua longer might cause others to feel compassion toward this prisoner. Instead he turned back to Saul. "Well, do you want me to crucify your 'King?'"

"Sir," said Saul, "we have no king but Cæsar."

Pilate appeared pleased with this level of devotion, but he continued to press the Sadducees to appear to be the ones calling for sentence to be rendered. In reality, they would have done anything he wished.

"I will even offer you a choice. I will let one prisoner go. This will demonstrate how just the Roman rule really is. You may choose either your 'King' or the murderer Jacob Bar-Abba to go free today."

Saul knew his part well. He chose Bar-Abba. It probably would have meant his life if he had chosen otherwise.

Pilate was always the fox. He had learned from experience that direct abuse of power caused too much unrest, and that would soon get back to Rome. The way to keep his power was to have it appear that his wishes were those of the people governed. "Then it is done. You have chosen. I will free Bar-Abba and sentence this man to the cross. Let every man see that I have been a just administrator and have regarded the wishes of the leaders of this client state. I therefore wash my hands of him and follow your wishes."

Jeshua appeared to be in pretty bad shape physically, but I doubted that this would have stopped him from disappearing or freeing himself by force if he so wished. The problem was <u>when</u>. Would he let himself be hung on a cross? I must follow and be there to act if he needed help. I ducked into an alley and spied some clothes hanging out to dry. Women's clothes would serve me better as a disguise, so I covered myself in half-dried clothes and rushed to catch up to Jeshua.

The Roman guard was already pushing him at sword-point through the street carrying the cross on which he would supposedly die. He could not make it all the way with that burden and collapsed. A disciple in the crowd, Simon of Cyrene, picked up Jeshua's cross and carried it all the way to the hill of the Skull, beyond the city gates.

Thoughts wildly careened through my mind. What if he would not do anything? It would all be over. My lifetime would be wasted; all of this would just be wasted!

In the garb of a woman, I was able to get closer to the site than if I were dressed as a man. If I were dressed as a man, they would have recognized me as a follower and I would have been taken into custody. I bent over and attempted to look old and frail. Before I got close to the site, I pulled out one of my blades and made a small slit in my palm to get some blood, which I spread on my lips. I then felt more confident with my disguise. It had been quite some time since I had practiced my skills as a Sicarri, but not so long that I would forget them.

I was able to get very close but halted in my tracks. Mary, Jeshua's Mother, and Mary of Magdala, Martha, Ruth, and a number of female disciples were there and they would have recognized me, so I did not approach further. The soldiers stripped Jeshua, placed him on the cross, and would have bound him as they did with the Zealots who were to die on either side of him. Saul feared trickery and told them to use nails to lessen the chance that Jeshua would find some way of escaping. The soldiers offered Jeshua a sedative to drink before using the nails but Jeshua refused.

The nails were driven in, shattering bone and tearing flesh. I felt every blow inside my very essence. I quickly lost any kind of courage. Any hope that I had quickly evaporated. Why would he allow himself to go through this?

After nailing Jeshua to the cross, the soldiers nailed a quickly formulated sign in Hebrew, Greek and Latin. I focused on the Greek that said "Jesus, called Christ, King of the Jews."

They raised his cross between the other two and sat down to watch him die. I felt a cold wind on the back of my neck. I turned around and saw that James and John had come. Their faces were shrouded in grief and disbelief.

There were a few Sadducees remaining and they mocked Jeshua. "If you are who you say you are, come down from the cross and all will believe you." "You rescued others from the grave, why can't you save yourself?"

Jeshua did not answer them directly, but looked up and said, "Forgive them, Lord, for they do not know what they do."

He then called out to John to come closer. John approached the cross and was eyed suspiciously by the Roman guard. The guard searched him and found no weapon. Then the guard backed off.

"John," said Jeshua, "I am leaving my mother and sisters in your tender care."

"Master, while they live, my home shall be theirs," said John.

The Zealot on the left said to Jeshua, "If you are the Messiah, you have the power to speak the Word and free yourself and me."

The other Zealot, on Jeshua's right merely said that he had seen Jeshua's entrance into Jerusalem and that had reawakened a desire to know God inside of him. From there, he received a glimpse of the Kingdom of which Jeshua had spoken. He said: "It just seemed so natural, so right that it would be present here and now." This man told Jeshua that he was sorry to see him treated in this manner. Jeshua's countenance brightened and he weakly smiled.

"I also grieve," said Jeshua, barely audibly, "but only that God's plan should need to come about with the wounding of so many hearts. I am rewarded by the knowledge that all did not ignore my words and deeds. You will be rewarded also. I will see you today in the realm of the soul…" He hesitated looking out at the small crowd until he found my eyes and looked deeply into them. "…And others, too."

It was midday but the sky had become unnaturally dark. Jeshua looked up and exclaimed, "Sun, sun, why have you left me?"

He looked so alone, so vulnerable, and so <u>human</u>. He may have been a high spiritual Master and the most advanced being on the earth, but it was his humanity that touched me so deeply. I cried, as did the others in woman's clothing.

"He looked up again and said, "Abba, into your hands I place my soul." His eyes closed and his knees buckled.

A Roman soldier, a veteran of these executions, knew too well that often people would feign death on the cross to escape it. He took his spear and pierced Jeshua's side to the heart. Blood poured from the wound. And I saw a glow arise out of Jeshua's body where it hovered for a minute and then was gone.

Gone was my friend from childhood. Gone were all the dreams that I had of bringing change to the world. Gone were my visions of Jeshua's kingdom on the earth. It was all gone. I was also gone. I was a walking dead man. There was not one thing left for me. Not one thing left that would bring me any comfort in this world. I once told Jeshua that I would follow him to the ends of the earth. I will now do more. I will follow him to death. I looked for my blades, but I must have dropped them. It had begun to rain steadily and I could not find anything on the ground that shone like metal.

I would follow Jeshua into death, but it would have to be a different way. I was wearing a long sash. This could possibly be used for a rope to hang myself if it had the strength. I did not want to hang and choke to death for hours; I wanted to end this wretched existence as soon as I could. If the sash was long enough I could do this properly. I unwound the sash from around my waist and found that it would suit my purpose well.

I found a tree overlooking a gorge that had sturdy limbs that would easily hold my weight. I climbed the tree and stood on the lowest and thickest branch. Not only was I able to get the sash tied around the trunk, I was also able to stand upright with the other end of the sash tied securely around my neck. It would then be quick and decisive. The rain had increased to the point where it was almost impossible to see to the next hill. I tested the sash. It was now soaked and appeared to be even stronger and the wetness would prevent it from sliding off the limb. I relaxed every part of my body.

"Jeshua, I'm coming," I said out loud.

The last thing I heard was my neck snap.

After the gavel sounded, Chris glanced at me with a look that I could describe a pleading, pleading that I had something he could use.

"This may or may not help, but I'm sure of one thing," I said.

"What's that?"

"I know who Hastings is, or <u>was</u>. Saul! He was Saul. I knew I knew him from before, and now I know for sure."

"Now <u>that's</u> good news," Chris said sarcastically.

"Well, Chris," I said with some excitement, "what if you put me on the stand and regress me to that lifetime. I could explain…"

"In Aramaic!"

"What?"

"Do you know Aramaic?"

"If I did, I wouldn't have needed a translation of the manuscript, would I? Chris, what are you planning?"

"Something that may buy us a whole lot more time," he said. "By the way, would you give me the phone number of your archeologist buddy in Jerusalem?"

Over objections from "Saul-Hastings," Chris asked for and received a two-day recess.

On the day we reconvened, we stood nervously at the terminal waiting for Dr. Wilder's plane to come in from Jerusalem.

When his face appeared in the crowd, I rushed over and got a big bear hug.

"When I got the call, I came as quickly as I could," he said. "I am really eager to help in any way I can."

"You are set to testify in just a few minutes," said Chris. "So let's not keep the judge waiting."

We happened to come in a few minutes late and got a withering look from Judge Wainright.

Chris quickly called Dr. Wilder to the stand.

"May we have your name please?"

"Dr. Ernest Wilder."

"What do you do for a living, Dr. Wilder?"

"I lead archeological expeditions."

"Just what qualifications do you have that would allow you to do that?"

"I am an archeologist, historian, and an expert in a number of ancient languages."

"Tell me," asked Chris, "would Aramaic be one of them?"

"Yes, sir."

"Is it not true, Dr. Wilder, that you are one of the most accomplished living experts in this language?"

"Well, some say so," he said modestly.

"Come now, Dr. Wilder, I think you are much too humble. Wasn't it you that Mr. Hammer approached with the copy of the original manuscript while you were in Jerusalem?"

"Yes, sir."

"Then you took that manuscript and translated it from Aramaic into English, is that correct?"

"Yes."

"How long did it take you to translate the entire manuscript?"

"About four weeks."

"Is that fast, Dr. Wilder?"

"It took the Foundation about three months to do the same thing I did," he said, a good part of him beamed with pride.

"By the way, Dr. Wilder, does Roy Hammer know Aramaic?"

"If he did, he wouldn't have called upon me to translate it for him, would he?"

"Thank you, Dr. Wilder. That will be all."

Chris then called to the stand Dr. Collins, the psychologist who did past-life regressions. He asked her how many years she had been doing the regressions and she answered "twenty-one."

He called me to the stand and handed me a sheet of paper with some scribbles on it and asked me to read. It was in Aramaic. "I can't read this." I said.

"OK, said Chris, "can we dim the room?"

I could barely see the scribbles on the paper still in my hand.

"I would like to call Dr. Collins to the stand to regress Mr. Hammer," said Chris. "Take him back to the Judas lifetime."

It was an incredible experience. It was like I was living in two times, then and the present. A flood of new memories came back, but Dr. Collins asked me to concentrate on the sheet of paper I had just tried to read. I read it as it was, in the original Aramaic. It was like reading the newspaper. I was then asked to write a translation of the text into English using my present self as a source for English. When I was done, I was asked to read both translations, which I did.

Chris called Dr. Wilder back to the stand.

"Dr. Wilder, could you tell me how well Mr. Hammer did on his translation?"

"Mr. Hammer got an estimated 96% of the words, phrases, and nuances correct."

The part of me from two thousand years ago became irritated. I blurted out: "Nonsense! My translation was completely correct. The errors are Dr. Wilder's. There are some slight differences in Judean and Galilean Aramaic that he missed. He's mixing the two. It sounds ridiculous."

Dr. Wilder's face drooped, but he perked up after he understood what had happened.

Chris picked up on that and asked, “Dr. Wilder, would you say that Mr. Hammer or should I say ‘Judas’ knows Aramaic?”

“Better than I do, it seems!”

Chris continued, “So in his normal consciousness, he does not recognize this language and in his previous persona, he is fluent. Would you say that the only explanation would be that he grew up with Aramaic two thousand years ago?”

“Objection!” bellowed Hastings. “This man could have learned Aramaic, perhaps even from Dr. Wilder, himself.”

“Then why would he need to see Dr. Wilder to get it translated?”

“To establish this nonsensical idea, that he was Judas in a previous life, so he could claim the manuscript as his.”

“That would mean he would have had to translate it in four weeks. Could he have done that, Mr. Hastings?”

Hastings was silent.

After the proceedings were over, I was brought out of that shared state of consciousness and back to the present. “Chris, it looks like we’ve finally got him!”

Chris did not smile. He shook his head slowly. This just set him back a little. “There is not enough evidence to prove beyond doubt that you are who you say you are. Hastings will always be able to cast doubt on evidence that is not solid and physical. Unless we can convince Hastings, we will not convince the jury.”

An ocean of doubt flooded me. First, having to read this account brought back a feeling of disgust for myself. I felt the experience of letting my desires for importance and my fear of loss affect my support of my teacher. I knew that I wasn’t the monster that is depicted in other accounts of the New Testament, but I still fell prey to judging myself for weakness and profound spiritual failure. I felt like throwing myself at the mercy of the court and let them sentence me. I felt what I needed was punishment. Then inside of me I heard Eric speak: “Roy, you are just getting another test from Spirit. Remember, tests do not attack you on your strong points, but at your weak ones.”

I withdrew my emotional attachment to the events of the day, and knew at once that I was letting negativity and depression run away with me. A past failure was one thing. I don’t have to fail now! In my entire life I had never done something for a cause larger than myself, never committed myself to a project that was “for the highest good,” as Jeshua described it. This was what I was being offered — an opportunity for service. It was a chance to erase my judgment of past failure and perhaps be of service to others by showing how important self-forgiveness is in man's understanding of himself. How could I do that if I was having trouble forgiving myself?

As I drove home I kept asking myself that question. Home, in the solitude of my bedroom, I went through the steps Eric described would work for me. I did nothing for half an hour but watch my breath. My mind ran everything as if it were a movie on a loop. I let go of my desire to control it. I allowed myself to become an observer. Whatever came up in my mind or emotions I did not participate in it. I was outside of it. I could finally see myself in a somewhat neutral fashion. I saw myself as a small child trying to do the right thing — making errors and learning to correct those errors. I opened in myself a sweeping feeling of compassion and understanding that I really was that child. I fell in love with that child. I saw the preciousness of my own being and experienced a feeling of forgiveness that brought a sweet flowing of tears from my eyes. So this is loving oneself! I felt the presence of what Eric had called the "inner master." At last I had reached the "core" of myself that could not be swayed by ignorance, doubt or fear. I realized that I was facing a point of choice. I could surrender to this inner guide or do things the way I had always done them. I could follow this inner direction and possibly look to the world like a great fool, or sacrifice the importance that I placed on the opinions of others and be the living expression of this inner wisdom that asked my attention. If I did fail, at least I would finally have been true to that essence within me. I had found my inner messiah. The question was: would I again betray that inner messiah by ignoring what it called me to do or would I be true to it?

I knew my next step.

CHAPTER 14 - THE TIME IN HELL

"You've got to put Hastings on the stand." I told Chris. "If we regress him, I've got a few questions to ask. They might bring back some convincing memories."

Chris just shook his head. "We're just not ready to do anything like that. I'm just a step away from being charged with contempt. That will push the judge over the edge and you'll be without a lawyer to represent you."

For the first time, I saw fear in Chris' eyes. If I were going to take my leap of faith, he would have to also.

A new day brought a new session of reading. I began:

At first everything was dark. Then a dim light appeared from far away and edged closer. I could make out shadows approaching me from the left. My vision began to clear. There were others in this dark place, all moving toward the light. I turned to look at them. I didn't seem to know any of them. We all kept moving toward the light. The light became just bright enough for me to recognize the boy who first led me into the ambush. He must not have escaped the guard and they must have killed him to assure his silence. "Here is the betrayer of the Master," he shouted. "And I am even lower than he, for I am the betrayer of the betrayer." One who I recognized as dying on the cross with Jeshua came forward and shouted in a rage of disgust, "This is the betrayer of The Messiah." At that point my calm disappeared. I felt a fear that I would come to harm, but more than that, I felt the pain of being not understood. Would I now forever be reviled and despised? I just wanted to leave this place. I looked around at the souls who were converging upon me. And from the left side of my vision came a shadow.

It appeared to be a beautiful blue angel with outstretched wings. The angel floated closer and reached out to me. I started to reach out to the angel but a hand from the right grabbed my hand and pulled me up into a light-filled room.

"Just got you in time," said a familiar voice. As my vision cleared further I saw the face of Jeshua shining like a sun. It hurt my eyes. I had to turn away.

"Sorry," he said, "I should cover up a little."

Most of the Light disappeared. "In the physical world, to be seen, one must reflect light, on the inner realms, one must BE Light," said Jeshua.

I put my hand on my neck, moved my head and found everything working properly. I tried it out with a small question. "There was this beautiful angel… Where am I?"

Jeshua looked at me as if I really should have known the answer to this question myself. "That was the Angel of Death. The normal process of death and rebirth has been interrupted for you. I have need of you with me. That is why I grabbed you from that place. We are on the Soul Realm, our true home. You have been here before, feel the energy, the calmness and the bliss. It is the kingdom of which I have always spoken."

Yes, I did recognize it. "The rooms, the structures, are they part of this realm?"

"Only in a manner of speaking, Yehudah. On other realms they would be part of the creation of those realms. Here, creation is not complete. You see what we have both created. The room is only here because your higher self wanted it and was comfortable with it."

"You mean we can create whatever we wish on this level?"

"Again, in a manner of speaking," said Jeshua. "On this realm we truly reflect who we are as children of God, and that means that we are also creators."

"Master, couldn't someone create something terrible that would harm others?"

"It is not permitted. Before we can actually create here on our own, we must prove to be responsible creators. Why do you think we spend so much time on the physical level? It is the schoolroom of the divine.

When we have accepted our birthright there, only then can we move to it here."

"Oh, that is why you have taught us continually to 'not harm ourselves or others and to take care of ourselves so that we could take care of others.'"

"It is the wish of the Most High God, that we now begin to move into our roles as co-creators with Him. My life is supposed to be a demonstration of what we all can do if we accept, finally, our roles as responsible children of God. Because of the work we do now, this Soul realm will be opened to humanity as a whole. Now there are only a very few who can reach it. Kal[12] and his plan have prevented it. That will be changed very shortly."

My guilt overcame me. I fell down on my knees. "Please, Master, forgive me. I have cut your life short with my unthinking selfishness and lust for power and acknowledgement. I feel as if I have committed a grave spiritual crime, one for which I'm not sure I could ever forgive myself."

I was lifted from the floor by unseen hands and placed on a soft couch.

Jeshua frowned and said: "You have not committed a spiritual crime in your past actions. However, you are <u>now</u> committing a spiritual crime upon yourself. You are denying your own divinity. The result is that you are betraying the spirit in you. I am also that spirit, so in a manner of speaking you betray me also. You have fallen into a trap set by the negative forces."

"I am confused. What could I have done differently?"

"You took in the judgment and condemnation that the world, in its misunderstanding, offered you. It offered the same to me, but I acted differently. I left the wilderness with greater resolve. You could have lifted in your expression and gone beyond your limited earthly character, but you allowed earthly logic to rule you. If you had only waited, held in your assurance, to witness my return, you would have seen that everything is right and proper, and you would not have condemned yourself. The result of your actions has set in motion grave consequences for yourself. For ages your name will be linked with betrayal of me, but at the proper time you will finally learn to forgive and accept yourself. Until you learn self-forgiveness, you will not be worthy of the spiritual gifts that will be offered you, because you have denied them within."

---

[12] Kal (Lucifer), the Lord of the negative realms.

"What can I do about this now?" I asked.

"I am asking you to look at all this differently," said Jeshua. "Your 'mistakes' were necessary for me to fulfill my mission to conquer death. When I return this illusion will be pierced for all time. This would not have worked without you, Yehudah. Your personal drawbacks, your Karma, are being used to lift and to teach yourself and others. When we return to the physical level we will finish what I have started. I need you to give me your focus and your energy. What did I tell all of you continually?"

"Use all things to the greatest advancement of the Soul."

"And, Yehudah, you will find out truly what that means."

"But, even on the lower realms, I am cursed by those who see me."

"You are 'the unforgivable.' You will come to represent all that people hate and despise most in themselves. Then you will teach them all a great lesson. Before this life you asked from the core of your being to be of service to the Christ-action. What you did in your unawareness was necessary for what I am to do on earth: to bring people closer to their own knowledge of their Christhood within. You are getting your dearest wish, to be the Sojourner's right hand. But it will be more painful and more difficult than what I went through physically on the cross. You will be tempted to despise and condemn yourself at the level of your very being. But you have the will and the strength to resist this. You have asked for this in spirit and it will be brought forward."

"But you are the Sojourner, the Christ, the Elder Brother. I am…"

"I am but the first one to do it. Remember: 'This too you shall do, and even greater.' Do you think that I ruled you out of that? Do you trust me?"

"Master, with all my beingness!"

"Then the time has come for us to do some work on this side of the veil. You will have a special task to perform for me, if you so desire. It is one that will set the stage for changes for at least the next 2000 years, the beginning of the next age. This will involve shifting the power relationships of the levels of spirit beneath the Soul.

"As you know, the Kal holds sway on the levels below the Soul. So the Realm of the Imagination, Realm of the Emotions, The realm of the Mind, and The Realm of the Unconscious are the kingdom of the 'loyal opposition.'"

"Why do you call the forces of darkness 'the loyal opposition?'"

"Didn't I tell you that everything is a part of God and therefore has value? The Kal forces act as our testers. Kal will test us on all our weakest areas to see if we are really ready to assume our true positions as co-creators with God. Let me give you some information without hiding it in a parable: A long time ago, before Lucifer was cast out of heaven, he was God's greatest angel, his firstborn. He was a splendid co-creator; in fact he was so good that he got caught up in his own creation. He wanted to manage it his way. It was not so much him being 'cast out of heaven' as him rejecting what he perceived as God's 'status quo.' He is just as trapped in these levels as humanity is. Man left the Garden (which was just another name for God's kingdom), because he learned to judge, to see things as 'good' and 'evil' rather than as all a part of God, and therefore right and proper. When man left the garden, Kal put forward his plan to test us in order that we prove ourselves worthy of returning. His plan was that we are re-embodied on the earth until we perfect our consciousness. His plan failed. The 'School of Karma' did not produce any graduates, but instead locked humankind into the bonds of the lower levels. Our inner divinity cried out for release. And now, at this time, the sum total of all our divinity, that which is the cosmic Christ, offers another plan, the 'School of Grace.' In this school there is but one lesson and that is to learn to accept oneself as a true child of God. When that happens, you and your Father are one and you transcend the lower levels into the realm of the Soul, your true home. Nothing will be able to keep you from your home at that point. It will be a matter of your choice. I have been given the opportunity to free the souls who have been locked into this trap. This will be most unsettling for Kal. His home ground is going to be invaded by Spirit. It would be another indication of the failure of his plan. He will try to hold on tight, but it will avail him not."

"Is the Grace plan 'new' or was it always available as a choice?"

"It was always available. It has been hidden and secret and kept from the masses for such a long time that there are few left who are aware of it. It is a much simpler way, but also more difficult. The trap is for us to let our conscious selves think we are therefore 'special' as Sons and Daughters of God. It is really a quite ordinary state. Spirit is ordinary, God is ordinary, it just IS. To learn to be a child of God, we must learn to be perfect in our ordinariness. This means that on our conscious level we make mistakes and we learn to accept that. Our basic self, our animal nature, has desires; we accept that and we educate this level of ourselves. And since we all are children of God, we also accept these things in others."

"Does this mean that we have to allow ourselves to be subject to the will of others?"

"It is our divine right to just get up and leave, to take ourselves from a negative situation. When we cannot move we can change our attitude toward a situation. I have spent many lifetimes battling against my own spiritual ignorance. I can safely include myself when I say that there is not one of us who has not betrayed, at one time, the Anointed One within us and chosen the path that leads to pain and sorrow. It often feels like that is the part of us that we just can't avoid. The Kal Power would wish us to fight it. That gives it energy and keeps us here. Yet Kal provides us a service. When our pride gets too big concerning our spirituality, the forces of Kal will give us a nice smack on the rear to let us know that we also need to watch our levels of responsibility. Our Father has offered us the path of forgiveness, to forgive our humanness. My best advice is that if Grace is offered, take it! This is a time of Grace and if you wish to help me, you will also be offered that. But, heed well, you must truly know yourself worthy of it from inside of you."

Jeshua bade me to sit and listen. "I will try to explain to you what we are about to do. You must not speak of it or even think about it on the lower levels because Kal will pick it up immediately. You will be meeting Kal in his own domain. I will be with you very closely, in fact, you will be overshadowed by my consciousness. You need not fear at all for I will share your form and will not allow anything to happen to you. We are going to release the trapped souls on the lower levels. You will only be in peril if you lose sight of yourself as a spiritual being. Keep chanting your tones and if things get too frightening for you, don't forget to call on the Sojourner. In that, you will not only be calling on me personally, but also upon all the Sojourners across the Cosmos. This is good practice for you, since it will serve you well in the future. The only thing that you will be armed with will be a tone. This is an initiatory tone that comes right out of the Sound-Current of God, the highest energy there is."

He chanted it slowly for me.

I felt great power, energy, and joy bursting through me. It almost made me forget my life as Yehudah.

"I forgot to tell you," Jeshua said. "This will also be an initiation for you. The distance that has often separated you from the other disciples will be erased. So much of your life defined you as an earthly warrior. Now you will become a warrior of the spirit. Take in well what I have told you, we have very little time in order to accomplish what we must. You have been given the keys to Kal's defeat and the opening of what is to come."

"I am ready," I said, looking up at him.

"So am I," he replied, "and don't worry. I am with you always and will guide you through this and beyond."

In an instant I was transferred back to the tunnel with the light at the end. No one was moving. I heard Jeshua's voice: "There is no such thing as time in the Soul Realm. To everyone here you will not have left."

As he said that, the scene came to life. As hands reached out for me, I grabbed the outstretched arm of the Angel of Death. For a moment I soared above an endless blue sky. The Angel then dove straight for a huge lake and as we entered it, all became black. I could see that we were going through some type of cavern because both the Angel and I were giving off light. When we exited the cavern, the Angel left. I found myself on a tall mountain that abutted over an immense plane.

A huge Angel the size of a world stretched out before me. I felt a booming voice that made me ache, "I've been waiting for you, Judas. You are damned and I've got your Soul for eternity. You might as well give up on your Master; he has given up on you."

A shiver went up my spine.

Jeshua was right about Kal. Kal was extremely clever. He is adept at using our worst fears against us; taking away our integrity and offering us something to make it all feel better.

"Renounce him here with me and I will give you all in life you didn't have, recognition, fame, the pleasure of being called a 'holy man.' I will make you a Master of Light both on earth and on all the inner planes of existence."

What he was offering sounded very inviting, indeed! I was conscious enough to consider the results of such an action and so I held to my tone and kept chanting internally. I felt the inner power of the tone and it kept me from turning in fear and running from this overpowering presence before me. I had no longer any doubt. I knew that I was under the protection of the Sojourner. The word of the Sojourner was given. The word of Kal could never be trusted. Kal had the most power here on the Causal Realm, the realm of the emotions. Here he was most powerful. I feared being overcome, but kept on chanting.

My inner chanting was beginning to irritate him. He taunted me: "You have the gall to defy me, worthless human trash. Don't you know that words of power that bring in Light Initiations have no power other than what I give them?" His beautiful visage became distorted with anger and beamed with more hatred than I had ever witnessed. "All can be corrupted." His eyes were shining with a mixture of ecstasy and lunacy.

I was feeling fear but also resolve. I could feel the presence of Jeshua with me. Kal gloated like a captor ready to torture his captive. "You are ignorant of the law here. Mirror images of the words of power cancel out the Light with darkness."

I could feel the strength and assurance being built up inside of me. "Then whatever I chant to you, you will chant the reverse?" I asked.

He nodded his immense head in the affirmative, holding his hate-filled gaze upon me. "I have you for eternity. The time will come when you will willingly turn to me and serve me better than you served your previous master. I know your lower nature perfectly and will not let you stray from your path of service to me. You will worship me in my glory and brilliance — for I am perfect and fully formed — the greatest creation of God. I alone perform His will on these levels of creation."

I spoke… no, a voice spoke through me: "You have no idea what perfection is, fallen angel and brother. I pity you for the eternity you will spend here." It felt like Jeshua.

"Amilius!" he gasped. His smile vanished and he appeared shaken.

I began to chant out loud the tone that Jeshua gave me. It started small, but soon it occurred to me that the whole universe was vibrating. I could sense massive fear and anger from Kal. He focused his hate-filled eyes at me and gleefully chanted what I assumed was the mirror image of the tone I had chanted. The result was different than he expected. Instead of canceling out my tone, his chanting intensified it. I could feel tingling on all levels of my being. The sky appeared to break apart with a rush of purple-white light that was almost blinding. It filled and surrounded everything.

The voice using me spoke again, "Yes, it is me, and the time has finally come for lifting. All these lower levels will now be bridged into Light. You will never again hold souls in bondage who do not choose to be bound. You will have no power over the students of the Sojourner, for if you try to hold one, he will free himself and all the other souls within your grasp."

I then saw the radiant form of Jeshua standing before me, brighter than countless suns. Kal shook with fear. There were choruses of angelic voices and shouts of joy from souls in ignorance from bondage and permitted to leave and travel into the higher realms.

Kal's fear again turned to anger. He looked directly at me and I realized that he could not see the radiant form of Jeshua. "You are not who you appear to be. This was all a deception."

Jeshua continued to speak through me. "I am a son of the Most High. I no longer follow your plan. I have been transmuted, and you have failed." It was as if the "me" that was speaking was a composite of Jeshua and myself. For the first time in my life, I was given the gift of knowing what it was like to be Jeshua, to share his consciousness.

"Tell me how I failed," said Kal. "I must know."

The "composite" me began again: "It will do no harm to let you know, now that my task here has been completed. While it is true that Light initiations can be corrupted, the initiations of the Sound Current of God are above and beyond your realms and cannot be affected by you. In fact, it was you who assisted me in the initiation of your realms. In essence, we did this together. The mirror image of the Sound Current tone is the same as the tone itself. You added your power to the tone and together we have created a bridge from Light into darkness so that all those in darkness from now on will be able to find their way into Light. When one who holds the Light dies to the physical, he will be protected, not lost. You will no longer have a claim on him. Now I am free of your pull and will freely travel upward."

"I will be watching you very carefully; I will make sure that you fail."

It was more me that spoke now: "I might very well stumble, but I have seen how I cannot fail."

"Perhaps, then I should fall down at your feet and worship you," Kal said with a sarcastic grin.

Both Jeshua and I answered, "You would do much better to worship the Sugmad, the Most High God. To worship anything less is to worship a false God."

"Yes, I am aware of that, but certain of your followers, Amilius, may not be. You should know how close their adoration comes to worship."

I was not aware of what Kal meant at this point but I was certain Jeshua did. He answered Kal with some sadness in his voice, "Even that will not stop the opening of mankind to its true nature. You are still capable of interfering with the process, even slowing it perhaps, but you are no longer capable of stopping it. As for me, I have overcome death and overcome the earth; I think I can also overcome being worshipped."

In an instant we reappeared in the same room we had occupied before this trip through Kal's domain. I assumed that we were back on the Soul Realm.

"Yehudah, I will be leaving soon. There is more for me to do on earth. I must return. We won't be separated for long. You also need to return to complete the life you left. I have arranged the means for this."

"But…"

"I will make this all clear for you later. All this change has left you weary. You need to rest."

As he placed his hand on my eyes, I fell into a deep, dreamless sleep.

CHAPTER 15 - A SILENT MINISTRY

"There is little time," said Jeshua.

I opened my eyes and saw myself in a strange house. I tried to move but my body was unresponsive.

"Do not speak. I will tell you all you need to know," Jeshua began. "It was in the best interest of all concerned that you finish out this lifetime. It will soften the trauma of what has occurred to you and erase some of the karma which you have accrued. Your Higher Self has agreed to live out this life in your present consciousness. Your body… well, that's another story. It is better for you to return here without being recognized. You are occupying the body of a scholar and disciple named Matthias. The consciousness, which inhabits that body, has agreed to share that body with you. You will be in charge. He is a student as you were sharing your consciousness with me. However, all decisions of life and death must be made mutually. Is that agreed?"

I nodded in the affirmative and I began to ask a question but Jeshua put his finger to his lips and said, "Your Higher Self has contracted you for a silent lifetime in which you are allowed to say one thousand words so you will have to choose them well. After that you will be physically unable to say more. If you need to communicate, you can write or learn to sign."

I bent down and wrote in the loose dirt on the floor: *"Won't people become suspicious that I do not communicate as they do?"*

"All you need to do is to indicate that you have taken a vow of silence, which from the level of the Higher Self, is true."

"The Discipline of Maun," I thought, remembering that Jeshua once said it would be to my advantage.

Jeshua continued: "This is a time when you will gain greatly from observation. Find your book of notes and keep them current. They will be of some value to those who come after. Peter knows you in your present form. He will introduce you to become the successor to… well, yourself. From this position you will keep your eyes opened at all times. Erase any notion that you can be 'the power behind the throne.' You will be learning the discipline of acceptance and the path of forgiveness. As a Warrior of the Spirit, the only way you can really change things on the outside is to first change them within yourself. Remember the times before you went out on a mission of combat and wondered if you would ever be coming back?"

I nodded.

"Well, you won't be coming back from this one. And that's good news. Meet me in Jerusalem in two days, during the Pentecost. There you will be chosen as the twelfth apostle."

Jeshua saw the look of concern on my face.

"After all that we have been through and you have experienced, would you not trust me now?"

I smiled and nodded my head.

"Peace, my friend," he said and he started to become transparent and finally disappeared.

I still could not easily move my body, so I sat and silently chanted some sacred tones and began to listen to that other consciousness inside of me. It was a very gentle and harmonious consciousness even if a bit unworldly. It reminded me somewhat of the disciple Stephen. I suddenly realized that I could access the thoughts of this consciousness and it could do the same with me. I found memories of a close friendship between Stephen and Matthias. I was even able to see myself, or my former self, through the eyes of this other consciousness. I appeared as a somewhat frightening figure to this entity, a harsh and combative personality, too close to the master to be a peer for Matthias, yet not close enough to be revered such as Peter or John.

I finally was able to move myself from where I was lying. I felt very stiff and uncoordinated. The body I now occupied was taller, more muscular but less fit than the old one. I stumbled outside. The sun was bright and felt soothing on my skin. I went to the water trough in the front yard. I studied the reflection I found. My new face was without the lines of care I noticed the last time I gazed at my previous image. I liked looking younger, yet this body! I would have to do something about it. Even after I had cut all ties to the *Sicarri*, I kept myself fit through a regular regimen of exercise. I instinctively began my training exercises and felt exhausted in short order. I had trouble catching my breath and I could feel the gentle consciousness that shared this body cringing. It wondered if I really was that harsh consciousness I had portrayed to him.

I realized that I needed to learn and practice acceptance and tenderness with my new self, if I wanted the full cooperation that I would need to carry out this ministry. In my previous life as Yehudah I had only one inner voice to consider. Now I must learn to keep myself open to a measure of inner cooperation.

During my trip to Jerusalem, I had plenty of time to think and consider. I felt as if this was a totally new world where none of the old rules that I had lived by before were valid. I wanted to adapt, yet my ties to the old patterns and actions were part of my identity. Who am I? Would I be able to function under these new life circumstances?

I remembered leaving my journal in Jerusalem and I headed directly there, but there was a sudden impulse for me to stop at the home of Lazarus, Martha, and Mary in Bethany. On the way I remembered an old quarry where there was slate I could use for writing. I took along chalk and some stones to polish the edges of my piece of slate. Writing was now almost as important as my next breath. It is amazing how we as human beings can take the ability to communicate so much for granted.

When I knocked at the door, it was Mary that answered. I wrote on my slate, *"Matthias, disciple of the Master Jeshua."*

"Can't you speak?" she asked.

"Yes," I wrote, *"but I have taken a vow of silence."*

"A silent ministry," she mused.

I had forgotten the warm silkiness of her voice. My heart beat faster hearing it. Her voice was somewhat lower in pitch than the average female voice, so when she talked it felt like the purring of a cat. Her presence excited me but I tried not to appear nervous.

"I am going to Jerusalem," I wrote. *"Jeshua told me to find and keep the book of Yehudah."*

"You've seen the Master also?" she asked.

I nodded. She appeared to gain interest in what I was saying, and me, and I admit that I liked the feeling, to be the center of her attention.

"He has appeared only to a few people that I know of since his... crucifixion. I must have been the first because, initially, no one would believe me. Peter said that it was probably womanly hysteria, but he also saw Jeshua and then, after that, was able to believe that I did also. Oh, by the way, I have Yehudah's book."

She not only had the book but the leather bag I used to carry that held the book and the tools of writing.

"How come you had this?" I wrote.

"It's... personal," she answered and said nothing more about it.

A flash of feeling crossed her face. She was skilled at showing a hard exterior, but her countenance appeared to soften for a moment. This intrigued me. Did she still have some good feelings toward my former self?

"Jeshua told me to come to Jerusalem to replace him." I wrote. *"Did you know Yehudah well?"*

"I think only the Master knew him well, but I think I was getting to know him. There were times when I actually felt quite close. The last words I said to him were in anger, and I regret that. There are those among us who still blame him for the Master's crucifixion but, reading the book, I know that he meant no harm and I forgave him. It's just a shame that he isn't here to hear it in person."

I wrote: *"I'm sure that wherever he is, he is aware of your feelings on the matter."*

She then seemed to open her heart wide and extend this new me the trust that I never received as my old self. "Just reading that... I know it and feel it. I've felt it ever since I saw the Master reappear after his crucifixion. Now I know for sure that life is eternal and we are all sons of God and that we have not been abandoned on this physical level."

I scratched my question on the slate: *"What happened when you saw him?"*

"I had been despondent ever since Jeshua was taken and when I saw him on that cross I truly felt that all was at an end. But on the third day I went to the tomb to pray with Mary, Jeshua's mother, and Martha, my sister. When we got there, we saw the tomb was open and Jeshua's body was not inside. Being the youngest, it was I who ran to Jerusalem to try to find some disciples in order to spread the news. I saw Peter, James and John just outside the gate of the city and told them what I had seen while trying to gasp for breath. John was gone before I finished. He raced off to the tomb to see for himself. When the rest of us got there, it remained as I had said, empty. They did not know what had happened. They thought that perhaps Romans or Sadducees had broken into the tomb and stolen the body. Something inside told me to remain. I had time on my hands and did not know where I was going to go from there so I sat down on the burial slab and tears began to flow. I had lost my master teacher and one of two men who treated me with kindness and respect." A tear rolled down her cheek.

I felt touched that she actually spoke of the former me in the same breath as Jeshua. I reached over and took and her hand. She held mine tightly and continued to tell her story.

"By this time Mary and Martha had caught up to me and sat beside to comfort me. I heard a voice from the shadows that said, 'Why do you cry?' I turn around to see from where the voice came. It was a man with a white coat and hood. I said to him, 'The body of my spiritual master has been taken.' The man removed his hood. There was something vaguely familiar about him but I did not recognize him immediately. Then he looked to Mary and said, 'Mother.' 'Jeshua!' she answered with unbridled joy. We were ready to embrace him but he held us at arm's length. He said, 'I have not yet come fully back into this realm so this form is not ready to be touched.' We approached cautiously and could see that his form was ever so slightly shimmering and translucent. I stared at his face and then I saw the resemblance to the Jeshua that I had known before. It was he, but the body, complexion, and features were more like an idealized copy of the original. I was ready to question when he held up his arms to me. I could see the scars from the wounds where he was nailed. He said with a comforting smile, 'I said that I would return after three days, why did you look for the living among the dead?' I managed a self-conscious laugh. James and John arrived at the tomb and also talked with Jeshua. We told the other apostles later, but they thought that we had just seen a vision of the master. Jeshua appeared to each of them, some scattered by long distances, at about the same time. Thomas still would not believe. He actually demanded that he see the wound made by the Roman spear. Jeshua was happy to oblige. By that time his body had fully materialized and Thomas was able to touch the wounds for himself. There was finally no doubt among any of the disciples, the Master had returned as he had promised! He told the disciples that he had, at last, fulfilled his mission, having both demonstrated the Christ in man and the immortality of Man. He said that death should no longer stop people from reaching their potential as spiritual beings, and that there was nothing to fear. He mentioned that now even the Negative Power itself could not hold those who wished to be free."

I wanted to tell her of that occurrence myself, since I was a part of it and had fully experienced it, but my duty now was to listen and record.

I told her that I needed to leave if I was to meet the other apostles in Jerusalem. She squeezed my hand and told me that she was glad that she would be seeing me again. I left, carrying my resurrected book on my way to find my resurrected Master.

I was again on my way to Jerusalem. I went inside myself to learn more about this Matthias whose body I shared and whose identity I was to take over. Matthias was not trained by the Essenes as I had been. He was born an Israelite but he was well versed in the mysteries learned in the Egyptian mystery schools. I would have considered him a worthy replacement. In many ways he was my opposite: a very quiet and shy man, not a man of action, who rarely spoke up or took an initiative, yet he was still a loyal disciple who rarely questioned authority. In the days before the crucifixion he would be as a lamb among wolves among the strong personalities of the other apostles. I realized that this joining was a learning situation for both of us. He was to learn from my outward personality and I was to learn from his more reserved character. A good plan. Perhaps together we could make one effective apostle! I could feel his consciousness chuckling inside. There was an aspect we both shared: a quick wit and a slightly off-center sense of humor.

I was so deep in thought I did not notice that I was approaching the gates of Jerusalem. A loud voice called my name off to the right of the gate. It was Peter. A part of me was afraid that Peter would see me as Yehudah and condemn me, but there was only relief and joy in his voice.

"Matthias, I was worried that you might not come. I guess you have heard that the Master has reappeared."

I wrote on my slate: *"Yes, it was he that visited me."*

He looked at me strangely. "Why are you writing?"

"Vow of Silence," I wrote.

"Isn't that an Eastern practice?" he asked.

"I will use whatever is for my greatest growth, enlightenment and expansion."

He seemed to accept that simple explanation. "There were eleven of us who voted, and you are now an apostle. One was needed to replace Yehudah who committed suicide after the Master's crucifixion." He shook his head. "Some say it was because of guilt, some say it was remorse, some say it was despondency, no one really knows for sure."

"It could have been emptiness," I wrote.

"Emptiness?"

I wrote: *"If you feel that all is gone and nothing is left in your life, you are empty."*

Peter laughed. "That is a simple and reasonable explanation. You may be our silent apostle, but you may actually speak the loudest in your silence."

The other apostles were all there. Peter brought all of us to a hill just outside the gate. We stood there, milling around, not knowing what was to come. A figure approached from the direction of the gate and headed directly toward us. It was cloaked in dark robes and hood. When the figure got close the individual threw off the dark cloak and we could see that he was clothed in white. It was the Master!

He held up his hands as a gesture to keep all where they were, but one could also see the scars of crucifixion prominently on his hands. He first went to Peter and talked with him alone. Then he went to John and his brother James. He saw each of us, in turn, separately, as if saying good-bye. It was as if he was giving each of us directions on how to continue. He took time with each of us, sometimes a long time, and sometimes a short time, depending on how much instruction he wanted to give. He spoke to Mary of Magdala before he spoke to me. It was a surprise to me when he pointed once in my direction. Was he telling Mary who I was just recently? I would not have courage to ask her, so I guessed that I might not know unless she volunteered the information.

He got to me. He used my new name. "Matthias, my brother, I will be leaving you again. This time I will not return in human form. I have grown beyond this form and it is a limitation for the continuation of my work with humanity. I will always be with you, all of you, inside. I have made it easy for anyone to talk to me inside of himself or herself. If you go to that special place inside yourself that yearns for union with God, you will find me there with you. A person need not say my name or call on the Christ to be there, for there are many names that men have for this spirit that I represent. The Spark of God that is in me is the same Spark that is in you. If you will go there, I will be waiting for you.

I wrote: *"What about other lifetimes? I might forget you or be born into a family who does not know you."*

"At an appropriate time you will be able to remember all your lives. It is a gift that you will give yourself and it will not occur until you are ready to be responsible to use this gift for your upliftment and the upliftment of others. Keep reaching for the best inside of you." He seemed to be ready to move on, but he noted, as if a postscript to a letter: "Do not be afraid to reach out and love Mary. In many existences you have been close. The two of you have the power to heal each other of the imbalances that you have accrued over millennia. It will not always be easy, but it is a partnership, which will benefit you both. Farewell. I will be seeing you 'inside.'"

Jeshua spoke to a number of other disciples and followers. Finally he stood on a rock above the heads of all and gave us his final instructions: "I will be leaving soon. I have other flocks that need tending. There are brothers and sisters in a place very far from here, on the other side of the world that I have not yet contacted. You may not understand this now, but I will try to explain the reason for my going. As you, I am still growing and learning. I have reached the point where one human existence is too limited for my awareness. That which is my spirit is about to embody this entire world. To do that, I must make preparations. I am leaving you and will not return in the form of man but I will always be with you. Not only in the inner realms where you can reach me but also in every rock, every tree, in every eye of every person you meet, in all things on this world, I will be there also, if you remember to look."

He shifted his balance on the stone. "You are not the only group who is being made aware of this. I have talked to many groups and individuals since my return. I do not belong to any one group; I have equal responsibility to all on this world. I have already appeared to Pilate and the Priests of the Temple. It was not my purpose to have them react in fear but they have done so. You will be unmolested for a time but soon this memory will fade and you will have many hardships to endure yet on this level. Be soldiers and warriors of Spirit; use all of it for your advancement and growth. I have also appeared to those who supported me in the counsel. I have appeared to our friends in the East to demonstrate man's immortality. I have appeared to my fellow Sojourner Apollonius at Heliopolis where I was given the honor of standing on the sacred pedestal for the demonstration of resurrection, where no one has stood before. I have even appeared to a counsel of Watchers who are observing this world. They have seen that one of us has demonstrated that death cannot hold the spirit of man. They have reported to me that our world will soon be ready for the next period of growth. At that time, the 'miracles' that I have demonstrated will be commonplace, where all will know God from within and will greet each other with open hearts and loving gazes as the brothers and sisters we all are. Those days are coming. I have brought my will totally in tune with the will of God, and therefore my tasks on this earth are at an end. You will not see this body again, but I will be with you always in your heart of hearts. Remember the Baptist's words to be vigilant and to keep in preparation for the days that are coming. I have passed the keys of the Sojourner to John and he shall be reborn here until I return in the hearts of all. The Sojourner wisdom will guide you. He will be your wayshower. To my brother James go the keys to the Christ Consciousness. Look to him to demonstrate what it is to know your own divinity. Supporting both of them with the practical aspect of administration will be Peter. He is the rock on which the foundation rests."

The Master reached out with both hands and a blazing white light leapt from them and touched the heads of the twelve. It felt like my entire being was being cleared, cleansed, and purified.

"The blessings of our Father, all the Holy Ones, the Christ that lives inside you, and the Holy Spirit itself will be upon you until you sit with me in God's Kingdom."

Chapter 16

His body grew more and more bright and yet more transparent. Just when the brilliance was more than we could endure, his image faded.

No one moved for what appeared to be ages. Finally, John and James rose in front of us and led us, as Jeshua did, in chanting the names of the Lord. I found that humming outwardly and chanting inwardly did not violate my silence, so I too, was able to participate. As we all chanted, a mighty sound was heard that drowned us out. It felt like all the light of heaven was pouring out upon us and we were being baptized by the fire of Spirit. We were all filled to capacity by the Holy Spirit and began talking in tongues alien to us. The amazing thing was that we understood each other. We were receiving lessons in time and space. Others, who did not hear the sounds that we did, thought we were all drunks, but, in truth, we were drunk on Spirit.

Peter explained to those who mocked, quoting the prophet Joel: "…I will pour out my Spirit in those days and they shall prophesy… and it shall come to pass that whoever shall call upon the name of the Lord shall be saved."

James said: "We have chanted the Lord's name and have received His blessings as we were taught to do by our Master. We then received the bounty of God's abundance. We have undergone a miracle not seen by human eyes or heard by human ears. We shall however, manifest what we have been given in ways that you can see and know."

John stood and continued saying, "The Patriarch David prophesied that from his loins would spring one who would bring to us the message of the Messiah. This, Jeshua, son of Joseph, who some call Jesus, has demonstrated to us that there is no death of the Spirit and that we are all the children, the offspring of God, and are therefore Holy and divine. This he told us. It is then our task to manifest what we already are, to choose every second in favor of our divinity and leave behind our weakness and our corruption."

The Spiritual Light was so great that day that as we went into the crowd and touched people, they shed burdens of Karma that had been on them for ages. More than a thousand became disciples that day.

In the days after Jeshua's departure I helped Peter with organizing the followers. Even though Saul was not bothering us, we made it a rule for Nazarenes never to travel alone. Groups gave us some protection. Because of our growing numbers, we had many more places to stay in Jerusalem. I had some trouble making myself understood to those who did not read. Peter was not a very good reader, but at least he understood my communications. When it was necessary for him to write something, he always called on me to assist him.

When I was not with the other apostles, I found myself spending quite a lot of time with Mary. She was interested in knowing how to write, so I found myself becoming her mentor. She began using my slate and then graduated to some unused scrolls I was given by friends at Qumran. She was an extremely fast learner and very much enjoyed expressing herself. What seemed to motivate her most was reading spiritual texts and philosophy and writing her own interpretations. This was a part of her that I had never seen before. She not only had a quick mind but also an intuitive grasp of spiritual truth. In all the years I had spent with Jeshua, I was the student, always taking. Now I had the pleasure to be giving back, imparting some of the wisdom Jeshua had personally shared with me over the years. It was also thrilling just to be close to her.

I also spent time getting my new body into shape. It was younger than the previous one but less fit. I took the advice of the scholar inside who shared it with me and trained it gradually. I changed my diet, eating mostly fish and a wide range of vegetables. Getting back in shape proved to be quite fortunate since one day I spied a familiar face on the streets of Jerusalem. I had to get his attention & I used a word, the first one since coming back into a body, "Petronius!"

He turned and looked at me. "I don't believe we have met? Who are you?"

I wrote in Greek, *"A follower of Jesus, son of Joseph."*

He gave me his puzzled look and expressed irritation and impatience. "You are capable of speech. What is this foolishness? If you are toying with me, you'll soon regret it!"

"Jeshua gave me only 1000 words for the rest of this lifetime. I spent one calling you. I would use the rest without fully explaining. I am Yehudah... returned."

Now he really appeared uneasy. "You cannot be Yehudah, he is dead and buried."

I jotted down a number of things about Petronius that only Yehudah would know.

"You could have read those things in Yehudah's book. That does not prove anything."

"How can I prove to you that I am Yehudah?"

"One way, and one way only," he said, drawing his sword.

Here was where I was really grateful for continuing my physical training. The reaction time was slower but the knowledge and the training was still there. I brought him to the ground with one quick move.

"You never did learn to counter that move," I scribbled.

"That's because you never would teach it to me," he complained. Suddenly he realized that I was who I said I was. He was still the larger man and easily picked me up with a hug that squeezed all the air out of my lungs. "I really did miss you."

"The last time you saw me you threatened to kill me."

"I did not understand at first. Now I understand that it was a necessary part of what Jesus had to do. What can I do for you?"

"Two things: reveal my identity to no one, and bring Tuzla to me."

Lucky for me Tuzla was in Greece at the time and not home in Tibet. It took him a little over a month to get to me.

In the meantime I was getting even closer to Mary. She became much softer in her expression and I always felt so blessed to see her eyes light up when she saw me. This woman brought tears to my eyes when she smiled. The beauty of her being was like the air around me. I felt like I would surely suffocate if I could no longer see her. We were a community where everything was shared but I was still able to get a few extra things, which I gave to Mary, Martha and Lazarus. People who saw us together knew immediately what was going on, but I still could not gather the courage to tell her how I felt. One day she did not say a word, but crossed the distance between us and placed both hands on my face. "You have shared with me so much… but I'm still in the dark about how you feel about me." She went to pick up my slate to hand it to me when I took hold of her arm.

"I love you," I almost shouted.

She dropped the slate, realizing that I had broken my vow of silence.

I picked it back up. *"It's all right,"* I wrote. *"This is a situation…"*

She pulled the slate from my hands and kissed me. It was a kiss that was at once passionate and innocent. It was the most stirring kiss I had ever felt and I wanted it to linger. Suddenly she pulled back and looked me in the eyes and said: "I know so little about you. I asked Peter and he gave me only general details about your life, but there is so much I don't know about you, the man I want to share this life with."

I picked up the slate. *"You already know all that is necessary about my life before I met you. You may never know how true the statement is that my life began anew when you opened your door to me. Everything before that is unimportant."*

This time she could not diminish her enthusiasm for marriage. She was puzzled yet glad that I didn't want to know about her life previous to meeting her again in my new body. As far as I was concerned I didn't want anything to come between us. I was afraid that if I revealed my true identity, she might only want to be friends. It seemed easier to keep my silence than to risk having to overcome her feelings of shame for a life that was dead in the past. It suited me just fine that both of us had another life and another attempt at happiness together.

Mary was always eager to see me when I came up from Jerusalem. One day while we were sitting outside, under the shade of a tree, two familiar faces, Petronius and Tuzla approached us. Tuzla saw into the soul and recognized me immediately, but was aware of my wish to remain in present character. Since Tuzla had been a master at sign language I suggested that he teach both Mary and I how to sign. Since Mary and I were soon to be married, we would be spending a lot of time together and we could spend a good deal of it learning this new form of communication. Mary thought it was a great idea and even suggested that she could act as my "interpreter" when I was in Jerusalem. She said that it would speed up communications between others and me, and get her into a more active role in our community. I was not one to belittle the importance of a woman in any undertaking. Jeshua used to rely as heavily on his female disciples as on his male disciples. I valued Mary's enthusiasm for her work. Through this arrangement we enjoyed closeness and the ability to work together.

James was stepping more into his role as the holder of the Christ consciousness. He would appear in full priestly vestments in the Temple to the chagrin of the Sadducees. As a leader of the Essenes, he could not be barred from the Temple at any time. On days of festival, he wore simple vestments of white with spun gold and a gold colored miter. The Sadducee priests dressed in black with jewel-encrusted breastplates and dark miters. Their clothing was more expensive, but James looked so much more a priestly figure. He appeared quite imposing but was well loved by the populace. Meanwhile, the High Priest was jealous of the popularity and power that our group was amassing. He looked for some way of stopping the growing popularity of the Nazarenes.

John and Peter came to the Temple during a festival to teach of the Kingdom of God. He also taught of Jeshua who demonstrated how everyone could attain this kingdom. They were met by Sadducees who were looking for confrontation.

"Where is your prophet, Essene?" asked Caiaphas.

John remembered that Jeshua used everything to teach. "Our teacher Jeshua, son of Joseph, attained the highest level of spirit one can have while still being in a human body. The Romans crucified him because they were frightened of what he taught and what he did. Jeshua taught that all are sons of God. He awakened others from the dead to show there was no death. He, himself came back after three days, to overcome death. He taught nothing and did nothing that was not a truth in scripture. He fulfilled the Law and transcended it."

Caiaphas was livid. "They speak of that which is evil and unnatural. They lie and blaspheme in the house of the Lord. Arrest them. Take them before the council."

In front of the full council of the Sanhedrin, Peter, filled with the Holy Spirit, stood and spoke: "We are here because of the truth. We spoke the truth and were arrested. Our teacher, Jeshua, performed miracles, spoke the truth and was crucified. The things that he did in his life you say no ordinary man could do. But he showed that a man <u>could</u> do them. That which appears to be a miracle is just something we do not yet understand. We are afraid of what we don't understand or we are in denial of it. What does that accomplish? The pain of this life presses down on us and we are sick. We look for all kind of "medications" out in the world to heal our inner illness, but the truth is that all healing comes from within, and miracles are just a manifestation of what is. We come and offer truth that will bring you back to healing inside. Where is the crime here?"

They released Peter and John and told them not to spread the teachings of Jeshua. But Peter and John said that they could not stop telling of what they saw and heard. The people had great praise for them, so the Sadducees had to release them, but not before further threats.

It seemed as though the friction between the Essenes and the Sadducees had subsided for a while. It was the day of our wedding. We had James officiate and John was going to do the actual ceremony. It was held in the Court of the Gentiles so that all could attend. Right from the beginning it was a wedding that defied tradition. I signed instead of speaking my vows and Mary spoke for both of us. Rather than the usual wedding contract, we both vowed to keep each other and ourselves in the experience of God's kingdom and to be good partners and friends. There was no subjugation of the female, and all responsibilities and honors were to be shared.

John and Peter used this time to teach more about God's kingdom and how it was available to all. They told the populace that God's Anointed one had come and left them with the experience of God's Kingdom that was present right now, available to all.

Caiaphas entered the court with a cadre of guards. Not a thing was said.

John asked the reason why they were being arrested.

"Blasphemy," said Caiaphas.

"Is it blasphemous to tell others that the Kingdom is present?" Peter asked.

No answer was given. The guards taking them to prison handled them roughly. We followed at a discrete distance dressed in our wedding clothes. Mary and I did not speak, but the understanding between us was that we would wait until they were released, no matter how long it would take!

The sun had set and we kept our vigil as long as we could. Finally sleep overtook us and we drifted off. It seemed like an instant later when John and Peter shook us awakened.

We were happy to see them but confused. "Did they just release you?" Mary asked.

"No. It must have been the Holy Spirit that opened the door to the prison and released us," Peter said. "A bright light poured into our cell and the guards dozed off. I touched the lock and the door opened for us."

"Come with us to Bethany. There you will be safe," said Mary.

"We will come with you, but only for a while," said John. "There is much more to do."

We sent out to all the people who were at the wedding to come in the middle of the night to celebrate both our getting married and the release of John and Peter from prison. They stayed for only a short time. Later we found that they had gone back to the Temple and taught about The Kingdom. When the Sadducees sent their guards to the prison to bring the apostles, they found the doors locked and the apostles gone. The guards did not know how they had vanished. Then another man informed them that the apostles were at the Temple. They went to the apostles but not in force, because they were afraid that might cause a riot.

John and Peter were again made to stand before the entire Sanhedrin and Caiaphas, the high priest.

Caiaphas asked, "Did we not forbid you to teach?

Peter answered: "We were given a choice whether to obey God's law or man's law. We chose God. He urges us to teach the truth to men. We do not teach the overthrow of any earthly power, we merely want to let the people know that The Kingdom is here and available to all. The Kingdom provides the forgiveness that the people need to change to a better way of living."

The Sadducees were enraged and would have had John and Peter stoned to death. But we were not without friends in the council.

Gamaliel, a teacher of the law and revered by all rose up and ordered the guards to take the apostles outside while he spoke to the council.

Gamaliel was clever and used their fear to reduce their desire for blood. He said to them: "Be wise and listen to history. If you kill these men you will make them martyrs and many more will die following them. If you let them alone, it would be best for all. Pay no mind to what they teach. If what they teach is false, then it will fail and pass away, but if it is true then God will not judge you as unrighteous for your actions. If you kill them, however, you will have to answer for many lives. Is the favor of the Romans worth the lives of your people?" He left them to their deliberations and went outside to speak alone with the apostles.

"My friends," he said, "I was the student of Jeshua's teacher, Rabbi Hillel. I believe that Jeshua's teachings should be made available. Yet, in this time, there is great unrest. Confrontation may not be the best policy at this time. The Romans will do anything to maintain their power and the Sadducees, in their fear of retribution, are doing all they can to please the Romans. These are times where ears are not open to new ideas for fear they could bring destruction. Do not judge these men for their weakness, they are driven by fear."

John responded, "They have been placed in slavery by their own creation. When people focus on their fear they bring to themselves the worst of their expectations."

"I would still caution you," Gamaliel noted, "That which is not your creation can still harm you. If you are destroyed, who will survive to pass on the teachings? I would say that the best alternative is to, whenever possible, avoid confrontations."

Peter and John returned to us and told us of their experience with the Sanhedrin. I signed and Mary spoke for both of us.

"I feel that they will make more use of Saul in the future," I began. *"He is a worthy adversary. And although the things he does are despicable, he is a talented warrior."*

"That is something that Yehudah would have said," noted John, his gaze boring deep inside me.

I was careful to not arouse any more suspicions. *"I have been spending some time with his book. There are many thoughts on this man Saul. I am sure we have not seen the last of him."*

For the next two years there was no direct action against us. Mary had given birth to a beautiful baby girl who we named Rebecca. Even though I got this body into shape, I was happy that she looked more like her mother. These were times when there was not much for me to write about. I was busy at Qumran copying scrolls, and Mary was busy taking care of our daughter. We were building a strong Essene congregation or "church" as our Greek and Roman converts called it. There were a surprising number of them. I found that the prospect of circumcision kept all but the most pious male converts from our church. But those that joined, like Petronius, were model congregants. I told Mary, jokingly, that women had it easy. She stood there with her hands on her hips. It seemed as though thunder rolled while she spoke: "While all men born into Jewish families were circumcised at birth and have no memory of the deed, most men assumed that the same thing occurs for women's brains and that is why there is a traditional bias against women." While most men would have realized that it was time to keep quiet for the peace of the household, I chose to sign. *"Well, my Love, if this bothers you so much, do something about it."*

"Just what do you propose I do?"

"Thomas has moved his ministry to the East and has no plans to return. His spot is vacant. Be an apostle. Why shouldn't you at least try?"

"M…m…me, an apostle?"

"If you really are serious about equality for women, then I would say, put more than your attitude on the line, put your body there and don't move until you are an apostle! I think that's what Jeshua would have said."

She threw her arms around me, held me tight and shook her head. "Sometimes you are just maddening, but your support for me as a Soul is unfailing. I love you Matthias, and I always will!"

"Then it is settled. We will meet with the other apostles as soon as possible."

On that day Mary was radiant. She was filled with the Holy Spirit and spoke with the power and persuasion of any man. "Do we not worship a God who is both male and female in its divinity? Why should the feminine be avoided?"

"It is our tradition that the men should take care of the spiritual matters and the women take care of the home," argued Peter, the strongest advocate for tradition. "It is not inequality, but there have been roles set aside for thousands of years and to change these is to destroy the foundations of our society."

I signed my response to Peter as another apostle: *"Tradition is often a betrayer of the present truth. I read in Yehudah's book that Mary was never sent away when he was teaching. If the teachings of the Christ and the Sojourner are not for women, then why was she permitted to stay?"*

Mary then reflected on an experience with Jeshua and the Apostles: "Do you not remember, Peter, when you spoke up against my participation in Jeshua's teaching sessions? You said that women were not worthy of receiving the teachings of Spirit. What did Jeshua say? I believe it was, 'I myself shall lead her, to manifest the male within her, to awaken her living Spirit, resembling you males. For every woman who awakens her male part will enter the Kingdom of Heaven.'"

"Does this mean that every female has a part of her that is of the male?" asked Peter.

"Just as every male has a tender part within that is female," replied Mary. "Like God, we are androgynous beings that express male and female on the level of the physical. Peter, does the Holy Spirit have gender?"

"No."

"Then each of us is that in truth, would you not agree?"

It's not often that Peter was taught a lesson. After a very active session of conferring, we came to one accord: Mary would be the first female apostle.

Rebecca was getting older and we often invited Petronius, Julia and their two boys, Titus and Marcellus. Titus, the younger boy, was now five and his brother Marcellus, six. Titus would usually ignore Rebecca since she was only three. Marcellus always tried to include her in their games and was always very kind to her.

I brought my slate so that I could talk to Petronius alone. *"You said that it would be our grandchildren that would be playing together. It seems as though you were somewhat conservative on your estimate."*

"Well what I said might still come to pass, unless Saul manages to kill us all."

"Is there something you know? What do you hear?"

"Only that he has been given more authority to take matters into his own hands. He can be pretty brutal, as you know."

It wasn't long after that Saul found one of us who would not travel in a group. It was Stephen. Stephen had been an old friend of the part of me that was Matthias. As a precautionary matter, I found it useful to limit our contact. Stephen probably thought that I made new friends after getting married. Stephen followed more the ways of John the Baptizer and eschewed family. Stephen was one of the original seven disciples chosen to be ordained to preach the Kingdom of Heaven. Stephen knew the power of debate and there were few that could stand against his wisdom and the Spirit that was in him. This made him particularly dangerous to the Sadducees. The Sadducees claimed that he said blasphemous words against God. They appointed false witnesses against him and brought him to the council. This could have been the work of Saul. The council's charge was that Stephen was supposed to have said that Jeshua would change the customs that were given by God. The High Priest asked Stephen if these accusations were true.

Stephen answered that he was following the Holy Spirit that has precedence over the laws of men. He also said that there would always be ones who are stubborn and self-righteous in their ways, and would resist the Holy Spirit in them and in others in order to follow the ways approved by men. Those who have the courage, insight and devotion to follow Spirit are often condemned, persecuted and murdered. It was the same self-righteous ones who did not defend their prophet Jeshua against the Romans. The Sadducees were angered and threatened by this powerful Nazarene.

Stephen then saw a vision of Jeshua standing at the right hand of God. The Sadducees were panic-stricken. They did not want word of this to get back to the Romans. They ordered Saul to have Stephen stoned. As he was being stoned Stephen cried, "Lord, do not hold this sin against them."

Saul was pleased to have a part in the murder of Stephen. His power with the Sadducees kept growing. There began severe persecution against the church in Jerusalem. However, our apostles were not harmed. Saul vowed to continue to persecute the church, sending many to prison.

The part of me that was Matthias' essence screamed with pain. There was anger and hurt and outrage that flooded my being from my companion inside. He was aware of everything about my life as Judas. He said that if I were half the warrior that I thought I was I would seek vengeance for this act. I was not swayed by this taunt but I considered what he said carefully. He was not acting rationally. Stephen was Matthias' best friend, one who had introduced him to the way. I could feel the devastation inside him. On one hand, Stephen was never close to me. I felt myself more "special" in my relationship to Jeshua. Part of my vow of silence involved staying out of political battles.

On the other hand, I never gave up my opinion that Saul needed to be killed. Getting rid of Saul would protect fellow Nazarenes and perhaps my family would be a little safer if he were gone. It would be quite easy to kill him, I thought. When he is in Jerusalem, he stays in the home of one of the priests. Each time another priest, so as to protect him. Finding out which should be easy. Then all I would have to do is slip in at night and quietly slit his throat with my *twin blades*… but those no longer existed. I heard Jeshua's voice inside of me: "Matthias, you must not kill him. Yes, he does belong to Kal, but he also belongs to me. I will take care of him."

I carefully considered all the voices inside of me and decided that I would act. I knew that Saul loved his wine. He could put away quite a volume without succumbing to its effects. Under the pretense of shopping for wine for the Essenes for a festival, I found out from the most prestigious wine merchant in Jerusalem which priest had been ordering more wine lately. I asked Petronius to get me the black outfit of the *Sicarri*. I filled a small pouch with gravel. I found some herbs and filled another pouch. He must have had an idea about what I was going to do because he actually answered me, "Yes, Judas."

When all things were set, I waited until nightfall and found easy access past guards and into the home of the hospitable priest. I went to the kitchen and chose a sharp knife. It was the home of an elderly priest so there were no children in the home. I first found the door to the room where the priest and his wife were sleeping and made sure that it was tightly closed. I found Saul's room opened the door and threw pebbles on the floor, just enough to wake him. He got out of bed and lit a candle to investigate. Finding nothing on the upper level, he proceeded down the stairs to where I was waiting. I realized that I was going to have to waste words on this man, and words were more precious to me now than all the gold in the Temple. I grabbed him from behind and held his chin up with the dagger at his throat. "Make any sound and it will be your last," I whispered.

He was so scared that he wet the floor. "There is only one man who could have found me…but you're dead!" he whispered.

I wanted to appear as menacing as I could be. "I came back from the grave for you, Saul."

He shook with terror. "Are you going to kill me?"

"Not unless I have to, so shut up and do everything I say if you value your miserable life," I growled. "You are going to take an extended trip. See Alexandria, see the East, but do not return here until you change your profession. If you're still in Jerusalem tomorrow, I will come again for you. Is that understood?"

"Y…y…yes!"

"Then before I go I have a little present for you." I began to run my knife along his neck, from ear to ear.

He started to resist. "DON'T KILL ME!"

"Quiet. I'm not going to kill you unless you move." I finished the wound, which bled freely. He was in a panic, so I had the job of comforter. "If I meant to kill you, you would be dead now." I got a handful of the herbs and pressed them against the wound. The herbs seared and burned the wound and he let out a whimper. "This will heal in a matter of days but the scar will remind you of your agreement. You will look at this scar and remember that I could have easily killed you."

"Why…why didn't you?"

"God has other plans for you. Quiet! I've wasted enough words on you." I brought the handle of the knife down on his head hard enough to render him unconscious and carried him back to his bed. I wrapped a towel around his neck just tight enough to cut back on bleeding, yet not to suffocate him. It would be a shame for him to die that peacefully. I made it back to Bethany just after sunrise. I tried to clean up and got back into bed before Mary woke. The minute my head hit the pillow, she rolled over to face me and said, "You're up early."

"I just couldn't sleep," I signed.

"Stephen?"

"Yes, Stephen."

About mid-afternoon I heard that Saul had left Jerusalem at noon, traveling east.

Chapter 16

CHAPTER 16 - FROM SAUL TO PAUL

There are few things in this life that give me more pleasure than to watch my Mary teach. My heart fills with pride when I see her instruction reaching men as well as women. Her sweetness and wisdom are matched only by her enthusiasm for the Light. I am thrilled with her radiance and beauty as Spirit flows through her. She has taken up her burden of being an apostle with a combination of earnestness and joy that is truly inspiring. It has been a joy to watch spirit blossom in this marvelous woman who God has, by His grace, made my beloved. When I find it difficult to see the God in others, all I have to do is to look at Mary and it awakens it fresh inside of me.

The home of Lazarus, Mary and Martha in Bethany has become a small Nazarene center because of its strategic location: it is near enough to Jerusalem to arrive within a few hours and yet far enough away to avoid any unrest from Jerusalem. Lazarus and I have built an addition to his house so that there is space for Mary, Rebecca, and myself to live. Our life often takes us to Jerusalem.

There is still time for a few precious moments every day (when we do not have intrusions from the outside world) for us to share our experiences of Spirit and of Loving. It is a busy life. We both spend as much time with our daughter as we can, but when we cannot, others in our community are only too glad to mind her. I'm sure she misses us when we are busy. She has so much of her mother's determination and strength she never lets on that she misses us. I see the makings of a fine woman in that girl.

I have again taken over the job of scribe, this time as Matthias. James the Just, brother of Jeshua, gave me this task to set down the teachings as they came through Jeshua. He wished an accurate account of these teachings that would reflect as little of the current intra-sect politics as possible. A mutual mistrust between the "Pillars" of our sect, James, Peter, and John, surfaced and expressed itself as both Peter and

John starting work on their own separate accounts of how our movement began. In response to this, James gave me the task of writing, not an account, but a volume of the sayings of Jeshua. This was the most joyful blessing I could hope to have. I was given free reign to pull from all my experiences, from the earliest memories I had of Jeshua until his last words to me before he left. James was helpful, from time to time, supplying his own remembrances and experiences concerning Jeshua's teachings. I have been spending quite a bit of time with my brother Simon, who, among his tasks, took over the role of translating my signing.

Under the leadership of James our Nazarene sect has flourished. When Jeshua was physically among us, it seemed that life was easier. In those days, the only job we had was to bring the joy of his teachings to others and to try to live them ourselves. By looking at James, you could see that the pressure of organization was exacting a toll. His presence was required both at the Qumran settlement and on the counsel in Jerusalem. Essenes were now either Nazarene (followers of Jeshua) or Mandaean (followers of the Baptist). While the old saying that "true prophets do not fight, but their followers do" is accurate in many cases, it was not the case between the followers of Jeshua and John. While all "took sides," the competition was friendly and often the two groups shared fellowship. Our Nazarene sect was more powerful and numerous, so James represented the Essenes on the counsel.

But of greater concern was the politics of running a sect. James would hold frequent meetings at our home at Bethany. Along with James (Jeshua's brother), John, Peter, James (John's brother) usually attended. One late summer evening James called a meeting of apostles.

"As you know," began Peter, "our numbers are growing throughout the Empire. Jews in every area are accepting the teachings of Lord Jeshua[13]. Our preachers are in the Synagogues and have been met with interest by many there. This brings a problem, however. As you know there have also been gentiles who have heard our message and accepted the teachings. Most of these have converted to Judaism and therefore are fully accepted as Nazarenes. Others, God-fearers, have not made a complete commitment to Judaism and the question is 'Can these gentiles truly be members of our sect?'"

James said, "This question has never come up before because, except for the Roman occupiers, there are few gentiles in Judea. In the

[13] "Lord" is a term of great honor that is reserved only for the greatest of spiritual leaders

Diaspora[14], however, the followers of Jeshua and Jews in general are more ritually lax as they become more cosmopolitan. There is much more mixing of Jews and gentiles. It is also easier to become a Jew. In Judea, however, things are different. Do you remember how upset the *Parush* became when we opened our brotherhood to Samaritans! The Sadducees were enraged and threatened excommunication of all Nazarenes. It is good that the *Mandaeans* and the *Hasids* along with us outnumber the others on the counsel. Yet I think we would surely lose even these allies if we included gentiles in our sect. We are not on the steadiest ground and a move to include gentiles would hurt us politically."

John, silent up until now, began to speak. "I think what we must do is ask what Jeshua would have wanted us to do in this situation."

"Do you speak for Lord Jeshua, then?" asked Peter.

"No, I would not presume to do that," answered John, "Although he told us to preach only to Judeans before his return, the last thing he instructed us to do was to make the teaching available to all mankind, and that must include gentiles. The kingdom is everyone's inheritance, whether they follow Jewish rituals or they do not. During his life in flesh, Jeshua ate with the outcasts of our society, with Samaritans and even with uncircumcised gentiles. It seems that Spirit cares less about ritual purity than the brotherhood of all mankind. I know that it is sometimes difficult to follow the dictates of Spirit when the politics of the world presses in on you. I am open to counsel on how to solve this dilemma."

James then suggested: "What if we allow them to be Nazarenes, but they stay in their own separate communities. Then the question of ritual purity would not come up. They would not be eating with those fully Jewish. In that case we do not risk opposition from all the other sects on this question."

James was the leader appointed by Jeshua so his decision always carried the most weight. He expressed understanding for John's position, yet he felt he was acting in the best interests of the entire sect. This seemed to me to reflect the low-level distrust among the three "Pillars". I had never heard these things talked about in the open, but I could sense that there were seeds of disharmony present. This was built around the politics of where each stood politically and spiritually. The political landscape of our sect appeared to mirror the nation as a whole.

---

[14] The dispersion of Jews outside of Israel from the sixth century B.C., when they were exiled to Babylonia, until the present time.

Peter was the most "traditional" religiously and politically and John seemed to have the most desire to be at the head of whatever was happening at the moment. James tried to remain connected to both and not take sides. Also, both Peter and John may have mistrusted James due to the fact that he did not become a Nazarene until after the crucifixion of Jeshua. Either or both could have resented the authority given to him by his brother. I am considering that this may be totally my imagination, the part of me that sees plots where none exist. If that is the case, then I make none of this as a judgment.

I followed John back to his quarters after the meeting. He looked so sad.

"What is troubling you, Master?" I wrote, using the title we reserved for a Sojourner.

"Jeshua was for inclusion, not exclusion. We have allowed our apprehension and fear to dictate to us and turn us from the straightest path to Spirit. I fear that this a position which will ultimately bring us harm."

"How is that?" I asked, *"What is the importance of gentile converts? There are certainly not all that many."*

"It is true there are not many in Judea, but the rest of the world is potentially full of them. In the Diaspora, Jews and gentiles naturally interact as a part of the prevailing Greek culture. Becoming a Jew in the Diaspora is less arduous to begin with and is made easier there because we are in the minority. I fear that we may be underestimating the importance of this source of converts and, more importantly, not demonstrating in our actions what we are teaching."

"Of all present today," I wrote, *"you sounded most like Jeshua."*

He looked at me with an inquiring gaze. "Just how would you know this?"

"I was there when he gave his final message to us, remember," I wrote.

"What do you think he would tell me?" He looked intently into my eyes.

"I think he would tell you to forgive yourself for your weakness and keep moving to the Light," I scratched hurriedly.

"Just as he told you to do for your part in his capture by the Romans, Yehudah?"

I stood there without moving for a full minute while he looked into my eyes.

"I have known for a while," said John. "The Master told me before he left. I have also noticed many familiar traits in you. The years have mellowed and refined you, but you are still Yehudah. Do not worry. I will keep your secret. Tell me, does Mary know?

"No, I wrote, *I was afraid..."*

"...To lose her, I'll bet. You do her a disservice by not trusting in her love for you."

"I just can't bring myself to tell her," I wrote. *"What if she judges me, finds me the most horrible creature upon the earth and leaves me?"*

"It can't be any worse than the way you have judged yourself. But this is for you to do and I will say no more about it. Peace be with you... Matthias."

I didn't even have time to write "and with you" for he was too quickly gone.

I saw Mary later that day at the home of a disciple where we stay in Jerusalem. We were the only ones home. I told her that we needed to spend some time alone together to talk. She met my serious demeanor with an attitude of playfulness. "Is this really going to be <u>important</u>?"

I took a deep breath and signed a question to her: *"How did you feel about Yehudah?"*

"Are you jealous?"

She just loved to answer a question with a question. I fought to regain my composure. *"No, but I would really like to know. It is important to me."*

"He was a good enough man. He showed me kindness and caring and was even willing to have a deeper relationship. But he was <u>not</u> you Matthias. And you don't ever have to worry that I am comparing you unfavorably with anyone who came before you. You are the only one with whom I would have chosen to spend the rest of my life."

Her sweetness and loving almost brought me to tears. How could I say something that might hurt her? I decided to put it off indefinitely and just be her Matthias from then on.

I felt that it was a miracle that, despite the differences of opinion in our community, we managed to maintain a brotherhood that had room for so much diversity. An even greater miracle was the way differences seemed to get resolved in a consciousness of acceptance and loving.

When Peter returned from Cæsarea we could all see a marked change in him. He was in Jerusalem for only a very short time before he called a meeting of apostles.

He spoke: "It is difficult for a man to change, especially a man such as I, often headstrong and full of pride. Yet when the Lord speaks, it is only the fool who does not listen. It happened in Cæsarea. I was alone, preparing for a meal, when I had a vision. A tablecloth descended from heaven and all manner of beasts were on it. A voice loudly proclaimed: 'Peter, arise, kill and eat.' I saw that there were beasts not proscribed for us to consume according to the Law. I answered the voice: 'I have never eaten anything unclean and defiled.' Then the voice answered, 'If God has cleansed it, you should not call it unclean.'

I did not know what this meant. But it all became clear within the month. I met a god-fearing centurion named Cornelius in Cæsarea and spent some time with him. According to the Law it is unlawful for a Jew to associate with a gentile, but I realized that God had shown me that I should not call any man unclean. God is no respecter of persons, but He accepts all that love Him and do his works. John, I realize that you were right, perhaps God has also granted repentance to gentiles. After all, if God has equally given blessings to the gentiles who are followers of Jeshua, who am I to dispute with God?"

John added: "Since all men come from Spirit, so all men are equal. Men are not to be evaluated by their background, but by deeds alone."

"We must still be careful," said Peter. "There are many who will fault us for going into houses of uncircumcised men to eat with them."

"Peter," said John, "this is where one must decide who it is that we will serve: the god of Man's Opinion or the One True God. If we do not live what we know is Holy, we are preventing God from serving through us. It is time to have courage; to follow the heart."

Peter remained silent.

Eight years had passed since my Master Jeshua was in flesh. I remember a day that had a profound impact upon me. It was a cold, rainy day, where the water came down in sheets and there was not much more to do than to sit near the hearth and meditate. I heard a knock at the door. It was Petronius.

"Matthias, I must talk with you… alone." Mary looked at him in mock frustration and said, "You are not going anywhere until you put on some dry clothes. I have some of Matthias' which are dry."

In my present form, I was about the same size as Petronius. He would never have been able to fit into Yehudah's clothes.

After he had changed, he took me up to the loft where we would be alone. "I have news. Saul has been to Judea."

I could feel the old anger grow inside of me but checked it in order that I might hear the whole story.

Petronius continued: "I know what you must be thinking but it is not that way at all. He has undergone some type of change. He now seeks to follow Jesus with all the zeal he summoned to persecute us. He has gone to study with Philo at Qumran."

"This must be some kind of trick," I signed. *"He is spying on us from the inside by merely pretending to follow The Way."*

"No. I assure you that's not the case, Matthias. He was given the teachings of a novice. He knows nothing of the Initiations. They are not fools at Qumran. They were open to trusting his motives were pure, but only so far. The secrets are safe."

"Is he still there?"

"No, but let me continue. Saul came from a Hellenistic background, as did I, so Philo's own brand of *Merkabah* mysticism and Gnosticism were what attracted him. I am familiar with this mysticism since is it much like other Hellenistic cults such as Isis, Mithras, and Elensis. After his study with Philo, he returned to Tarsus and joined a gentile community of Jesus followers.

"I am pleased that he is no longer here. I have too many bad memories that stem from his presence."

"So do I. But it seemed as though he caused no trouble during his stay and only wanted to learn. Perhaps God has a plan for Saul."

"Away from us!"

Petronius laughed. I realized that I still had little forgiveness in my heart for Saul who had murdered so many of my brothers in the Christ. Saul joining us seemed only to cheapen their memory. Then a thought came in that sent a chill into my Soul: I still had not forgiven myself in my complicity in the death of Jeshua. If I could not forgive myself, I certainly would not be able to forgive Saul.

"Any other news, Petronius?"

"Only that God has spared us a war!"

"How was this?"

"Our late Emperor Caligula was becoming more and more mad. As his delusions grew, he became outraged that anyone would worship other than himself. After all, he considered himself to be all-powerful. He decided to erect a statue of himself inside our Temple, right before the Holy of Holies! He was planning to support this desecration with two Italian legions. The Romans finally assassinated their self-proclaimed "god" Caligula and made Claudius emperor. Just in time for us. Caligula's excesses and cruelty became too much even for them to tolerate. At another time, I would have welcomed this intrusion and challenge for war, but my sons Marcellus and Titus are nearing the age where they could take up arms, and frankly, Judas… Matthias… I worry for their safety. I have lived many years, experienced many things, and would not mind dying as a soldier. But my boys have yet to find their way in life. They have not fully come into the understanding of who they are and have not tasted the joys of raising their own families. Why should they be cheated out of this by war? I know that this may sound strange coming from an old soldier and gladiator such as me. I gave up my life for death when I was young, only to discover real life later through loving God, through studying with our Lord Jesus, and through the goodness of family and friends. I would still fight and die to protect the things I hold dear but I would want to spare my sons from having to do the same."

I signed: *"While I have no sons, my family is just as important to me. I would also fight to protect their lives, yet there is also part of me that would prefer allowing myself to be martyred to save them. I have learned over the years the true meaning of the Christ, what Jeshua meant us to know, and that is that <u>we are all the Christ</u>. He wanted us to get to know that part of ourselves that is divine. Yet he spoke of giving to Cæsar what is Cæsar's. We cannot ignore the responsibilities of the physical existence. It is like I am standing here, not only as Matthias the follower of Christ but also as Matthias the Christ speaking to Petronius the Christ, another part of God who stands before me in physical form. On that level of being there is no separation between us; we are like two fingers on God's hand. How can one finger hurt another? I fear that only when all men know that they too are brothers in this divinity will man's inhumanity to his brother finally cease. But, I tell you, Petronius, it is supremely difficult to keep my focus on divinity when I see what goes on in this world. Jeshua was always able to keep his focus positive. He had a great strength. I am much weaker. I often distrust myself... and God."*

"Our world has a long way to go, Matthias. Many have difficulty acting human, let alone divine."

There was nothing more to say to one another. We embraced and looked into each other's eyes, trying to see the divinity behind the sadness.

Finally I had finished the "Sayings Gospel." It took me four years to complete, even though I spent as much of my free time on it as I could throughout the day and evening. Mary used to chide me for always having ink stains on my hands. I admit that I borrowed time from family life to spend on this blessed work, but Mary always seemed to understand. James instructed me to get a copy of my finished work into the Library at Alexandria, Egypt, so that it would be safe, no matter what occurred in Judea.

I took Simon with me as interpreter and traveling companion on my way to Alexandria. We stopped in synagogues along the way to teach The Way to our fellow Jews. My approach to teaching had changed over the years from the confrontational style of the Baptist to the sensitive and understanding style of my Mary and the other consciousness of Matthias that shared my body. I have learned much from her (and from him!). Simon would have been surprised if he knew that the one who calmly taught and debated with the elders of the synagogue was the one-time cutthroat Yehudah the *Sicarri.*

When we reached the library at Alexandria, we had an interview with the curator, Filias.

"Just what is this work that you would like me to keep for you?" He asked.

I signed to Simon who did the talking. *"A compilation of the sayings of our teacher, Jesus, son of Joseph, a Master of Wisdom from Nazareth."*

"We have many works by Jewish sages. Just how is this one different?"

"Our teacher is the first to herald this new age where the Kingdom of Heaven is now available to all of mankind."

He looked at me with some amusement. "What is this kingdom?"

"It is difficult to explain in words, so our teacher always spoke about it in parable. But from one who occasionally experiences its closeness, I can tell you that it is knowing that the core of your beingness is one with the creator of all, that you are inseparable from God."

"That is interesting..."

"It goes further. He has also said that we are God's children and we have always been such. The task that we have is to regain our knowledge and experience of this. There is no separation between God and ourselves except that we place it there. God does not reside on a mountain or in a Temple, but in and through all things. God is available to us and speaks to each of us through our hearts."

"So, if we all are these spiritual beings, how come we don't have an awareness of this? What is it in our nature that brings suffering and misery?"

"We are all Souls, and Souls are units of God's being. Just as God is a creator, so are we, but on a lesser scale. Maybe I should say we are creators in training. We are given free choice in this life to choose where we are to place our awareness and therefore our direction. We are here to learn through our errors. Our Master Jesus once walked the streets with his disciples and passed the carcass of a rotting dog. While others were focused on the obvious, the ugliness of the putrid flesh, the Master noted how beautifully white and shiny the teeth were. He was not blind to the ugliness of this world but it was his conscious decision to focus his awareness on a positive direction and action for life. We all have the same choice and it takes a lot of strength and practice not to be seduced by the terrors of this world. We can all create this kingdom for ourselves because we <u>*are*</u> *all the Soul, a part of God. The nature of this Soul is joy because it knows this."*

"These teachings carry a powerful message. I presume that you also teach this message."

"We do."

"Then you must be spiritual masters in your own right."

I laughed somewhat self-consciously. *"It is also said that you often teach what you most need to learn. Yes, I know the words and follow these teachings the best I can, but I find that in my everyday actions, I betray that which is spirit inside. I often know better, but fail to do better. But I am not through with learning, and Spirit is not done with me."*

"I would be honored to accept these teachings as a part of this library. Do you have any questions for me?"

"Would these writings be safe in this library?"

Filias laughed as if the question itself was nonsense. "This is the safest place in the world for all manuscripts."

"Was there not a fire when Cæsar was at Alexandria?"

"That was a freak occurrence... wartime... it could not happen again, the world is pretty much in a state of peace. Believe me; your book is safe here!"

Both Simon and I were glad that our mission was a success. We were instrumental in preserving the teachings for future generations. We could all be swept away, but as long that there was a record of The Way, we would have passed on our legacy.

We returned home to a sad and troubled group of disciples. Herod Agrippa had put John's brother James to the sword. Up until now the new King, Herod Agrippa, had left us alone. We had been able to preach freely without difficulty.

James the Just told us that he suspected Agrippa had been making overtures to the priests, trying to win their favor. Since our sect seems to be the ever-present thorn in their side, what better way to accomplish this than to eliminate one of the rivals of the Sadducees? It was a good political choice for Agrippa; he may have achieved his aim with minimum carnage.

We were pretty much in a state of shock. Many Pharisees joined us in our service for the dead. It was somewhat consoling to see that James was respected outside of our sect. After the service, John asked us to gather with him. He said a few words concerning his brother and then reflected on a chilling dream.

"What you may not have known concerning my brother was that he had shared the consciousness of the Sojourner with me. It was difficult to hold this energy at first and he was there to assist me in coming into it fully. Now he is gone and I have assumed a fuller part of this role.

"Last night my spirit was troubled and cried out for help. I was greeted by a dream most frightening. It started as a joyous occasion when we were celebrating the kingdom together. We raised our voices in song and our hymns were so sweet that the angels appeared and joined us in song. It seemed as if our songs of praise would illumine the whole world. But then a dark wind from Rome came and grew in strength. One by one it took us. There was no longer any escape from this wind of darkness. Matthias, you were the last to be taken. But before you left you asked for my blessing. As I touched you, I lost my voice and you regained yours. You kept on singing as you were swept away, but the fury of the wind made it impossible to hear you. At last I was left, alone, the wind all around me, touching me not.

"There are many interpretations one could give this dream. Even if we carry the kingdom inside of us, the world is still a dangerous place.

All we can do is place our faith and trust in the Lord that we will be guided for the highest good."

Our numbers were also being reduced naturally. Disciples and apostles were being called to missions outside of Judea. Thomas was in India. Andrew and Philip left for Scythia. Thaddeus, son of James the brother of John, selected Armenia.

When Herod Agrippa died of an unknown ailment, many saw that as a sign that the Lord was watching over us and that things were changing for the better. That feeling was short-lived for the Emperor Claudius appointed Cuspus Fadus procurator of Judea. From his first day Fadus proved to be a cruel and corrupt administrator.

There were a number of people in these times that believed themselves to be a messiah who would lift the people out of their subservient position to Rome. One poor individual, Theudas, must have thought himself to be Moses come again because he promised to part the river Jordan and allow his followers to cross. Like so many other self-proclaimed prophets, he predicted that the end of the world was at hand, and that the destruction would fall first upon Jerusalem. He had persuaded a few hundred from the area of Jerusalem to follow him. It is ironic that a number of these were escaped slaves that he had promised to free from bondage. There were others who just came to see what he would actually do once he reached the Jordan. Theudas never reached the River. Fadus sent a troop of horsemen out against them, surprised them from behind, and slew about half of them. He also took many others alive — including Theudas himself. The poor man's head was cut off and taken to Jerusalem. This type of ruthlessness was unnecessary against someone who was, at worst, a harmless crackpot. This overreaction was a hallmark of Fadus' administration and only served to point out the level of his procuratorial misconduct.

The numbers of *Sicarri* and Zealots were increasing, but from what I had seen the quality of their training has greatly suffered. These looked like they could be the sons of the soldiers that Petronius and I trained. In another time I would have enjoyed whipping them into fighting shape. However, that was now out of the question.

It had become a tradition for us in the last few years for Petronius and his family to spend the Sabbath with us at Bethany. Petronius and I would go off together, walking, silently chanting the names of God. Mary and Julia would be at the house with my daughter and Petronius' boys. I found that I could stand much more out in the world with the knowledge that every week I could look forward to sharing the Sabbath with our dearest friends. There were many times that other disciples and their families would join us, but Petronius' family never missed a Sabbath.

I sensed something was brewing because Petronius' younger son, Titus, was sent to bring us back to the house. We hurried because Titus refused to tell us what was going on and we feared that someone might have come to some harm. Even at our age Petronius and I kept up with Titus on the run back to the house. (In fact, Titus was the one that was out of breath!) When we saw that no one was in danger, we suspected that the women were up to something. I looked at Petronius and he shook his head. He had no more idea than I did of what was going on.

Finally someone spoke. It was Rebecca: "Father, I ask that you arrange my marriage to Marcellus." Before I could answer, Marcellus asked Petronius the same. There we were, tongue-tied seeing my daughter and Petronius' son looked at each other with eyes that only spoke of the greatest loving and respect. I looked at Petronius who was smiling. A feeling of joy welled up inside of me and I nodded my head. Our children threw their arms around us amid tears of happiness. I signed to Petronius: *"Well, it looks as though you could not have been more correct when you said that we would someday watch our grandchildren play together. Now it appears that your grandchildren and mine will be one and the same."*

"With all that is going on in Judea, it is a blessing from God that we have a joyous occasion to celebrate," added Petronius. "It is humbling to see my children get older. It is also sad to think that there will be a time when I will not be there for them."

"For me," I signed, *"it is the realization that I had no idea this was going to happen. Have I been so removed from my family that I was not present when I needed to be?"* I looked at Rebecca. *"Did I totally miss your childhood?"*

"No, father. I have felt your love and caring all of my life. Except for the times you were traveling you were always available if I needed you. Both you and mother gave me a good home. I feel very grateful for that. If you were preoccupied with other matters, it didn't take away from your expressing your loving for me."

I felt a wave of remorse. *"Mary,"* I signed, *"You and Julia were aware of this from the beginning, were you not?"* Both she and Julia nodded their heads. *"Mary, could I have been more attentive to your needs over the years?"*

"Julia, have I failed you?" asked a confused and somewhat overwhelmed Petronius.

"Dear one, you must not torture yourself about the past," she answered. "I know that we have all been doing as well as we can with what we have been given in this life."

Mary nodded and answered with humor in a way that lifted the spirit in the room: "You men have the uncanny ability to spoil a happy occasion. And you call women emotional. There have also been times in our life together that I wish that I also had reached out and we can't change that, but we can change the future. Let's enjoy that together, shall we?"

James, himself, officiated at the wedding. It was a feast that all contributed to, a truly joyous occasion. The part that I remember most clearly was when John, demonstrating the consciousness of the Sojourner, stood and talked of Loving in Marriage: "My friends, it is a joy to be present at such a celebration where loving is so visibly confirmed. Not only do we come together in the unity of the Christ and Spirit, but also we recognize the unique love of this man and woman. When so many marriages are little more than business contracts, we have the joy to behold the model of right relationship between spouses. The most important aspect of coming together is communication. Your mate is the one closest to you, the one who shares your being in the most intimate manner. Be the Soul for each other. Let your minds share the same mind that was in Jeshua. Do not just follow the law; fulfill the law through loving. What is loving between a husband and a wife? Many may see it as each looking into the eyes of the other with great devotion. I say it is also looking in the same direction, looking into the face of God. If they both do that, they will find that they are also looking into each other's eyes and seeing God present as living love. At that point, it matters little what either does, for each knows God is present in the other. The love that is present depends not on what happens in the world but in the knowing that each loves the other as God would. This is the way to become an expression of God to each other. There can be no higher service."

John took a deep breath and continued: "Part of loving is also honoring each other. This is a must for a husband and wife and, in fact, it should be this way for all of us. This man and woman have come from different cultures. In choosing to come together they have also chosen to break down barriers of separation, hatred and mistrust that have been built over many generations. The real enemy is the one that lives inside of us as separation, hate and judgment toward others. We can overcome this enemy only by a conscious choice of unconditioned loving. This is not a choice that we make once and forget but one that we have to continually choose into. Begin inside. That is where God is; that is where Jeshua is."

Nineteen years had passed since Jeshua was in flesh. During a meeting of apostles, James told us of some difficulty in Antioch. "Brothers and Sisters, many of you are aware that our sect is growing in the Diaspora. We are adding whole communities as well as increasing our numbers. You may also know that there are gentile communities who follow The Way rising up at even a faster pace. Much of this is the work of Saul of Tarsus, who now calls himself Paul. Many of you are familiar with this man under his old name. He caused us much difficulty during our early years when Lord Jeshua was among us. By way of a vision he has proclaimed himself apostle to the gentiles. More gentiles have been attracted to his communities because he offers them all the benefits of Judaism without the need to be strict in following our rituals. True, they practice baptism and the communal meal, as do we, but are otherwise as God-fearers. Now I believe that God-fearing is the moral equivalent of Judaism but without our rituals such as circumcision and dietary laws. Since they are in their own communities, I am inclined to accept them as such. However, Saul… Paul has been causing problems with our communities. He rebuked the Antioch community for not being converted to his approach. He stated that only those who had a similar metamorphosis and followed his way were true followers of Christ. He said those that followed the Jewish traditions in addition to Christ, he felt followed not grace, but law only. All of this caused the leaders of the community to contact us to speak to Paul. This issue has become serious enough where it necessitates a general conference of all apostles."

Paul was called from Antioch to appear before the counsel. There was a wide spectrum of views represented at this counsel. It ranged from those followers of Jeshua who were almost indistinguishable from the *Parush* to followers who were as fully Hellenized as Jews of the Diaspora. Many were curious to see what changes had occurred in Saul to have him "become Paul."

Paul was led into the Temple chamber usually reserved for the Sanhedrin. Peter was elected to represent the more conservative members of the community. It was in this role that he opened the questioning of Paul: "We are familiar with a certain Saul of Tarsus who has persecuted us with impunity. We are not yet familiar with this Paul who claims to be an apostle. Why do you claim to be an apostle when you were Lord Jeshua's enemy during his life?"

Paul was in his element. He began: "Yes, it is true I persecuted our Lord and killed many who are now my brothers, but I am not the same man who did those things. While I was traveling to Qumran, looking for

Essenes to capture and bring back to Jerusalem, a brilliant light from the sky surrounded me and held me in paralysis. I lost my sight. I fell to the ground. Then I heard a voice, and the voice said, 'Saul, Saul, why do you persecute me? By fighting the Holy Spirit, you only hurt yourself.' I was deathly afraid, but I was able to ask the voice who he was. The voice answered, 'I am Jeshua of Nazareth whom you persecuted.' I asked what I should do and the voice said, 'Go to Qumran and you will be told what to do.' Those with me who could still see brought me to Qumran. There I met a disciple of Jesus, Ananias, who had seen me in a vision. He placed his hands on my eyes and restored my sight. I had heard that Jesus had risen from the dead, but I did not believe. It was not until he spoke to me that I believed. I have always been a pragmatic man, this… this completely removed my life from the logic that I have always lived by. Anyone who can arise from the dead must be the direct link to God. From then on I have pursued my Lord Jesus spiritually with the same total fervor I had pursued the Law as a *Parush*."

Peter continued his line of questioning. He asked, "So does this mystical experience give you the right to be an apostle? Most of us who are apostles were appointed by Jeshua himself."

Paul was just as clever as Peter in matters of law. He answered, "My right comes from the fact that my vision was of the resurrected Christ. He came to me in the Spirit body and I then knew what I was to do in this life. Since he appeared to me <u>after</u> his ascension into heaven, my claim to be an apostle is at least equal to yours. Perhaps my claim is even more worthy since I met the spiritual Christ and you only knew Jesus the man."

"And what is your mission, as you see it?"

"I am the apostle to the gentiles. There is no other. It is a job that none of you would have and so it has fallen to me. In the scriptures it talks of 'bringing a Light to the nations.' It is my job to fulfill this prophecy. The messianic age that was prophesied has arrived with Jesus, and this is the window of opportunity to bring the gentiles into the elect status of being divinely chosen along with the people of Israel."

Paul had a way about him. I could see him using words as his new weapons to cajole, convince and inspire others to his way of thinking. He never lost his cunning or his ability for drama and sense of his own importance. I admired his brashness and the cleverness of his arguments. Peter, in his role of fact-finder for the conservative Nazarenes, appeared to be toying with Paul. I knew that soon he would get into the heart of the matter — the theological differences.

"I have heard that you have suggested that your gentile converts not undergo circumcision. How can they be Jews without adhering to the covenant with God?"

"Peter, the question we must ask is does one need to be fully Jewish to follow the Jewish messiah," asked Paul. "God-fearing gentiles are considered the moral equivalent of those who are fully Jewish. A conversion in Christ is a spiritual transformation. I see the Essene ritual of baptism replacing circumcision for gentiles. In baptism the entire being becomes a sacrifice to a spiritual way of life. And these people are truly hungry for Spirit! Why should we keep them from their faith through an adherence to rituals and ceremonial law that have little meaning for them? As I see it, it is our duty to make it easier for gentiles to more freely join the Chosen People. We have a divine opportunity to change the face of our world by converting pagans to a belief in the One God through faith in His son Jesus who is the Christ."

As I listened I was struck with Paul's sincerity, and especially the love he was demonstrating for his gentile converts. This love must be quite great for him to plead his case among many who did not share his point of view. I looked over at John and saw that he was looking at me. The communication was unmistakable. We were to help Paul reach at least some of his ends without alienating the more conservative delegates thus tearing apart the entire conference. It would not be easy. Paul never lost his ability to make enemies. Paul, growing up as a Hellenistic Jew, was less sensitive to the concerns and sensibilities of those in the homeland. His tendency to be somewhat heavy-handed, arrogant and egotistical made him enemies, most of the time without his knowledge.

Those who were *Parush* were angry with Paul. His negative judgment toward their tradition and piety disaffirmed their entire way of life. It was ironic that he still saw himself as one of them. They insisted that circumcision was necessary for salvation and that gentiles must also submit if they were to share the communal meal. They said that the coming of the messiah fulfilled Judaism and made following the Law ever more important. It was their view that all the rules of Jewish life be imposed upon all gentile followers of the messiah. Peter framed his question in the most neutral form: "Just how can baptism replace circumcision? Circumcision is part of our covenant with God."

"My dear brothers," Paul began, "as you are aware, when Jesus was resurrected, he overcame the earth. This is the beginning of a new covenant with all of mankind. I had a vision that I would like to share with all of you. It is of a New Israel embracing both Jew and gentile, all those who accept this new covenant based on faith in the Jewish Messiah. All are one in Christ. To achieve this, both Jews and gentiles must undergo a conversion as did I, a transformation, a radical reorientation and commitment to this new community. The path to Righteousness depends upon perfect faith in the Christ. I see Judaism changed, simplified, permitting the greatest numbers to participate in their own salvation. This new community would be based on sharing the Spirit, with all the virtual distinctions between Jews and gentiles be removed entirely. Both would have to give up the factors that separate each from the other and completely revalue their lives. If gentiles must give up their idol worship and hedonism, then Jews must give up their traditions. Only in this way can a single community be formed."

This time it was James who spoke. "You make a distinction between faith and the Law, as if these are two different pathways, is that correct?"

"Yes," answered Paul, "one is based on the rules of men and the other relies on divine grace."

"What is faith, then, without action?" asked James. Paul was silent. "It is one thing to profess faith. It is quite another to breath life into your words through changing your behavior to reflect your faith. You cannot say you believe and then not act in accordance with your belief, for you are fooling yourself. You do not fool God, however. Faith without action is dead. For most, this means continuing to live a Torah-observant life, as did Jeshua. We are not inflexible. Otherwise why would there be so many different sects? There are Ten Commandments written in stone; the rest, then, is open to interpretation. Some will be very literal; others will be guided by their hearts. I am for unity, but not at the price of our sacred traditions, the things that have defined us as a people for thousands of years. It has been our shared traditions that have held us together. You would cast away that which makes us strong as a people. I have heard that you are a Roman citizen. Is that so?" James asked.

"I do not hide this fact," said Paul.

"What would <u>that</u> mean without the rule of Roman Law? Laws are defined as a roadmap for righteous behavior. And still there are laws of Spirit higher than the laws of man that must be followed, since they are the roadmap for us along our pathway to God. Did not Jeshua tell us to love God with all our heart, soul, and mind and to love our neighbors as ourselves? He told us that this was the distillation of the entire Torah. The ceremonial law is our heritage as a people and some may follow it more closely than others, but it is revered by all since it defines who we are."

John added a final comment. "It is a great service that you do in bringing The Way to the gentiles. I would caution you to also be mindful that your focus on faith brings you a community of believers. May I ask you what it was that brought you to accept our Lord Jeshua as your Messiah?"

"It was the experience in the desert..."

"Exactly. Before that you had no faith. Would you agree that an experience of the Christ was instrumental to your faith in Christ?"

"I would have to."

"Then you will want to do all you can to provide that experience for your converts. Paul, turn them from believers to knowers." John handed Paul the 'sayings' book that I had helped to compile.

"I will give this to my companion, Luke." said Paul. "He has wished for a book such as this."

"I will speak with you later," John concluded.

The time came for James to make his decision. He spoke with Peter and John for some time before coming to the center of the gathering. "The decisions we make here today will have repercussions far into the future, so none of this has been taken lightly. We can only choose what is to be for the highest good of all as we see it. In that, I have asked God's help. We have heard from Paul and seen the changes that have occurred in him. We are impressed with his commitment to his converts. We cannot accept his formula for uniting the Jewish and gentile communities, for the 'solution' would cause a more serious shattering of the unity of the Jewish people. As far as we are concerned, no conversion is necessary for Jews. If a Jew accepts the fact of his own divinity, the Christ within, that is all that is needed. As far as the dietary laws are concerned, Jews and gentiles could eat together if they followed the same dietary laws. If they did not, there should be different communities. Dietary laws are only one of the differences. We cannot remain Jews by giving up our heritage. This is the heritage that Lord Jeshua loved and built upon. If he thought there was value in that, who are we to disagree? As I see it, we are not yet at a point where we can all be in the same community. I do see this as a real possibility for the future. Gentiles are new to The Way. Many behave as though they have special wisdom that the rest of us do not. They need to mature and see that there is unity in our diversity. Paul is teaching his converts that his approach is the only way to follow the messiah. That may work to prevent his converts going to other preachers, but in the end, it will bring forth only intolerance and bigotry. True unity <u>will</u> occur someday, but it must be based on an answer that will work for all, and I welcome it. We can, however, love and support each other in the present. We support the work that Paul is doing with the gentile community. He can continue to convert gentiles and allow them to forego the Jewish tradition and the Mosaic Law."

Some of the *Parush* members were unhappy with the compromise. "Are all people Jews, then, even if they do not follow our laws?"

Peter, seen as most sympathetic to their concerns, answered. "In a broad sense, this is true. We have been chosen by God to perform a sacred duty to bring Light to the nations. In this new age of the Messiah, it is the nations who have awakened to our call. The chosen people are now the ones who are choosing back. We cannot shirk our duty to the rest of mankind on account of ceremony. We are being called again to rise above this. The question is, will we choose back? Lord Jeshua has told us that the Christ is inside of each person, with a kingdom so close they do not have far to go for the door to Spirit. If we have made it too difficult for some to join us, can we at least support someone who will make it easier? These people are being called and they are choosing back and becoming part of Israel. And this seems to happen regardless of one's religious practice."

The meeting ended and John motioned for Paul to sit and wait while the hall cleared. I found myself alone with Paul.

"Do you happen to remember me?" I asked out loud.

A look of surprise and a wave of fear swept across his face. "Yehudah?"

"I am Matthias now …Paul. Do not worry. I will not harm you. But I must be brief. I counted you as my enemy for a long time, but I see that God may yet use you for good. I have forgiven you for all that was in the past." I smiled. I pulled back my cloak. "See, I have no more knives."

He smiled nervously and felt the scar I had left on his neck.

"That is all that is left of our enmity." I said.

I led Paul into a smaller room. John and Simon (acting as my interpreter) were there already.

"Paul, there is one thing that truly saddens me," said John. "That is your willingness to change the teachings to your liking. You have spun a tale of a Jesus who was more Greek than Jewish. You have created a Christ who seems more like the mythical pagan gods, Dionysus, Adonis, or Tamuz, through whom their followers gained eternal life in mystical union provided by their mysteries or rituals. Why have you done this, Paul?"

"John," began Paul, "I am a practical man. Most of the new converts are familiar with Greek philosophy and the mystery cults you mentioned. To get converts I must compete with those things with which they are familiar. They are familiar with worshiping a human figure of divinity along with God, a second God, a pre-existing deity predestined to rule as God. I will make sure that the figure of divinity will be Jesus. It will spread our message and reach the most converts. We need numbers for our survival."

"Jesus never once told us to worship him," said John. "He did say, 'follow me.' In fact, Jesus rejected all the labels men placed on him because he saw that God was working on something ultimate through him — the manifesting of the co-creatorship of man and God. Jesus attained that co-creatorship with God by allowing God to manifest through him with ultimate clarity. Until Jesus, that which is the Christ — the divine expressed through man — was a potential within us. Jesus demonstrated that it could be physically manifested in the world. He told us that we will do as he, and perhaps even greater. Why would he say that if our legacy were not the same as his? We who knew him can say with assurance that he was fully human, and still he reached the divine through surrendering to his divine nature, as is our potential to do. The Christ is also inside of you, as you, waiting for you to ascend, as did Jesus. Jesus never said this but it is my understanding in working with him: 'Worship what is unattainable, seek to become what is attainable.' No one can become The One, the God of all things, it is unattainable; but we all can, as Jesus did, become one with The One by becoming one with the divine Christ. Just as the divine Christ is still <u>part</u> of God, the One, it is also part of us. We may never completely understand the One, but we can start to understand the Christ by experiencing the divine Christ inside of us. Call on Jesus, call on the Christ, and worship the One.

John took a deep breath and continued. "By calling Jesus different from us in essence, you separate from him and make him less accessible. Is that what you want to teach your converts? Jesus is our elder brother and he is waiting for us to follow him along the road to Christ-hood, as he said was our divine legacy. How could you so thoroughly misunderstand?"

"No, said Paul, "it is not <u>my</u> misunderstanding. Jesus MUST be different! I am well acquainted with my own unworthiness. There are many things that I would like do to be more in Christ but do not."

"It is like that for all of us Paul," said John, "we are only reaping what we have sowed. But, in spite of our past actions we keep surrendering to that which is Christ inside. Don't be fooled into arguing for your limitations."

Paul started to shake. "My past actions have been transformed by my faith in Jesus Christ. God's Grace will support me."

At this point I had a flash of understanding. I saw clearly Paul's frame of reference. I signed and Simon spoke: *"To have grace, one must lead a grace-filled existence. This is a state of activity in full acceptance of life. Anyone can have faith that the cow will give milk, but faith is useless unless you actually act to do the milking. God's grace will serve you as long as you have the wit or the courage to actually move toward God by changing your behavior. I have known you, Paul, longer than you were Paul and I feel that there is a good reason for your insistence that faith replace law. If faith were everything, you could bypass the burden of guilt and fear of judgment you must feel about your persecution of Jesus. You might even feel the pressure to condemn yourself under the law. Under grace you would be forgiven and you might even be able to forgive yourself. If there were still a law of karma, you would feel yourself in serious danger to reap the results of past actions. Grace will only help as far as you are willing to move to grace through action. You need to put your body on the line and have the faith that God will meet you. I, too, struggle with regret for my past actions. But Jesus forgave me and he forgives you as well."*

Paul remained motionless. His face became contorted and he started sobbing uncontrollably. "I… I thought suffering and pain were an integral part of the faith. I believed that Jesus came to save sinners, I hoped that this was why… because I believed the greatest sinner was myself."

"Jesus would just have said, "Go and sin no more."

When Paul had composed himself he had become more thoughtful. "My brothers, you have given me much to think about."

"Paul, will you continue to hide the truth from your followers?" asked John.

"I will change what I can but I fear if I reveal all there will be confusion and doubt. My communities need to survive. Faith will hold them together, one belief will hold them together, a belief that most can subscribe to. I must not confuse followers with things too deep, it will make them question and lose faith."

"Does this mean you have little faith in your followers?"

"No. It means that I have faith in the gradualness of revelation. They will see the truth eventually, when they are ready. There is no need to dump all of it on them at once. The more simple the gospel, the easier to adhere to it."

"<u>If</u> the whole truth can survive."

"I believe that it will. You in Jerusalem will keep it alive. That is <u>your</u> ministry. Mine is preserving the community."

The conference was finally over and Paul prepared to depart for Antioch. John, Simon and I sat in the small room silently.

I looked over at John, who was deep in thought.

"Paul, I fear, will bring us separation and trouble. He is breeding followers who will be ignorant of the true teachings." I signed.

"Not of his own accord." said John. "He is doing what he feels is for the highest good of his communities and does not act out of againstness toward us. What saddens me is that I see forces that are pulling Judaism apart. We have always had differences between our sects. Sadducees, Pharisees, Essenes hardly every agreed. Yet there was a common bond between us, our traditions as a people. Faith alone cannot replace that which cements us. This is more than just a split between the followers of Jeshua; this is something entirely new. Our group here in Jerusalem is the keystone holding Judaism together. But, I fear that if we are destroyed there will be a chasm that cannot be breached. And, if that is God's will…" John let out a sigh "…then we can do nothing but cooperate with that."

I signed: *"I sense the feeling of urgency Paul is experiencing. He feels that he has found a plan that seems both right with him and in alignment with God. He is then driven to complete it."*

John reply was hardly audible: "Paul must follow his own way. We do not know where it will lead, so we cannot judge. We can only pray that the Christ will be a part of whatever he does."

When the gavel sounded I looked over at Chris. He knew what was on my mind — our time was running out. I whispered, "We have to get Jack on the stand. As Petronius, he came to surpass me in espionage. He is certain to remember many things which I've forgotten."

Chris shook his head. "Jack will never agree. It will make him useless as an agent. By testifying, he blows his cover. There has to be another way."

"Could we make an agreement with the court to hold his identity in secret?"

"That's not the way it works, Roy. I have to furnish the opposition information about every witness <u>before</u> I introduce that witness so they have a chance to cross-examine. If Hastings gets the information on Jack, then *Empire* will also. If *Empire* finds out about him, he won't be able to get close to them. So it's a no-go, Roy. He's paying the bills."

"Then what about Hastings? If we can regress him I am sure that he'll be convinced."

"I'll be honest with you, Roy," Chris said. "I really don't know that I could handle that. He is at his best when backed into a corner and I really don't want to experience that firsthand."

Time was on our side this day. The reading of the next-to-last chapter went longer than expected and the judge said it would be better to wrap things up the next day.

We had an extra day but no clues as to how to proceed. As I left the court to go home I asked inside for guidance and any grace that the Sojourner could provide me. This was my last chance and I was feeling desperate. But something else appeared. It was a feeling that everything would work out as it should. It was the strangest feeling. In the midst of a mind going into frantic overdrive was a trust that things were as they should be. I actually became calm. It asked of me a leap of faith, a trust in this inner knowledge without a shred of logic to substantiate it. Even if I lost, I allowed myself to feel content that what would occur would be for the highest good. By the time I got home, I was clear on how to proceed. I would continue to look for clues in all the material which I had read and maintain a positive attitude.

As I cooked dinner, I made diagrams of my entire previous lifetime from the beginning as a young Judas to an old Matthias. I went over all the memories of that life to the minutest detail to try to find some that could be used to prove that I was there. I was so engulfed by this project I grabbed hold of a hot tray and couldn't drop it fast enough. Food went all over and I slipped on the mess that I had made and came crashing down on my face. At the same time I heard some glass break at the front of the apartment and something whizzed by my head.

"Roy, stay down!" I heard. Jack burst into my apartment with his gun drawn. He took aim and fired at a shadow on the roof across the street. The man took another shot, which didn't even come close to us. We waited. Nothing.

All of a sudden, Jack jumped up, "Bastard's trying to get away." He said and bolted out the door. I followed about two steps behind. When we got to the street we saw a man in front of a café, gun in one hand, trying to steal a motorcycle. He put the gun in his belt, started the bike and left just as we arrived. Two more bikes remained. Jack had a key, which started one of the bikes. I grabbed it from him, "I'm good at this, believe me," I said. I started my bike as Jack pulled out. We raced around the corner and saw his taillights. He must have seen us in his mirror and accelerated. I hadn't been on a bike for a couple of years. It sure felt good!

We kept inching up, closing the distance between him and us. The rider tried everything — weaving in and out of traffic, hairpin turns; nothing could shake us. Jack was really good on a motorcycle. He got close, but not too close to allow the man ahead to take another shot at us. The rider ahead of us took a turn to the left and I knew we had him. The street dead-ended at the beach.

In a few minutes we were flying across the dunes. I loved jumping the dunes in the daytime. At night, it could be dangerous. Sometimes it seemed as if we were suspended in the air for minutes at a time, each time landing on a cushion of soft sand, but sand also as dangerous as a carpet that could be pulled out from under you at any time. While Jack was on the rider's tail, I swung around to the side and ran parallel with the rider. He now had two targets. Which would he see as the most dangerous? He fired at Jack, hitting Jack's headlight. Jack continued following the rider's taillight. At the same time I made my move, accelerating and coming in ahead of the rider, dumping my bike in front of the rider's front wheel. This time I was able to get off before being injured. His bike hit mine and sent him flying. He landed in the sand, unconscious, and hopefully alive.

Jack cuffed the man and called for help. After half an hour, a helicopter arrived took all of us to a track of land in the suburbs. Jack finally spoke to me. "I owe you one, mate. In your lingo 'we've got a real badass here.' His name is Saad Saleh, an al-Qaeda assassin. A few weeks ago he was reported to have entered the country illegally from Mexico."

"Why was he interested in me?"

"You're getting close to winning your case, too close for *Empire*. This guy's mates don't want the funds to dry up, which would happen if you won the case. The only way to stop that would be to stop you — permanently."

"You said you owe me. Well, I need you to testify, Jack."

He stopped what he was doing and was absorbed in thought. Then he spoke. "Love to, mate. If we have all we need, I guess there's no harm in it. Then cover won't be so important. I'll know by tomorrow. What's involved?"

"Just come to court and do whatever Chris tells you."

The thought of that didn't sit too well. He frowned.

CHAPTER 17 - END TIME

As I approached the closed door to the courtroom, I saw Jack sitting on a ledge waiting to enter. This in itself was a sign that it was to be a good day. Jack flashed his roguish smile and said, "Well it looks like Judas and Petronius together again, eh, Mate?"

"So far, we've fought with guns and motorcycles. I hope we can do as well with motions and evidence."

"Well, remember, we've been through worse."

"Just as long as nothing outrageous shows up."

Immediately Chris appeared to punctuate that prophetic comment.

"Hi, guys!"

Jack and I both had a laugh.

"What's up?" asked Chris, feeling somewhat left out.

"We were wondering what was going to go on today."

"Well," said Chris, we're going to listen to the last chapter being read and then put you, Jack, on the stand. Hopefully you can come up with some information that will make our case more favorable. Right now, it's too close to call. The jury could go either way, depending on whether they had time to have their coffee this morning."

The doors to the building opened.

"You guys ready?" Asked Chris.

No answer was necessary. No other choice was possible.

I took the stand and read.

Every day there seems to be more unrest throughout Judea, Samaria, and Galilee. Not only are there more attacks by Zealots and *Sicarri*, but there are also more religious figures preaching to crowds about the end of the world being near. Many of these were just those acting upon their faith, but that had been seen as dangerous to Roman rule. So much so that the new Governor, Antonius Felix, had many of these preachers placed on crosses right beside the Zealots.

Even among the followers of Jeshua, there are many who still cling to this notion that there would be an "end time." One of these, surprisingly enough, is Paul. I do believe that, in this instance, Paul is not trying to delude his converts, but really believes in the imminent return of Jeshua at the end time, and that time is near. It is my sincere wish that he actually reads the compilation of the sayings of Jeshua that I gave to him. In that text, I wrote that Jeshua told us that we would not see him again in this form and that he would send the Holy Spirit as a comforter to us. To those who are awaiting his "Second Coming," it would tell them that already occurred at the resurrection. To those who await the coming of another, I would tell them that the time is over for looking outside; it is time to look within, for therein lies the Messiah.

When Jeshua spoke about "the end of this world," it was not in the sense that all would be swept away and a New Kingdom brought forward to replace it. That was the mistake in belief that I, too, made as Yehudah. I should have realized this when he said that his kingdom was not of (or in) this world. Since then, I have learned that Jeshua was talking about the end of a way of seeing this world. I found that when we discover that we are already in the kingdom he spoke of, all IS changed in the twinkling of an eye. Can it be that simple? Can the answer to man's questioning on the right relationship with God come down to that of clear seeing, a joyful attitude, and giving yourself over to God as His agent? Jeshua, my dear friend and master, Jeshua, what silly absurd fools we in this world must be not to see what you have so clearly pointed out to us.

I made my concerns and ideas known to John, who fully supported me. We were in one accord with Paul's desire for unity within Judaism, but we both recognized that Paul's formula could not work. There is no way that all parties would accept it. Since our group in Jerusalem was the intermediate between Paul's view and that of the more conservative groups, our group would logically be the position from which to forge links between the two "extremes." John suggested that I draft letters to both the Sanhedrin and to Paul. Perhaps in this way I could influence both sides to move more to the center.

In the letter to Paul, I carefully explained to him that it was the experience of those who knew Jeshua, had known him to be fully human, and had earned the experience of his own divinity by keeping his focus on the Lord. Not only this, but I stressed that he had always insisted that we do the same. (Therefore we CAN do the same).

I was not yet aware at this time there had been a serious argument between Paul and Peter, which, for a time, closed Paul's ears to compromise. Peter told me that he had visited one of Paul's communities, basically to check up on Paul. Paul invited Peter to dine with him and a number of gentile followers of Jeshua. This went on for some time while Peter was with him. When they were visited by some of the more conservative Pharisees (who were against any mixing of Jews and gentiles at the table unless they followed precisely the ritual aspects of the Torah), Peter had to choose whom he would offend. He thought that Paul would understand if, for a time, he did not share meals with Paul's converts. But Paul was enraged, calling Peter a hypocrite and accusing him of not being true to Christ. It seems that Paul's temper had gotten the best of him and he stormed out in a huff. Paul then decided to travel to Syria on a missionary journey. I do not know whether or not my letter reached him, and if it did, whether he was in the mood to respond.

My letter to the Sanhedrin fared little better. I told them that all that was required for their participation was to accept the teachings of Jeshua. The Pharisees who were followers of the Hillel line of teachers were willing to do this but they were not in the majority. The more conservative Pharisees and the Sadducees blocked any reconciliation by demanding proof that Jeshua was The Messiah. They argued that The Messiah would come and lead his people to victory against the forces of darkness (the Romans), and Jeshua did not do that. I had explained that he was not the Military Messiah but one who came to teach. It was also their belief that the end time was soon and they must be prepared to give their all to one who would lead them out of Roman occupation, as Moses led us out of Egypt. Their opinion was always: "Why should we pay any mind to a dead Messiah when there may be a live one just over the next hill, waiting to take us from the clutches of the Romans?"

As conditions worsened, all reason evaporated from both faith and politics. Among the Sadducees, those who considered themselves our enemies, came a desire to have all followers of Jeshua excommunicated. This was an extreme measure that had little following outside of the priests, but because of the fear and hatred surrounding anyone who proposed change, it was considered a stalling tactic to prevent the Nazarenes from gaining more power in the counsel. I was dejected. Not only had my pleas seemed to have fallen on deaf ears, but also my attempt to have driven a wedge further between the sects. I needed the wisdom of the Sojourner. But even John did not bring calmness to my troubled soul. He sounded somewhat fatalistic: "Matthias, perhaps now would not be the time for unity. Perhaps there is nothing to do now except to see this to its conclusion."

I had not felt as much pain since Jeshua's crucifixion, but I had learned that there was always something to do in support of the Spirit. I offered John a weak smile and said: "Don't be concerned. I won't be hanging myself once again. Jeshua may need me just right where I am."

It has been twenty-five years since Jeshua was in flesh. Three years ago, the emperor Claudius, no friend to the Jews, sent us Antonius Felix, who has turned out to be just another corrupt governor. Since that time the number of *Sicarri* has grown, and differences between the different sects have grown into blood feuds. I do not care for the Sadducees, but I doubt that I would have killed Jonathan, the high priest, without due cause as did our present *Sicarri*. Many innocent people in Jerusalem were slaughtered that day, when Felix sent troops to put down what they thought was a revolt. It seemed to me that if these Romans really did fear rebellions, they would stop committing the very acts that might cause them.

The people of Jerusalem can be hotheaded and follow a hot-blooded leader, but they also want to get back to their everyday lives and maintain a kind of normalcy. It is not wise to continually remind them of their continual subjection to Rome. This has been going on for some time, and something has changed in the awareness of the average person. There is a growing <u>expectation</u> of war and death. This just adds to the fervor that was expressed when another false prophet, called The Egyptian, came along declaring that the end time was near and prepared an attack upon Jerusalem by people armed only with the "prophet's" assurance of their victory. When Felix sent his troops, The Egyptian fled, leaving the ordinary people to be either captured or slaughtered.

It is now a world gone mad. There is certainly no reason in it. For example, when the Romans, who proclaim that their order and civilization are good for those they have conquered, cannot maintain the order of their own affairs. Case in point, Claudius was poisoned and Nero became emperor. Having become the most powerful man in the world, he protects this position by killing his wife, brother and mother. A government founded on death and cruelty will not last long and will certainly decay from within.

It is easy to wonder how people could continually make the same error and judge themselves as witless fools each time, but then Karma is where one does not see the pattern of one's mistakes (or they would not repeated). The cycle begins and ends with pain: the pain of occupation, the pain of humiliation, and the pain of loss. Pain makes a man turn to

God (and, unfortunately, anyone who uses God for their own gain). Following a false Messiah is just part of that desire to find someone to release them from pain.

I spoke to James and found that he was open to supporting a new direction for our people. Over the years James had built up quite a following, not only among the people but also in the Sanhedrin. He was even respected by his traditional enemies, the Sadducees and the Parush, for his piety and knowledge of the Law. When James spoke, it stirred the hearts and minds of those who listened, even if they were not in agreement.

James felt that it was time to address the assembly on matters gravely important to the survival of the Jews as a people. "My brothers," he began, "we stand here at the beginning of a new age, one of great promise and of great danger. All that we put into motion at this time will overshadow our destinies for hundreds and perhaps thousands of years. Many of you knew my brother, Jeshua. Some of you were familiar with his teachings. Even fewer of you agreed with them. My brother was dedicated to God, dedicated to Spirit. He knew the peace that flows from a strong inner connection with God. He was not against a fight when he was fighting for a spiritual principle, but he always fought FOR and not against. Rome has caused much suffering in our country and, without a doubt, will cause more. How are we to deal with a cruel occupying force? We have seen the merciless way Rome deals with those who even appear to be her enemy. Every day they get stronger militarily. We do not. The heavy burden of taxes keeps us poor and hungry. Many of us are waiting for a Messiah to arise and drive out the ungodly foe. We hunger for relief; we look with anxious eyes — anywhere, everywhere. As a nation we have not learned the lessons of loving. My brother was killed by these Romans and yet he believed in loving his enemies right to the end."

Delegates who had connections with the *Sicarri* and Zealot factions started to shout James down and prepared to leave the chamber.

He stopped them in their tracks when he raised his voice above the din. "But I am not asking you to love the Romans. I am asking us to love each other and ourselves. If we continue to think of ourselves as a conquered people, that is what we shall always be. It is hard to hold onto our faith and pride in ourselves when every day bring a new Roman insult. But I say that we MUST not give into being a victim of the Romans. The first step to loving is forgiveness. We can forgive ourselves for our weakness. Let us forgive ourselves for our inability to weave our own destiny as a nation. Let us forgive ourselves for being at the mercy of a treacherous giant. We can still be God's own people. They cannot take that away from us, even if they tear down this Temple and scatter us to the four winds. What God has given us, no one can take away!"

All the tumult had died, James' voice was the only thing we heard. "If we forgive ourselves these things, we will stop hating what we have become. In the eyes of Rome, we are a conquered people. That does not matter. It's who we are in our hearts that truly does matter. Let us choose to be God's people by letting go of the hatreds of the past, and living in the loving of God and the appreciation of what He has given us. Peace must begin inside of each of us. We must first make peace with ourselves. Then, and only then, can we make peace with the world."

"Do we give up and become sheep, like the Sadducees would have us do?" asked a Pharisee.

"No, we do not. But neither can we afford to fight them in the open. I do not want to see more of our people killed. We can resist by not supporting their evil. God will meet us if we substitute love for hatred in our hearts. Do you remember when Pilate brought Roman images into the city? Do you remember how we resisted this? Every man, woman, and child stopped what they were doing and sat in place. It brought the city to a stop, nothing could get done and even Pilate would not slaughter so many unarmed innocents. We used Roman law to our own advantage that day. What we accomplished as a people that day was truly great! Have we forgotten that?"

A feeling of pride swept through the chambers.

James continued. "The difference is that at that time we were not trapped in the evil cycle of insurrection and defeat. My brother taught that when someone slaps you, you turn away from that action. You are not giving into to the other person, nor do you attack that person, but you are actively seeking another way, another path. The essence here is in not returning the againstness, not returning the conflict. If you give up, you give the enemy power. And when you enter into conflict with the enemy, you still give him power. When Jeshua taught, 'Resist not evil,' what did he mean? How then do we deal with evil? Not giving it power. Instead, focus on what is righteous and constructive in our lives and do not enter into any againstness. We replace it with a stronger 'for-ness' in supporting each other and ourselves. If Jerusalem is ever to live up to its name of being a city of peace, we must re-learn what it is to be peaceful; practice that inside ourselves and with each other. If, each and every day in our lives, we keep choosing the peace, it will absorb the evil and will not be perpetuated in the world. If we do not, there will be more bloodshed and greater suffering. Those are our choices. Do with this what you may."

James did not stay to hear what followed. He left quickly. I could tell there were some mood shifts in the room for some very strange reasons. Those who were of a pious nature saw the wisdom in James' approach. For the most part the Zealots and *Sicarri* were very skeptical but were open to listening. The most resistance and anger came from the priests, whose job it was to act on behalf of Rome in administration. They saw this as a way for James to take away their power. They condemned any kind of resistance, peaceful or otherwise. They saw James as a very dangerous man.

Petronius was always my source of secret information. He still was known by and had contacts with the Zealot and *Sicarri* camps. Since I became Matthias I had no connection with these organizations, but it either pleased Petronius to inform me or it was by force of habit that he did so. It seems to me that I am, for the most part, still Judas Iscariot (a *Sicarri)* to Petronius. I am his link with times gone by, in which he may have felt more comfortable. It seemed that someone in one of those groups was keeping a very close eye on Paul, because Petronius got word of Paul's intention to come to Jerusalem months before his arrival date. I admit that there was a part of me that also reveled in this intrigue. I wondered if we looked foolish to our wives: two gray-haired warriors recapturing their youth in the joy of secret meetings and discussions in the shadows.

As usual, Petronius' news was accurate. A few weeks later we got news that Paul had landed at Cæsarea and was headed toward Jerusalem to meet with James. Petronius really did shine that day. He could hardly wait to tell me of his plan: "Let us go like we did as *Sicarri* and hide in his following. We will get a first-hand look at what Paul is planning!"

It was an exciting thought for me too, to get back into some action, some danger and some suspense. This was the only time that I had ever lied to Mary other than not telling her that I had been Yehudah. I told her that I was going to the Sea of Galilee to rest and meditate. I knew that she would be very upset if she knew what Petronius and I were about to do. This was something that Yehudah would have done and she would be certainly smart enough to figure that one out… It was better just not to tell her.

I packed the things that I would take on a retreat. I buried them in a safe place in the woods. Petronius met me at the assigned place and handed me the robes worn by a follower of Paul. We moved by night so that we might not be seen by anyone until we got to Cæsarea.

Once at Cæsarea, we blended in with the crowd of followers of Paul, learned their special vocabulary, and developed our "characters" as if we were taking over these identities. All the techniques that we had practiced as *Sicarri* were still as effective and new as the day we introduced them. I was fortunate not to be recognized by Paul in my disguise. Perhaps too fortunate? I was not really sure if he recognized me, or if he just paid no attention to the situation. During the time when he was Saul, he would have been very wary of such a thing. But here was a changed man. Everything that he did was done in a consciousness of giving to the Lord, which I admired. But, that was only part of it. What he was doing was not without a certain degree of pride. It seemed as though he actually saw himself returning to Jerusalem as a conquering hero. He appeared to be acting as if the entire world was his grand play, and the rest of us were merely actors in it. Paul was a driven man, driven by his faith, perhaps mixed with ambition, and I didn't know whether to envy him or pity him.

By the time we had completed the trip from Cæsarea to Jerusalem, we had "become" these followers of Paul, to the point where we had learned to think like them. Paul was very careful to not keep around him anyone who disagreed in the least way with his gospel. As a teacher, he preferred to be the stern father figure. All were fair game for Paul's testing to make sure that we were all pious enough. This evening he took his own second in command, Titus (a Greek) to task.

"Have you sinned, Titus?"

"Yes, I have."

Titus hung his head. I was not sure if it was because of shame for his actions or the calculated humiliation that Paul used to make sure that no one in his group rose above him.

"Do you believe that Jesus is the only Son of God and that only He can save you from your sins? Do you believe that only through the divinity of Jesus can we hope for salvation and acceptance by Our Lord?"

"Yes." said Titus, almost in a whisper.

"And how can we achieve this," asked Paul.

"Through unwavering belief and obedience," spoke Titus.

I turned to Petronius and whispered that I had much more fun being a disciple of John the Baptizer. Petronius laughed silently, but it was only half a joke. I really would have preferred that Paul had known the loving strictness by which John guided his disciples, not to mention the presence of Jeshua…

Paul could tell there was some whispering going on and raised his voice. "AND… how do you know this to be true?"

"Because of what was shown to you by Jesus in your vision," answered Titus.

"And when will this occur?" asked Pau.

"At the end-time…"

"…In the day when God shall judge the secrets of men according to my gospel by Jesus Christ."

This group was a highly disciplined lot. They took degrading and humiliation as a sign of piety, and it seemed to strengthen their faith. The boundaries between insiders and outsiders were so dense you could almost reach out and pound the wall. Paul had managed to exchange the inner discipline of the law with an outer discipline of exclusiveness. He kept a tight rein on almost every aspect of the lives of his followers. He often judged quite harshly those outside of his sect but, strangely enough, condemned his detractors for their judgment of him. Paul had gone from a henchman of the high priest to the role of judge for God. I think he desperately sought the status of spokesman for God, as a prophet of old.

"We shall be among the false apostles," he said. "Therefore we must condemn their heresies. They have been blinded by the physical presence of Jesus so they have not recognized His true nature. It is clearly impossible that James could actually be His brother. Jesus' birth must have been different. God must have given birth to Him directly. He could not be related to such an imperfect individual. These false apostles are so high and mighty with their secrets and initiations. But it is <u>WE</u> who shall survive and they who will be swept away!"

I was not surprised to hear Paul talk of our Nazarenes in that way. I had suspected that Paul was jealous of and also hungry for the legitimacy of our group at Jerusalem. He often communicated with Peter as a slight to James, whose position he may have coveted. All of these traits were being learned and absorbed by his followers as part of the Gospel.

Despite Paul's harsh treatment of them, his followers remained quite loyal. Many were having discussions on why he should not go to Jerusalem. They felt that only danger and death waited for him there. There was widespread fear among his followers. Paul's own guilt had reached the level of doctrine with his followers. Instead of spreading the knowledge of the permanent presence of the risen Jeshua among them, accessible to everyone, they yearned for his return as a savior. They practiced the separation that Paul himself must have felt from his savior, believing that if, in the end, He judged you worthy, you would be able to become part of the body of Christ, what Paul assumed to be a flesh connection with Jeshua. Jeshua, in so many of his teachings, stressed that we are the Immortal Being we seek; we just have to accept the vast responsibility that goes with the status of being a co-creator with God.

Paul reveled in the prospect of stirring up antagonism toward himself. It appeared to me that he took persecution as a sign that he was acting out of Christ. The logical explanation for me was that he still felt overwhelming guilt for his persecution of Jeshua. If he himself were persecuted, it might alleviate some of the pain he felt. If I could have, I would have told him that suffering was not necessary for a spiritual life. Life is already a mix of joy and sorrow -- best appreciated from an attitude of surrender to Spirit. If he were not so afraid of his guilt he could actually have used it as a vehicle for inner purification. But it would be unwise for us to reveal our identities, so all I could do was pray for him.

We attended a communal meal and partook of wine and bread. The simple act of sharing in Jeshua's name had become more ritualized. There was a part of Paul that would always be a Pharisee. He had replaced the ceremonial law with his own form of ceremonial ritual.

In Jerusalem we were treated with respect and warmth but also with much caution. Paul had a reputation with the Nazarenes, of being unpredictable (with good reason). James listened quietly to what Paul had to say. Paul talked mostly about his efforts to win converts among the gentiles.

James said to Paul, "I am encouraged by the work that you have done, but there are also some problems that have arisen from your ministry that we must correct. We have heard rumors that you teach the Jews of the Diaspora to forsake the Laws of Moses, to not circumcise their children, to not follow the ceremonial law. These rumors, whether true or not, are harmful to the purpose to which you have committed yourself. I ask you to put our people's fears to rest by undergoing purification and meditation."

Paul consented to undergo daily baptism for a week, along with fasting and prayer as is the traditional Essene custom. When this period of purification had ended, Paul gathered his followers together and said, "What I did I did so that we could gain more converts among the Jews of Jerusalem. If I can show them that I am one of them, they may listen and accept my gospel over the false gospel of James and Peter. I have learned to be all things to all men so I can gain their confidence. Afterward, they will be more open to hearing the word of God through me. Remember, the only reason we fight is to win, and because we are doing this for God and His Son, Jesus, we win any way we are able."

For Paul to challenge James in a political battle was truly an exercise in futility. To the people of Jerusalem, Paul was called the "spouter of lies," while James was almost universally revered as an inspired leader, to some, almost as important as Jeshua himself. He was called, among the populace and especially among Essenes, the "teacher of Righteousness."

But Paul misjudged the breadth of his authority. He came unannounced to preach in the Temple. He had heard that James was of the habit of doing this and he wished no less of an entrance for himself. As he started, Jews from Asia Minor who had heard him preach before in their native lands recognized him. "Men of Israel," one of these cried out, "this is the spouter of lies who teaches against the law and the Temple and brings with him uncircumcised gentiles to defile this holy place."

Petronius and I shed our disguises and melted into the crowd in case the angry mood of the people spilled over onto Paul's followers.

They dragged Paul from the Temple. As he was being roughly handled, he shouted, "I did not bring a gentile inside our Temple, I am innocent of any wrong-doing."

The crowd looked angry and would probably have hung Paul eventually. I figured that even Paul did not deserve such a fate, even though he was a consummate liar. I approached a Roman guard and told him that a Roman citizen was being attacked. The guard told his captain who quickly dispatched a centurion with his soldiers to investigate.

As the soldiers menacingly approached, the crowd let go of Paul, who had lost nothing but his dignity. A shouting match ensued between Paul and his followers, the crowd, and the Centurion, poor man, who was trying to follow all the arguments.

Tempers ran hot and were not easing. The Centurion had the presence of mind to take Paul toward the fortress of Antonio, where he would be safe for the moment until the soldiers could ascertain what was to be done with him. As they reached the steps, Paul asked the Centurion to speak with him.

"Aren't you that Egyptian that caused so much trouble in the desert?" asked the Centurion.

"No," replied Paul "I am a Jew of Tarsus in Cilicia, and a citizen of Rome, and I beg you to allow me to speak to the people." The officer shrugged and stepped back.

"My brothers," Paul began, "give me a chance to present my defense. I admit that I have been wrong in the past. I persecuted the followers of Jesus of Nazareth. It was for the priests that I put both men and women into prison."

Paul again told the story of his vision, but it had the effect on the crowd of enraging them all the more.

The centurion received a message from his captain that Paul should be brought to the fortress, and there be scourged[15].

Paul was taken to the fortress but was not scourged because of his Roman citizenship. The captain was a just man and wanted to find if any of the charges against Paul were true.

The next day, the entire counsel and Paul were commanded to appear before the captain. Paul was a very clever man. He knew that in the present company, playing the Pharisees against the Sadducees would be an effective way to split the forces against him. "I am a Pharisee, the son of a Pharisee, and it is because of my views of rebirth that I am being judged." The Pharisees were angered and took Paul's side in the argument. Petronius and I looked at each other in mock surprise. Paul was accomplished at crowd manipulation and we expected him to demonstrate his expertise. The leaders of the Pharisees stood and said, "We find no fault with this man, and if a spirit or angel talked to him, that causes no harm."

The priests were incensed. Paul had once again proved himself a more able politician than the priests. He had made a few friends, but he had also made some very powerful enemies. The priests wanted Paul dead and had chosen forty of their class to do the deed. However, Paul had the good fortune to have a nephew who was a zealot sympathizer. Through Zealot sources Paul became aware of the Sadducees' plot against him. An additional irony was that Paul's nephew wrote a letter to Governor Felix asking protection for Paul due to Paul's Roman citizenship. That request was taken quite seriously, for Paul was taken from Jerusalem in the middle of the night and brought to Cæsarea for his protection.

Petronius had a first-hand account about what happened at Cæsarea from a female servant of Felix and Felix's wife Drusilla. Her duty was to tend to all guests as well as to her employers, so she pretended to see little, but was able to report much to her lover, a Zealot named Simon bar Asher. She had either a fantastic memory or an incredible imagination, because she was so precise in her details.

She told Petronius of a trial before Felix in which Paul faced his accusers, the Sadducees, priests and scribes. The priests could offer only

---

[15] Whipped with metal chains that tear the flesh.

vague charges that Paul had sought to defile the Temple and that he tried to turn Jews away from practicing their religion.

Paul was brilliant in this encounter as well. He knew that Felix would have positive and open attitudes toward him if he said and did the right things. He again played the Pharisee/Sadducee card to his advantage. Felix's wife, Drusilla, was Jewish, you see, and a follower of the teachings of the Hillel school. He then explained that he did believe in the dead coming back, as did the Pharisees, and that he had the same zeal for the law and the teachings of the prophets. He said that if he committed any crime it was to purify himself in the Temple, as is the Essene custom. And for this, and his belief in afterlife he was being persecuted. Drusilla was adamant that he should be allowed to go free. Felix would have let him go then, but it was his custom to receive a bribe, which Paul was either ignorant of or refused to do. Felix, hoping to get a bribe, kept Paul as a prisoner, albeit a well-kept one. He had Paul come many times and talk to Felix and his wife. Felix made himself available to be bribed, but Paul just preached about righteousness, holiness, and the judgment to come.

Felix never did get his bribe, for he left Paul to the next Governor, Porcius Festus. This new Governor still had to follow Roman law in the fact that men still were able to face their accusers and have the chance to defend themselves.

Other Zealot and *Sicarri* spies told us of Paul's trials before Festus and Agrippa. Paul stated before them: "I have committed no offense, either against the Law of the Jews or against the Temple or against Cæsar."

Festus had begun to receive bribes from the priests, so he was willing to place Paul into their hands: "Would you be willing to go to Jerusalem and be tried of these things before me?" He asked.

Paul played his Roman citizen card again. But once he played this one, there was no going back: "I stand before Cæsar's judgment seat, where I ought to be tried; I have done my people no wrong. If I had done anything worthy of death, I would not put up a fight; but if there is no truth in the charges made against me, then no man has the right to deliver me to death to please him. My only true justice will be before Cæsar."

Festus turned and conferred with his counselors and spoke: "You have appealed to Cæsar, you will go to Cæsar."

Paul was then placed back into custody. After a few days, King Agrippa and his wife Bernice came down to Cæsarea to push for Paul's trial. The Sadducees saw Paul as a great danger and were pushing for a judgment against him. Festus told Agrippa: "I would like to be able to accommodate you, but two things stand in the way. The first is that I have heard the complaints of the priests and they were not able to prove any serious charges against Paul. Most of these charges were arising from differences in worship between two sects. This is hardly ground for judgment. And then there is the matter of Roman law, which prevents me from handing over a man for execution without giving him a chance to defend himself. Finally, this matter is now fortunately out of my hands. Paul has appealed to be kept as a prisoner until such time that he might have a trial before Cæsar."

"Well, if neither of us has any further to say in the matter, would there be harm in allowing me to hear this man tomorrow?" Asked Agrippa.

"None," said Festus. "Tomorrow you shall hear him."

The next day Agrippa and Bernice came to the courthouse with great pomp. Festus commanded that Paul be brought in. Festus then said, "I have heard many things from the priests that say that this man should die. But I have found nothing worthy of death. And, since he has appealed for trial before Cæsar, that is where I shall send him. The problem is that I do not know what to write as his charges. After all, a prisoner cannot be sent without charges, it's just not done! Well, Paul, you now have permission to speak in your own behalf."

"In view of all of which I am accused," Paul began, "I consider myself blessed to defend myself before you, King Agrippa. I also appreciate the fact that you are familiar with all the customs and laws of our people. I beg that you hear me patiently. The Sadducees who accuse me are well aware of who I am. I came to Jerusalem as a boy and grew up with the excellent doctrine of the Pharisees. And now I am on trial for that very doctrine that states that God can raise the dead. I learned later that one Jesus of Nazareth had accomplished this. But in the beginning I worked for the Sadducees who were sworn enemies of Jesus and his followers. I did persecute them at every turn, until the day when I…"

Paul told his story of how he became a follower of Jeshua, and his life until the day of his capture.

"…And then I was seized in the Temple by those wanting to kill me. Yet I did or said nothing contrary to Moses and the prophets, but rather in line with their teaching. That is the Messiah, the Christ, should suffer and rise from the dead and preach to all, and come to me and have me to preach to the gentiles."

"Paul," said Festus, "too much study has driven you mad."

"Not so, my excellent Festus," said Paul, "I speak only truth and King Agrippa is also familiar with these things that I present. King Agrippa, do you believe the prophets? I know you believe."

"With a little effort, Paul," said Agrippa; "You could almost persuade me to become a Nazarene."

"I pray God, that not only you, but also all present could be as I, except for these bonds," said Paul.

They left and Paul was taken back to his chamber. He knew that he had again won his life, but he also must have realized that he might have gone free, were it not for his appeal to Cæsar.

We had heard of the trial and the outcome. Petronius and I decided to visit Paul in his confinement at Cæsarea, to see if there was anything he needed. We expected to find him in a cold, dark and filthy cell but instead he seemed at home in a spacious Roman-type dwelling. Except for the two guards at the door, we might have thought that he was a wealthy man on an extended holiday. He did not notice us as we entered.

"Thank you for coming. I do not get that many visits from followers these days and…"

Petronius interrupted Paul's welcome: "…It is Petronius and…"

"Yes, Judas."

"Matthias," I corrected, signing with Petronius giving voice to my gestures.

"I had wanted to talk to you again," he began. "It is said that when you want the truth, always ask your enemies. We are brothers in the Christ now, but at one time we would have tried to kill each other. I respect your views since you have nothing to gain from speaking to me from anyplace other than your heart. You also seem to know well the forces that drive me, perhaps, at times, even better than I do. But I find what you have to say intriguing, and I would like to hear more of your counsel. But first I need to tell you that I am a changed man. I thought all along that it was the Law that was weak and that men should abandon the Law and rely totally on faith. But it is not the law but the flesh that is weak. I know now that we are all heirs of God and fellow heirs with Christ, even in our sin and weakness. Yet, like all men, I look at my life and I see that there is a gap between my ideals and my experience. I am weak. And I feel the agony of this daily, for I know that to live by the flesh, you die, but by the Spirit, you will live. I have great dreams, Matthias. I see a future where all are in Christ and I will do anything to bring it forward; I will lie, cheat, and break my word to bring it forward.

I know full well what is right from what is wrong, but I see the dream and I am powerless to hold my tongue. My faith has not been strong enough to deliver me from the sins of my own body. What do you say to this?"

I held his hand for a long moment and then signed, *"Yes I agree we are brothers in the Christ because we both want God's kingdom to come for all. And I love you in Spirit but I neither like nor agree with your methods. I feel that you have corrupted the teachings that I love in order to appeal to the pagans. You have replaced knowledge with ritual, obedience for reverence. Still you have won over many who may at some time learn the truth, if it is to survive us. You also have the admirable quality of a strong devotion. It is much stronger in you than in me. I have come from a tradition of understanding my spirituality — a function of the mind, while you act through your devotion — an emotional state, but one with great power. We have different pathways yet they meet at the heart that encompasses both devotion* <u>*and*</u> *wisdom. If those two energies were brought together..." I mused.*

"...We might bring forward the New Israel," he replied. "But we have failed to do this in the past and part of this was my fault. I can speak with you even with our differences, but I have no common ground to work with the Jews who do not follow Jesus. In fact I had blamed them for complicity in the death of my Lord. It is because I felt all this guilt and they seemed to be totally unrepentant."

"That's not the whole issue," I signed. *"Your gentile believers are not seen as real Jews, either in Rome or in Jerusalem. That means that they will not have the protection of Roman law that Jews do. Your followers worship neither as Jews nor as pagans. The Romans might persecute them unless they have the same protection, as do Jews. Perhaps it would be in your best interest to become a separate sect. Perhaps you will be seen as less of a threat. Your followers have no real desire to go through the conversion processs, and the Jews that do not follow Jeshua will not accept you because you do not follow their traditions. You have defined yourselves in one direction and them in another."*

"And you..."

"I am afraid we are defining ourselves as a third. The world is pulling us all in different directions and my only hope is that the teachings of Jeshua survive no matter what happens to us or you or Israel."

"I will not survive this trip to Rome, Matthias. I have a feeling that it will be my last stop in this life. I fear I have condemned myself from my own mouth. Yet, if there is nothing I can do about that, I will try to use my skill for convincing the emperor that my followers should have imperial protection. For me, it is the communities that must survive, and I have seen a vision of how that could be and I would be sorry if I do not get a chance to see it occur."

"May we meet in the realm of the Soul," I signed. *"May we be One in the Kingdom."*

"And may the blessings of Jesus be yours," said Paul.

Petronius and I walked the streets of Cæsarea. It was summer, mid-afternoon, and few were on the street. Neither of us communicated for some time. Then Petronius turned to me and smiled. "Forgiveness feels really good, doesn't it?"

I turned to him with loving in my heart and a tear in my eye. *"Forgiveness is a rebirth without dying,"* I signed.

When I look back at what I said to Petronius, I had no idea that my belief in that teaching would be tested to hilt. It was thirty-two years since Jeshua was in flesh. The political scene had been moderately stable for the two years Porcius Festus had been procurator. People had become relatively comfortable, knowing what to expect from Rome's representative. There was one week of unbearable heat when even work was nearly impossible. That week Porcius Festus suddenly died of food poisoning, leaving the reins of government held by no one. Order began to break down. There were more raids by Zealots and *Sicarri* than there had been for many years.

My family and that of Petronius hardly ventured out of Bethany, where we watched our grandchildren grow up. I have been spending time creating two other copies of this book. Along with the Book of Sayings, this is my life's work, other than my children and grandchildren. It may be the only thing that will survive me to give to future generations.

One day when Petronius and I were sitting in the shade of a tree, a messenger came for Petronius. After some talk with the young man, Petronius shared the news with me. It seems that there was a plot by the Sadducees on the life of James. We dropped everything and moved with great haste to Jerusalem over the complaints of our wives, who thought the heat would be too much for us. But no matter how old the body, the Spirit was still young and vital. We moved like the *Sicarri* of old. We got to Jerusalem quickly, but not quickly enough to warn James.

We were two hours late. All that was left was a bloody, broken body that had once held the spirit of James and a young disheveled priest who was obviously in a state of shock. He kept mumbling, "With his last words, he forgave us," between paroxysms of weeping. Petronius was enraged and would surely have killed the poor fool, if I had not held him back.

I grasped the man by the shoulders and shook him. I let him go and signed to Petronius, who was at last composed enough to ask the question: *"What happened here?"*

After some manhandling the young priest regained his wits: "This day there were few who came to the Temple because of the heat. Ananas had been waiting for a chance to kill James and remove this perceived danger to his authority. As was James' custom, he came to the Temple unannounced, wearing the breastplate and the miter of a high priest. Ananas' Temple Guard seized him, brought him to the highest place in the Temple and threw him to the ground. But, it did not kill him. Both his legs were broken, but it did not kill him. This only fueled Ananas' hate and fear of this poor man. When he saw that James would not die, he commanded us to stone James to death, which we did. We have truly committed an offence before God today. As he was being stoned, he prayed for us. With his dying breath he forgave us. He forgave us. He forgave us."

Petronius and I took the body back to Bethany, where we helped prepare it for burial and later for the ossuary. Meanwhile, there was panic and rioting in the streets of Jerusalem. The Temple was closed due to the priests' fear of the mob violence against them. The mob was shouting, "The priests have killed the righteous one!" Only now did I see that James was beloved by most of our people, not only Nazarenes.

The Roman guard was powerless against the crowd without leadership. They stayed in the fortress, protected. The rioting went on for days and the populace was so offended, they asked King Agrippa to punish Ananas, the high priest, for his actions.

The King was a great politician. He banished Ananas to please the populace but placed Ananas' son in the position as a nod to the Sadducees. This most likely saved Judea from civil war, which, eventually would have been brutally put down by new Roman forces. It seems that Festus' successor Albinus arrived just in time to place the banner of Roman order again over Judea.

Meanwhile, we Nazarenes had our own problems. We needed to choose a successor to James. Jude, Jeshua's youngest brother, declined the position and Symeon, son of Clopas and Jeshua's cousin, became head of the Nazarenes due to his being one of the few remaining members of the "Royal House of Judah." He could not replace James, no one could. James was a master in the line of the Christ and Symeon was barely an initiate. His royal blood, his family relationship to Jeshua, made all the difference.

Albinus has proved himself to be another corrupt governor. It seemed that, in our part of the world, this is all we got. This one, at least, was even-handed: he stole from everyone. His official duty was to pursue the *Sicarri,* but he would often bend his principles for gold. In a way, he was good for Judea; all knew that he could be bought and influence peddling became rife around him. He was truly in his element. When you have three often-warring factions to govern, you can play politics for all they are worth. This is what Albinus excelled at. If you were a criminal of any type you could easily buy your way out of prison. The only "crime" that would keep you in jail was no money to give to Albinus.

In the Sanhedrin, our sect had lost some influence since the death of James. Only he could be so commanding in person and carry as much spirit in his daily activities. He is sorely missed by all other than the Sadducees.

I have little time to consider politics. I have finished scribing two copies of this book and will keep updating them as I write. Mary is happy. She is busy studying the mysteries and being mother and grandmother. I have approached her more than once to consider doing some writing of her own because I do see that talent within her.

It had been thirty-four years since Jeshua was in flesh. Having ties to the *Sicarri* was useful for Albinus, but it could not save him. He learned a month or two beforehand that he was to be replaced by Nero's favorite, Gessius Florus. Gessius Florus was appointed to his office because his wife Cleopatra was a friend of Nero's wife Poppaea. He found out that not only would he be replaced, but he was also to be tried for extortion. He knew this would be a death sentence for him when he returned to Rome, so he managed to have his revenge in advance by releasing all of the *Sicarri* he had imprisoned.

James' last wish was that someone of importance represent the Nazarenes in Rome. The logical choice was Peter but, when chosen by James, Peter dragged his feet, not really wanting to leave. It was only after the death of James that Peter resigned himself to carry out the wishes of our late leader. He sailed to Rome within a week of James' death.

Peter spent over a year in Rome, healing and preaching about the Kingdom of God. Then for months we heard nothing from Peter or our other, more secret, contacts in Rome. What news that followed proved more tragic that we could imagine. A fire began in Rome and the only group unprotected by Roman law was the followers of Jeshua who were not Jews. These were the ones blamed for starting the fire. Many said that Nero started the fire himself, and this group was vulnerable and therefore a perfect scapegoat. Persecutions of these followers began in Rome.

As the leader of the non-Jewish followers of Jeshua, Paul was finally brought before Nero for his trial. A servant who had ties to the *Sicarri* heard the trial and later recorded it on paper. He was not the only one to record this conversation. Nero had summoned a scribe to set down every word so he would not miss anything that was presented in this trial.

An official read the charges against Paul: "You are charged with being the leader of a group of seditious rebels and enemies of the empire who are followers of one Jesus, also called Christ." Paul countered with: "I am proud of my Roman citizenship and have never in my life worked against it. My faith and my citizenship are not at odds here. This I will attempt to prove to you. You will see that not only should I be allowed to go free but that those of my sect that follow Christ should be allowed to practice their faith unhindered, since they only wish peace and to bring honor to the empire."

"Paul," said Nero, "you are a Jew from a tiny, backward spot on the imperial map; what do you know of Roman citizenship?"

"Exalted One," Paul began, "it is because of my Jewish heritage that I know. In Judea religion and politics go hand-in-hand with our people. Most of the people do not know the difference between a military and scholarly messiah. This is the reason why they are such a difficult group for you to govern. Our relationship with our God is wrapped up with the national struggle. The stability of Judea rests upon God's view of its worth. In our minds, if we are worthy, God will destroy our enemies. If we lead a more holy, abstentious life, and God finds us favorable then we should expect the arrival of a Messiah to begin the process of a return to self-rule. That is the way of thinking of my people. On the other hand, Rome needs a climate of order in which to function. This requires and even necessitates a fair amount of social control of the people of the empire. At this time the forces of Roman rule are stretched thin and there will be areas and periods of lawlessness for a system that is based on fear — the control of people's bodies by threat of force. I propose that we work together and form a common solution. Controlling the minds of people is far more effective than just controlling their bodies."

Nero was intrigued. "Paul," he said, "I like what I am hearing, please continue with your idea."

"Most of my followers are not Jews, but are gentiles from all over the empire. They are very comfortable with the ancient mystery cults, such as the cults of Mithra and Zoroaster. As with my followers, these cults also include in their doctrines, baptism, a sacramental meal, belief in immortality, a savior God who died and rose again to act as a mediator between man and God, a resurrection, a last judgment and heaven and hell. The only difference is that those cults recognize the divinity of the emperor and my followers recognize only the proven divinity of Jesus. I have crafted a hybrid theology to meet the needs of the widest possible number of citizens. I know that it is the official policy of Rome to tolerate the superstitions of the plebeians. But I think that if the plebeians are to have their superstitions, why not have one that is state controlled? Eventually it could replace paganism as the state religion of the empire. Don't you see what an effective political tool this could be for the empire? Obedience to higher authority is built into my faith. They are offered a better life after death by following the teachings I have laid out. Part of that is to follow the wishes of those God has placed above us. Would you not agree that this could be a much more effective political tool for holding power? This way is more gentle and reassuring, where the process now is too ruthless and cannot last forever since it will surely breed rebellions in every part of the empire. We can avoid this terrible waste of your people and of your energy, my Emperor."

Nero sat and gazed at Paul for some time. This would have made other men extremely uncomfortable, but not Paul. Paul exuded the strength of a man absolutely convinced of the correctness of his actions.

At last Nero spoke: "Paul, you are a much wiser man than I thought you could be. Indeed, a much wiser man than even I. Such men can be very useful but also very dangerous. I like you. You have a sense of political manipulation that I deeply admire. In another time, I would want you as my partner and advisor. But an emperor, too, must think of his empire. The empire is at the height of its power. How did it get there? Certainly by following time-honored precepts of government that have been handed down from emperor to emperor. As emperors we are not insensitive to the need for change. What has transpired today is being written down and will be available for future emperors to read in the case that this sort of change becomes necessary. A break in tradition such as you propose would be warranted if this empire were crumbling, but it flourishes. I am convinced that we should continue with what is most effective until it becomes ineffective. Don't you agree?"

Paul was silent.

"Furthermore, Paul, I really enjoy being seen as divine. It is part of what makes being emperor so deliciously excessive! I am very grateful for having had the chance to talk with you. I was planning for you a death on the cross like your predecessor, but having met you, I wish to grant you a last great honor. Paul, you shall die a soldier's death for your emperor. If you are truly a Roman citizen, you will understand the honor I grant you. Your followers, I am afraid will not be so honored."

Nero motioned to his guard who dragged Paul away. Paul did not cry or plead. He simply began muttering to himself: "This was not supposed to end this way! We were supposed to create a New Israel. Oh, Jesus, was there something that I did which was not favorable to you? Please tell me what it was. No, I will be seeing you soon enough. Please, I pray, protect my followers. They are innocent of any wrongdoing that I may have committed. I will be another sacrificial lamb as were you…" He began praying out loud as he was taken into another room where he could still be heard. The servant who told this tale only knew when the deed was done when Paul stopped praying.

Peter did not have it that easy. He was condemned to the cross for being a supporter of a sect that Rome saw as trying to overthrow the empire. Many who followed Jeshua were singled out for persecution.

This was the first time that I understood the Essenic tradition of calling oneself "The Remnant." Circumstances were making us different from the rest of Judaism, as well as different from Paul's group of gentile Jesus-followers. I caught myself in a statement of judgments concerning the truth of the three paths. I, of course, considered our group to be the only true Judaism, the rest being hopelessly misguided. I found myself expressing the one trait that would have provoked Jeshua: that which he called "spiritual smugness": to assume with total assurance that I am righteous and to regard others (who presumably are not) with contempt. I had always felt myself angered by people who expressed this behavior of being smug and arrogant in their beliefs and quick to judge others, and feeling justified in that action. Now I was ashamed to find this within me also. I found that I really needed to find forgiveness for this trait that Jeshua found particularly galling.

There was only one person who could ease my pain in this self-discovery: John, the Sojourner.

John was tending his garden when he saw me and approached and put his arm around me. When he looked and saw the distress in my eyes, he asked what was troubling me. When I told him where my ache was being generated, he paused and began to speak: "None of us are above another on this planet. We are all like children in school. Some will be faster learners than others will, but all are students. If one displays a prideful arrogance on how fast they are progressing, they are in error because it is just that kind behavior that sends them to the back of the class. Why? Because there is always someone who is learning more quickly. And the one who really <u>is</u> at the head of the class has learned that we are all divine beings entrapped in this illusion of form. If none of us are extraordinary, and none of us are failures either. We are all ordinary, and the closer we can come to ordinariness, the closer we come to our divinity and to God, the Father. 'Those that humble themselves shall be exalted.' What does this mean?"

John didn't give me time to answer.

"It means not that you beat yourself into submission, but that you realize and come to love your own ordinariness including all your flaws."

It has been thirty-six years since Jeshua was in flesh. This is the year that open rebellion has finally broken out. I would say that the land was never the same after the killing of James, but also it was the barbarity and cruelty of Gessius Florus that provoked war with Rome. Compared to Florus, Albinus was a saint! Let it be shown for history's sake that Florus planned to incite the people to rebellion so that his own wrongdoing would be concealed. He stole money from the sacred treasury in the Temple. People came out into the street to protest this action. Others tried to meet with Florus to attempt to avert trouble. Florus demanded that those who demonstrated against him be turned over for punishment. None were delivered. Florus sent his soldiers to plunder the houses of the innocent, who were also captured and crucified – men, women and children. As these unprovoked attacks continued under Florus, the leaders of both the Nazarenes and the followers of Paul in Jerusalem saw the coming of war. Most did move out of the area, to the cities of Pella, Batanea, and Hauran; we did not. The sacrifices for the emperor at the Temple were stopped; and the Roman guard at the fortress of Masada were slain and it was taken over by Zealot forces, as was Jerusalem.

It seemed that the predictions of the apocalypse were coming true. Many thought the New Kingdom had at last come. Many of our sect joined with Pharisees and other Essenes to battle the invader. Petronius had a different view. He reminded me of the resources of the Romans, and that in a war such as this they would be able to outlast any army from Judea. There was great sadness among our people. Everything we loved and cherished about our country was being destroyed, both from within and without. Petronius kept talking to me about what a fortunate turn of fate this was. We were getting older, and Petronius was frightened that he would die in bed like a sick old man. He often spoke of his preference to die in battle rather than in bed. He swore to me that he would be joining the forces at Masada, but there was always something to do that stood in his way, that prevented him from making that move.

It had been forty years since Jeshua was in flesh. Roman troops have steadily hammered the walls of Jerusalem. I feel that I may have kept us too long in Bethany and that the family may be in danger. The Romans were getting ever closer to final victory over the city, and we suspected that no one would be safe against the random killing that would ensue. I suspected that the only safe place for us would be where the Romans were not. However, there is a spot that I feel would be perfect for us. There would be a home for us among the Celts. I have heard that these people descended from the Sumerians, as did the Jews. Their theology appears to be similar to Judaism and therefore would be open to the Nazarene philosophy. I have procured the whole family passage on a ship to the British Isles and perhaps I could get John to go with us. It would be an honor to be the one to carry the Sojourner to safety. But John was adamant. He said that he will not leave.

"At least come to Alexandria," I implored.

"There is still much to do here for me, my time to leave is not yet, trust me," said John.

I have succumbed to the desperation that one feels when all around one is crumbling. Jerusalem has fallen. The Romans are rounding up among the survivors all known leaders of Jewish groups. There are rotting corpses on crosses throughout the land. I can see no other path than to kidnap John and take him with us for his own safety. Old friend and fellow warrior, Petronius, is more than willing to help. In fact, he is positively joyful. He keeps muttering and laughing to himself that at last he will die a warrior's death. I am aware this might be my last battle as well. I made Petronius promise that if I did not come back, he would take care of our families on their voyage to the land of the Celts. He asked me to promise the same. I brought Petronius into the house and showed him the hiding place of my books. "*Make sure Mary finally gets to see this if I do not return*," I instructed. "*And make sure she knows how and why I died.*" Petronius agreed but said that I would be the survivor. He said that I had survived death before and would likely outlast all our children. I hoped that both of us could return, for I knew that our families could use our fighting spirit to get them all the way to the land of the Celts.

Petronius sighed and said that he found in his experience that even with the strongest of intentions, a man cannot escape his destiny (and he felt his was to die in battle).

He took my hand and forearm, with a grip that belied his age, in the traditional Roman handshake of the Gladiator.

"Matthias, you have been as a brother to me and I count myself fortunate to have known you in this life."

I let go his grip and signed: *"Petronius, you have been closer to me than my brother by blood, and I too, am grateful for your friendship."*

We embraced for there were no more words.

The gavel came down for what I though might be our last chance.

"I call Jack Highsmith to the stand," said Chris. Then: "What do you do, Mr. Highsmith?"

"I'm a government employee," He said wryly.

"How do you know Mr. Hammer?"

"Mr. Hammer is a key figure in an ongoing investigation."

"Can you tell us anything about this investigation?"

"Not while it's 'ongoing.'"

"OK. Did you know Mr. Hammer before this investigation began?"

"No, I didn't."

"Are you familiar with the manuscript?"

"Only slightly. Mr. Hammer indicated that he recognized me as one of the characters in that manuscript, that I was that character in a previous life."

"Objection!" Shouted Hastings. "This is hearsay."

"Your honor, this will only remain so for a short while," answered Chris. "I will show that this occurred as he stated. I would like to call Dr. Collins to the stand. Dr. Collins would you bring Mr. Highsmith back to the end of his lifetime as Petronius?"

Dr. Collins had the lights dimmed in the room and brought Jack under. She slowly and carefully brought him to the point in his life as Petronius, directly after Matthias died.

Dr. Collins began, "Who are you?"

"I am Petronius."

"Petronius, can you tell me how Matthias died?"

"Matthias was killed by Romans. We got to John and were making our escape when some armed Temple guard surrounded us. We fought our way free, while Matthias elected to stay behind and guard the rear. When I returned later, I found him dead among a pile of Roman corpses and dead Temple guards. The Romans must have come to the aid of the Sadducee guard. We laid his body in a cave near Bethany until the flesh was gone. As was the custom, we buried the bones in an ossuary. He received a soldier's burial. Tuzla came for the burial and brought a pair of twin blades to bury with Matthias' remains. I also brought the original ones that he had lost, and placed them in the ossuary along with the other pair. I had always meant to return them but never did. I felt guilty that he might have been able to save himself if he had them, so I never told Mary."

"Petronius, we read earlier the account that Roy wrote. Was that account accurate as far as you can tell?"

"Well, Matthias, or someone who had his experiences certainly wrote it. As for accuracy, well, it was Matthias' point of view. I would have written it differently."

"So in reading it, could you pick out the differences between the two books?"

"Only more details. But it was written by the same person."

"How can you be sure?"

"There were things in that account that only Matthias and myself would know, and the details were expanded in later version."

"Objection!" Hastings was on his feet. "How do we know this is not some elaborate hoax? Someone could have implanted those memories."

Jack, still as Petronius, heard Hastings' argument and responded, "If you doubt me why don't you just find Mary's section, the last part of the book?"

"Just where could we look for this section?"

"In the church, of course."

"Explain."

"Mary continued adding to the book after Matthias' death. What I said should be supported, at least to some degree, in that book for it has Mary's extra section."

Chris leaned over to me and whispered, "I don't think we stand a chance of winning this without Mary's copy, and I think the judge's patience has just about worn out."

Jack was just being brought back when a bailiff approached him and whispered something. Jack nodded his head and left the courtroom.

I looked into Chris' eyes. I looked further than the bravado, the wild sense of humor, and reached past a layer of fear and uncertainty and saw another soul. Then I recognized something I had not seen before. My face must have lit up with recognition – it was Matthias! The one whose body I shared, that "other part" of me about whom I had learned so much during that lifetime. I pulled my focus back and looked at his face. Something was going on inside him, but I really couldn't tell what it was. Was it recognition?

"Counselor?" Queried the judge.

Chris quickly composed himself. "Your honor, I wish to call Frederick Hastings to the stand."

"Your honor," shouted Hastings. "How long are we to put up with this foolishness? This is a court of law, not the psychic hotline."

"Counselor! Explain!" Directed the judge.

Chris look more focused and assured than I have ever seen him. This time he meant to stand his ground. "Your honor, I have taken this line of questioning on direction from Mr. Hastings. He rightfully questioned the testimony of my last witness on the basis of a possible hoax. I want to remove that ambiguity by bringing to the stand someone who has no reason to support our claim that Mr. Hammer was Judas Iscariot, the writer and owner of the manuscript. We wanted another person who was there at that time to confirm Mr. Hammer's identity."

"Your Honor, I <u>refuse</u> to be a party to this circus!"

"Counselor, it is not your turn to speak. You may continue, Mr. Woo."

"Your honor, I would like Mr. Hastings called as a <u>hostile</u> witness."

It seemed that Chris had prepared for this and didn't tell me. I could only assume that he never really chose to go ahead with it. I was extremely aware of the change that had overtaken Chris in the past few minutes. I knew what courage it took to stand against the doubt and ridicule that he must have felt. The spiritual essence that I had known before, the <u>original</u> Matthias, expressed courage to the extent that I never experienced in our life together inside the body of Matthias. I was grateful; but, more than that, I was just proud of him.

"So you are saying that I have had previous lives?" Hastings asked Chris.

"We have all had them. It seems as though we are normally blocked from these memories so we can concentrate on our present lives. We have seen one of Mr. Highsmith's previous lives. We wish to see one of yours."

"Well who was I?"

"We are going to let you tell us. Therefore we will avoid any question of suggestion."

It seemed that Hastings was at last opening to the possibility. He was curious! I chanted silently inside and sent the Light to Chris as a support.

Mr. Hastings took the stand and the lights in the courtroom were lowered. Dr. Collins administered the relaxant to Hastings and we all waited silently for about five minutes.

"Will you tell the court your name?"

"Frederick Hastings."

Dr. Collins then took him back 10 years. "What are you doing?"

Hastings answered, "I am preparing for my new position. It's been a sore point between my wife Valerie and me. She says that I don't spend enough time with her and the kids already, and this job will ask more of me, but I try to explain to her how important this is for me."

Dr. Collins took him back about four hundred years. He gave some information about a lifetime in what was Salem, Massachusetts. It was clear that he was really there explaining things in such detail.

Finally Dr. Collins brought him back to the year 29 A.D.

"Who are you?"

"I am Saul of Tarsus."

The silence in the court was deafening.

"Are you familiar with Yehudah, son of Joseph?"

"The bandit Judas Iscariot? Yes. Of all the rabble that oppose the priesthood, he is probably the most dangerous. I admire his ingenuity but that does not make me hate him less."

"Did you know that he wrote an account of the life of his spiritual master, Jeshua, son of Joseph?"

"No, I did not. If I did I would have found a way to destroy it."

"What do you mean to do to this Jeshua and his followers?"

"I mean to find a way to have him taken out of the picture, either have him arrested for blasphemy and have him stoned, or convince the Romans he a danger to their rule and have him crucified."

"Why?"

"Because that one man could bring down Roman armies on all of us. He must die so that the rest of us can live."

Then Dr. Collins took him ahead to 50 A.D.

"What is your name?"

"Paul of Tarsus."

"Paul, do you know Judas Iscariot?"

"He died long ago. But somehow he lives in Matthias. After all these years I still do not fully understand it."

Chris got the attention of the judge and motioned to her asking if he could communicate with Dr. Collins. He whispered a few things and she nodded.

The next thing I knew she had again put me under and took me back to the same year.

"Matthias, do you know Paul?" Asked Dr. Collins.

"Since before he was Paul."

"What is your relationship with him?"

"He used to be my mortal enemy. I had a number of opportunities to kill him, but it was God's will that he should survive, at least by my hand."

"Paul, is this Matthias?"

"Yes. He the only person who could have gotten that close to me."

"Did you know he wrote an account of the life of Jesus?"

"No. But I knew that he wrote a book of sayings attributed to Jesus."

"Is it possible that he could have written an account of the life of Jesus?"

"It was possible. He acted as the scribe for the Essenes, and could have been writing a history all along."

"As your present-day self, you have heard this account. Would you consider it accurate?"

"I could not tell you about the whole document, but the places where I was mentioned you could say that they were accurate from his point of view."

"What would you consider inaccurate?"

"Before I became Paul, when he threatened me, I did not fear death as much as he believed. I was merely acting so I could get out of that situation. So I could fight another day."

"Well, it seemed real to me. Why didn't you, then, come back?"

"I intended to, but my conversion occurred and I dropped all hatred. I ask for forgiveness for my previous life as Saul."

"It's already done."

"I'm sorry. We were never really on the same team. You had the concerns of the Jerusalem Church and I had my mission to the gentiles."

"Our politics were always at odds, Paul, but one thing that I appreciated about you was your willingness to follow what Spirit presented to you."

"Even if it led me in a different direction than your Essenes?"

"Only God knows if things would have been better if we had become the dominant sect rather than your churches. I could hypothesize but I really have no knowledge. So I am left with my trust of Spirit, that it did bring forward what was for the highest good of all concerned. It is something that I trust even if I can't see it."

On a sign from Chris, Dr. Collins interrupted: "I going to bring you both back now with full memory of this exchange."

Being an old hand at these trips back to past life memories, I got my bearings almost immediately. Hastings, on the other hand, first looked like he was in shock. He laughed, cried, howled and finally settled down.

"This changes everything," He said. "I am only a deacon at my church. Now I find out that I was the man who started the religion!"

"Are you all right?" Asked Dr. Collins.

"Yes, I will be. But there is something that I must do now. I must recuse myself from further participation on this prosecution team. I will have my associate, Merissa Crane, take over the prosecution; she is highly capable."

It was then that Jack entered the courtroom and sat back down next to Chris. He wore a smile that could only be described as "the cat that ate the canary." I heard a beep from a laptop at Hastings table. Merissa Crane whispered something to Hastings. She held a look of triumph on her face. He must have just received an important email, something that did not bode well for him.

Hastings stood up. He sighed deeply as if a weight was lifted off his chest. "Your honor, The SEC and NASD will be bringing charges of money laundering against Empire Investments. Oh, and I seem to be out of a job." I looked over at Jack. He smiled, winked and nodded. Meanwhile Hastings handed over his voluminous files to Ms. Crane.

Hastings slowly rose from his chair and moved over to our table. In a gesture I never imagined would happen, he approached Chris with an outstretched hand. "Congratulations. You did exceptionally well. I truly enjoyed the competition." He turned to leave, but something pulled him back. "By the way, since I am now out of a job, I'd like to join you in your suit to regain the original manuscript. You're going to be up against some powerful foes. You may need some help."

I knew that Chris had not thought beyond what was happening today, but he quickly regained professional composure, cleared his throat and said, "Certainly! It would be an honor to have you on our team!"

Chris stood up with the confidence of someone who had already won his case. "Your honor, I consider a missing section of the manuscript crucial to our case. Would you consider giving us a stay so we could obtain that evidence?"

"Just how long would this take?"

Chris looked over in Dr. Wilder's direction. Dr. Wilder held up four fingers, then three.

Chris answered, "Three months. At the most."

The judge's gavel came down. "This court is adjourned for… is four months sufficient time?"

Chris shot a glance at Dr. Wilder who gave him a thumbs-up.

Jack grabbed Chris' attention. "Chris, will you be wanting me to go? I have to be back here in the states in three or four month's time. Got to prepare for the *Empire Investments* trial."

"Are you kidding, we can't do this without you."

I remembered Eric's advice to catch the thrill of the adventure of my life. "We need to find that last chapter. My book needs a last chapter! I'm coming too. And I'm bringing my camera. Jack, with you as Petronius guiding him, I'm sure that Dr. Wilder will find that church."

So we quickly formed an expedition and left for Ireland. I figured that I would be just an observer on this one, but that did not still my excitement about finding a complete version of the manuscript. A possible find of this magnitude attracted many donors and expert scientists. This time Dr. Wilder led the expedition along with Dr. Collins and Jack. In taking Jack's consciousness back to Roman-era Ireland, Dr. Wilder found the ruins in a short time under a very large mound. Jack (as Petronius) furnished us a floor plan for the church and we finally found a vault under the floor of the basement.

Dr. Wilder was excited. This was a chamber that had not been opened in almost two thousand years. I was just prayed that the book that was promised would be in the condition where it could be read.

When we opened the vault there was much dust, but only one item that was left intact. It was a stone container similar to an ossuary. We careful opened it and found what looked like a huge egg made of tar. The tar had hardened like an eggshell. Dr. Wilder tapped it and found that it was hollow. He shook it gently. A faint rattle was heard. The Book? Carefully he pierced the tar shell. Some foul air escaped. That was not a good sign. Something had rotted inside the layer of tar. But this did not daunt him. He chipped away the layer of tar. Inside was a mottled membrane with the texture of cloth. It took him hours to peel that away. Finally, he heard a rush of air. It was from inside the membrane. There was the smell of burnt leaves. We were worried that the book was damaged by fire, but this turned out not to be the case. The edges of the book were only slightly discolored. Dr. Collins brought Petronius under to explain that this was a way that was used to seal and preserve books and scrolls for ages. It was not widely known but was ancient in origin. All the air was replaced by carbon dioxide from the leaves before the book was sealed in the membrane. The membrane itself was not only impervious to the elements, but also removed any acidic residues from the pages.

The book inside smelled of burnt leaves but was preserved intact. Dr. Wilder made sure to handle it carefully, because it was very fragile. As it turned out the pages were in pretty good shape but Dr. Wilder warned that the book was now exposed to the damp weather in Ireland and had already begun to minutely deteriorate so it had to be placed in a controlled environment and deciphered quickly. He went to work on the last chapter. It took him two weeks to complete the translation.

CHAPTER 18 - ACCORDING TO MARY

Each night in the crisp evening air of a remote section of Irish countryside we found ourselves around a blazing campfire going over the past day's progress. These were times that I had to truly relax. Everyone here was a working member of the team. It was my job to film as much of the process as I could. Even though we had brought along two very large SUV's, space was at a premium, so I was not able to bring all the equipment I had planned to bring.

This night was special. Dr. Wilder had completed his work and was going to present his translation to us. The rest of the manuscript was faithfully reproduced and placed in a vacuum chamber. I photographed this manuscript as I had done with the incomplete version. The only difference between them being the additional final chapter that Dr. Wilder called the "Mary Manuscript." Throughout the trial we had grown accustomed to the reciting of the manuscript, so we all agreed that this would not be a break from that tradition.

The late sunset of the Irish summer came at about 10PM. As the sun dropped from view, Dr. Wilder emerged from his tent with a printed copy of the Mary Manuscript. As the light faded and the temperature dropped, he switched on his flashlight, zipped his jacket, and began reading:

I was cleaning the room and talking with Spirit inside, with the Beloved, as I swept and straightened. "Thank you for this day, beloved Father. Look at the dust speckles in the sunlight. There certainly is a lot of clutter in here. Matthias had quite a knack for accumulating piles of papers and things."

I have long found conversing with God comforting. In my younger years, before my heart awakened, the conversation of my mind was deafening with negativity, and frankly boring in its repetition. It had the same script, over and over, sounding much like Pharisees of the Shammai School, the *Parush*, who intone the same sermons about social retribution and proper religious behavior, again and again and again. I chuckle to myself when I remember what I was like then; I often stood inside my own consciousness blank, like a gazelle frozen before a charging lion, seemingly incapable of helping itself. I give thanks for the day when I set myself free in Spirit, and opened my heart to the love and kindness within.

This sweet reverie, this moment of being present with my Soul, faded slightly as my focus shifted back to cleaning the room. A wave of sadness came over me. I do miss Matthias. I miss his silent ways, his twinkling eyes, and the generosity of his spirit. Although I know he lives inside of me — in some ways more now than ever before — I do miss the communion of our love and living together. It is a precious gift to share life with someone who shares a sacred focus, someone looking in the same direction of love and caring for all.

I bent beneath the bed, and found I had to crawl beneath it to liberate piles of books and scrolls. My hand fell upon some paper with a very different texture — it felt soft and inviting, like pages that had been referenced over and over again, worn with love and enthusiasm. I sat on the floor, and wiped my forehead. I looked out the window for a moment and closed my eyes as the late afternoon sun touched my face. I felt myself relax, and received the warmth. For a moment, I felt completely innocent, fresh, and new as a child. I looked at the pages before me, and smiled as I recognized Matthias' tight, looping scrawl. I started to read:

> "I was again on my way to Jerusalem. I went inside myself to learn more about this Matthias whose body I shared and whose identity I was to borrow. Matthias was not trained by the Essenes as I had been. He was born an Israelite but he was well versed in the mysteries learned in the Egyptian mystery schools. I would have considered him a worthy replacement. In many ways he was my opposite: a very quiet and shy man, not a man of action, who rarely spoke up or took an initiative, yet he was still a loyal disciple who rarely questioned authority. In the days before the crucifixion he would be as a lamb among wolves in regards to the strong personalities of the other apostles. I realized that this joining was a learning situation for both of us. He was to learn from my outward personality and I was to learn from his more reserved character. A good plan. Perhaps together we could make one effective apostle!"

What is this? What could this be? I felt my brow furrow as confusion set in. How could Matthias know these things? What is this that he is sharing? Matthias was not one to write fiction, or to speculate. He certainly wouldn't do so when it comes to Jeshua and the sacred teachings of liberation. There are things here that he could not know; that nobody in our lives would know. What can I make of this? I read on and on.

A strange buzzing sound filled my head, and I noticed that my breathing became very slow and thick. I felt a weight through my whole body as awareness came present inside of me. For a moment I felt I was standing outside of myself, watching a woman sitting on a floor, papers strewn across her lap, her face open and eyes wide. I saw my mind balking at what my awareness was suggesting to me, instantly recoiling as it tried to make sense of a truth beyond my intellect: Matthias had lived as Yehudah.

A kaleidoscope of imagery and information erupted in my consciousness in that instant, flooding me with more awarenesses: I could see Yehudah training with the *Sicarri*... I saw him sitting with Jeshua and the disciples... I could feel his mind and the tension between his heart's call to the loving and grace Jeshua taught, and his mind's demand for justice... The imagery came faster and faster, rolling through Jeshua's life, to his crucifixion, to Yehudah's death...

I felt dizzy as I experienced what seemed like a golden orb of energy exploding from Yehudah's chest and skipping lightly into the consciousness of Matthias, and his decision to live in silence as he healed from his life as Yehudah...

I slowly became aware that my body was slumped to one side, and the book had tumbled from my lap onto the floor. How long had I been sitting there? Night air was already blowing through the window. The air was still and silent and I found it difficult to move. Slowly, I was experiencing acceptance with my experience and the information that I had received. My mind started to retreat to its servant's position, in loving homage to Spirit and trust in a larger order at work. I chuckled as I thought that there were certainly stranger things to realize in life than that my husband had lived as someone else within the same time that we were both walking the earth.

My body jumped with a start as I heard a knock upon the door. I was on my feet in a flash, suddenly aware that my lap was filled not only with revelation to me, but with sacred information that I would protect with my life. I scooped up the book and tucked it back under the bed as I called out to the door:

"A moment, please!"

I recognized the voice that answered me immediately: "Of course, Mary. Are you well?"

“John!” I exclaimed, relief flooding through me as I made my way to the door. With my relief, a note of caution remained with me: “Are you alone, my friend?”

My body relaxed further as I recognized the next voice that responded: “He's all alone save for me, Mary. You know I can't leave this man to his own devices.”

I looked through the window nonetheless, to confirm with my eyes what my ears and intuition avowed. A sense of calm and strength filled me, and I opened the door wide in welcome.

John and Petronius entered quickly, closing the door behind them before exchanging hugs.

“We are glad you are here, Mary, and glad you are well. Have you any news from the city?”

“No,” I replied. “Though by your tone and manner it would seem you have some to share.”

“Indeed,” Petronius said, smiling briefly. “I wish it were happier news. There is much tension between the factions in the city. The *Parush* and those who were Sadducees are clamping down on all spiritual teachings. They are aiming to form a union amongst themselves – though I daresay if such a thing were even possible, I don't think it would long survive their mutual deceit and distrust. Their goal is to proclaim a single doctrine for all to follow. Sadly enough, so are the followers of Paul. They are turning Jeshua’s teachings upside down and twisting them, turning them into another rigid code for people to follow perfectly or fail.”

John chimed in: “As much as this turns my stomach, I must say they all excel at finding ways to keep themselves in business.”

My thoughts dashed instantly to the scrolls in Matthias' bedroom. Their existence took on added value in light of this information. But whom could I trust? And what did John and Petronius know? Here were two of Matthias' closest friends, and people who also knew Yehudah. I needed to center myself, and listen inwardly for guidance.

"Would you like some water?” I asked to create some space and pause.

Within a few minutes, we were seated together around the table. John began to speak. "Mary," he said, "There are some things about Matthias that I think you need to know."

I nodded, bracing myself to hear how Matthias had died. Though I had received word two weeks ago, I did not yet know the details. News and people traveled slowly — when it comes to painful news, it is hard to say whether that be good or bad.

As much as my feelings were mixed to hear the tale, John's gift for storytelling helped to soften the delivery. After the Temple was destroyed following Matthias' death, the Sadducees fell apart as an organized group, their numbers joining the ranks of general Roman sympathizers. They had set their sights on John as a scapegoat for their anger with the Nazarenes, and considered his death a start toward avenging their lost ambitions. They found John, Petronius and Matthias together. John related, "Matthias had been walking in the lead when the Sadducees seemed to appear out of nowhere. Mary, you know Matthias — again he showed his uncanny capacity to seem never taken completely by surprise. He turned the energy of our surprise back toward them, and rushed the Sadducees while waving Petronius off to get me out of harm's way. The last thing I wanted to do was run from the fight, but it was clear that was what I was to do."

Petronius reached out his hand to take mine. I felt his warmth, and his tenderness spread like a glow of comfort through my body. I relaxed, as I knew the final blow was coming.

"By the time I returned, Mary, Matthias was dead. Dead Sadducees and Romans surrounded his body. Some Romans must have joined the fight after we were safely away. I have no doubt Matthias would still be alive if their numbers hadn't grown." Petronius let out a long sigh. "I buried Matthias in a cave with the twin blades from Tuzla. We came here straight away."

I patted Petronius' hand; I could feel his struggle. He looked at me, wanting to comfort me in some way.

"He died a fine death, Mary — a warrior's death. If anything, I feel he denied me that death, for I would have been happy to meet my end defending him."

I smiled and patted his hand again as I stood up. "We don't always get what we want in this life. That is certain. I would rather Matthias were still here." A wave of pain moved through me and I felt my eyes fill with tears. I breathed deeply, to relax and ride the wave of emotion. "Now we have to look to what is next. I still intend to journey to the land of the Celts."

Petronius stood as well. “And you will not go alone. If I could not support this family by returning with Matthias alive, I commission myself to see you safely to the land of the Celts.”

John had been very quiet up until now, and then he spoke again, very directly. “Mary,” he said, “I need to ask you if you have had a chance to go through Matthias' things.”

I turned to John. “Yes, John. And yes, I have the manuscript. The work must continue. I will continue the writing, and make copies of what Matthias wrote.” John looked surprised only for a moment, before nodding abruptly.

In a couple of months, I managed three copies of the original writings.

We agreed to stay at the house for a couple of months, and then planned to move to Pella. I continued writing, and John and Petronius took time to rest, heal, and make contact with as many of our friends as possible. As that time came to an end, I knew that I needed to go and find Matthias' remains and give them a proper burial. While I knew that all was well with Matthias in the Spirit, I also knew this would be an important way for me to complete my relationship with him in the world.

John and Petronius were kind enough to offer to accompany me on my journey. I made my preparations and laid out provisions for Petronius and John for the journey. I felt like God was expressing His love for me through those two heavenly beings, Petronius and John. On the way we met an old friend of Matthias/Yehudah — Tuzla. I was glad to have another along but I explained that I did not pack enough provisions for another traveler. He just smiled and said that it would not be a problem.

Petronius found the site where Matthias fought his last battle. I told them I wished to just sit at the spot and be alone for a while. They seemed to melt into the scenery and I was alone with my ache of missing him. The pain began to leave and it became bittersweet as I remembered our lives together. At last I was complete with that place and did not need to see it again.

As I was getting up I again found myself in the company of my three guides and protectors. Petronius led us to where he had buried the body of Matthias. The body had been wrapped with obvious loving care, and the sweet smell of lavender, mint, and other herbs gathered from the nearby brush still lingered. There was not much odor of decomposition present; enough time had passed, and enough care had been put into the wrapping to minimize those effects. I gathered up Matthias' bones and was struck by how much I was aware they were simply bones — that Matthias was alive and well in my heart. It was profound to experience

Matthias alive in Spirit, inside of me, while my hands picked up his bones and placed them in an ossuary; while I felt my own tears in their mixture of sadness, joy, appreciation, and completion.

I sat down in the cave with the ossuary, and spent time in silent spiritual exercises, singing God's name through my heart, listening to the silence, and allowing it to enfold me. The darkness of the cave, the cool sand beneath me, the vibration of my chanting within my consciousness — a deep experience of peace came over me, and my consciousness traveled freely.

There was something joyous in opening my heart to feel the pain of the loss anew, and the joy in Matthias' passing, and the gratitude for the time we had shared together, and the wonder at the mystery of his life, and the choices he had made, and the silence he had kept, and all that was unknown to me in my conscious mind. When I opened my eyes again, I felt complete.

I lifted myself from the ground and came into the light again. Tuzla made a short bow and entered the cave. I could hear him chanting inside that cave. I assume it was in Tibetan. I know it was only one man chanting, yet it felt strangely amplified as if the angels themselves were chanting with him. I felt as though I might have been pulled out of my body again, if not for my disciplined focus on things physical. He came out and Petronius entered. There was not a single sound until I heard the sound of Petronius sealing the ossuary. He left the cave and the three of us stood together. I was ready to return home.

I packed all my belongings and we made our way to Pella. I started writing about the events following Jeshua's crucifixion-not only with an aim to chronicle them with accuracy, but also to practice observation with the changes I saw taking place around me.

After Jeshua's death and the destruction of the temple, the Essenes were either killed or took flight. Many made their way to Masada, the desert fortress by the Dead Sea. Petronius' son Titus was among them. He sent us periodic reports of skirmishes there by way of messengers. In Pella, we came to live amongst other Nazarenes. They began to call themselves Ebionites, or "the poor," those who had left everything behind in the face of social upheaval and Roman tyranny. Many of these people knew nothing of Jeshua directly, as the Essenes had; to them he was a great teacher and savior, and known as Jesus of Nazareth. Whether in Pella or Alexandria, the Ebionites cherished openness and freedom for all, regardless of beliefs. It was easy to see why so many Essenes joined with them, to find safe haven as well as to share the teachings Jeshua had given to us.

Factions are everywhere in this world. Jews who do not follow the ways of Jeshua meet in synagogues and call themselves "congregations." Followers of Jesus are now also gathering together into churches, (using the Greek word for congregation). What was left of the Sadducees have joined the *Parush*. The council is no more. There are no others to stand up to the *Parush.*

What is broken can no longer be fixed. They recently issued an edict excommunicating all of the Ebionites. The *Parush* gave this reason: "it is impossible to follow Jesus and still be Jews." This is absurd. What Jeshua taught was Judaism in its highest form. On the other side, the followers of Paul, now calling themselves Christians, organize themselves like the Romans. It cannot be healed now. There can no longer be unity, now that both larger groups have rejected our group, the Essenes/Ebionites. There is no middle ground to hold them together. The Jews and the Christians have divided themselves and set up their camps, and the Christians have taken to absolving the Romans for the death of Jesus while blaming the Jews for it. It is their desire to prove their loyalty to the empire and gain the security of becoming an established religion.

I sighed as I pushed back from my chair and put down my quill. I boiled some water over the hearth, and mixed in some herbs and freshly squeezed lemon, and returned to my desk. These days the Ebionites are considered dangerous, simply because they are more interested in ideas than rituals, and they are not welcome among either Jews or Christians. The Ebionites have not placed Jesus on a pedestal as a god, separate from them. They saw Paul as an enemy of truth offering an abundance of rules to obey, but very little that leads directly to an experience of the Spirit. I chuckled to myself as I thought that even a follower of Paul may come to simple bliss, if only by way of exhaustion from trying to follow every practice, ritual, and rule. I also felt a moment of compassion for the fear that drives that behavior, and an understanding that this compassion was second to my resolve to continue supporting a message of love and divinity for all, no exceptions and no exclusions. The work before me seemed more important than ever. With so many voices clamoring for power, control, and order, looking to fashion God in their image, I felt strongly motivated to do everything I could to keep Jesus' teachings circulating and available for all.

A knock at the door interrupted my work, and I rose to find a young man at my door.

"What business brings you here, brother?" I asked.

The young man bowed nervously. "Good lady, I am called Marcus. I come from Asia Minor, where we have a community of Christians — both Jews and Gentiles — living and working together. I have been charged with writing a chronicle of the life of Jesus of Nazareth for my church, and I have heard that you have accurate information about his teachings."

I handed him a copy of the teachings scroll that Matthias compiled.

He took the book and said, "I would be most grateful to have this to write a gospel, to help keep Jesus' teachings alive. I also hope this will help us to stay together to live in the true Spirit of love that Jesus taught."

I smiled, partly due to the young man's pluck and sincerity, and partly due to my experience of Spirit's perfect timing: that he should show up at my door as I was writing about these very dynamics in our world. His spiritedness did much to quell the sense of disturbance I had experienced in seeing a world filled with lifeless rules, regulations, and power plays. I was filled with a sense of hope for the future.

Marcus stayed at the house with us for a few days, and asked me to give him an orientation to the book of sayings. He knew no Aramaic, which I registered with some surprise. He couldn't get enough of the teachings. He poured over the parchment with his eyes wide and soft. He paused often and asked me to share stories from my own experience. I felt such gladness in spending time with him, to be in his peaceful, gentle company. Marcus had a quality of innocence about him that was born of deep love and appreciation of life's true purpose. He was not naive to the politics of power and personalities, or the subtle forces of doubt and judgment; he simply consistently chose to stay connected with his heart through it all, and had the wisdom to ask questions or be still rather than engage in what could be folly or painful for him. I was confident he would go back to Asia Minor well seasoned in the teachings, and would share them with his congregation openly, yet with good care.

After Marcus left, I was filled with a sense that something new was on the horizon, though I didn't know what. The house suddenly seemed complete, and so did my work — at least this portion of it. As I prepared to lay down my body for the evening, the soft night air carried whispers that seemed mystical in nature. I went outside and walked around the house, looking up at the stars, feeling the wind blowing softly along its mysterious route. Every atom in my body tingled and I felt love moving in my awareness. It is hard to describe, yet it is a very ordinary experience — it is that feeling, that sense, that quiet that stirs deep within. "Beloved, I am open. I am available to you; I give you my eyes, my ears, my heart," I prayed, as I returned to the house and climbed into bed. I began to chant, and my awareness moved.

I found myself traveling in consciousness. The experience had the quality of a dream, except I was awake, alert, and aware of my movement and experiences. I was moving very slowly, toward a point of light, and as I drew close the light became like a flower slowly opening, and I found myself in a different space, I suppose I would call it a sort of room. John and Petronius were there.

"Mary, it is time to move to Ireland," John said.

"The tribes there have been successful in warding off the Romans," added Petronius.

I nodded, and we joined in a circle together, holding hands and chanting. I felt a golden Light stream move through my awareness, that gentle energy that lets me know everything is on course.

I was not surprised when Petronius arrived the next day. My inner experience was confirmed as he simply looked into my eyes and said, "Ireland?" I nodded, and we hugged each other.

Our preparations for departure went quickly. I readied my family. Petronius provided me with information about Celtic traditions, and I managed to read some of it during our voyage to Ireland. I was delighted to find much there that indicated a readiness and openness to Jesus' teachings. The seas were kind to us, and the sailors were men of impeccable knowledge, practice, and generosity. Petronius and I were only too happy to cook for the crew during our journey, and they delighted in experiencing dishes unique to our former home.

While living in Ireland, I realized that everything about my life had been a preparation for that time. I never felt as much like a physical instrument of Spirit as when we were living there. My every moment was filled with purposeful activity. With Petronius' able support, we established the first Celtic church based on the Essene/Ebionite tradition. While I was uncertain about creating any kind of church, Petronius persuaded me, pointing to the value of having a church as an anchor for people to use to direct themselves to Spirit. It has always seemed a tricky proposition to me when we create things to support us in our spiritual awareness and focus — it can be so easy to fall into the slumber of allowing the structure to take over, and the direct experience to fall by the wayside. Petronius reminded me that all is part of the learning that each person has the opportunity to fulfill, to decide whether to live consciously or by habit, ritual, and rote.

In talking with Petronius about this, I realized that some of my discomfort about establishing a church stemmed from my own lack of self-trust that I would consistently use the church, the teachings, and the rituals as a support system for my direct experience of my divinity and the divinity of all. In my humanity I could be as susceptible as anyone else to the temptations of personal power or vanity that can so easily come with a public role and position of authority. The gift of responsibility can be corrupted into demand and a sense of entitlement with startling speed — I knew that from observation and from personal experience.

I had worked myself into quite a dilemma around this, and Petronius helped me cut through it one afternoon with a simple question: "Would you rather be right, or loving?" At first I did not understand. I didn't see myself as being righteous or forceful, though I did feel quite earnest and preoccupied. Petronius shared the perspective that wanting to be right can also take the form of wanting to guard against mistakes and errors; to prevent "failing" in some way. While that may be well intentioned, it is still a distraction and illusion. The way of Spirit, the way Jeshua shared with us, is one that is open, ever full of opportunity, and always choosing to offer myriad options and methods of support. People will do what they do with them; and we never know when a fixation or slavish observation of form may give way to an authentic experience of the divine, of essence, of truth and love and Light.

I realized that my deepest commitment was to that freedom and fullness, rooted in a deep confidence and knowing that all is well and always unfolding in accordance with the divine will. This understanding has reached into me profoundly, and is beyond a philosophical statement or concept; it has reached to a place of understanding and knowing that fills my heart with joy and a great calm, as an ocean of love and mercy.

I felt deeply grateful for Petronius and his clear-sightedness and devotion. He died while we were in Ireland, after helping to see the first church spur the creation of churches throughout Ireland, Wales, Scotland, and into North England. While he may have preferred to die a warrior, in my eyes he died a saint, for his love and compassion helped bring the teachings to so many who were looking for them.

I experienced a deeper calm with me as time rolled on after Petronius' death. Daily tasks and challenges came and went, and my perspective kept shifting. To be sure, I still experienced my personality flare and my likes and dislikes announced themselves regularly. Through it all, I observed greater flexibility in my attitudes and behavior. My commitment to authenticity and sharing what Jeshua had shared with us was still strong, yet even stronger was my commitment and devotion to living those teachings. More and more I realized that the way I live my life is the greatest statement I can make about what teachings I follow. I even noticed that as I backed away from talking about the teachings to simply living them as best I could, more people actually wound up asking me about them.

I was in the marketplace one day, reflecting on this, as I had just been sharing with a woman about my experiences while we pondered which fruits and vegetables would best blend into a lamb stew. As we parted company, a young man, sweaty with afternoon heat, trotted into view and approached me.

"Lady, be you known as Mary Magdalene?"

"Indeed!" I said, instantly charmed by his manner and courtly speech. "How can I help you?"

"I am a messenger sent by John. He told me to bring you these words in all haste." He handed me a bound armful of scrolls and bowed. Before I could open my mouth or offer him refreshment, he sped away. I stood for a moment, marveling at how a day can take sudden turns, and felt appreciation for the young messenger and his obvious love and devotion for his duties.

I took the scroll back home and sat down with them, leaving thoughts of stew and produce behind. John's note piqued my curiosity:

Dearest Mary,

I hope this message finds you well, healthy, and in good spirits. I am sending to you a copy of a gospel document, written by Mark. It claims to be the latest and most accurate presentation of Jeshua's teachings. Please review it, and send me word about how you find it. I am most curious to hear your experience.

All my love and peace be with you,

John

I sighed and settled back into my chair, and asked Spirit to fill my consciousness and my eyes as I received the words Mark had written. I asked for clarity, calm, and perspective. Overall, I found Mark's gospel to be more accurate than the others I had read — it was more like what really happened on the level of actual events. What I did not find was a clear communication of the teachings Jeshua shared. It read very well as a journalist's account, but when Mark wrote that Jeshua stood against the Temple and said it had to be destroyed because it was desecrated — at that point, I laid the scrolls down and rubbed my forehead. Jeshua would not have advocated destruction of any kind, no matter what the offense — real or perceived. His entire message had been a call to change the practices of the Temple to reflect more of the living spirit, the living truth, and let go of empty rituals. People had become so concerned with ritual that they were not experiencing the presence of the divine within and among them, and that was the whole point of having a temple in the first place.

Mark also portrayed Jeshua as a rather strange, enigmatic character – almost as if he were otherworldly. While Jeshua was truly mystical, he was also very real and practical. The Jeshua I knew danced with abandon, laughed raucously, told off-color jokes, and had a mischievous quality that brought out the joy in me and in everyone. Even at his most serious, Jeshua was someone I could relate to completely; more than anything else, that ease of relating with Jeshua helped me to see that I, too, was divine and cherished by God, and that I, too, had a responsibility to express as much love and kindness as I can, toward my own human faults and foibles as much as anyone else's.

I jotted a note to John sharing my experience, and left it to send by messenger in the morning. I then turned to the business of making a supper, and found the smells of my kitchen called a neighbor to come and join me. We spent a happy evening sharing each other's company, watching the sky turn to night. As I looked up at the stars, I felt as if I could feel them inside of me. Somehow in the midst of that experience I found a deeper calm. While I still worried about how Jeshua's teachings could be misrepresented and put to all manner of uses, I also felt a deeper trust and relaxation within myself. I knew my purpose was to do my best to maintain the integrity and purity of the teachings, and I also knew that nothing could happen that would not be part of the divine order.

I chuckled to myself as my mind balked, saying "How can you say that? People can use Jeshua's teachings to justify hurting each other. How can that be part of divine order? We have to make sure that does not happen!" The intensity of the mind's protest still shakes me a bit. I still find myself doubting at times. But I am starting to recognize that whenever I think those thoughts; underneath it is usually some struggle for self-importance, to have a role, an identity, a mission, something to live for on one hand, and a fear of punishment on the other. The deeper truth is that whatever people do with Jeshua's teachings is part of the learning process – learning how to love more, even if that involves periods of hatred.

None of this is to justify misuse or abuse, of course, but it did bring me back to the simple commitment to live my life practicing love as best I could, and doing my best to see that love is the focus of the world I live in.

I knew that I was changing. I felt as if my life was winding down in some ways, and expanding in others. Mostly, it seemed to me that those things that had triggered my ambition, my sense of urgency, or mental intensity were dissolving into a calm that reminded me of sailing. I loved to sail, and to be out on the water in the stillness, hearing the gentle lapping of the water against the sides of the boat, and the steady rocking with the water's movement. This was especially my experience in spiritual exercises, my time each day to go sailing with Spirit. The things I judged, the things that used to provoke my emotions – all of those things were losing their intensity. I was learning to accept myself and others in new ways, in deep ways, and this helped me to see more goodness and blessings everywhere.

More time passed. On the outside, my life settled into a normalcy that was new to me, and at first alien. The drive I used to feel to do, to accomplish, and to contribute faded into an easygoing life that, frankly, I would have rejected when I was younger. I spent much time keeping house, strolling in the marketplace and spending time with neighbors and children. I started taking long walks, and would paint by the light of sunset. I felt myself less as "Mary Magdalene," and more often felt that I was sharing in a precious presence throughout my day – the presence of my Soul, of myself as divinity. I was both stunned and amused to realize that this was the ordinariness of divinity; to walk with God is simple and unadorned, and does not ask any great feat or ability of any of us. The more I relaxed into the simplicity of my life, the more I came to know this presence and a deep, constant peace. I was experiencing an intimacy with myself and with Spirit that I cannot put into words, yet if I could I would speak of it endlessly. So I decided to let my heart sing with it throughout each day. Surely there are worse ways to live, than to live as a singing heart through time in this world!

It was amidst these revelations that one day I received a visit from Lucius, a former companion of Paul. He arrived at my door one afternoon, asking to see the "sayings book" Matthias had written.

"I have heard this book was the inspiration for the Gospels written by Matthew and Marcus, and I should very much like to see it for myself, to use as a foundation for a new gospel."

I was instantly amused at the prospect of a "new" gospel — on one hand, there is nothing new to say. Yet I understood Lucius' point of view and could feel his sincerity.

"The only copy I know of is in Alexandria, Lucius," I told him.

Lucius looked at me, perplexed. He seemed nonplused that I was not as eager to charge forward with a new gospel project as he was.

"Well, good Mary, perhaps I could use the sayings from Marcus' gospel. Is there any additional material?"

I thought to myself silently, "Oh, well, now you're getting practical, dear Lucius." Aloud, I told him about this book.

"Ah! I didn't know of this, but had such a sense there was more!" Lucius said. "What title does the book have, Mary?"

"Mmmmm, well, Lucius, truth be told that is a bit of a mystery. There is no title for the book as of yet," I said.

Lucius again seemed perplexed. "Well, what do you suggest for a title then, Mary? Surely you would be best to speak to this, as you are closest to the material."

I laughed — how true that was, and how little did Lucius know! "Fair enough, then, Lucius. How does 'The Gospel According to Judas Iscariot' strike you? For that is who wrote most of it!"

Lucius looked at me as if I had just thrown cold water in his face. I handed him a copy of the book, and still looking dazed he thanked me and went on his way. I knew he would be back, and I knew it would be a while. Mixing a companion of Paul with what Matthias had written to convey a direct taste of Jeshua's teachings was sure to produce some interesting reactions.

What I didn't know was that five years would pass before I saw Lucius again. He returned to my home, to find me pretty much as he had during his first visit — at least to outward appearances.

"Lady Mary, it is good to see you again. The Judas Gospel has created quite a stir amongst the Gentile churches. They mean to have all copies of it destroyed."

I looked at Lucius intently and nodded. "Well, then, Lucius, it is good to see you, too. Thank you for your report of the Gentile churches. Tell me, what do you think of the Judas Gospel?"

Lucius shifted uncomfortably on his feet, and then his body stiffened a bit as if he were girding himself for battle. "Mary, in truth, I feel the book has no place in the creation of a new faith. I think it is dangerous. I come to you out of courtesy to warn you of this, and to return your copy of the book to you." He handed me Matthias' book. It was evident that it had seen much use and reference, and it was also evident that whatever Lucius' feelings about the content, he had treated the book well, much as one can hold deep honor and even cherishment for a worthy adversary. I felt my heart open to his warrior-like commitment to a sense of honor and duty, and appreciation for his gesture even as he struggled with obvious disapproval and a sense of threat with the material.

"Lucius, you are truly an honorable man. Thank you for returning this to me and God bless you with all manner of peace and fulfillment in your life." I touched his arm gently as he handed the book back to me, and experienced a moment of deep understanding pass between us. Without a word, Lucius turned on his heel and left, like a soldier on the march.

I sighed, and thought how if this had happened ten years ago I probably would have had a more alarmed response to the encounter. It seemed clear that the forces of order and control were again asserting themselves, and the freedom of Jeshua's message brought discomfort to those comfortable seeing spirituality as a sort of social project or blueprint to order behavior and society.

I did know I had work to do, however, and set about enlisting a number of scribes to make as many copies of the book as possible. I felt each day a great sense of importance with this project — that it was essential to do, and yet I went about it with a deep calm and without a sense of urgency. I knew that nothing could stop the truth of Spirit from coming to anyone who was looking for it. Nothing is more powerful than the power of love. No worldly threat can overcome the truth and power of love, of the indwelling Spirit.

During spiritual exercises, I was filled with a sense of guidance to take the copies and bury them in different locations throughout the world to make sure they would be preserved, like seeds planted for those looking for these teachings and the direct experience of divinity. I made my plans to set sail.

How funny and perfect, to go sailing again, out into the world. All of the years sailing with Spirit inside my heart seemed to be perfect preparation for this task, and I knew that when it was complete, my work, and perhaps my life, would be done. The blessings always are, and my heart fills with simple joy, peace, and calm.

If you read this and find pieces of your heart here, read no further of these words but go to your heart and gather yourself in the current of your essential being, and flow with the Spirit you are. I wish nothing more than this for every person, for every being, for if there is anything life has brought me it is knowing this as the simple great reality and common heritage of all of us. Glad tidings, blessings, and best wishes to us all.

Dr. Wilder put down the translation.

I was touched by the expression of a woman that I had loved in a previous time and began to feel a desire to seek her out. I had no idea if she existed in this time and no idea how I would find her, but I placed my trust in Spirit that if that would be for the highest good, I would find her. Had I been with her other times? Where there other stories we shared? My mind raced for what must have been thirty minutes, not being aware that our campsite had been silent since the conclusion of the reading.

Throughout most of my life I had not taken the lead in my life and followed my heart. I had been afraid of ridicule and judgment if I appeared to be different than everyone else. Since I took the pictures of the manuscript, all that began to change. Now I was more open than ever to my inner direction. I felt truly whole. My direction and purpose were clear. A blissful calm came over me. As I opened to it a thought gently came in — I knew how to prove my identity as the owner of the manuscript!

"The ossuary! We must find the ossuary!" I shouted.

All eyes were upon me. It got very quiet. "Look. How many sets of twin blades did Mary mention?"

"One," volunteered Ernest.

"Right. One was brought by Tuzla. But what about the pair that Petronius had kept for so many years?"

"So?"

"There should be two pairs of knives buried in that ossuary!"

"What's that prove?" asked Jack.

"Just about everything, Jack. You mentioned two sets of knives. If that turns out to be correct, then it proves you were there. If then it becomes accepted that you were there, then your placing me there carries a whole lot more weight. The ossuary is the physical evidence that would confirm any claim of ownership I might make for the manuscript. What do you think?"

There was buzzing immediately from all sides.

"We would have to pull up stakes and travel to start another dig," said Ernest. "We might go over the time limit — we've got six weeks more — plus the money has to come from somewhere."

"I don't have a lot of savings, but I would be willing to put it all on the line to help finance this dig." I said.

"What if we don't find what you're looking for?" Asked Hastings.

"Well, if we don't come up with anything conclusive, the court could take the rest of what I have anyway. At least I would be spending it for a good cause."

"I'll toss in a few bucks," said Jack.

Hastings looked troubled, but appeared to shake it off. "I've made and saved millions through my practice. There is no reason I couldn't help finance this expedition."

"He'll find some way of writing it off," joked Chris.

Hastings lumbered over to Chris who looked like he was in danger of being flattened within the next minute. Instead Hasting put his bear-like arm around Chris and gave him a squeeze. "Not a bad idea, Chris," he said. "Now you're thinking like a lawyer!"

Relieved, Chris laughed out loud. So did we all.

Some say it was the fastest relocation in the history of archeology. Any time would have seemed long for me, but the enthusiasm of the group calmed my fears. I was uncertain how long this could take, but Ernest moved swiftly and got us to the general area. When he got us to what he thought was within two miles of the site, he turned to Dr. Collins and said: "It's up to you now." We set up a base camp and prepared a dinner fit for weary travelers.

The next morning, at breakfast, we gathered together. "Dr. Collins, we need you to access Petronius' memory to take us to the site," said Ernest. A wisp of concern flitted across his visage. He added: "We really don't have much time."

"OK, Ernest," said Jane. "Jack, we're going to go back to your life as Petronius. We are taking you back to the burial of Yehudah's ossuary." It took her more time than ever before to get him there. It seemed that everyone was feeling the pressure, even a man from 2000 years ago.

The now familiar, deeper voice of Petronius boomed out: "Things have changed so much, I don't recognize this. There was a village near the rocks, near the cliff under which was the burial spot. It's gone now."

"The village you speak of was destroyed by Saracens a few hundred years later. You will have to find another landmark. What else can you remember?" Dr. Collins did not sound very enthusiastic. Faces fell as if the feared dead end had finally come upon us.

I felt emptiness in the pit of my stomach that felt a whole lot like failure. I pushed back the pain and sadness that came up from within me. I crouched down and felt drawn back inside. I had a choice just then to go with this expansion or resist it. My surrender to it was total and complete. Immediately thoughts, feelings and experiences came flooding in. It was like Yehudah was talking to me inside of me. Then I understood. "There, it's in that direction." I pointed to a similar ridge about two miles distant.

"Is that Judas?" asked Dr. Collins.

"Just his experiences, Jane," I answered. "I am fully conscious as me, yet I know things that I learned then. And I know it is in that direction. Give me the binoculars! There should be a rock shaped like a three-tong fork." I looked along the ridge and saw the odd-shaped three-humped rock. "There, it's there."

"You are now controlling this flow of information?" Jane asked.

"Not so much controlling it as asking with a certain assurance that it will appear. I do see your point of it being a gift. If I turn out to be correct, that is."

We moved the SUV's to the prospective site. "Petronius, does this look more like what you remember?" Jane asked.

At first bewildered, Jack (as Petronius) started to recognize the surroundings. "Yes, a little further up the trail." He took a few steps and then lifted his right hand. "Dig here."

We cordoned off a rectangle about eight by ten yards. It was all carefully staked out as to not miss anything in the area Jack (as Petronius) had chosen. At about four feet we came to a layer used as a burial site. The caskets looked like they were built quickly, with the top fashioned as a shield with intricate Latin lettering. Ernest took one look at it and placed it during the first crusade. We opened what appeared to be the most elaborate one and found a knight buried in his armor. We carefully cataloged what we saw and removed it, attempting not to disturb what we found, intending to return it so we could examine it at another time. We were focused on the ossuary. After another two feet under the previous layer we found Roman and post-Roman artifacts. Ernest determined these were from the 5th century. We had perhaps only two hours of sunlight left. A determined Ernest quietly said, "We press on."

We continued digging. Another four feet and we struck something. Pottery; a few shards of bone. Ernest, looking concerned, removed some of his testing materials from a piece of luggage. "I sure hope I'm wrong," he almost whispered.

Everyone put down their tools and watched. "Just as I feared," he said, "these pieces are from about 200 B.C."

"You mean we missed it?" said Jack, "how could that happen?"

"I don't know," said Ernest. He was more than tired. His body language conveyed more than exhaustion, it was more like a sudden depression. It seems to have touched the entire company. "There's nothing more we can do today, let's get some sleep and find out what happened tomorrow."

I knew it was here. I was never more certain of something in my life. I went to bed and fell asleep immediately. Something pulled me from a dreamless sleep. Half awake, I saw the dig area outside my tent as it passed through the centuries. I saw something quite curious. The land that had started out in front of me had moved away. It looked like it was moving south. As the centuries passed before my eyes the land crept south.

I forced my eyes open. I fought against my own raging exhaustion to stay awake. I had watched Ernest and the others dig so I knew what tools to gather. I moved to the southern end of the dig area. I tried to remember the exact distance that appeared in my dream of the movement from the first to the 21st centuries, but this was beyond what I could hold in my mind. I went on instinct. I judged that the place for the first century was somewhere between the 5th century and 200 B.C. That was as exacting as I could get while fighting the urge to go back to sleep. I started digging into the wall left behind by our previous work. It was slow going and I was not sure how long I was at it. The last thing that I remember before collapsing and going back to sleep was that I struck something hard. I dug around it and found the end of a stone box and left that protruding from the wall before placing my tools on the ground for a rest.

The next thing I heard was a great commotion as I was being lifted up away from the place where I was digging. It was morning & the sun was again shining. I drifted back to sleep. A few hours later I felt Ernest's hand on my shoulder. "You found it. I don't know… how did you do it?"

I took a deep breath. I was ready for the new day. "I saw it in my dream, Ernest. I saw how the earth had moved over the centuries. We were digging in the right place for the first century, not for the 21st."

"Let's finish your job." He replied.

The object was carefully removed from the wall of the dig site.

"It's an ossuary, all right! Bring me the tools to open it."

Dr. Wilder took a deep breath, "There is a talent that you are starting to develop. I know I want you on every dig I organize."

"I am not really sure I know what it is. I'm just being sort of 'receptive,'" I answered.

Dr. Wilder pried open the top. He gazed into the box and kept nodding his head. "Roy, it looks like we found what seemed to be the bones of a first-century man with the remains of four long knives."

Chris approached the tomb and peered inside. "That corroborates Petronius', I mean Jack's story." He then turned pale and continued to stare at the contents. "It's like someone was walking on my grave and that someone is me. This is very unnerving," he said collapsing to his knees. He spoke softly as if only to me. "I beginning to remember things you read in the manuscript, Roy."

"I know."

"How long have you known?" He asked.

"A few days ago."

"For God sakes, Roy, why didn't you tell me?"

"Wasn't sure you could handle it, Chris. After all, you were my last best chance. Didn't want to frighten you away."

Dr. Wilder pulled me over to the opened ossuary. "Roy, this is actually you, two thousand years ago."

"Well, more correctly, the body I inhabited two thousand years ago."

"The body we inhabited two thousand years ago." Said Chris, still a little shaken.

Dr. Wilder's eyes opened a bit wider and he pointed at Chris, "Mat-thias?"

"Yeah, so it seems." Said Chris, somewhat bemused.

Ernest smiled. "Well you have certainly learned some self-expression over the last 2000 years."

"I'm going to need every bit of it when we reappear in court," said Chris.

Jack gave Chris his peeved look. "C'mon, ya drama-queen, it's pretty obvious to me that we now have direct proof that Roy is who he told us he is… was."

"Well, I wouldn't be so confident," Chris shot back, "any number of unexpected things could happen in a trial like this. It's best just to be prepared for the options you know and some that you don't know."

Hastings put his heavily muscled arm around Chris and gave him a powerful squeeze. "I never thought I'd hear you say that. Just the kind of partner I would like to have when I get back to the states."

Chris looked at him, somewhat puzzled. "You did say 'partner?' Is that right."

Ernest picked up his tools. "Speaking of getting back, we need to get back to camp. I figure we found what we were looking for and it's time to get back to the states."

Jack moved to the truck.

A shot rang out and Jack was thrown off his feet.

I could barely see a figure behind a dune about 100 yards away.

"I have you pinned down," said a voice from far away. "I do not have to kill all of you. You mean nothing to me. I just want Roy Hammer. I will prove it to you. Someone pull Mr. Highsmith out of my line of fire."

"No! Leave me alone," gasped Jack. "The man we captured, Saad Saleh, this is his boss, Yawar al-Sahl.

To my surprise, it was Chris who stood up and moved away from cover, keeping his eyes fixed on the dune where the shooter was. Heroics were not the original Matthias' strong point. "This is a rotten idea." He mumbled. He reached Jack and pulled him quickly behind the car. I could see Jack was losing a lot of blood and would be gone soon, if we did not get help.

"I'm proud of you Chris," I said.

"I just want to maintain bladder control," He said with a shutter.

From the voice far away: "You see, I did not kill him. I am no fanatic, I am a reasonable man. Only Mr. Hammer must die. All come out and bring him to me. I will let the rest of you go afterward."

Chris started to get up again.

"No!," said Jack. "He won't let any of us leave alive. Believe me! Don't be fooled. This is now a matter of revenge. This bugger's *Empire's* Al-Qaeda contact."

Until that moment I felt myself frozen in time and space. Memories from other lives began to rush in and my heart beat so fast I felt it was going to explode. I felt the part of me that was Judas make its bid to come forward. No longer was I afraid to "give in," because I knew it was a part of me and would not hurt me or allow me to be hurt. I opened to it and my heart slowed down; everything appeared to slow down. I knew what to do. It was about ten yards from the car where Jack lay. I rushed and dove for cover. Shots rang out and bullets whizzed past my head.

I saw Jack lying in a pool of blood and my heart again raced, but this time it was under control. Judas was no longer a separate entity but was being engulfed by a larger me that held this life, that life, and many others. What could I do? I remembered what Jesus taught us about healing. I focused my attention and called the names of God in a mixture of Aramaic and other ancient languages. I placed my hand on his chest where the bullet went in and focused the sense that I had of spirit on that area. I felt pain run all the way through me, yet I held onto him. I looked into his half-opened eyes and said half in English and Aramaic, "Now you won't die."

I turned to a shaken Hastings and said, "He's lost blood. Give him water."

Chris had a look of surprise and joy on his face. "He's no longer bleeding!"

"Try not to move him. We don't want that wound to open up again."

I popped my head out for a second to see if the shooter was still there. Nothing.

"Maybe he's gone," said Chris.

"Not very likely," I thought.

Other memories, other experiences began to surface. I remembered how a *Sicarri* would handle this. I saw that there was only one flank that the shooter could reach to get to us and still have cover. I pulled two of the knives from the ossuary, the ones that seemed to have resisted the years the most. They felt familiar in my hands. I did what I could to be invisible in my surroundings while placing myself in the path most logical path for an attacker. I slowed my breathing and waited.

It may have been about five minutes. I heard some movement about ten yards from me. A man in a checkered headscarf was advancing with a sniper's rifle. He had a clear shot into the group hiding behind our vehicle. I saw him crouch down. I had the advance of surprise for he did not see me. He had someone in his sights.

"Here!" I shouted.

The rifle went off and he missed his mark. That would not happen again. As he whirled around I took aim and threw one of the twin blades. It sliced through his right bicep and stuck in his rib cage. He dropped the rifle and pulled the knife out with his left hand. He came right for me with the knife. He was good, but he wasn't a *Sicarri*. I hit him in a spot which cut the tendon of his right forearm without damaging too many major blood vessels. I wanted this one to be incapacitated so Jack could question him later.

"Why didn't you kill me?" He managed to ask.

I felt for a split second that I was back fighting Roman soldiers in Judea. I said first in Aramaic, then again in English: "I would only kill you if it was absolutely necessary. And, quite honestly, you weren't that much of a threat."

I collected his rifle and I directed him toward the group still hiding behind the car.

Hastings saw us coming. "Any more of them?"

"Nope," I answered, "this is the lot."

We drove to the nearest hospital. Jack was rushed to ICU. We waited hours and finally a doctor told us we could come in and see Jack for a few short minutes. He was just coming out of anesthesia and it took some time for him to recognize us. The doctor gave us the news: "He's going to be OK. I can't figure it out. With his wound and the length of time past, this man should be dead."

"Reckon I'm lucky bugger!" Said Jack.

"Well, we're just glad you're going to make it," I replied.

Jack managed a smile. "Wouldn't be dead for quids. Anyway, I've got to testify at two trials back in the states." He looked me in the eye. "Thanks for everything. I turned our friend over to the Israeli security people. They'll know how to handle him. This guy's real big. Used to be Bin Laden's number two. Left to form his own group. Guess he thought his boss got house-broken and he wanted none of it. Anyway, he's the one who made the deal with *Empire*. They're really going to be up that well-known creek after this. You guys go. I'll get better as fast as I can and join you."

He had enough strength to lift his hand. I gave him mine but instead he took my forearm with the handshake we did two thousand years ago. He managed a smile. "Like old times."

Exhausted and most likely in pain from this activity, he closed his eyes.

Eric was waiting for me at San Francisco airport. "You've had quite an adventure haven't you?"

"Eric, this has been more than an adventure…"

Eric laughed. "When you write the screenplay, make sure I'm played by Brad Pitt."

Chapter 18

"Yeah, right."

He smiled and shrugged.

"Listen Eric, the abilities that I remember having, they're coming back. What's more, I'm really clear on my direction for this life…"

"Well, now's not the time to tell me. You need to be in court. Chris is waiting for you. Focus on that now. It's what's right in front of you. The future depends on how you handle the present."

When we got to court, I could see that there was already much activity that had gone on before our arrival. My future, perhaps the course of my life hung in the balance.

This time Chris and Hastings were sitting on the same side, across from Merissa Crane, who had take over Hastings' position with *Empire*. They looked positively dour. For a moment Chris seemed to lighten up, but was elbowed by the more massive Hastings. They resumed visages I found indistinguishable from that of Crane sitting across the isle, who by the way, was doing her best to not notice us at all. Something was going on here. Eric always told me to wait and observe. I took a deep breath and became totally calm. I figured I was going to know everything eventually.

"The Court will come to order," shouted the Bailiff. "All rise…"

As I stood I watched Chris and Hastings body language. They were hiding something that was obviously joyful for them.

The judge took her seat. Down came the gavel. "I have been in conference with counsels and a settlement has been reached. All charges against Mr. Hammer have been dropped. Furthermore, Mr. Hammer is acknowledged to be the author and owner of the original document. But since the original intent of the document was that it be made public, and because of the length of time involved since its creation, the original document is hereby deemed a public document. However, Mr. Hammer's additions to the original document are his under copyright law."

I gazed severely at Chris and he avoided my gaze but could not hold back the laughter. I tried the same with Hastings. He just gave me a big smile. "So, you guys wanted to surprise me? OK, you did."

When he was able to stop laughing, Chris said, "You guys need to restrain me. I'm about to do my legal victory dance! *Empire* now has their hands full with their own suits, some of them criminal. So, they wanted to handle this matter as quickly as possible."

I felt a wave of gratitude. "You know, I really have grown to feel close to you guys..."

Almost immediately I became sandwiched between Chris and Hastings. Chris began, "My life has changed so much for the better since all of this started..."

"Me too," interrupted Hastings, "and I have you to thank. I was against you at the start. I saw you as an obstacle. But since you took me back in time, I'm starting to really enjoy my life again. I'm just sorry the adventure has to end."

"Does it?", Asked Eric. "All of you found the pathway inside to who you really are. You have discovered the adventure in life and as long as you follow those inner directions, as long as you follow what gives you joy, the adventure's there too."

Eric placed his arm around me. "I am now ready to hear what you have to say."

"Oh, right," I said. "The Martial Arts training from that life have come back to me. The ability to hide myself, the healing abilities..."

"Yes, you are luckier than most in that some of your previous lives are remembered so vividly. Most of us, if we are aware of them at all, do not have access to the skills and abilities we developed there, at least on a conscious level."

"For the first time in my life, Eric, I have real direction. I know my purpose. It is to share this knowledge that we are all divine beings having a human experience."

He smiled. "Life truly takes on a different flavor when you realize that. You may do the same exact things afterward, but you'll being doing them in love and service to your fellow divine beings. You can't help yourself. You see God in yourself and everyone you meet."

"I have the same annoyances and irritations as before, but they mean much less. I have this new core of assurance that everything is just as it should be – it's just perfect."

"One word of caution," he said. "In all cases, maintaining must follow attaining. Don't forget your connection to God. You have attained this in other lives; you forgot and had to return. It's too easy to get sidetracked by all that's in this world."

"You mean there's more for me to do?"

"Yeah. To whom much is given, much is expected."

"You mean my Karma's not all complete?" I asked.

He laughed. "I can assure you it's not."

"How come?" I asked, knowing, but not minding, that was I stepping into the role of Eric's straight man.

"You're still alive, dummy!"

Information from the Author

This is a story. It is fiction. But the concepts and wisdom behind the fiction are very real. For anyone who might be interested in learning more about "the real thing," a good place to start would be at: www.MSIA.org.